Unspoken RULES

ELIAH GREENWOOD

www.eliahgreenwood.com

Warning: This book contains graphic mature scenes and foul language. You have been warned. Read at your own risk!

ISBN: 978-1-9994390-2-6
Editing by One Love Editing
First printing edition 2019
Reality Survivor Publishing (Eliah Greenwood)

For my Wazers, the center of my universe.

PROLOGUE

"How could you do this to her? I always knew something was wrong. I knew your friends were trouble."

I can't move. *Why can't I move?*

"I didn't mean to. Mom, you have to believe me. It was an accident. She followed us to a meeting and—"

"Stop. Just stop. I can't deal with this right now."

Dark. It's all so dark.

"Kendrick, keep applying pressure to the wound for me. I'll be right back. Tom should be here any minute."

"Mom, I… I don't know if I can do this."

"Kendrick, now!"

A door closes.

"Are you fucking kidding me? We don't have time for this. Winter needs help now."

Haze.

Haze is here.

"Shut up, Adams. You're not helping."

"I thought your mom was a nurse."

"She is, but she was a doctor first. She went to nursing school when she lost her first patient."

"Wow, years of studies to change your mind right when you get the job? Wish we all had that luxury."

That's Will.

"Maria was loaded then. She'd just gotten her inheritance."

"Now's not the time for a biography, dickheads."

Haze's voice… it's filled with fear.

"Why does she need her friend if she's a doctor, too?"

"It's not him we need, idiot. It's his clinic."

It hurts. Everything hurts.

"Why did we let him stay again?"

"I knew this was a bad idea. She needs proper care."

"And what do you suggest, Haze, huh? That we bring her to the hospital? Don't you think that's the first place they'll look? Not to mention, people will want to know what happened to her and we can't answer those questions. We're lucky Maria's friend can treat her."

The door opens.

"Get out of his way. Let him do his job."

Maria.

"As soon as she's treated, you're gone, you hear me? You're out of her life for good."

"Are you deaf, East side? I told you I'm not fucking leaving until I know she's okay."

Footsteps…

A sigh…

Then complete darkness.

ONE
New Beginning

I've heard my aunt's voice a lot in my life.

I could pick it out in a crowded room without the slightest hesitation. I'd recognize it anywhere. How could I forget the voice of the mother I never had? As a kid, her voice was the last thing I'd hear before I fell asleep every night during the summer trips my mother and I took to Florida. Weird that my own mother wasn't the one singing to me, I know. But that's not who my mother is. If she'd been the type to sing her kid a lullaby, maybe I wouldn't be so messed up.

I'd listen to Maria sing until sleep took my hand and swept me away. But now, as I lie with my eyes closed and my body numb, the voice that was once upon a time so reassuring is filled with a pain that could make the coldest heart ache.

"Winter, my poor baby. I'm so sorry. It's going to be fine. You're going to be okay, I promise." Her voice is weak, faint.

My eyes fly open.

"Thank God."

I sit up straight. My sight is blurry. My thoughts, too.

Maria immediately pulls me into her familiar arms, holding me like it's the last thing she'll ever do.

"What the hell happened?" I blink repeatedly.

"I'll tell you everything, I promise. Just… let me have this moment."

When she pulls away, I glance around the room and wait. That's all I can do: wait for my senses to come back to me. But along with my senses comes the worst part.

The memories.

I remember the fight at the Downside, watching Haze and Kendrick beat each other to a pulp, getting kidnapped, figuring out that Tanner, Haze's brother, was behind the whole thing and that Blake was—sorry, *is*—a traitor.

I remember our escape and cutting my leg open with a piece of glass. Haze carrying me in the chaos. His panicked voice in the dark. But most importantly… I remember the last words he said to me. The words I will never forget.

I love you, Kingston.

That awkward moment when your crush tells you he loves you because you're dying.

My vision clears up, and I take in my surroundings. I know I shouldn't be sad when I'm hit by the cold hard truth, but it doesn't stop my heart from crumbling.

He's gone.

Of course he is.

The pain in my leg is almost as bad as the disappointment that courses through my veins when I stop searching for his face. I've been slipping in and out of consciousness for a while.

I think I fainted. They must've put me to sleep while they removed the glass from my leg. I could hear snippets of conversations here and there—let me rephrase: snippets of *arguments*—but I couldn't move or talk. Like my mind was awake, but my body wasn't.

We're not in the clinic I heard them talk about earlier, that's for sure. They must've had no choice but to move me.

We're in a crappy motel room. A sad shade of blue covers the walls, and an orangey lamp sits on the nightstand next to me. On my left is another bed and a desk.

"What happened?" I ask again.

My aunt draws in a breath. "Kendrick called. He said you needed help, and they couldn't take you to the hospital. He..." She pauses, her eyes full of pain. "He told me everything."

It takes my brain a while to digest the piece of information it's been fed.

She knows.

I'm pretty sure this isn't how Kendrick intended for his mother to find out about his street fighting secret.

"I called an old friend of mine. He's a doctor. He told us to take you to his clinic. All you need to know is you're going to be fine. We managed to remove the glass from your leg. You are so lucky it wasn't fragmented. It wasn't deep enough to do any real damage, but you've got a fracture. It's not going to be fun, but you should be able to walk again in six weeks."

I look down at the heavy blanket weighting on me. If the

pain tells me anything, it's that this is not going to look much better than it feels.

"Do I even want to see my leg?" I ask, well aware that I'm not going to like the answer.

She forces a smile on her face. "You'll heal."

"That means no."

"I said you were okay. I never said it was pretty." She reaches for my hand and intertwines our fingers.

"So… he told you everything, huh?"

She heaves a sigh. "From beginning to end."

"How are you holding up?"

"As good as a mother can after finding out that her baby boy likes to beat up people for fun, I guess."

To my great disbelief, she manages to get a faint laugh out of me. Why am I laughing right now? Must be the exhaustion. Ironic that I feel completely drained after sleeping for so long.

"I'm not surprised, to be honest. I'd hoped the fights had stopped since my days, but…"

"Wait. Rewind. You knew about this?" My eyes widen.

"I was young once, too, you know. The fights have been around a long time. I knew about them, but I just never thought Kendrick could be…" She doesn't finish her sentence, but she doesn't need to.

"I'm so sorry we didn't tell you. We were trying to protect you."

Her face twitches in frustration. "That's exactly the thing,

Winter. Protecting you is my job. Mine. I'm the one that's supposed to take care of you while your mother's away. I'm so sorry. I'm an awful guardian." Her eyes are bloodshot.

"No, stop. It wasn't your fault. You didn't like them from the start and I… I should've listened to you. Please, don't blame yourself for this."

Guilt darkens her face. "If only it were that easy."

I don't say anything. Simply because no words seem strong enough to ease her pain.

"How did you find out about the fights?"

She wipes her eyes. "Let's just say I've had a few bad boys of my own in my days. Like your boyfriend… Haze, is it?"

I wince at the reminder.

Great. Thanks, Auntie. I almost went two whole minutes without thinking about him.

I look down. "We're not really together."

"I figured." She gives me a weak smile.

It must've been pretty obvious that he wasn't my boyfriend when she heard him and Kendrick bicker about how he could never see me again. A boyfriend doesn't usually leave his girlfriend's side when she's unconscious.

"But there's something going on, isn't there? That boy… he means something to you?"

"He's…" I pause, searching for words that refuse to be found. "Complicated."

She smiles warmly. "Well, if you ever want to talk about it, I know a thing or two about complicated."

"Where are the guys?" I realize that Haze isn't the only person missing here.

"Kendrick went back home to get your things."

"What?" I ask, my gaze drifting around the room.

This can't be true.

She squeezes my hand, pain apparent on her face. "He's getting you out of town."

"But… why can't we go back home?"

She pauses for a long moment. "There's no such thing as home anymore, Winter."

Deep down, I knew she would say that.

I have no idea how I could, even for half a second, think that I'd simply slide back into my routine after getting freaking kidnapped. After all this, a foolish part of me still dared to believe that everything could go back to normal—whatever "normal" means.

"Or at least, not for a while."

I fidget with my fingers, the truth burdening me. "Where is he taking me?"

"You'll be staying at Tom's summer penthouse four hours out of town. He was nice enough to offer, and I'd much rather have you there than in dirty motels like this. You're leaving in a few hours."

It comes back to me when his name escapes her lips. She mentioned him earlier.

Tom.

As in Thomas, Maria's ex-husband's best friend. They'd spent their entire college years together, all three of them. But he ended up growing closer with my aunt after she divorced Nick, his supposed best friend. I think they always had a thing for each other, and from what I can see, that hasn't changed, but she was his best friend's girl and they could never make it work.

She was right. She knows complicated.

Now that she's officially single, he probably wants to give it a shot. Letting her family stay in one of his properties sure is a big sign that he's not over her. Not that I'd mind her with him. He's a gentleman and a very successful doctor who recently opened a clinic downtown. She deserves it after what Nick did.

"What about school?" I ask, unable to believe that I'm trying to use school as an excuse.

"Thomas will get you and Kendrick a doctor's note. We're working on getting you online classes until you can come back."

"And when do you think that might be?"

The look on her face tells me that I'm seeking an answer she can't give me. I get it. Florida isn't safe anymore. Not when Tanner and the East side's countless enemies want my head. Whether I'll even make it to the school's prom is uncertain. I'll probably graduate online and go back to Canada as soon as my mother and Harry, my stepfather, come back from their work trip.

"That bad, huh?"

"It's for your safety. Kendrick made a lot of mistakes, but I know he only wants what's best for you. He's going to keep you safe while I take care of everything at home." She leans in to kiss my forehead and gets up, heading for the door. "Tom said to notify him when you're awake. I'll give him a call."

I nod and watch her walk out of the room. A few minutes pass. I close my eyes, trying to ignore the throbbing pain in my leg, and enjoy the silence. Unfortunately, it doesn't stick around for long.

"She'll be fine." I hear distant voices in the hall.

The walls are paper-thin. Great to see the rest of the motel is as shitty as its rooms.

"She's already fine. The question is will she walk again?"

I recognize Will.

"Wait, did you just say she was hot?"

And Alex.

"Yep."

"You're an ass, you know that?"

"Yep."

I repress a smile as they struggle to unlock the door. When they walk into the room with pizza boxes in their hands, it's a wonder I'm not drooling.

Okay, I'm awake now! Give me the pizza.

Fainting like an idiot does require a lot of energy. I can't believe I passed out the second I saw my blood. I've always been terrified of it, but I thought I'd gotten that under control.

Obviously, I was wrong. Just a drop of blood and there goes my punk ass again. I turn into a damsel in distress in need of a savior.

It's a good thing Haze was there to fulfill that role.

Stop thinking about him!

"Good, you're awake." Alex smiles, resting the box he's holding on the washed-out desk a few feet away from the door. "I told you she'd be okay." He shoots Will a quick glance.

"Of course she's okay. She has me to watch over her."

Even in moments like this, Will finds it in himself to make lame jokes, and I'm not surprised.

Some things never change.

"I mean, now that Haze is out of the picture, she might need a real man." He wiggles his eyebrows, flexing his bicep and creating a "let me just barf real quick" feeling in me.

I roll my eyes. *Typical Will.*

"You're a shitbag, you know that?" Alex says.

"I love you, too, bro."

I know Will's kidding, but it doesn't ease the discomfort flickering in my chest. He's right. Haze lost the fight. He has to respect the deal he made with my cousin. He's out of my life.

I can never see him again.

Alex turns to me, tearing me away from the unwelcomed thoughts floating around in my brain. "How are you feeling?"

"She almost died. How would you feel?"

"Shut up," Alex hisses.

"Honestly?" I wince. "Like I got run over by a truck."

"Told you." Will takes a huge bite of pizza.

Alex picks up one of the boxes and opens it. "You hungry?"

"Starving."

I'd be lying if I said that I don't almost shed a tear of happiness when I shove the pizza in my mouth in a not-so-classy manner a minute later. I chew on this crappy pizza like it's the best food I've ever had. I can't remember the last time I ate. I've just finished my slice when someone knocks on the door.

"Open up, my hands are full," a familiar voice calls on the other side.

Will gets up. "What's the password?"

"You have got to be kidding me."

"This ain't it."

"Will, open the door or I'll kick your ass to China."

"Fine. Don't get your knickers in a twist."

Will unlocks and opens the door. On the other side is my cousin. The very first thing he does when he walks into the room is drop two large suitcases on the stained carpet of the four-walled shithole. My entire life for who knows how many weeks is in there.

"Tell me you brought everything," I beg.

"Most of it." Kendrick shrugs.

I don't bother asking him more questions. In Kendrick's language, "most of it" means "I brought whatever I could find." Something tells me he didn't exactly pick coordinating outfits. It's a good thing I don't need to look cute locked inside Tom's penthouse.

"When are we leaving?" Will asks, throwing himself onto the other bed.

"I talked to my mom on the way in. Tom should be here soon. He needs to speak to Winter, then we're gone. It's a four-hour drive."

I don't have a phone anymore. How the hell am I going to survive the boredom of a four-hour drive? Not to mention I'll be stuck with Kendrick in an unknown town for a while. I won't just sit around Tom's luxurious penthouse all day long, will I?

"I need to get a new phone when we get there," I say.

Kendrick turns to me and slides his hand inside his back pocket. "That won't be necessary."

In his hand is the phone I thought was gone forever. The screen is completely shattered. I can't believe it still works.

This is some Nokia-level shit right there.

"I thought I'd lost it at the Downside."

"You did. Haze returned it to us. That's how we tracked Tanner, remember?"

I nod, shifting uncomfortably. Am I going to feel this way every time someone brings up his name?

If so, I didn't sign up for this. I want a refund on my feelings, *thank you very much.*

At first, I'm surprised that he'd just give me my old phone back when it contains Haze's number and all of our messages. I unlock it and it doesn't even take a second for me to understand that I was right: it was too good to be true.

He erased the data.

I'm far from the type to memorize numbers. Would I even call Haze if I could? I can wonder all I want, but it's useless. It's not an option. Kendrick made sure of that.

My cousin notices the torn-up look on my face and sits on the edge of the bed.

"I'm sorry. I know it's a bit radical, but I promise it's for the best. This guy is toxic, Winter. You have to see that. He's the one who put you into this mess in the first place. You're never seeing him again. I mean it. He's… wrong for you."

"He's wrong for you. Seriously? That's the best you've got?" I mutter, fighting the urge to give him a piece of my mind.

That's the thing: *I know* he's wrong for me. Knowing it is exactly what's driving me insane. I know Haze Adams is the last thing I could possibly need on this earth. I know I should run as far as humanly possible. But just because I know it, doesn't mean I don't replay every moment we shared in my head. Just because I know it, doesn't mean I'm going to stop thinking about the way he pinned me up against the wall and kissed me in that motel room. Just because my mind knows, doesn't mean my heart agrees. And that's exactly why I can't get him out of my system. I can't shake him. No matter how hard I try.

He's about to answer when Thomas and Maria walk in, Tom holding a bunch of medical tools I can't identify and Maria carrying crutches.

"You've been given a second chance, Winter. Look at it as a fresh start. It's a new life. It's over. You'll be safe until you graduate. What else could you possibly want?" Kendrick says before stepping aside.

He didn't say what he truly meant, but I know him well enough to read between the lines. What he means by a new life is… *a life without Haze.* And he's wrong. I don't believe it. It's not over. In my heart, I know…

It's just the beginning.

TWO

She's not you

Haze

"Wake the fuck up, man. It's two o'clock."

I can barely open my eyes, my eyelids so heavy it takes everything I have not to fall right back asleep. I let out a groan as an answer, hoping that Trevor will take a damn hint for once in his life, but of course, he doesn't, turning on every light he can find and drawing the curtains.

"Get out," I growl, my head buried under the uncomfortable pillow of his guest room. I'm exhausted from passing out at around five last night.

"I'm not going anywhere. I've been waiting for an explanation since last night. What the hell happened, man? Why couldn't you go back to your place?"

I let out a deep sigh, rub my eyes, and wince at the sunrays lighting up the room.

Where's the rain when you need it?

I don't reply, sitting up straight and stretching. I take my sweet time, yawning, picking up my shirt from the floor and throwing it on. Trev grows impatient, his sighs louder with every second that goes by.

"Remind me why I let you crash here again?"

"Because I'm your leader and you don't have a choice. That a good enough answer for you?"

He waits for me to look somewhat alive before he speaks again.

"Rumors are spreading, Haze. We're not dumb. We can barely get a hold of you these days, and you've been MIA since the fight—the fight that we lost miserably, by the way."

"I know. I was there," I hiss.

"Where have you been?"

"I've been busy." I reach for my phone on the nightstand. It's dead. Not that I have any messages worth reading on there anyway.

I look up at Trev. His eyes clearly say "I smell bullshit." I have no clue how I could explain this to my fighters.

What's up, guys? Yeah, so, the rumors are true. I fucked up big-time. Remember the girl I wanted to make fall in love with me to piss off Kendrick? Well, I kind of, sort of ended up falling for her instead and kind of, sort of lost the fight for her because I'm a whipped little bitch.

I know they suspect that I let Kendrick beat me. I just have to be grateful that it hasn't been brought up yet.

"Busy? Cut the crap. You've been looking for the East side girl. You think we don't know you've been seeing her? We're not clueless. It was fine when we thought you were just chasing some piece of ass but—"

"But what?"

"Man, it's more than that this time, and you know it."

"Says who?"

"Says you and everything you've been doing since you met the girl. Some of the guys are even wondering if you lost the fight on purpose."

There we go.

"You were looking for her, weren't you… when she got taken?"

"Yes, I was. And no, I didn't lose the fight on purpose. Not that it matters anyway. She's gone. She's not coming back."

Word travels fast. They might find out I was working with the East side. And if that happens, I have no idea how I'll justify myself.

"Can't you see? That's not the point, Haze. We don't care that she's gone. We want to know what you'd be doing if she was still here."

Stop asking me about her, damn it.

"What kind of stupid question is that? I'd be here, training for the fight on Friday. Where else would I be?"

He stops annoying me—sorry, I mean talking—for a short instant.

"Are you like… in love with her or something?"

I immediately want to punch him in the face. No warning, nothing, just a good old punch right in the nose.

Truth is, I don't know what the fuck I feel. I know I told her otherwise, but my head is a huge mess right now.

I don't reply, once again, my gaze traveling from the ceiling to the floor.

He sighs. "You're not going to answer that, are you?"

I get up and head for the bathroom that's linked to the bedroom.

"Nope."

"Are you at least going to tell me why you couldn't go back to your place?" He trails behind me.

"Long story short, Tanner's the one who took her. Then, he kidnapped me for finding out and, well, let's just say we won't be having dinner at Thanksgiving anymore. I'm looking at a place next week."

His mouth drops. "Seriously? You're going to stop talking to your brother and move out of your house for some chick?"

"Did you forget the part where his guys kidnapped and almost killed me?"

He nods, but I can tell he's biting his tongue not to talk back.

"Just thought you should know, word on the street's that the North side's preparing something against us. Our alliance apparently went to shit. Any idea why?"

I mentally curse. The East side and I showed up to Ian's lair when we were looking for Winter. I almost forgot about that tiny detail. I'm assuming throwing in a smoke bomb and threatening Ian's girl did the trick. To think we did all that for nothing. We gave my traitor of a brother exactly what he wanted by going after them.

"No, no clue. Sorry," I lie, closing the door.

"One last thing." He blocks the door with his foot.

I sigh in annoyance. "What?"

"The East side girl. What's her name? Willow?"

"Winter."

I almost smack myself for correcting him this fast.

Way to look like you don't give a damn, Haze.

"Was she worth it?"

I pause, memories flashing in my mind against my will. I remember all the time she spent pushing me away only to pull me closer when I kissed her at the motel. I see my hands on her hips, her body against mine, my lips on her skin. I remember how much I wanted to tear that dress off her when I showed up at Kendrick's fake-girlfriend dinner and she dragged me to her bedroom to yell at me.

I see the day she got my helmet stuck on her head, the day I took her out for coffee and she got rid of the girl flirting with me by telling her I had STDs. I see the time she threw her phone in the freaking toilet to make sure no one could locate her when, in fact, I was the one calling her.

The girl sure knows how to make me laugh.

His question echoes in my brain.

Was she worth it?

Yes, she was.

"No, of course not. I don't know what came over me."

He beams, satisfied with my answer, and steps out of the

room. I lock myself in the bathroom. I need a shower. A cold one. But what I really need…

Is to get this girl out of my head.

THE FIRST THING I SEE WHEN I enter Trev's living room is Ryan sitting on the sofa with a few empty beer cans at his feet. I turn my head and notice Emmett, Andrew, and Trevor spread across the large leather couch pushed up against the wall. With a joint between his lips, Trevor stares at me with an apologetic look in his eyes.

It doesn't take a genius to figure out he called them.

The fact that they're all here isn't a good sign. We never meet this early.

"There he is." Ryan chortles, taking a sip of his beer.

I haven't seen him in a while. He was out of town for the past month. I had no idea he was back. I used to be on top of my game and know things like that before… well, her.

"Drinking at two in the afternoon. Glad to see you haven't changed, Sutter."

Ryan shrugs. "Look me in the eyes and tell me a drink doesn't sound good right about now."

Unfortunately, he's right. I could use a shot, *or five*, to numb whatever it is that I've been feeling since I left her at that shitty motel with the East side.

He sees the hesitation spread in my features and smiles.

"I get it. Love does that to you."

"Oh for fuck's sake, this again? I already told Trev: I don't care about the girl. She's gone anyway. Can't you just let it go?"

"We want to believe you, man, we do. But we can't take any chances," Trev says.

"You don't have to worry. I'm telling you, I don't care."

Silence ensues. Ryan is the first to speak again.

"So you really don't care, huh?" He raises an eyebrow.

"Not even a little."

"Well then, you won't mind telling me how she was in the sack, will you? I was thinking maybe when she gets back in town I could get a go at it. I bet she's a virgin. Looks real tight."

I instinctively clench my fists.

Don't give him what he wants.

Don't kill him.

He's testing you.

If you let yourself kick his teeth out of his shit-eating mouth, he'll have won.

"You did sleep with her, didn't you?"

No.

"What do you think?" I feed them the lie they crave.

"And you didn't share? Man, I thought we were friends."

I thought you had a brain.

"What is this? An intervention?" I ask, eager to change the subject.

Ryan shrugs. "Something like that."

"Thanks, but no, thanks." I spot the door and start walking.

Ryan steps in my way faster than I anticipated.

"We weren't asking."

I'm not surprised that Ryan's the one on speech duty. He can say what he wants, but he lives for the power. Out of all of the boys, he's the one who'd take my place in a heartbeat if he could.

He wasn't so cocky when he first started fighting a year ago. You'd think the fact that I taught him everything he knows would owe me some gratitude. But that's just Ryan being his self-centered, arrogant, and power-starving self. I used to think that hunger made him a good fighter, but now I know it just makes him an asshole.

"Is it true?" Emmett asks, a frown upon his face. Emmett's always been Ryan's sloppy second. They're friends. He got Ryan into the fights, but we all know Emmett secretly admires him.

"Is what true?"

"You're against Tanner now?"

I hesitate at first but say it anyway. They'll find out the truth soon enough.

"Yes, I guess I am."

Their faces grow pale, and I curse under my breath. I should've known they'd react this way. My brother and I have been the West side's main fighters for the longest time. Main is what we call the fighters who win the most fights in their areas. Each side has one. The main automatically becomes "the leader." It may sound stupid, but it's the only way we can maintain some semblance of order. Why would one deserve to lead more than another? You have to earn it.

Tanner and I were always tight on our victories, almost even. Until a few months ago, when I beat him. Things went downhill from there.

Just like I made Ryan, Tanner made me. Being the oldest gave him a head start on being the troubled Adams kid, and he got into this street fighting mess long before I did.

He started training me when I was fourteen. He took pity on me after what happened. Fighting was the only thing that made me feel alive back then.

I guess having the student beat the teacher didn't sit well with him. He started getting all up in my business, almost becoming controlling and needy. Maybe because he was afraid I'd end up being more of his competition than his brother. We don't have plenty of family to go around.

It got a hundred times worse when I met Winter. It's like he was terrified that I'd be happy and leave him alone in the misery we've shared ever since we were kids—courtesy of our not-so-loving parents.

He's not the main anymore, but that doesn't make my guys any less scared of him. The tables can turn at any time in our world, and we had the proof of that multiple times in the past.

Tanner's been around a lot longer than I have, and they know it. So they might be following me now, but I don't doubt for a second that they'd side with him if I lost my title, especially Emmett, who's the type to support whoever wins when we watch football.

They're afraid of standing up to him in case he takes the title back overnight. I get it. Whether it's me or my brother, no one wants to get on our bad side.

"I'm not after revenge, if that's what you're worried about."

As soon as the words leave my mouth, their shoulders relax and the color finds its way back to their faces.

"We're glad to hear that, man," Trev says.

"He just wanted his brother back," Ryan adds.

I can't believe they're agreeing with him. *He just wanted his brother back*. How ironic that all he managed to do was lose him even more.

"Have you thought of going after her?" Andrew speaks to me for the first time today.

Yes.

"No. Wasn't planning on it. Will that be all, officers?" I shift from one foot to the other impatiently.

Andrew nods, his ginger hair covering his eyes as he stares at the ground. He's always been the quiet one of the gang. But in contrast to Emmett and Ryan, he's loyal. He and Trev have been with me since the beginning when we first formed our alliance. They're more than my fighters; they're my friends. Which is why it stings like a bitch that Trevor called up this "saving Haze" intervention behind my back.

"One last thing," Ryan continues. "Do me a favor and go pay that Bianca chick a visit. Maybe she could…" He stops like he's looking for the right words to say. "Get your mind straight."

I almost puke right there and then.

I know exactly what he means by that. They want me to go sleep with Bianca as proof that I don't care about Winter.

"Whatever." I make my way to the front door, the urge to get away becoming impossible to ignore.

"Haze," Ryan calls out from the living room.

I turn around. What else could he possibly want? They're blackmailing me into hooking up with some girl in exchange for their trust. Isn't that enough?

"Today."

I feel like I should laugh because there's no way he's serious.

"You're joking, right?"

They avoid my gaze in silence.

"What? Did I become a hooker and nobody told me?"

Ryan ignores my comment and gets his keys out of his pocket. "Here, I'll drive you."

"I'll drive myself," I say, slamming the door and rushing out of Trev's house.

Next thing I know, I've reversed out of the driveway and disappeared down the street in a deafening roar. I hook my phone to the charging cable I keep in my car and drive with no direction for a few unbearably long minutes.

I wait for my phone to light up. For the screen to show that I have a message from her.

Just one.

But of course, when it does light up, it reveals messages from everybody on the damn planet but the person I want to talk to.

There are four messages from random girls that I don't even bother opening and a few from Trev, who's trying to apologize for the group therapy he just tried to pull. I don't know why I hoped that she'd have contacted me.

She's gone, Haze. She could be anywhere in the world by now. It's time to move on.

I turn the corner rapidly and set up the GPS.

Bianca's place it is.

THREE
Miles Apart

Winter

"This place is insane." Will's voice bounces off the walls of the semi-empty living room as I sit on the couch and glance around the too-good-to-be-true penthouse that lacks any sign of human touch.

It's spacious and wide but so clean it feels cold. I love the white, modern house as much as the next girl, but I can't see myself ever feeling at home in a place like this.

Thomas wasn't lying when he said that he barely ever went to the penthouse. His place looks like an IKEA commercial. An IKEA commercial that the boys will have wrecked before tomorrow.

I look through the draughtproof windows at the distant buildings hovering over the whirlwind of motion in the city. We're on the last floor of a twenty-story building, so high up the cars and pedestrians are barely visible. I doubt that anyone will find me here.

It took us way longer than expected to get to Thomas's place. It's already six o'clock. I finally got a good look at my leg, and all I could do was wince as my eyes flew over the stitches and swelling from the fracture. I'll have to walk with crutches, and I'll be in a splint for the next six weeks. Tom said I was lucky, that I should be able to recover from the fracture quickly.

Sure, okay, but what about my broken heart?

I can't believe I just thought that. This is worse than I thought.

"Anyone hungry?" Will walks in and shuts the door with his foot, his hands full.

He drops the Chinese food takeout boxes on the gigantic marble counter in the kitchen. Kendrick and Alex instantly get up from the couch they haven't left since we arrived. Only food could be enough motivation for these boys to move.

They sit around the counter and start eating like actual pigs. I eventually have to remind them of my existence and my current inability to walk.

I could've made an effort to get there, but just thinking of moving is exhausting after everything that's happened in the past twenty-four hours. It's crazy to think that not so long ago I was trapped in a cave and now… I'm watching Kendrick throw kung pao chicken at Will.

After request number three, Alex brings my noodles over and I have no choice but to pray that Thomas's white couch won't become a canvas for my Chinese food.

The boys are leaving tomorrow. Kendrick might be on "Protect Winter" duty, but they aren't. They have school and a life to get back to. Not to mention it'd be way too suspicious if we all just happened to disappear at the exact same time. The last thing we want is to draw attention to ourselves.

They say they'll be back every other weekend. They better. I'll lose my mind if the only human interaction I have for the next few weeks is with Kendrick.

My cousin's phone ringing interrupts his classy inhaling of the Chinese food. He gets out onto the balcony to take the call.

"Who do you think it is?" Alex goes to throw his empty box in the trash.

"My money's on Nicole. She must be wondering where he ran off to. They did just get back together. I'm curious to see what he comes up with to justify this one," I say.

Alex nods. "Yeah, well, whatever it is, something tells me she's not going to buy it and she'll dump his ass again."

Will decides now is a good time to bless us with his wisdom. "Hey, would you look at that? Winter won't be the only heartbroken sap in the gang anymore."

"Will," Alex chastises him.

"What? It's true. I hate to break it to you, Canada, but by the time you come back, Haze will have probably found himself a new East side girl."

I won't lie. That hurt. I'm grateful that, from where they are, they can't see me miserably trying to stop the pain from taking residency upon my face.

"Yeah, right. That's why he said he loved her," Alex starts. "Because that's something Haze Adams would say if he didn't give a shit. We both know that's not who he—"

One severe look from Will is all it takes to shut him up. Alex makes the face of a child who's just done something forbidden and lowers his eyes to the tiled kitchen floor.

They have *got* to be kidding me.

"Let me guess, Kendrick told you to talk me out of ever wanting to see Haze again."

"What? Of course not," Will says in his high-pitched "I'm lying" voice.

I know Will won't be the one to crack, so I focus on Alex. He can't keep a secret for the life of him. He's way too honest and kind. It's a miracle he didn't spill the beans to Kendrick about Blake and Kass secretly dating back then.

Hard to believe this guy can throw a mean punch and show no mercy in a fight.

"Fine. He did." Alex puts his hands up.

Will elbows him in the stomach, and Alex makes it his pleasure to punch him right back.

I want to ask them how they still see Haze as a monster after everything he did to help them but decide to save my breath. It's pointless. They don't know him the way I do. He's different with me. Here I am, still thinking about him. I wonder if he's thinking about me, too.

Oh my God, I'm totally that pathetic girl, aren't I?

"Winter, do you seriously think he's going to sit around waiting for you? He's probably already found a girl to spend the night with by now. Not to mention that he left you when you were unconscious and hurt. Does that look like love to you?"

I remember hearing his voice when I was half awake, half passed out. *"I'm not fucking leaving until I know she's okay."*

They're lying to me. Just how far are they willing to go to keep me away from him?

A text message comes through on Will's phone, stopping him from going on another "let's break Winter's heart" rant. He shakes his head in disapproval and nudges Alex with his elbow to get his attention. Alex glances over his shoulder at the text and displays the exact same reaction.

"Trust us. The best thing you can do is move on." Will puts his phone away and looks at me with pity in his stare.

"What just happened?"

"Nothing." Will gives Alex a look that says *"Tell her and I'll kill you."*

"Don't 'nothing' me. I have eyes. What's in that text?"

"I told you. Nothing. Just let it go."

"Alex?" I glare at him. "Alex, tell me. You know you want to."

He shifts nervously, his eyes darting back and forth between Will and me.

"Alex, don—"

"Haze was at Bianca's three hours ago." The words fall out of his mouth so quickly it's a wonder I even understood him.

I swallow the pill or at least, really try.

"Says who? It's not like you saw him."

"No, but I trust my sources," Will says.

The emotions that creep inside my heart when he says that are indescribable. I'm happy because I got him to answer the question. But I'm also broken, because sometimes…

The truth is worse than the oblivion.

FOUR

Chasing You

Haze

My phone rings a few times. Then, Kendrick's stupid voicemail comes on. That's all I've been hearing for the past month. None of the guys are picking up, and I'm pretty sure it's not because they're busy.

I glance at the empty apartment and breathe out a bitter sigh. It's the third I've seen this week. It needs some work, but it'll do. It shouldn't be too long until Trev gets sick of me eating his food and kicks me out. I really need this place. The apartment lady asked me why I needed to move so quickly. I really wanted to tell her, "Well, long story short, my brother, who's also my roommate, locked me in a basement and tried to kill me," just to see her face, but I'm guessing this wouldn't be a winning tactic.

I glance down at the messages I've sent Winter. She would've answered by now. I've tried calling her too, but it doesn't even reach the voicemail. My guess is either my number's blocked on her phone or she doesn't have a phone anymore. But blocked by who? Did she do it? Not knowing is driving me insane.

Weeks of silence and I still can't stop thinking about her. This girl who, for all I know, could be on another continent right now. It's been one freaking month. It should be getting better. Why isn't it getting better? Why can't I stop obsessing about where she is and if she's okay?

My guys are even more suspicious than before, and the frown that's plastered on my face twenty-four seven isn't helping. I'm sloppy in fights. I'm not down for anything other than sleeping. Going over to Bianca's last month felt so wrong. It made me realize that maybe… I don't want this life anymore.

Speaking of Bianca, she's been texting me nonstop, asking me about what happened when I showed up to her house. I haven't texted her back once, but she can't take a hint.

"Thank you for waiting." The Realtor walks back into the room after taking a forty-five-years-long phone call. I don't have all day, but she obviously doesn't care.

"Have you made up your mind?" she asks.

I glance at our conversation on my phone and reread the last few messages Winter sent me before this madness started. Yes, I've made up my mind. I lost the fight. I lost her. But I don't care about the deal. I'm chasing that girl… *again.*

I look down at the lady and nod.

"I'll take it."

Winter

I need to have a chat with whoever said that time heals all. That's the conclusion I came to while lying awake in Tom's guest bedroom at three in the morning last night.

You'd think I'd be used to this reality by now. After all, it's been a month. Well, five and a half weeks to be exact, but I'm not sure that's enough time for the famous quote to be effective.

It feels like I've been locked inside the IKEA penthouse for years. Kendrick spends every day playing video games while I read or watch *Friends*. That's all I do: read, watch my favorite shows, think about Mr. *I-Say-I-Love-You-and-Go-to-Another-Girl-the-Next-Day*, take online classes, and eat.

It'd be slightly better if I could explore the city, but my leg disagrees. Not to mention, we're supposed to be undercover, and "going out to play tourist" doesn't come close to fitting the word's description. Although, that doesn't seem to stop the boys from going out to get food every chance they get.

I lie awake in the oversized bed that's become my best friend in the past few weeks. Distant voices fill my ears. Today is Saturday, and Will and Alex are back for the weekend. I listen to their conversation until the front door is shut closed. I assume they went out to get Chinese; it's almost lunchtime.

I push the heavy cover off me and yawn. The only things I did today were go to the bathroom and shower, which, by the way, isn't a piece of cake with this injury. Bright side is, my fracture has really improved since we got here. Only a week and a half before I can walk again. I'm even kind of good with my crutches now. And by good, I mean that I no longer fall on my ass every time I use them.

I get dressed and stare at the empty closet in the corner of the white bedroom. I can't bring myself to unpack. Part of me fears that unpacking would be like accepting that this is where I'm going to be spending the last of my senior year, and I'm not quite ready for that.

So, for now, I keep my suitcase open next to my bed and pick what I need in the morning.

Oh, and needless to say, I was right. Kendrick didn't do color matching and picked around two flattering outfits in my closet back at Maria's. The majority of the clothes he brought scream "single with twenty-four cats."

"There she is," Kendrick says when I enter the room. "Slept well?"

"Maybe if I'd slept at all." I groan, rubbing my eyes. "Where are the boys?"

"Went out to get food. Where else?" He shrugs, turning on the TV.

I nod and hop to the fridge—since hopping on one foot and holding on to furniture are now my main ways of transportation—and pour myself a glass of juice. I'm about to take a sip when a knock on the door reverberates throughout the penthouse. I turn my head to see Kendrick just as confused as I am.

"Must be the guys. They probably forgot something." He gets up and goes to check through the peephole.

The way his face collapses when he peeks inside tells me he

was wrong.

It's not the guys.

"Who is it?" I ask.

I can practically hear the million thoughts racing in his head from where I am.

"How the fuck did he find us? You told him, didn't you?"

"What? Who?"

"You know who."

No.

No way.

Haze?

"He's… he's here?"

Kendrick nods, panic written all over his face.

Haze is here.

On the other side of the door… is the guy I haven't been able to stop thinking about for the past month.

"We have to leave. Now!" Kendrick starts running around like a headless chicken in a miserable attempt to gather all of our belongings.

"Are you serious right now? He's right here. You can't stop me from seeing him for the rest of my life. What are we going to do? Escape out the window?"

"We will if that's what it takes," Kendrick says.

"You do know I can hear you, right?"

Kendrick jumps at Haze's voice and stares at the door.

Oops.

Well, we do now.

What is he doing here? He can't be here. He lost the fight. He should be miles away.

"I just want a minute," Haze pleads.

"We had a deal, Adams," Kendrick says, his voiced raised, and heads for my room to get my things. Again, how he plans for us to escape without using the door, I have no idea.

"I know, I know. Listen…" Haze pauses, his voice raspy. "I want to make another deal."

"Not an option."

"Kendrick, you know damn well I can pick the lock if I want to. I'm not here to start shit. I just want to talk to her."

That's why he's here.

He came for me.

That came out wrong.

This finally seems to be enough for Kendrick to admit defeat. He knows Haze is right. He'll find a way in. It's just a matter of time. He takes a very hesitant step toward the door and slowly unlocks it. I can't help but hold my breath.

There he is.

In the doorway…

With his hands deep in his pockets, his tousled brown hair a perfect mess, and the bags under his eyes displaying his lack of sleep. Even in this state, he manages to look like the guy up there dropped the whole "hotness" package into the mix while creating him.

That's it. I can't lie to myself anymore. The past month changed nothing.

I still have feelings for an idiot.

"I tried to keep my word. I did."

He turns his head, and our eyes meet for the first time since the night I blacked out in his arms.

"But I can't."

A billion unwelcomed emotions infiltrate my heart.

"How the hell did you find us?" Kendrick asks.

"Gee, I don't know. Staying undercover 101: buy a burner, pay in cash, and maybe don't spend all your time out in public. It took me fifteen minutes to track you idiots." He stops and assesses the living room. "Whose place is this anyway?"

"Don't change the subject. What are you doing here? What do you want?"

"What part of 'it took me fifteen minutes to find you' didn't register? She's obviously not safe with you. Do you have any idea how many people want her head? She's coming with me."

"Like hell she is! You can't seriously think it's going to be that easy, do you? If so, you're an even bigger idiot than I thought."

Haze steps inside the apartment, a smirk settling upon his lips. He looks unbothered by Kendrick's statement, his gaze locking with mine again as he lifts an eyebrow. I know he's going to do something just by the cockiness radiating off him.

"If you're making me choose between not breaking the

stupid deal or keeping her alive, I know exactly what my choice is."

I'm so conflicted. On one hand, I can't ignore the butterflies literally destroying my stomach, but on the other, I also hate him in more ways than one. He's here. He went through all this trouble to find us. Yet, he went to Bianca not even a day after I left. His mouth says that he cares…

But his dick said otherwise.

Haze continues. "So yeah, you're right. I didn't think it would be that easy."

He glances at me. I know that look.

"Which is why I have to do this."

I let out a gasp when Haze sends Kendrick flying with one strong and precise punch. My cousin drops unconscious, collapsing on the couch right behind him. It's like he calculated it all. Like he knew Kendrick wouldn't hit the ground.

That's kind of nice of him.

Winter, stop finding a bright side to every shitty thing this guy does.

As senseless as this may sound, at first, I wonder why he doesn't do this trick on all his opponents during the fights, but then I come to the simple conclusion that this probably would suck the fun right out of the street fighter experience. You'd assume the whole point is to win the old-fashioned way.

"Why the hell did you do that?" Panic consumes me as I kneel down next to my cousin.

"Oh, relax. He'll wake up in a little while and still be a self-righteous imbecile." His eyes wander around the room. "Where are your things? We need to get going."

It doesn't take him long to find what he's looking for. Kendrick brought my luggage in when he was planning a realistic out-the-window escape.

"Wow. You've got some nerves. You can't just casually ask me that after you knocked out my cous—"

He takes a step forward. "Hold that thought."

Next thing I know, he's out the front door, but this time, he's walking out with something he didn't have walking in: *me.* He threw me over his shoulder so quickly I couldn't even put up a fight. With one hand carrying my stuff and the other supporting me, he walks around like I'm weightless. And I know I'm not. I'm pregnant with Chinese food. The boys spent the last month making sure of that.

He enters the elevator leading to the underground parking where I'm sure his car is waiting for us. I can't help but wonder what he'll say to the other residents of the building if they use the elevator at the same time and see him carrying me out.

"Don't worry, you'll thank me later." I can picture him grinning as I wiggle around for freedom. I quickly give up. It's no use. He's stronger than me, and I only have one leg available.

Then, as the doors slowly close, he hits me with a sentence that brings back a thousand memories.

"I told you I wasn't done annoying you yet, Kingston."

FIVE

Friends?

I wake up with a start, the honking of a car pulling me out of a dreamless sleep, and open my eyes halfway as the smell of leather and car freshener fills up my nostrils. I blink repeatedly and wait for my eyes to adjust to a light I did not anticipate. The first thing I see is a blue blanket covering me. We're on the highway, and the sun is rising in the distance.

That's when it comes back to me.

Haze showed up at the penthouse yesterday.

And knocked Kendrick out.

And sort of kidnapped me.

And I'm sort of pissed at him for all of the above.

I turn my head and see him driving. He's been behind the wheel all night. This can only mean one thing: he's taking me a lot farther away from Florida than I thought.

I refused to say a word to him from the moment he put me into the passenger seat of his ridiculously expensive car. He tried. He really did. But I have nothing to say to his player ass.

After keeping quiet for several hours, I ended up falling asleep. I have no idea where the blanket came from. Haze must've had it in his trunk and put it on me.

There he goes again doing the nicest thing ever to confuse

me about the *not so nice* things he did before that.

"Good morning, sunshine," he says, the sunrays illuminating the left side of his face giving him a freaking halo. Because he doesn't already look like an angel enough as it is.

I ignore him and rub my eyes.

"Still not talking to me?"

I look out the window, resting my chin in the palm of my hand.

"Can I at least know why?"

I turn the volume to the radio up until the music is loud enough to cover up the awkward "I'm mad at you because you slept with Bianca" silence. Haze turns it down right away.

"You're welcome for the blanket, by the way."

No reply.

"You've got a little drool right there." He points to the corner of his mouth.

My eyes widen and I quickly wipe away the drool from my mouth only to find out that it doesn't exist.

"I do not!"

"I know, but you talked to me." He grins.

"Idiot." I mutter to myself.

"Seriously, what's wrong? I thought you'd be happy to see me."

"And why would you think that?" I huff.

"Man, I don't know. Maybe because of what you said to Kendrick yesterday. You said and I quote, 'You can't stop me from seeing him.' Now, I may not be an expert on female emotions and all, but that doesn't sound like hate, does it?" he mocks.

"No, you know what? You don't get to do that. You don't get to make jokes after you just basically kidnapped me and punched my cousin in the face. Leave me alone."

"So that's what this is about."

"Yes, it is," I half lie. "Why did you do that?"

"Must I constantly repeat myself? I had two choices. A, take you away; B, respect the deal and leave you to die with your moronic cousin. I'd rather see you alive, thank you very much."

A bit ironic that it took him a month to start worrying about my safety. I smell excuses.

"You don't know that I was in any danger with the East side."

"Yes, I do. They just lost a member to another gang. Word spreads. Everybody knows there was a traitor. They're considered weak at the moment. Plus, like I said, it took me fifteen minutes to find you. You weren't safe there."

"What? And I'll be safe with you?" I give him a challenging look.

"Of course, we'll *always* be safe." He smirks.

Why do I feel like he's talking about something else?

I ignore his innuendo and go back to watching the passing trees through the window.

"Fine. I'm sorry. I shouldn't have hit him. Is that better?"

I sigh.

"Oh, come on, what do you want from me, woman? I had no choice. I did it for your protection."

I scoff. "Ha, for my protection. Speaking of, I sure hope you used some with Bianca last month."

His jaw drops.

Crap. *Did I say that out loud?*

The last thing I expected is what he does next. He takes the upcoming exit, gets us off the highway, and pulls over on the side of the road next to a gas station that's beyond sketchy. He turns to me and stares until I have no choice but to face him. I can't believe I said that. It just slipped.

"Who the hell told you that?" He asks.

"You mean, who told me the truth?"

He scratches his neck. "Winter, I…"

"Look, Haze. Don't waste your breath. It's okay. I get it. You really don't owe me an explanation. You're free to do what you want. It's not like we're together."

I see a hint of annoyance glimmer in his stare, and panic stirs up in my chest. Why'd I have to say that we're not together? I'm not saying that I don't want us to be. I want us to be. But the question is, does *he* want us to be? Because sleeping with Bianca right after I leave town doesn't exactly give me clear "let's be a couple" vibes.

What do I say? What do I say? What do I say?

"I mean, we're just friends." I stumble on the words.

"Right..." He pauses, his jaw clenched. "Just friends."

And just like that... I regret ever learning to speak.

He clears his throat, making it his life purpose to ignore my eyes locked on him, and stares into the emptiness.

"Good. At least, we're clear on that."

Shit.

Shit.

Shit.

Shit.

Did I just say the *F* word?

Yep. I definitely did.

I just said the *F* word. I, Winter Kingston, just friend-zoned the guy I want to make out with until I can't breathe. Is there some kind of award for most likely to die alone? Or for the world's best at sending hot guys the wrong signals?

Why are you so worried? You shouldn't even want him. He slept with Bianca right after you left town, remember?

Like he's reading my mind, he speaks again.

"And, for the record, I didn't sleep with her. Hell, I couldn't even kiss her for two seconds."

"So... you did kiss her?" I ask even though I fear the answer.

He doesn't reply right away, easing himself deeper into the driver's seat like he's trying to disappear. "Yeah."

My heart aches. I try to cover my wince. At least he's honest.

"Well, was it any good?" I feign carelessness.

Please, don't answer that.

He glances at me in silence. Then, his gaze travels downward to my lips for an everlasting moment that sends shivers down my spine.

"I've had better."

Is he talking about what I think he's talking about?

Without a word, he leaves my thoughts to spiral out of control and fires up the car to get us back on the highway. I spend the next fifteen minutes reprimanding myself for letting the word friend out of my mouth. We can't be just friends. Not after everything that happened. Not after he almost stripped me down in that motel room the day before the fight. He seemed to agree with my word vomit. He didn't fight it. Does he actually want to be buddies? Did I ruin my chances?

We ride in heavy silence for about half an hour until he says, "We're almost there."

"Almost where?" I watch the approaching exit.

When he takes it, I dare believe that maybe, just maybe, wherever we're going… it's somewhere where we won't be "*just friends.*"

He turns to look at me and smiles. "Home."

SIX
The Lake House

"No way. This is your place?" I shamelessly gawk at the wood-built house that overlooks the most breathtaking lake I've ever seen.

"Kind of. It belongs to my parents, but they haven't used it in years," Haze says, taking a slow turn and pulling up to the long asphalt driveway.

I admire the tall trees circling the impressive property and the sunrays peeking through the waving leaves. Haze parks the car and the engine dies down in a rumble.

"Don't worry, it's prettier inside."

I fight the urge to punch him on behalf of all middle-class people everywhere. If he thinks this is ugly, he needs to see the one-bedroom dumpster I used to live in with my mom.

I can tell from the way he bites back a grin that he doesn't mean it and he's just trying to get a reaction out of me. I know Haze is rich. Allow me to revise: I know *his parents* are rich. But this is on a whole other level.

"Hold on," he says, getting out of the car.

I watch him walk around the vehicle and open the trunk. He gets our luggage and my crutches out, drops them onto the porch, and comes back to open my door.

In a week, I'll be able to walk on my own again. Until then, this guy who's just a "friend" is going to have to give me a hand. He's the one who showed up and claimed he wanted to protect me. Well, now he's going to have to play nurse whether he likes it or not.

When he helps me out of the car, tightly wraps one arm around my waist so that I can find my balance, and pulls me closer, I swear the eighteen years I spent breathing properly vanish and I have to learn all over again.

Standing on one foot, I have no choice but to press my body to his. I instinctively look up and regret it when our eyes connect. Again, I think I see his gaze drop to my lips for one fleeting second, but I'm way too focused on trying not to kiss him myself to be sure. I'm brought back to reality when he clears his throat and looks away.

Note to self: Haze Adams and close proximity means dysfunctional brain.

"Is that all you brought?" I say, eager to break the silence and tension between us, and point to the tiny black bag he left on the porch.

"Yes. I used to come here all the time. I'm sure I left some clothes in my old bedroom."

"And how long ago was that?"

"Like two years." He shrugs, helping me to the front door where my crutches are waiting. "Let's hope they still fit."

"And if they don't?"

He grins. "Well, I guess you'll have to tolerate me walking around naked."

Cue the scarlet cheeks.

I'm thankful that he doesn't notice the flushed expression on my face when he unlocks the door with a number combination and pushes it open.

A loud creak indicates how long it's been since the last time someone was here. I step inside and a cold breeze scampers down my spine, every hair on my body standing up.

The inside is just as beautiful as I expected, although the ceiling-high windows covered by thick curtains dim the sun and soak us in darkness. Two large gray couches are symmetrically placed in the center of the living room, and a large TV hangs above a marble fireplace. I glimpse to the kitchen on my right. The wooden decor is a recurring theme all throughout the first floor. This house would probably feel cozy if it wasn't freezing and gloomy.

Shivering, I run a hand up and down my arm.

"Yeah, sorry, it's cold. No one's been here in a while," he says, noticing my slow but very real transformation into a Popsicle.

He proceeds to draw all the curtains and let the sun invade the main areas of the house. The direct view of the calm water through the uncovered windows knocks the breath out of me. Many luxurious houses surround the lake. The sign I saw earlier read "Colton Gate. Population: 9,564." This is basically a small town for rich people.

I didn't ask Haze about it, but I'm pretty sure this place means something to him. Could it be his hometown?

"I have to go turn the heater on. I'll give you a tour when I get back. Make yourself comfortable," he says and disappears down the hall.

With the help of my crutches, aka my new best friends, I begin making my way to the couch but stop in my tracks when I notice three framed pictures above the fireplace.

I hop toward them. The first one is empty, and I'm immediately under the impression that someone took out whatever picture was in there in a hurry without bothering to replace it or put the frame away. I wouldn't expect such carelessness in a house like this.

Maybe Haze's parents did it the last time they were here. I wonder if they knew they wouldn't be coming back when they walked through the door that day.

The second picture is a family portrait. I know something's off the second I capture it in my hands to get a closer look.

On the picture is Haze, Tanner, a man with hard features, and a brown-haired woman showing off what looks like expensive jewelry. That would be Mrs. And Mr. Adams. Sad to think this is probably the closest thing I'll ever have to meeting Haze's parents.

At first sight, everything about this picture screams "typical family." But when you look carefully, the photograph looks like it's been cut off on the side. It's barely visible, but the slightly uneven paper gives it away.

Something tells me whoever was in the empty frame is the same person who was removed from this portrait.

Haze looks so young, innocent… carefree. I'd put him at twelve years old tops. Obviously, he looked just as adorable then as he does now. Not that I'm surprised. Of course he would be the "you're going to be hot when you grow up" kid.

As for me, I was some other type of kid. I was the "don't worry, there's hope for everybody" kid.

What rubs me the wrong way is the third and last picture. It's a portrait of Haze. Alone. He looks older. I'd say around fourteen or fifteen years old.

He's still so young, but something in his eyes is different, darker. No sign of that boyish smile from the first picture. As sad as it is, the only word that comes to my mind when I analyze his perfect features is "broken."

He's broken.

Now that I think about it, I still see this exact same look in his eyes to this day. Something happened between these two pictures, no doubt. But what?

I hear distant footsteps and jump. My instinct tells me to get away from the pictures, which I do as best as I can, before he turns the corner.

By the time he walks back into the room, I'm sitting on the couch and pretending that my crappy phone is somewhat interesting. He starts to say something but quickly cuts himself off when his gaze lands on the pictures I was looking at barely ten seconds ago. His face twitches in irritation. He just noticed them. If he'd known about them sooner, they wouldn't have been there for me to see, I'm sure of it. He'll probably just snatch them and put them away when I'm not looking.

"Ready for that tour?" He turns to me.

"Seventy-five rooms later," I say in a ridiculous narrator voice that draws a small laugh from him.

"You think this is big? You should see the one we have in Arizona."

"Brag much?"

He smiles and holds out his hand to get me up from the couch. "Always, Kingston. Always."

The tour goes by a lot quicker than I anticipated. When we reach the second floor, I'm astonished by the numerous closed doors surrounding me. Haze said that the house has nine bathrooms. Nine.

What the hell did the Adamses do with nine bathrooms?

"Where's my room?" I ask.

He opens the door on his right. A bedroom. My eyes scan over the large room that's obviously a boy's. Probably his.

"You mean our room."

My lips part.

"Oh, come on. You didn't really think I'd let you sleep alone, did you? I mean… my house, my rules."

The look on my face must be priceless because he starts laughing seconds later.

"Relax, I'm kidding. It gets cold around here. That's the warmest room in the house, so it's either that or pneumonia. But, hey, it's your choice." He puts his hands up.

Dang it.

"Look, I promise to stay on my side of the bed. Plus, it's only for a few weeks. What are you afraid of?"

I bite my tongue so as not to talk back.

"So this is where you used to sleep, huh?" I change the topic.

"Yep." He sits on the edge of a bed he knows all too well.

"Where are these clothes of yours?"

He gets up, walks to his dresser, and opens a drawer.

I can't help myself. "Five bucks says it doesn't fit."

He arches an eyebrow, accepting the challenge, and reaches for a blue T-shirt in the bottom drawer.

"Oh my God." I gasp.

"What?" He jumps a little.

"Colors!"

I catch his grin. "You're an idiot."

"What? It's true. You never wear any. Do you actually own something other than black T-shirts?"

"Colors aren't my thing," he says.

"Could you be more of a Casanova cliché?" I roll my eyes.

"I mean, if you insist."

He casually removes his shirt and throws it on the floor. I

can't help but pry my eyes away.

"Haze!" I yelp.

"What? You asked."

Right. Because this is totally helping me in the "let's be friends" department.

"Did you put it on yet?"

"Yeah."

I turn around, only to find him still very much half-naked. "But you said…"

"I know what I said." He smiles.

Oh freaking hell.

I miserably lose the fight and let myself stare at his toned body. It's almost like he's doing it on purpose. Like he wants to see me drool over him.

"Enjoying the show?" he asks after a few seconds of me gawking.

I come back to the land of the non-drooling living and shake my head in the hope that it will shake the embarrassment off my cheeks, too.

"Just put the damn shirt on."

Finally, he does. No, wait—he *tries*, but it doesn't go quite as planned. Uncontrollable laughter crawls up my throat at the unexpected sight offering itself to me.

Haze. Stuck in an undersized T-shirt that stops in the middle of his stomach.

His broad shoulders stretch the fabric that holds on for dear life to his sculpted body. It might not sound like much, but it's hands down the most hilarious thing I've seen in a while.

"It's not funny," he hisses.

This only makes me laugh harder. This is definitely Karma punishing him for all the teasing he's been doing. Needed to kick the sexual tension down a notch.

He tries to remove it but struggles to free himself.

"Winter… I can't take it off."

I'm suffocating at this point.

I try to speak between chuckles. "Are… are you serious?"

"Do you think I'd still be wearing this ridiculous thing if I wasn't?"

"You said you used to come here two years ago."

"Maybe it was two. Maybe it was five. Same thing." He growls in annoyance.

This strangely reminds me of the motorcycle helmet incident. He had to get the helmet off of my head, and now I need to free him from a T-shirt.

Oh, how the tables have turned.

"Don't just stand there. Help me."

I barely swallow my laughter when he motions to come closer. Swiftly, he grabs my wrists and places both my hands on his chest.

"There," he says.

I wait for him to tell me what to do next. But he doesn't. Instead, he stares. All I can do is feel his torso through the light fabric of the nightmare he calls a T-shirt. The fact that I'm still attracted to him when he's stuck in a kid's T-shirt just shows me how far gone I am.

Like he can hear every forbidden thought clouding my judgment, he fixes on my lips and nibbles on his lightly. He starts to lean in.

He wouldn't…

He wouldn't kiss me again, would he?

As though he's come back to his senses, he stops.

"Never mind, I got it."

He pulls away and takes the shirt off like it's the easiest thing in the world.

"Wait… You clearly didn't need me," I stutter.

"I know. I wanted to feel your hands on my chest." He grins and heads back for the drawer.

This guy.

Haze Adams masters playing with my emotions like there's an instruction manual.

Amused by the shock I'm drowning in, he picks up his old shirt from the ground and throws it back on.

"Come on. We have to go."

"Go where?"

"Shopping. I need new clothes, and we're eventually going to need to eat to, you know, survive," he teases.

I hold back a sigh. I haven't even been here with him for a day yet and I already feel like the tension's going to end me. His careless words sneak their way back inside my head.

It's only for a few weeks. What are you afraid of?

And all I have to say to that is…

Oh, Haze. Do you have *any* idea how many things can happen in a few weeks?

SEVEN

Jealous Much?

As we drive around Colton Gate, I watch the small but luxurious town parade in the rearview mirror of Haze's black car. I can't stop myself from wondering how I went from crashing at Thomas's place to living with Haze Adams in less than forty-eight hours. How I went from eating takeout food with my cousin to going on a shopping spree with his enemy in a town whose mall is meant for millionaires.

I wonder how his parents could even afford a place like this.

"What do your parents do for a living?" I try.

He shifts in his seat. "Nothing that would interest you."

Predictable.

"You must have one hell of a boring life according to all the topics I wouldn't be interested in."

"Something like that."

I grow annoyed. "You do know that the more you dodge my questions, the more I want to know, right?"

"Yep."

I roll my eyes. "Jerk."

"Prude." He smiles.

I can't erase the grin creeping in the corner of my mouth. I have no idea when or how "jerk" and "prude" became our thing, but somehow, it did.

Haze takes a right and pulls up into the mall parking lot. It looks just like any other mall, but the sign at the parking entrance indicates that mostly expensive clothing stores are located inside the building. I've always had a slight problem with expensive clothes. Unfortunately, to me, expensive doesn't always mean "pretty." And, from what I can tell looking at the clothes displayed in one of the shops' windows, the millionaires in this town have strange taste.

This won't be easy.

Haze stops the car and makes a face, indicating that he's having the same train of thoughts as I am.

We exchange looks and smile.

Let's go shopping.

"YOU ARE NOT GOING TO BELIEVE it," I say, my fingers fidgeting with the price tag of the most hideous polka dot slash floral dress I've ever seen.

"How much?" he asks.

"A hundred and fifty."

Haze smothers a laugh, on the other side of the changing room. We've been going around the mall and trying on the most ridiculous clothes we could find for two hours now. Haze found what he needed in like minus two seconds. Finding plain T-shirts isn't a very demanding task, apparently.

As soon as we walked inside the mall, a million missed calls and messages came rushing in on my cracked phone screen. My dinosaur could barely get signal at the lake house, but it's way stronger at the mall.

They're all from Kendrick and Maria. They must be worried out of their minds.

I don't even want to think about how Maria reacted when Kendrick told her that I left Tom's "safe" house.

"Who on earth would pay almost two hundred dollars for this?" I take off my clothes the best I can to put on the dress.

"Yeah, well, it's either this mall's clothes or driving two hours out of town. I told you, we're a bit isolated."

"What is this place anyway? Like a top-secret town for the Kardashians?" I struggle with the tight fabric.

Haze cackles, then speaks to someone. The clothing store employee, I assume.

"Yes, Mr. Adams, right away," I hear a female voice say.

I furrow my eyebrows. Mr. Adams? First, how the heck does the employee know Haze's last name? And why so formal to someone who's younger than her?

He brings his attention back to me. "It's just a wealthy area."

It's a gated community with huge houses and a mall filled with luxurious brands. I'd say this is more than just a wealthy area, but I guess for Haze this is an everyday thing.

"This isn't even close to *a bit isolated.* We're in the middle of nowhere. If you left me here, I'd die. Especially since my ancient phone won't let me use the GPS." I laugh, catching a glimpse of myself in the mirror. Good thing this dress doesn't have a zipper.

"How's that going, by the way? Living without your phone? It's been a while since you…" He pauses, erupting in laughter. "Since you threw it in the toilet."

Here we go.

It's official. He is *never* going to let me forget this one.

"Shut up."

It takes him a few seconds to stop laughing. "Are you done yet?" He knocks on the door.

Someone's getting impatient.

"I don't think it's a good idea." I wince.

"That bad, huh?"

"More like disastrous."

"I'm sure it's fine. Come on out."

I fidget with the sleeves of the dress. "Okay, but if you take a picture, I'll stab you in the eyes, rip your eyeballs out, and slowly make you swallow them, are we clear?"

"You're creepy as fuck, Kingston, you know that?"

"Are we clear?" I ask again.

He chuckles. "Yes, ma'am."

I get on my crutches and push the changing-room door open. Haze instantly starts laughing, and truth be told, I can't really blame him. I don't consider myself to be a fashion expert with unbeatable style, but this… this is something else.

"You look like my grandma's curtains." He snorts.

I mean, he's not wrong.

"You know what? I think I'm good with my clothes. Like you said, it's only for a few weeks."

Again, special shout-out to Kendrick for making sure I only had the ugliest clothes in my closet to wear during this "let's keep Winter safe" adventure. Sometimes, I think he did it on purpose.

Maybe somewhere, deep down, Kendrick knew Haze would show up and that's why he decided to have me wear hideous pajamas every single day. What better way to make sure Haze wouldn't make a move on me than to make me look like a hobo? My oversized sweatpants and band T-shirts aren't very attractive, to say the least.

"This isn't just ugly. It's uncomfortable, too." I wiggle, the dress itching. "I need to change."

Haze checks the time on his phone. "There's something I have to go do real quick. I'll be thirty minutes tops. You going to be okay on your own?"

"Sure. As long as you don't leave me here—you're supposed to protect me, remember?" I taunt.

He smiles. "Don't worry, I'll be back. Plus, you have the nice employees to keep you safe. Not that anybody would want to make a move on you dressed like this." He looks me up and down.

"Jerk," I mutter under my breath.

"Prude," he says as he walks away.

I watch him disappear with an idiotic grin on my lips and turn around to find myself alone with the pile of clothes I have yet to try on. I did find some decent clothes in the discount section. Nothing was below fifty dollars, but this will have to do. I'm hoping they'll fit and I'll be able to look semi-cute from now on. I spend the next thirty minutes making faces and throwing clothes in the "never again" pile. I'm happy to get at least a few items to bring back with me.

I'm about to step out of the changing room when my phone rings. My heart sinks at the caller ID.

Maria.

I take a breath and pick up.

"Winter, thank God. Where are you?" my aunt says as soon as I press the button.

"Hey, Aunt Maria," I say, careful not to be too loud.

"Are you okay? We've been trying to call you since last night." She speaks rapidly.

"I'm okay, I promise."

She sighs in relief. "What in the world happened?"

"Kendrick didn't tell you?"

"He just said you're with this Haze kid. Tell me where you are. I can come get you right now."

I proceed to tell her exactly what happened. I start with how easily Haze tracked us down, and she listens to every word. No matter how much I wish I could stay, I know that she's probably right. This is insane. She's my guardian. I can't stay here if she doesn't want me with Haze.

"I'll text you the address," I say in defeat when I'm finished with the story.

She doesn't speak for a few seconds.

"Don't."

"What?" I ask, certain I heard that wrong.

"I hate to admit it, but we don't know what we're doing. We can't protect you right now. If what you're saying is true, if it really took him fifteen minutes to find you, I… I think the safest place you can be right now is with him."

Joy, surprise, disbelief—so many emotions fill me when she says that. Deep down, I'm happy because I don't want to leave.

"Are you sure?"

"Trust me, I don't like the idea, but this is for the best. You just need to stick it out until school's over and you can go back home. Can you do that for me?"

"Yes," I agree.

"We should really tell your mom about this though," she says, guilt overwhelming her.

"Please, like she would care. She hasn't called me once in the whole time I've been living with you. I've only talked to my dad. She's happier not hearing from me, believe me."

"Oh, sweetie, don't say that. You know how she is. Lauren's not too good with emotions. I'm sure she's just been busy traveling with Harry," she lies to make me feel better.

"Busy hating me maybe," I grumble to myself. My aunt doesn't want to admit it, but there is a reason my mother jumped at the opportunity to join my father—well, technically stepfather, but I consider him to be blood—on his work trip. The less she has to look at my face, the happier she is.

Maria fights my claims for a few more minutes and makes me promise to call her often. She also tries to get into a very awkward safe-sex conversation that I dodge like a pro.

"I have to go. I love you," I say.

"I love you, too, honey. Be safe. I'll be waiting for your call."

I hang up and shove my phone in my jeans pocket. I step out of the changing room with all the clothes I don't want in my hands, and the employee from earlier walks up to me with a black dress hanging from her left arm. She tells me that Haze wanted me to try it on. This is probably what they were talking about earlier.

"How much is it?" I ask.

"Two hundred and eighty."

How about an organ with that?

I begin to decline but tell myself that there's no harm in just trying it on. Minutes later, I'm out of the changing room and beyond conflicted. The dress looks like it was meant for me, even with my splint on.

"You looked fabulous." The ginger employee smiles when I hand her the dress. I almost didn't take it off.

"Thank you. But I really don't have that kind of money for a dress."

"I do."

I'm a bit surprised when an unknown voice reaches my ears. I turn my head and see a guy who's around my age standing a few feet away from me. Black hair covers part of his eyes, and his jaw is so sharp I'm sure you can throw a cucumber at it and have instant crudités.

"I'm sorry, manners. Name's Ryder."

He's cute and all, but his offer pushes him into the slightly creepy category.

"Hi, I'm Winter," I say politely.

"Are you new in town? I think I'd remember seeing you around."

I almost scoff. *Original.* There should be a limit of uses allowed for cheesy pickup lines so you have to pay a fine every time you use one as old as time.

"I'm on vacation. Not staying for long."

"That's a shame. Well, enjoy the dress. It's on me."

"You really don't have to d—"

He cuts me off. "I insist."

The employee motions to follow her to the front of the store where the cash registers are.

Okay? Because this isn't weird at all.

All I can do is stand back and watch this perfect stranger spend three hundred dollars on me. He pays and comes back to hand me the bag.

"There you go."

I thank him. He starts walking but stops midway and turns around.

"Oh, and good luck for next Saturday."

I nod faintly, confusion pouring over me. What is that supposed to mean?

What's happening next Saturday?

Ryder waves goodbye and exits the store. At the same time, Haze walks back in with a bag of his own. He frowns and stares at Ryder until he's out of sight.

"What was that about?" he asks.

"What do you know? Rich people are more generous than I thought. Dude insisted on buying me a three-hundred-dollar dress for no reason, can you believe it?"

"And you let him?" he blurts.

I'm a bit shocked by his reaction. "What was I going to do? Punch him? He didn't give me much of a choice."

The kind employee comes to my rescue. "It's true, Mr. Adams. He didn't give her a choice."

I frown. This Mr. Adams thing again. Why would she call him that?

Haze barely acknowledges her, too focused on being angry for no reason. The employee knows how to take a hint and goes back to the storefront. I follow her, pay for the few items I'm getting and return to his side.

"Let's go." His tone is cold.

Am I sensing… jealousy?

We walk side by side for a few minutes until I can't take it anymore.

"Why are you so moody?" I finally let myself ask.

"I'm not."

"Yes, you are. You've been moody since that guy got me the dress," I say.

"We have to go grocery shopping next."

"Way to change the subject."

"I mean, who does he think he is? Buying a perfect stranger a dress? That's creepy. I don't trust him."

"Haze, it's just a dress."

"Whatever." He shrugs.

"You know, if I didn't know you any better, I'd say you're jealous."

He stiffens up. "Jealous? Please. I'm just wondering what motive this guy has. He's probably never going to see you again, so why? Not to mention that we're trying to keep under the radar."

"It's not like I'm ever going to wear a classy dress like this locked up in the lake house anyway."

His shoulders seem to relax, his anger decreasing. He's about to speak again when someone beats him to it.

"Haze?"

I can tell from the way his face crumbles that he knows that voice. I'd even go as far as to say that he'd recognize it anywhere.

We both turn around simultaneously and come face-to-face with a beautiful, short red-haired girl and a guy with loose brown curls. They look slightly older than us.

"Vic?" Haze seems a bit uneasy.

"I can't believe it. How long has it been? Like two years?" The guy who answers to the name Vic pulls Haze into one of those bro hugs guys do to show their affection. I don't speak male, obviously.

"Who's this?" Vic asks when they pull away.

"Winter, this is Victor, my oldest friend. Victor, this is Winter, my…" He pauses, hesitant as to what word he should use. "Friend."

There goes the *F* word again. I mentally curse, feeling myself fall deeper and deeper into the friend-zone hole.

"Nice to meet you, Winter," he greets me. "This is my girlfriend, Beatrice."

"But everyone calls me Bea." She grins shyly.

I return their smiles. "Nice to meet you both."

"What happened to you?" Bea asks, noticing my leg and crutches.

"I…" *Think, Winter, think*. "I fell."

Haze holds back a small snicker.

What? That technically isn't false.

Bea and Victor nod, satisfied with my answer, and bring their focus back on Haze.

"Why didn't you tell me that you were back in town, man?"

"Because I'm not." Haze shifts uncomfortably. "Well, not really. We're just passing by. You know, not staying for long."

"Still, you should've told me. How are things with you? We've barely even spoken since…"

Haze slightly clenches his jaw, and Victor cuts himself off like he just got too close to talking about something they promised to never bring up again.

He said Victor's his oldest friend. They must've grown up together. I knew Haze had a past in this town.

This has got to be his hometown.

What else?

"I'm good. I'm great, actually." Haze quickly fills the uncomfortable silence before it gets too thick. "How are you?"

A bunch of chitchat follows, and all Bea and I can do is stand by while the boys catch up.

"Good to see you guys are still together. How long has it been?" Haze asks.

Vic circles Bea's shoulders with his arm. "Four years in a few days. We're actually having a dinner party with a few friends next Saturday to celebrate our anniversary."

"That's great." Haze nods.

No one speaks for a few seconds. Bea lightly elbows her boyfriend as if to make him realize something. On hit number two, he takes the hint.

"Oh, hey, do you guys want to come?"

Immediately, I feel Haze pulling away. Not physically, but

mentally. He doesn't even move a muscle, but his body language and the energy oozing off him scream that he's not a fan of the idea. But I mean, that's pretty much what he does every time someone tries to get somewhat close to him.

"We'd love to." The words escape my mouth faster than I thought possible.

Haze tenses up by my side.

"Wait, really?" Vic's eyes widen. "I mean, that's great," he corrects himself. He looks in disbelief that Haze said yes.

Well, technically, I did. But I spoke for the both of us.

It's obvious that Vic's tried to reconnect with Haze in the past and got repeatedly blown off.

"We have the day of the party off. What do you say we all hang out at our place beforehand?" Vic suggests, pushing it even further to see how long his luck will last.

"Sure," I speak again.

Haze clears his throat, and I know it means "What the hell are you doing? Shut up," but I ignore him.

"Awesome. Let's exchange numbers," Bea suggests.

Haze doesn't oppose, nor does he entertain the idea. We all exchange phones. Vic and Haze are the only ones who don't have to as they already have each other's cells. Minutes later, we're all set.

"This is going to be so fun. We'll text you the time and address." Bea claps her hands in excitement and looks at the time on her phone. "Oh, we have to get going, babe."

"Okay. Well, we'll see you next Saturday," Vic says, turning away. "It was really nice meeting you, Winter."

"You too." I wave.

Haze forces a smile, and I bet to them it seems real. I think I'm the only one noticing those details because I've spent way too much time looking at his annoyingly perfect face. I could tell his fake smile apart from a real one with my eyes closed.

"Oh, and dress up." Bea glimpses at us one last time before they walk away.

As soon as they're out of sight, Haze turns to me.

I am so *not* getting away with this one.

WHEN WE ENTER THE LAKE HOUSE, Haze drops the many grocery bags he's carrying on the counter. Silent, he starts unpacking and filling the empty fridge up.

"What's the big deal? It's just some dinner party." I try to get him to warm up to me. He's been cold since we left the mall. First, it was the dress, now this.

"You had no right to say yes," he says and puts a cereal box away.

"Why don't you want to go?" I hop to him and grip the counter to find my balance. "They seem really nice. Plus, what else are we going to do stuck in here for the next few weeks?"

"Just drop it. You already said yes anyway."

"That's not an answer."

"You don't get it, Winter."

"Then explain it to me." I stare at him.

"It's complicated."

I scoff. "It always is."

I put the last of the groceries away and move over to the living room to get away from him. He can't be upset with me and not want to tell me why. This whole "closed book" thing is really starting to get on my nerves.

A few minutes later, he joins me. He's holding the bag he had walking in the store earlier after his mysterious departure. He tells me to scoot over and sits next to me.

"Remember what we talked about today?" He grins like we weren't arguing barely a minute ago. He seems so excited I don't question his sudden demeanour change. "About you not having a phone?"

"Yeah?"

"I thought it was time we did something about that." He gets a box out of the bag, opens it, and takes my ability to speak away from me.

In the box… is a brand-new phone.

"Haze, you didn't."

How the heck am I supposed to be annoyed with him when he does things like that?

My eyes fly over the phone for a few seconds. It's very recent—like this year's recent.

"Are you insane? I can't accept this."

"You kind of threw yours in the toilet because of me. I

figured I owed you one. Plus, having you walk around with a dinosaur kind of defeats the purpose of keeping you safe, don't you think?" He grabs my phone on the table next to the couch and analyzes it. "What can you even do with that piece of crap anyway?"

"I mean… I can text and call."

"Can you even take pictures on that thing?"

"Of course. As long as you don't mind them looking like they were taken with a potato."

"Do you have any?" he asks.

"No, it's kind of useless."

"What about apps?"

"Server doesn't allow it." I shrug.

"So, basically, you don't have anything that matters on there." He raises an eyebrow.

"Pretty much," I give in. "But it's not that bad. It survived a lot more than the new phones do." I refer to the whole kidnapping hell.

He smirks and glances at my prehistoric phone in his hand.

"Let's see if it survives this." He gets up and starts running.

Dang it, Winter. How could you not see that one coming?

"Haze, stop! I can't chase you. That's cheating."

I watch him open the large glass doors leading to the balcony. Before I know it, he's on the floating dock next to the house and throwing my phone as far as he can into the lake.

He walks back into the living room seconds later, laughter

wrapping him up, and sits back down next to me. I immediately punch him in the arm with all the strength I can gather and scowl at him. After a few minutes, I give up. It's not making a difference. If anything, it's just amusing him more.

"Please, I did you a favor throwing that nightmare away. You should be thanking me." He leans forward and glances over my shoulder to see what I'm doing. "What are you waiting for? Open it."

"What's the deal with everyone giving me stuff today?" I admire the phone—forced to admit that it's much nicer than anything I've ever owned before—and press the button to turn it on.

"Haze, I… I don't know how to thank you." I flip the phone around and assess it some more. It's huge. How am I even supposed to put this in my pocket?

"You can call me Master for the next few weeks and we're good."

"You wish, you sicko." I chuckle.

He tears his eyes away from me. "Had to try." He gets up from the couch. "You hungry?"

"Famished."

"What do you want? We got pizza, pizza, and pizza."

I swallow a small laugh. "How about pizza?"

"Good choice. Coming right up." He glances at me one last time before turning the corner. Deep down, I'm glad that Maria allowed me to stay here with him. I found out more about Haze in the one day I've been here than in the whole time that I've known him…

And something tells me there's way more to come.

EIGHT
Close And Personal

"Okay. Why the fuck is the car flying?" Haze says, and I break out into laughter, sinking deeper into the couch. We've reached the end of *Grease.* Just because I'm watching it with him, it feels like I'm rediscovering the movie—even though I've seen it a hundred times—and finding every joke funnier. I'm guessing this might have something to do with the alcohol coursing through my veins.

Haze thought it'd be a good idea to drink the beers he bought earlier and watch a movie while we ate dinner. One thing's certain: he sure didn't expect the only DVD left in the house to be *Grease.*

"Are we going to another dimension? Or space?" He frowns, tilting his head to the side.

I laugh. "Just go with it."

"I mean, I get it. They graduated, they're happy, the girl got hot, and the bad boy's gone soft, but what the hell is this? A flying car? Is this a sci-fi movie and I missed it?"

The closing credits begin, and after arguing with me about the necessity of the flying car scene for a few minutes, Haze gets up and scoops the beer bottles off the ground.

"I'm going to throw these out. Be right back." He turns around one second before he leaves. "You want another one?"

"Sure. Why not?"

He walks out of the room, and I let myself gape at the stars through the living room's high windows. This is breathtaking.

"There you go." Haze walks back into the room and hands me my beer.

"Thanks."

When he sits down next to me, we're left with nothing but silence and this tension that follows us everywhere we go. My eyes divert to the grocery store pizza box on the table.

"That pizza was beyond disgusting, by the way."

"Yeah. Next time we'll get it delivered." He takes a sip of beer.

I look up at him. "Does that mean we're going to be eating pizza this entire time?"

"Well, unless you cook, yes," he says.

"What about you? Do you cook?"

He avoids my eyes. "Nah."

He's lying.

"Bullshit. You totally do." I point an accusing finger at him.

He throws his head back with a sigh. "Fine, I might know how."

"No way! Haze Adams cooks. You have got to show me."

"How do you do that?" he groans and slumps farther into the couch before I can ask him any more questions about his past as a chef.

"Do what?"

"See so clearly through my game."

"What can I say? I know your lying ass pretty well by now." I push my hair over my shoulder jokingly.

He scoffs, impersonating me and pretending to push his nonexistent long hair to the back in a ten-times-more-ridiculous manner. I chuckle and throw a pillow at him.

"There's a nice restaurant downtown. We could go grab a bite there tomorrow morning if you're not feeling pizza for breakfast."

"Sure. I'd love that." I can't help but wonder if this is his way of asking me out.

"Hey, can I ask you a question?" A seriousness covers his features out of the blue.

I nod. "Ask away."

"Are you a virgin?"

I smile, remembering how he tried to get the info out of me via text many times in the past. I never answered.

"Wouldn't you like to know?" I tease.

"Oh, come on." He puts his hands up.

"What do you think?" I challenge him.

"I don't know. That's why I'm asking. I can't read you." He squints his eyes like it will help him uncover my secrets. "On one hand, you totally give me *innocent girl in bed* vibes, but on the other…" He smirks, giving my imagination a million chances to finish his sentence.

"On the other what?"

I'm not sure I want to hear the rest. He lets my thoughts run unnecessary miles before speaking again.

"You also look like you could blow a guy's mind if you wanted to."

I ignore the suggestion dripping from his voice, biting on the inside of my cheek. Why am I all of a sudden even more drawn to him? It's like I'm battling this urge to pull him closer and say "let's find out." *So much for being friends, huh?*

He speaks again. "So, are you?"

"What?"

"You know what."

Only then do I notice that we've gotten closer to each other without even realizing it. This couch is huge, but our bodies didn't get the memo. We're a bit too close to be talking about things like this. Especially after the numerous beers I've had.

I draw a breath. "I wish I was."

"Ooh, *dark*." He rests his chin in the palm of his hand and stares at me intently. "What happened?"

"Let's just say hearts were broken and it got real awkward real fast." I take a long sip of beer. I don't want to get into this with him. Not now. Not ever.

"Bad sex, huh?"

"Haze," I say, a small smile covering my lips.

"What?" He puts his hands up. "Isn't that like a universal

rule that most first times suck?"

"You mean the romance stories where the girl's been saving herself up for nineteen years only to end up having the perfect first time with the oh-so-perfect boy isn't always real?" My mouth drops open in mock disbelief.

He laughs. "Go figure."

Quickly, the harmless questions become more… personal. And as much as I want to think of myself as someone private, the embarrassment I usually feel every time someone asks me about sex is nowhere to be found. We end up telling each other about our favorite positions—not that I really have enough experience to know which one I like best—and I'm not uncomfortable at all. Not with him.

On beer number seven, I've officially had enough.

"Your turn. What about your first time?"

"It was…" He pauses. "Okay, I guess. It was her first time, too, so."

I hate myself when a hint of jealousy burns within my stomach. They were each other's firsts. It wasn't just sex. They were intimate. She must've been really special to him.

Don't do that, Winter. He obviously had a lot *of "intimate moments" with girls, so if you start feeling bad about all of them you'll be wallowing in bed until next year.*

I remember what Blake said to me at the hotel about how Haze got a girl pregnant at sixteen. We never really got around to talking about that since, the very next day, I was out of town.

Riley. That was her name.

"Was it Riley? Your first time I mean?" I ask.

Instantly, his smile fades. He sits straight and away from me.

"We never really talked about what Blake said that night..."

He doesn't speak, staring at the hardwood floor.

"You know, about you being a father."

"There's nothing to talk about." His tone takes me by surprise. "Blake's a fucking psycho, and she got an abortion. End of story."

How'd he go from nice to cold as ice in minus two seconds?

"Are you sure?"

"Yes, I'm sure. Can we change the subject now?"

Okay. Sensitive nerve right here.

"But why? Why won't you talk about it, Haze? It'd be good for you to—"

"Damn it, Winter. I said no," he snaps, raising his voice to the point of turning my blood cold.

I don't speak for a few seconds, shock plastered on my face.

"Fine. Gee, no need to freak out. I was just trying to be a good friend."

As soon as I pronounce the last word, his face darkens and he lets out a bitter laugh.

"Then, as a *friend*, I'm asking you to respect that I don't want to talk about it."

I know I shouldn't have said it, but my irritation with his infuriating habit of doing everything he possibly can not to open up to anyone got the best of me. I couldn't help it. I had to use the forbidden word to try and get a reaction out of him. It's like the dude would rather die than be vulnerable for five seconds.

"I'm tired. Can you help me upstairs?" I ask after a few minutes of heavy silence.

"Sure." He nods, his voice softer than before.

When we get onto the second floor, Haze leads the way to his room. I use my crutches to head for the closest guest room instead, and he stops me.

"What are you doing?" His eyes bore into mine. "That's one of the coldest rooms in the house. You might catch a cold."

"I think I'll take my chances." I pick up my luggage—that we left in the middle of the hall when we came up in a rush earlier—get inside the guest room, and shut the door behind me. Seconds pass. I hear him sigh. Then, his door closes, too. I fall backward and collapse onto the freezing queen-size bed.

He's never going to let me in.

No doubt about it…

These are going to be the most frustrating weeks of my life.

THERE ARE MANY REASONS WHY HAZE Adams and I can't be friends. The main one is that, as a friend, I don't think I'm supposed to drool when I see him in nothing but a towel in the morning.

I've been trying not to make eye contact with him too much since I ran into him walking out of the bathroom half-naked. All

I can see when I look at him are the drops of water slowly rolling down his abs, and I might need a bit more than fifteen minutes to get that image out of my head.

We're sitting in the car and heading for the breakfast restaurant Haze talked about yesterday. The atmosphere feels heavy. Mostly because of the mini fight we had last night. He's been acting like nothing is wrong, but I can tell we both have a lot on our minds.

I hold back a small cough and see him frown from the corner of my eye. That's the third time I've coughed today, and he's had the exact same reaction each time.

He was right: I froze my butt off last night. But I was trying to prove a point: that we can't get closer physically unless he lets me get close to him on a deeper, more meaningful level. I hope I'm not getting sick for nothing.

"We're here," he says and points to a restaurant on our left. Beck's, the sign reads.

Haze quickly finds a parking spot and helps me out of the car.

We walk into the crowded although very simple restaurant, and I think this may be one of the only places I've seen driving around Colton Gate that doesn't scream "exorbitant." It's welcoming, warm.

As soon as we step foot inside, a gorgeous waitress greets us. She immediately raises her eyebrows at the sight of Haze.

I know, girl, I know.

“Welcome to Beck’s. Table for two?” She smiles, shamelessly devouring Haze with her eyes. She could at least *try* to be subtle. We only nod as a response. “If you don’t mind me asking, are you a couple? We currently have a promotion for—”

He cuts her off. “We’re just friends.”

Ouch.

“Oh. All righty, then. Follow me.” She poorly tries to contain her joy and leads the way.

I do my best not to display any reaction, but I’m boiling on the inside. This is getting ridiculous.

It didn’t sound like we were just friends when you started undressing me in that motel room, Haze. Or when you told me you loved me right before I passed out.

We both sit down at a table next to the bay window and exchange looks that are packed with insinuation.

If you could read somebody’s intentions in their eyes, mine would say…

Game on.

FIDGETING WITH MY PHONE, I WATCH the waitress pull her third attempt at getting Haze to become more than just a customer. First, it was the “Oops, I dropped something” in front of him. Then, it was the “Oh, no worries. Dessert is on the house”—which, really surprised me, by the way. Turns out she’s the daughter of the owner—but this… this is the best one yet: her phone number on a napkin when Haze asked her to get us more after I made a mess.

I'll be honest, it's beyond annoying. But what eases the burn is the way Haze doesn't seem interested. He's made sure to pretend he didn't see her number on the napkin and ripped his eyes away when she gave him a first-class view of her behind. Now, that's got to take some skills. I think the whole restaurant looked, to be honest.

We spent the meal talking and, surprisingly, laughing. We managed to act like there weren't a million unresolved issues between us and went back to the way we usually are: chatty and random. But I'm not forgetting the friend stunt he pulled on me earlier. Not even close.

"There you go." She hands him the bill, her seductive smile fading away when she sees the napkin with her number on it has been used to clean up my mess. I think she's just starting to realize he has got to be doing it on purpose.

"I got it," Haze says and reaches for the bill, but I lean forward, stealing it away from his fingers.

"My treat. You've been paying a lot recently. What are friends for?"

I'm certain the emphasis I put on my last sentence didn't go unnoticed, but I don't dare look up at Haze to catch a glimpse of his reaction.

What I see instead is the waitress and the suspicion crossing her face. It looks like she's thinking, *"Well, damn. These two clearly have their own shit going on."*

"It's fine. I don't mind paying." He leans over the table and takes the bill back from me.

"But—"

He gets a look at the total and taps his credit card on the machine before I can finish my sentence. He offers me a victorious smile and leaves a twenty-dollar bill on the table. The waitress grabs it, tells us to have a good day, and awkwardly walks away. We exit the restaurant in complete silence.

When we pull back onto the road minutes later, I start coughing again.

That's when he snaps.

"Fine. You win."

I hold my breath, waiting for him to finally acknowledge the elephant in the room. We'll never be friends. He knows it. I know it. Let's stop this nonsense.

"What are you talking about?"

"Don't even try."

My heartbeat increases. I sink in my seat, ready for him to destroy the wall of lies standing between us since we got to the lake house.

"You're obviously getting sick."

Well, I didn't see *that* coming.

"How about this? I'll tell you one thing you don't know about me every day that you sleep in my bedroom with me."

A smile tugs at my lips. That's not what I was going for, but the fact that he's worried about me getting sick makes up for it.

I narrow my eyes, pretending that I need to think about it first, when, in fact, I know I'll take whatever he has to give me over pneumonia any day.

"Deal."

His mouth quirks up into a smile. "Good girl."

He turns on the radio and upbeat music bursts out of the speakers. What was left of the awkward tension from yesterday is now officially gone.

"So, shoot." I glance at him.

"What?"

"What's my first fact about you?"

He changes lanes and furrows his eyebrows like he's trying to find something to tell me that won't give too much away.

"My birthday's December twenty-third," he says after a while.

"Really? Do you only get gifts for Christmas since it's so close? Or do you only get presents on your birthday?"

"I don't really get gifts on either day. Or at least, not in a very long time."

Somehow, my soul aches for him. Not because Christmas and birthdays are all about gifts, but because of the way he said it. He sounded like he'd be really surprised to ever get one.

I want to ask him a dozen more questions, but, since I know he'll tell me that I already got one fact out of him today, I push my curiosity aside, watch him take the exit to get back to the lake house, and eagerly await tomorrow.

"IS THAT WHAT YOU CALL SLEEPING on your side of the bed, Adams?" I laugh when Haze sprawls onto the oversized mattress carelessly. The day flew by, and the moment I dreaded the most is here. The moment where I have to sleep in the same bed as the guy who's been driving me completely nuts since the moment I met him.

We woke up so late this morning that we got out of the breakfast restaurant at around 2:00 p.m. And, from there, hours became minutes and minutes became seconds. I only realized it was nighttime when I looked out the window. Time flies when I'm with him.

"I don't know. I guess we'll find out." He grins and gets off the bed, sniggering when he catches the look on my face. "I do have to warn you though: I'm a cuddler."

I'm tempted to tell him that I'm well aware he's the cuddling type from the night we spent together at the motel, but decide against it. He might've forgotten all about our moments—and the way we fell asleep in each other's arms—but I didn't. I couldn't even if I wanted to.

Then—because that's what any sane person would do—Haze rips me back to reality by taking his clothes off right in front of me. As in, his shirt *and* his pants. This is becoming a habit of his, I swear. All I can do is stand there and stare at his looks-like-it-was-photoshopped body.

"Really? Again?" I don't tear my eyes away this time. Might as well enjoy it.

"What?" He beams. "You're lucky I'm even keeping the boxers on, Kingston. I always sleep naked. But for you, I'll make an exception."

I can't help but flush.

You better keep them on because I'm not sleeping comfortably knowing I could turn around and accidentally hit your dick.

"Are you going to get changed or?" He arches an eyebrow and slides under the covers.

I nod and turn on my heels to go to the bathroom—let me rephrase: I turn on my heels to go to the *closest* bathroom, since there two million in this house—but he stops me with just one sentence.

"Let me guess, you're a granny pajamas kind of gal."

I glance back at him. "What makes you say that?"

He turns off the lamp on the nightstand, the only light occupying the large bedroom now provided by the faint moon rays coming in through the window.

"I don't know. I guess you're just predictable like that."

I have no idea why I do what I do next. I can't stop myself. The urge to prove him wrong outgrows my prudishness and I act on impulse, keeping my eyes on him.

Without a warning, I pull the dress I'm wearing over my head and let it hit the floor. I'm suddenly very thankful that I chose to wear my cute undies today.

Haze's eyes grow four sizes, and his lips part as he takes in my dimmed silhouette. It's too dark to see properly, but he sees enough.

How's that for predictable, Adams?

"I sleep in my underwear, too, but nice try," I say, my heartbeat pulsing through my body.

It takes everything in me not to pick up my dress from the floor and throw it back on. I know I would've *never* done that in broad daylight. I would've never undressed in front of him like this if he'd seen me clearly.

"I… You… We…" Haze blabbers.

His search for the English language destroys my anxiety and makes me feel empowered. He's not so cocky anymore. I get under the cold blanket, ignoring the heat radiating off his bare chest and the way it so desperately calls out to me.

"Good night, Haze," I whisper.

The tension between us is so thick I know I won't be falling asleep anytime soon. He doesn't say a word for a while, until eventually, he breaks the silence.

"Good night, Kingston."

I have no idea how long this teasing thing is going to last, or what it's going to take for us to stop lying to ourselves, but from what I can gather, neither of us intend to break first. I think back to what happened at the restaurant and mentally curse. Just friends, huh? Really, Haze? You want to play this game with me?

Fine.

May the best "friend" win.

NINE

Kiss Me

"Let's just say we're sick." Haze's voice echoes all the way from the kitchen to the second floor.

"Don't even try. We're going," I say from the bedroom and analyze the girl staring back at me in the mirror. I barely recognize myself under the winged eyeliner and mascara. This is the first time, since I moved into the lake house with Haze, that I've made the effort of wearing some of the makeup I bought—because Kendrick didn't pack mine as it would go against his plan to make me look like a hobo.

Today is Vic and Bea's dinner party. It's already been a week since I promised to make my "friendship" with Haze unbearable, and we're supposed to be spending the day at Vic's apartment. Since we won't be coming back to the house to get ready, I figured I'd pick out a dress to put on later and do my makeup in advance.

I open one of the many closets in the room—more specifically the one Haze told me to use—and reach for the black dress the creepy Ryder guy bought for me. I have two other dresses lined up, but I can't choose. I walk back to the mirror and hold dress number three up in front of my body.

Apparently, they weren't kidding when they said to dress up. Vic even called to make sure Haze wouldn't show up in a T-shirt. But what else did I expect from someone who lives in a town like this?

The six weeks are up and I've been able to walk again for a few days now. When I got my splint removed and put my foot back down for the first time in a while, I realized how much I'd missed it. Not needing Haze for everything I do felt strange at first, but I easily slid right back into my routine.

I throw the tight and fancy black dress on to refresh my memory. It looks even better than I remember. It rounds up my behind and accentuates curves I didn't even know I had. This is definitely going in my "catfish people into thinking I work out" pile.

"What's taking so lo—" I hear Haze come in and turn around quickly. My mouth opens on its own. I've never seen him look hotter. He's wearing a white shirt that looks like it was designed for him, the rolled-up sleeves revealing his inked left arm and making me wonder why he only got one arm tattooed.

The contrast is intriguing, endearing. One side is dark, intimidating while the other is bright and bare. One side says, "I'll make you scream my name," while the other says, "I'll meet your mama." This constant fight between good and evil, the troubled and the wise, the light and the darkness… this is such an accurate representation of who he is as a person.

I wonder if he knows his life story is written on his skin.

Escaping my thoughts, I stare and wait for him to finish speaking. I don't know if it's the makeup or the dress, but his words seem to have left him.

"What?" I glance back at my reflection, a bit worried.

"Winter, you look…" He doesn't speak for a little while. "Amazing."

I flush. "Thanks."

He stares for a few more seconds. Then, like he just remembered that we're still torturing each other, he looks away and clears his throat.

"What's taking so long? We have to be at Vic's in twenty minutes."

I hold back a sigh.

"I can't choose a dress. Can you help me?"

"Meh. I'm not sure I'm qualified, Kingston." He crosses his arms over his chest and leans against the doorway.

"Come on, do it for me." I let our eyes meet. "Be a good friend."

As they always do when I mention the word friend, discomfort and annoyance run through his face. Or at least, I love to believe it.

"What do you need me to do?" He lowers his voice.

"What do you think of this one? Does it make my ass look big?" I spin to get an overall look in the mirror. He shifts from one foot to the other, chewing on his bottom lip.

"No… no, it doesn't. It's not too big. Not that it looks too small either, I mean… it's okay. It's perfect," he rambles.

I smile.

Anyone who knows Haze knows he is not the speechless kind of guy. Moments like this are the only way I know I have any effect on him these days. His nervous answers, his furtive glances… they're the only confirmation I have that I didn't imagine everything that happened before the lake house.

He's really going along with this friends thing, and it's driving me crazy. What's a girl got to do to get a guy to wake up around here? It'd be so much easier if I just confronted him about it, but he could've made a move on me multiple times by now, and he hasn't. That's got to mean something.

Maybe he's just not *that* into me anymore.

"So I should go with this one?" I ask.

"Definitely." He nods.

He makes sure to avoid looking at my body, sliding his hands into his pockets and fidgeting with his keys.

An idea comes to me.

"Do you think you could unzip me? I'll change back into my dress tonight." I pretend to struggle to reach the zipper.

He seems surprised by my request but agrees. He clears his throat again and walks toward me with hesitation lingering in his steps. Shivers erupt all over my body when he places one of his hands on my shoulder and pushes my hair to the front with the other. I see from his reflection that his jaw is clenched and his eyes are darker. He's battling himself.

But over what?

He slowly brings the zipper to my lower back, his fingers accidentally brushing my skin on the way down. Or *is it* accidental?

When he's done, he doesn't pull away like I would expect him to. He stands there with his hand on my shoulder and his breath crashing against my neck. I can't move a muscle.

The air hitches in my throat when he leans in and stops next to my ear. My pulse quickens, the anticipation of a move that might never come driving me mad. It's been like this since the night I slept in my underwear. He somehow caught on to what I was doing and started giving me a taste of my own medicine. Either that or he developed an unexpected passion for walking around shirtless.

I've been sleeping in my underwear every night—say it with me: *every freaking night*—and nothing.

Nada.

Zero.

Not even a little cuddle.

The guy's cold as stone.

We've been going back and forth like this for the past week, teasing each other and waiting for one of us to finally make the first move. He pulls, I push. We're like magnets refusing to touch.

I don't want to push anymore.

Right now, I want to surrender…

"I'll wait for you downstairs," he says and brings me out of a hypnotic daze. By the time I comprehend what just happened, he's walked out of the room and closed the door behind him.

"IT'LL BE FINE. WHAT ARE YOU so afraid of?" I ask as Haze and I step inside the elevator leading up to Vic and Bea's place. He'll never admit it, but anxiety has been eating at him since we left the house. I don't know why reconnecting with his childhood best friend is so bad.

"I haven't seen the guy in two years. It's just… what if it's weird?"

"It won't be. I'm sure it'll be like you were never apart."

"I still think we should've bailed," he says under his breath.

"Can you be positive for like two seconds?"

"Sure." He counts to two. "Time's up. Can we leave now?"

I laugh and elbow him.

"Hey, you haven't given me a fact about you yet today." I try to get him to think of something else while we go up to the seventh floor.

"Seriously? You want to do this *now?*"

"Oh yeah." I snicker. "And none of that 'my favorite color is green' crap. I want something meaningful."

He draws a breath and starts thinking—probably of a way to get himself out of this one like he did the others—and rubs at the back of his neck.

He's been making sure not to give me the good stuff since

he started telling me one secret a day. In the past seven days, I've learned that his first dog's name is Buster, that he used to have a really hard time going to the dentist as a kid because he'd always bite, that he's left-handed, that he hates pickles, that he's allergic to bees, and a bunch of other facts, but nothing that might help me understand what happened for him to be so untrusting. As much as I appreciate the little things, they still feel like a gate keeping me from accessing his heart.

The elevator doors open, granting us access to a long hallway.

"Which apartment is it again?" I ask.

"It's 306." Haze walks ahead. I assume he remembers the way from the last time he was here.

We stop in front of the right door and knock. A dog starts barking.

"Just a minute," a female, most likely Bea, says.

I turn to him. "Don't think you're getting away with it. I want my fact."

Approaching footsteps can be heard in the apartment. Locks rattle on the other side. Just when I think we won't have time, he hits me with the one sentence I did not expect.

"I don't believe in male and female friendship."

Did he just…

The door opens in a creak, and it takes all I have not to let my jaw hang. A smiling Bea and a barking pug stand in the doorway.

"Hey, guys. So glad you could make it. Please, come in."

We step inside and exchange pleasantries. Vic turns the corner and joins his girlfriend in greeting us. I try to listen to what they're saying, but all I can think about is how Haze just acknowledged that we're full of shit.

He knows we're not friends.

Bea picks up her pug and drags me into the kitchen while Vic takes Haze to what he likes to call his sports room. The small talk begins. I pet Rory, the excited dog, and nod along to what Beatrice is saying, but deep down, I know…

This is going to be a long day.

Haze

"SHE SEEMS REALLY NICE." VIC'S VOICE echoes in the almost empty room. We've been talking and watching a football game for a good hour and a half now. I'd be worried about leaving Winter alone with someone she doesn't know if it wasn't for how often we hear her and Bea laughing in the kitchen. Vic and I keep discussing useless topics I'm sure he isn't really interested in. I know what he truly wants to ask me, but he can't. He promised.

He hasn't changed one bit. He's still the same good old Vic who's obsessed with anything that rhymes with sports. I'll never say it out loud, but I missed that. I missed just hanging out with him. I've been missing having a friend I could trust ever since the day I left town.

The West side isn't loyal, and I know it. They're loyal to whoever's the strongest. I've been dodging their calls. They're wondering where the hell I ran off to, and I get it. I don't know how much longer I can keep telling them that I'm off to take care of business out of town. They're not stupid. They probably know that I'm with the "East side chick."

"Haze?" Vic speaks again.

I'm brought back to reality. "Huh?"

"I said she seems nice."

"Who?"

"Your girl. Sorry, your *friend*." He snorts at the word I used to introduce her to him.

A small smile hangs on to the corner of my lips.

"She is," I say.

"How long you two been dating?"

"We're not. She… it's complicated."

"Oh. So it's just physical, then?"

"Yes," I lie.

"You know, Haze, you were a lousy liar when we were kids, and you're even worse now."

I'm not even surprised when the words escape his mouth. The guy's known me since I was five. What did I expect?

I throw my head back with a sigh. "What gave it away?"

"Come on, man. I'm not dumb. You brought her back here. Now, I doubt it's because she's amazing in bed or because she's just a friend. You care about her, don't you?"

I think for a few seconds, my mind racing.

"Yes, I do."

This is the first time I've said that out loud since the night I told her I loved her. No wonder she might want more after that. Might as well ask her to marry me and then push her away while I'm at it. Watching her eyes close felt like someone gutting me on repeat. She was losing a lot of blood and about to pass out in my arms and it just… it just came out, I guess. But now, I know it was a mistake. This can only hurt her more. I still don't know why the hell I said it.

"And we haven't, by the way."

"You haven't what?" he asks, but quickly puts the pieces together. "Oh. You mean…"

I nod.

"Not even a little?"

"Nope."

He scoffs. "Wow. Haze Adams saves himself. That's a first."

My mind wanders to the dress stunt she pulled on me this morning. Does she know that I'm this close to pushing her up against the wall and ripping her clothes off, or is she really just *that* oblivious?

She asked me to unzip her dress, and I genuinely have no clue how I didn't strip her naked right there.

Not to mention that she's slept in her underwear every single night since she agreed to join me in my bedroom, and I'm beginning to think she's testing me.

No, I *know* she's testing me.

Vic's words come back to me. *Haze Adams saves himself.*

If he only knew.

"It's not me I'm saving. It's her. And trust me, it hasn't been easy. She's driving me completely insane. I'm telling you it's like she's doing everything in her power to make me break. All I want to do is back her up into a corner and…" I clench my jaw and stop myself from sharing the very dirty thoughts I've been repressing. "My balls are as blue as the fucking sky at this point, but I can't do that to her. I know if I sleep with her, she'll want more."

"And you don't?" he asks.

Do I?

"I can't. You know that."

"Says who?"

I grow irritated. "Says my entire life, Vic. Where have you been the past four years? You know I can never give her what she wants."

A short silence follows.

"Does *she* know?"

"What? That she's wasting her time with me? I don't think so. Not yet, at least."

"Then why did you bring her here? If you really don't want to commit? Why bring her to your hometown?"

He doesn't believe a word I'm saying.

"Because…" I open my mouth and close it.

Truth is, I don't know why.

Why do I do *anything* when it comes to Winter Kingston these days? Question of the century, folks.

"Haze… it's been four years since—"

One look from me. Just one.

That's all it takes for him to stop talking.

He retracts himself. "I know, I know. I'm sorry. We said not to go there. But you're going to have to talk about it eventually. It's time to start living again. And that girl… she could be it."

Does he really think I don't know that?

"Boys, the caterers will be here soon. Get your asses off that couch and come help us set everything up," Bea calls from the kitchen.

We exchange brief looks that mean the conversation is over and get up. We walk to the door, and one second before he turns the handle, he glances back at me.

"Listen, I don't know how long you're in town for, but if you ever need to talk, I'm here. I've had your back since kindergarten. I'm not stopping now."

I crack a sincere smile and follow him into the living room. I can't believe he's saying that to me after what I did. I regret cutting him off and ghosting him for years. I don't deserve his friendship. I stopped deserving it the second I left town with my family and started ignoring his calls. But he reminded me of things I couldn't bring to my new life. And so, to leave those things behind… I had to leave him, too.

"THANK YOU SO MUCH FOR DINNER, guys." I throw my arms around Bea's neck and hug her like we're best friends—which is funny considering we barely knew each other's names a few hours ago. She's a sweetheart, and I couldn't have asked for a better person to be "stuck" with after Haze dropped the friend bomb on me.

We say our goodbyes to Vic, Bea, and Rory the pug and walk to the elevator in silence. It's around 7:00 p.m. We're leaving earlier than the other guests because we've been here the entire day and, frankly, we've had enough of this social thing.

Overall, the dinner party was great. It was fancy so, of course, the food was delicious. It wasn't even *that* awkward with Haze—okay, maybe the free champagne helped a little—and I managed to have some fun along the way.

A friend of Vic asked for my number halfway through dinner. Haze witnessed the scene and got pissy. He didn't say a single word to me for a good thirty minutes and kept shooting the poor guy killer looks.

There he goes again with his mixed signals. So you haven't made a move on me *once* in the whole time we've been alone, but you can't stand to see someone else flirt with me?

Thankfully, the ride to the lake house is filled with laughter and chitchat. The party put us into a good mood, and I'm not even interested in asking him about today's confession. I'm done forcing things. If he wants me, he better make it clear.

He pushes the lake house door open, and I sigh in relief.

"Thank the Lord," I say, collapsing on the couch and kicking my heels off. "Why did I do this to myself?"

I ask myself this question every single time I wear heels, no exception. One day, I'll learn.

"What's that smell?" Haze gags.

I frown.

"Found it." He points to my bare feet.

"Shut up." I throw the pillow on the couch at him, and he dodges it, grinning.

"Seriously, you should open a window or something." He laughs.

I'm about to send a snarky reply his way when my phone vibrates with a new text message. It's from the guy I met tonight. He seemed nice and he was definitely cute, but I'd be lying if I said that the way Haze glared at us isn't the only reason I gave him my number.

"Who is it?" Haze pulls an eyebrow.

"The guy from the party."

I think I see a hint of irritation flash in his eyes for one fleeting second.

"What's he saying?" He sits next to me.

"None of your business." I stick my phone two inches away from my face to text back without Haze seeing my reply.

"Give me that."

In the blink of an eye, he's stretched his arm out and stolen my phone away from me. I immediately bounce to retrieve it, but he's too strong, and I quickly find myself howling with laughter while I try to take back what's mine.

"Wow. You're actually a lot stronger than I thought." He laughs while we go back and forth on the couch.

"And you're a lot weaker." I tease.

"Am I?"

I can't repress a small yelp when he stops going easy on me and pulls on the phone with all his strength. I fall backward onto the couch, laughing so hard it takes me a short instant to become aware of the position we've gotten ourselves into.

He's on top of me, our bodies as close as can be.

The air gets stuck in the back of my throat when our eyes lock. Our laughter fades out until the only thing we can hear is the sound of our breathing merging. This is probably the closest we've been since the night he said he loved me. I expect him to pull away, the way he always does when we get too close, but he doesn't.

Not this time.

His gaze descends to my mouth as one of his hand moves up to my waist. He places his available hand on my cheek, his thumb slowly running along my lower lip.

Holy sweet mama of goodness.

My heart starts hammering in my rib cage. He leans in, his face a few inches away from mine. Our lips are about to tou—

"Anyone in here?" Multiple knocks on the front door make us jump.

Haze lets out a short sigh. He doesn't get up to open the door. Instead, he tightens his hold on my waist, the light fabric of my dress the only thing standing between his fingers and my bare skin. He's going to wait for the cockblocker to go away.

I find myself both hating and thanking the Universe for what's happening. I've been playing this exact moment in my head on repeat for so long, and now that it's here, I'm terrified. Until now, it was all speculation. But if we cross this line, there's no going back. No more lying to myself. No more denying what I'm feeling. If we kiss, I'll be all in.

I'll fall.

Falling for Haze Adams feels like jumping out of a moving plane, realizing your parachute won't open midair, screaming the whole way down and freaking out as you slowly watch the ground get closer, only to land on a cloud, get back up and say, "Again! Again!" The fall is fucking terrifying... but the landing is *beautiful.*

On knock number two, Haze sighs. We're both thinking the same thing. He's not going away. What he decides to do next renders me speechless. He leans in and whispers something against my lips.

That's it. I'm gone. *Someone reboot my brain.*

He uses both his arms to pull himself up, gets off me, and drags his feet to the front door. Here I am, lying on the couch with my mouth agape and the last words he said to me spinning around in my head.

Deep down, I wish he would've said, "I'm sorry. I don't know what got into me. It won't happen again." Then maybe I could get over his blue eyes and irresistible smile. Maybe I could forget the way he first kissed me on the beach and the sensation of his fingers tracing the curve of my hips.

But he didn't.

Far from it.

He said the one thing I was both desperate and afraid to hear…

"We're not done, Kingston."

TEN

The Storm

A man that looks around forty years old is standing on Haze's porch, his eyes wrinkled with worry. He looks like he's carrying the weight of the world on his shoulders, the exhaustion taking all he has to give.

"Yeah?" Haze's voice is dry.

"Hi. I'm so sorry to show up unannounced, Mr. Adams. I hope I'm not bothering you."

Here we go again with this Mr. Adams thing. Why do people in this town treat him like he's their superior? I furrow my eyebrows, waiting for Haze to clarify the situation.

"We were busy, actually." Innuendo laces his voice. I bite back a smile. The guy has no shame, whatsoever.

"I apologize. I saw your car in the driveway. I didn't know someone was home. I'm afraid your parents didn't mention that detail."

"That's because they don't know," Haze says, a hint of annoyance in his voice. "My parents sent you?"

"Yes. To check on the house for tonight's storm."

So, this man is an employee of Haze's parents? No, wait. Not the part I should focus on. There's a freaking storm coming?

"Hold on. What storm?" Haze asks.

He doesn't know either.

"Didn't you hear? It's been expected for a while now."

That's when the pieces come together. Today is Saturday. I think back to how Ryder, the guy who bought me the dress, said "Good luck for next Saturday" last week. I didn't think much of it at first, but now it all makes sense.

"I don't exactly come to town often," Haze replies. "So why are you here?"

"Your parents sent me to board up some windows and make sure the house would be fine."

"Of course. Bastards haven't come here in years but still don't want to lose a sellable property," Haze mutters more to himself than to us. "How bad is it going to be?"

"Violent winds, lots and lots of rain. We'd be really surprised if we don't lose power. Hope you have plenty of food, candles, and blankets just in case."

"Yeah, no worries. We still got some leftovers from the last storm."

The last storm?

Did he just say the last storm? How many of those do they have around here?

"When is it starting?" I ask.

"Two hours from now."

"All right. Well, I'll let you do what you came here to do. Oh, and if you could not tell my parents about us being here, I'd really appreciate it." Haze dives his right hand into his pocket and slips the man a hundred-dollar bill.

Just like that.

No hesitation.

Who casually walks around with a hundred-dollar bill in their pockets?

Haze freaking Adams, apparently.

And why would he waste that kind of money so that his parents don't know their own kid is in their house?

The man's eyes widen, and he happily accepts his donation. "Of course. I'll be an hour tops."

He tells us he'll be back to *un*stormproof the house tomorrow. We watch the man walk back to his car and open his trunk to get whatever he needs to do his job. Haze shuts the door and turns away, ignoring my partially opened mouth.

"We still got leftovers from the last one? Are you kidding me right now? You brought me to a town where dangerous rainstorms are a thing?" I follow him up the stairs.

"The last one was years ago. Back when we still liv—" He stops himself, probably thinking that he's oversharing. "Back when I was a kid."

Now, I know for sure that he must've grown up in Colton Gate. What I can't be certain of is whether or not it was in this house or if this is just his parents' summer house.

"What are you doing?" I try and catch up to him.

"You heard the man. We need to get ready for the storm."

"What's going to happen? Is this how we die?" I ask, and he chuckles.

"Nah, we haven't been evacuated. This one's a softie."

He pulls on the string of the retractable ladder leading up to the attic and disappears in the black hole embedded into the ceiling. He uses his phone's flashlight to find what he's looking for and comes back with a box labeled Emergency.

"Well, that's reassuring," I say.

"It's a bunch of candles, lighters, canned food, and like a few blankets. Big fucking deal," he teases. "I gotta get some wood for the fireplace if we don't want to freeze. Would you go around the house to make sure all the windows are closed?"

"Sure." I nod and watch him stride down the stairs.

The front door is shut, and I hear the rattling sound of a hammer hitting a plank outside. The Adamses' employee is starting the job.

I've become quite familiar with the house in the time I've been here, so I go through every room pretty quickly—even the thousand bathrooms—and find myself without a task after barely fifteen minutes.

Or at least, I think so until I spot the one door I haven't opened yet.

It's hidden and at the opposite end of the hall. Now that I think about it, this is the only room Haze didn't show me during the tour. I just assumed it was a closet.

I decide to go check just to be sure. I walk to it and slowly turn the handle. The door opens with a loud creak and immediately a cold—no, a *freezing*—breeze runs down my spine. It's clear that no one's opened this door in a very, very long time, and something tells me this goes back to way before Haze's family stopped using the lake house.

It's a kid's room. No doubt about it.

A tiny unmade bed is centered in the middle of the room. Everything looks so… untouched. It could almost make you believe that someone slept in here yesterday.

My eyes divert to the floor. A dollhouse and a bunch of toys are lying on the ground next to the bed. They look expensive. These are rich kids' toys. I know them all too well from the numerous commercials I saw on TV when I was younger. We could never afford them. It feels like whoever used them just got up in the middle of playing, left the toys on the floor, and never came back.

Could this kid have something to do with the empty frame and the cut picture I found on top of the fireplace?

"What the hell do you think you're doing?"

My heart jumps out of my chest.

I turn around and see Haze's tall frame standing in the doorway. His eyes are hard, dark. The arctic temperature of the room is nothing compared to the icy discomfort his words bring to my soul.

"I… I'm sorry. You said to shut all the windows, and I wanted to make sure I got them all."

"So the fact that I didn't show you this room when I gave you a tour didn't ring a bell?"

I don't move or speak, frozen in place.

"Get out," he says, and my body decides now is a good time to reconnect with my brain. I walk around him, and he locks the door. The Haze I know—or think I know—seems like a distant memory. The guy standing in the doorway was completely different. He was mean, harsh—*empty*. And in his eyes… was the same pain I saw on that portrait of him at fifteen.

"I'm sorry," I say again even if I don't understand what the big deal is.

So, he has a younger sibling. What's the problem with me finding out?

"It's fine. You didn't know. Just don't do it again." His voice softens although he is still upset. I follow him to the first floor where a bunch of wood is waiting next to the fireplace. I look out the window and see it's started to rain. I know the man boarding up the windows is not done yet. Hopefully, he will be soon. I wouldn't want to be outside when the storm hits if I were him.

"OKAY. CAN WE PUT THIS BEHIND us, please?" I blurt out the second Haze finishes lighting the fire. The rain has only gotten worse, and thunder has joined us, too. We heard the man's car take off in a roar around thirty minutes ago. It shouldn't be long until the power is out, so we thought we'd get a head start and make the fire now.

It's been awkward between us since he lashed out on me for no reason. I'd like to know why he's so mad about something so harmless.

"Please say something."

He turns to look at me, his eyes piercing into mine. I hold my breath, afraid of what he's going to say.

"Something."

Of course. *Haze will be Haze.*

I can't believe I held my breath for this.

"Jerk." I roll my eyes.

"Prude." He smiles.

That's how I know we're not "fighting" anymore.

I sit on the carpet in front of the fireplace and enjoy the heat the waving flames provide. Haze sits down by my side and stretches. It must've taken him five minutes tops to light that fire.

"How did you know how to make a fire? Was Hazie a Scout?" I snigger.

He frowns. "Don't call me that."

"Whatever you say, Hazie."

He sighs, but I catch his grin.

"I believe I asked you a question, mister."

He runs a quick hand through his hair. "I wasn't a Scout. I was a son. My dad taught me when I was a kid."

I'm surprised by the information. *Was* a son? As in, not

anymore? He refrains from saying anything else, but we're making progress. This is the first time he's voluntarily mentioned his family or a somewhat personal story since I met him. All the other facts I had to practically blackmail out of him. I'm about to ask him another question when loud thunder makes me jump.

Everything turns black.

There goes the power.

We thought the fire would be enough, but we were wrong. We can barely see anything apart from the living room. I don't know why we thought that one tiny fire would be enough to light up this freaking mansion. I stare out into the gloom.

"Wow, we really can't see shit." He states the obvious. "I'm going to get the candles. Mind giving me a hand?"

"I'm right behind you."

I watch him get up and do the same. I try following him, but I lose him barely two steps into the kitchen. Why'd he have to walk so fast? I can barely see one inch in front of me, so how is his silhouette, that's dressed in black, going to make it any easier?

"Haze?" I let out a nervous laugh.

I hear footsteps getting closer but can't seem to figure out which side they're coming from.

I hear a light scoff.

"Stop, it's not funny."

"You scared of the dark, Kingston?"

I can't locate his voice.

"No," I lie.

I swear I will *never* admit that I run to my bed after turning off the lights. I'll take that secret to the grave.

"Well, you're definitely scared of something."

"I'm not."

I jump, feeling a presence behind me. I have no idea how he could even find me in this cave. My heartbeat goes from uneven to nonexistent when he presses his torso to my back and circles my waist with his arm. Slowly, he leans in until his mouth is next to my ear.

"Then why are you so tense?" he whispers.

Static and electricity linger everywhere he lays his fingers.

"Personal space, ever heard of it?"

He snorts. "Right, sorry."

Without a warning, he grips my waist with both his hands and spins me around to make me face him. He's even closer.

"Is this better?" he taunts.

"I… I don't know." I almost choke on the words.

Damn it, Winter, speak!

A faint streak of moonlight peeking through the partially covered window allows me to see his chiseled features.

"Well, what does your gut tell you?"

"My gut gets me in trouble. I've learned not to trust it anymore." My voice comes out in a murmur.

"Why? I always follow mine." He seems intrigued.

"And it's always right?"

"Yes," he says.

Bitter thoughts flood my mind.

Don't say it, don't say it, don't say it.

"Like it was right when it told you to go sleep with Bianca after you said you loved me?"

I finally let the truth that's been dominating my brain for the past month come out. I never confronted him about what he said that night. I never really had a chance. I bet he wondered if I even heard him at all.

When he doesn't reply as quickly as I anticipated, a wave of nerves and regret drown me.

"I… I'm sorry. Just… Forget I said that." I turn away, intending to walk back to the fireplace, but he captures my wrist and yanks me back to him.

I suppress a gasp.

In the moonlight, I see everything, from the way he narrows his blue eyes, to the way he tries to figure out what I'm feeling, to the way he destroys my ability to think properly with just one look.

"It's fine. Really. I get it, Haze. You thought I was going to die and you felt bad, so you said…" I ramble. "I understand that it didn't mean anything. Plus, you tell everyone that we're friends. It's oka—"

He cuts me off. "Winter, look at me."

I don't move, my heart caught in a war against my brain.

"Look at me," he repeats, cupping my face with his hand.

He lifts my chin up to let our eyes come together. I hate that I shiver at the contact.

"I told you. I didn't sleep with her."

I refuse to let his pretty words work their magic on me but can't help but want to hold on for dear life to the sincerity in the back of his irises. I want to believe him. I really do.

"Right," I whisper.

"It's true. Yes, I showed up at her house, but I didn't sleep with her. I must've been there two minutes, if that."

He pauses and places a hand on my cheek.

"And, for the record, I didn't say shit because I felt bad or because I thought you were dying." He lowers his eyes to my mouth for a few endless seconds. "I meant what I said."

If I thought I was shocked before, I definitely wasn't ready for this.

"I still do."

A whirlwind of disbelief captures me. His words hit me so hard I know I won't be able to formulate a comprehensible sentence anytime soon.

He steps closer and I step back, reminded of the countless times we almost kissed. We've been there, we've done that. We've been through this before.

But… is this time different?

"So, no, I don't want to be your friend, Kingston."

Oxygen.

I need oxygen.

"I don't want to be near you knowing I can't push you up against the wall right now and do all the things we talked about last week." I know he's referring to our lovely favorite-positions talk. "I don't want you to give your number to another guy, and I especially, really, truly don't want to help you pick out a dress."

My back hits the wall, and I know that I can't run from my feelings anymore. I'm cornered. *Literally.* He keeps leaning in, and just before his mouth can touch mine, he stops.

"Not if I can't be the one tearing it off of you."

In a heartbeat, he closes the distance between us and crashes his lips against mine. I automatically kiss him back, my pulse quickening. When his fingers wander to my hair and he pulls my head forward to deepen the kiss, I swear I can hear my heart explode. I can't find it in myself to think about anything but his mouth moving in synchronization with mine when we embark on a dance we've been craving for longer than we can bear.

What if I actually died right there? What if my poor heart couldn't handle Haze Adams? Winter Kingston, died from kissing the guy she'd been crushing on. Rest in peace, *idiot.*

In moments like this, it doesn't seem too far-fetched.

I recognize the urgency from the day we made out at the motel, but this feels like more than just "making out." It feels like a step toward something else… something inevitable.

When we pull away for air, he brings his lips to my earlobe.

"Want to take this upstairs?" His voice is raspy, thick.

I swallow the pit in my throat, the desire in my lower

stomach agreeing with him while my head is screaming to escape before it's too late.

He reaches for my fingers and pulls on my hand, leading me to the staircase. When we go up the stairs in complete darkness, I almost trip—because I wouldn't be me if shit like that didn't happen in the worst moments possible—and he catches me before I hit the ground. He laughs at my clumsiness, and this simple incident calms my racing thoughts.

This is still Haze.

He's still the guy who can make you laugh until your stomach hurts. He's still the guy you spent fifteen minutes arguing about Grease *with. You* are *friends.*

It isn't long until my back hits the queen mattress and Haze kicks the door shut. He gets on top of me, his toned body calling my name, and places one arm on each side of my head to hold himself up.

His mouth finds mine again, but this time, his tongue pries its way in between my lips and I can't believe I wasted so much time being afraid. Here we are, kissing in the dark, in the middle of a storm, in a town nobody knows about to escape people potentially trying to kill me, and I've never felt more alive.

His kisses are eager, hungry. It isn't long until the clothes are peeled off his skin and he's in nothing but his boxers. He tugs at my dress straps, letting them cascade down my shoulders, and slowly kisses my stomach as he pulls the tight black dress all the way down to my feet. I want to feel his mouth everywhere, and when I say everywhere, I mean *everywhere.*

He throws my dress across the room and stares at my uncovered body. Strangely, I don't feel exposed. The look in his eyes makes me feel confident.

"You're so fucking beautiful," he exhales and leans forward to kiss me. He gradually descends to my neck.

Neck kisses… man, I am *not* responsible for what happens if you kiss my neck.

He sucks on the skin above my collarbone, and it's enough to make my thoughts blurry. Then, he pulls away, stares at my neck like he's admiring his work of art, and grins. I know that grin. It's the "I did something and you're going to be pissed" grin.

"You didn't." I catch up right away and bring my hand to my neck as if I will somehow fix the damage he did.

He beams as an answer.

I'm going to kill him.

I'm about to scold him when he places a hand on my stomach and slowly works his way down to my panties. I press my lips into a thin line, and his smile grows wider. He knows how to shut me up, and he likes that.

His hands are warm, but my skin is so hot they almost feel cold. He stops just under my belly button and glances at me. He's waiting for me to say yes. I know he won't make another move until he has my approval. I pull his face to mine and kiss him again, whispering a quiet yes against his lips.

Without breaking the kiss, he crosses the line we won't be able to cross back.

He slides his hand under the light fabric of my underwear, and his fingers connect with a spot I haven't let anyone touch in a really long time.

I tense up at the contact. He feels it and stills his hand, leaving it exactly where it is for a few seconds. He pulls away, his eyes searching for mine, and stares at me for a short moment as if to make sure that I'm ready to *really* listen.

"Just one word, Winter. Say it and I'll stop."

His sentence makes me feel better. Not because I expected anything less, but because having him say it to me makes me feel respected, comfortable. This, right here, is how we should always feel in a moment like this.

He starts moving again. Every muscle in my body relaxes all at once when he starts rotating his fingers exactly where he should.

Okay. Wow.

I don't know what I expected, really. I didn't think Haze Adams would be bad, obviously, but I'd somehow convinced myself that he couldn't possibly be attractive, funny, *and* good in bed. I told myself that it wasn't possible. That surely the Universe took pity on regular humans and put a limit of perfection on individuals like Haze. But apparently, there is no such thing as a limit of unfairness in this world. *What's up with that, Universe?*

He presses down on me in a rough way that drives me completely mad and listens to my body, adjusting his speed to every sound I make and every tiny reaction I have.

I throw my head back with a sigh and think I see something flash in his eyes when I bite back a moan. I find myself wrapping a hand around his arm without realizing it and tighten my hold every time my body ignites with delight. He takes his lower lip between his teeth, watching my facial expressions change.

I'm slightly surprised when his fingers travel downward. Again, he dives his blue eyes into mine, waiting for the green light. I tremble in anticipation and nod yes.

My heart gives a jolt when he pushes a finger inside me.

It slightly hurts at first, but the way he begins moving in and out of me all the while letting his thumb start up the circles again quickly shatters the pain. It's getting hard to be quiet.

He tries to add a finger but sees it's not going to work just yet, so he doesn't force it. Soon enough, the moisture between my legs tells him to add that second finger.

"How does that feel?" He brings his mouth to my ear, his voice packed with lust. I don't reply. When he sees that I'm not going to answer, he speaks again. "Does that mean you want me to stop?"

I bite on my lower lip and shake my head like I'm afraid that opening my mouth will release the moans building up in my throat.

"I'm sorry, did you say something? I didn't catch that." He

smirks. "Do you want me to stop?"

I shake my head again.

"I want to hear you say it, Winter. Tell me how it feels."

I have no idea how I could expect Haze not to mess with me even in such a heated moment. This is still Haze we're talking about. Sometimes, I think his entire purpose for existing is getting me out of my comfort zone. Oh, and annoying me.

"No?" he insists. "Okay, then."

He stops moving, his finger abruptly ceasing their thrusting and circular motion. *What the hell?* The sudden absence of sensation immediately drives me nuts.

"What are you doing? Don't stop," I pant, tightening my hold on his buff arm and clenching my teeth.

"Why not?" he whispers. "What? Does it feel good?"

He's driving me crazy on purpose. He won't stop until he hears me say it.

"Yes, yes," I relent, raw desperation lying between every word. "It feels good. It feels so good. Don't stop."

He grins, my begging satisfying him. He starts moving again, curling his fingers in and out of me faster than he did before and speeding up his circles.

He applies more pressure, and I go from holding his arm to sinking my nails into it. That's for sure going to leave a mark, but I know he's probably used to having girls leaving marks on his body.

The thought of his fingers entering another girl while her

toes curl leaves an unpleasant taste in my mouth, but it quickly dissolves when an overwhelming feeling starts building up inside me. I don't know how much longer I can take this.

I'm not going to lie and say I've never climaxed before, or that it took Haze five minutes to get me there, but I know from the way my body shakes that what's coming is about to make anything I've known in the past seem like a cheap knockoff.

My breathing grows louder, and Haze buries his face into my neck to feather my collarbone with kisses.

"You drive me fucking insane, you know that?" he breathes out.

"I…" I try to speak, like my brain needs to find words to put on such an indescribable feeling, but fail.

My eyes widen when I begin to lose control. This is so unprecedented for me. I have the reflex of covering my face, feeling so vulnerable and exposed to this guy who seems to know me better than I do. He made me say these things, and Heaven knows I don't do dirty talk—if you could even call it that—he got me to beg and I… *I liked it.*

I usually have control over myself but not with him. Not with this. Right now, my body is entirely his, and it scares me.

"Don't." He grips my hands and gets them away from my face. "Don't hide. I want to see you. Look at me."

I chew on my lower lip, my gaze refusing to find his.

"Look at me," he says again, this time in a demanding tone.

And so I do.

I look at him. I look at him when my legs start to shake. I look at him when my mouth drops open and I arch my back. I look at him when I reach the peak and can't repress the moans anymore. I come undone while we're looking into each other's eyes and… as stupid as it may sound, that's how I know that I'm in trouble.

That there is no going back.

The memory of his fingers moving recklessly inside me as I shudder throw the truth I spent weeks denying right in my face.

I'm in love with him.

I'm in love with Haze Adams.

I fall in love with the one guy everybody told me to run from. Yes, fall. Not *fell*. Because I'm still falling… every second, every minute, every single time he looks at me.

Let me fall. As far, as long, and as hard as it takes.

Because if this is what falling feels like…

I'll fall for the rest of my life.

I come back down to earth, and the calm after the storm—ironic considering the raging thunder outside—settles around us. I glance down at his boxers that are clearly tighter.

"You were… That was…" I tumble over my words.

Haze smiles at my inability to speak and kisses me again, his tongue caressing my lips as his hand traces along the curve of my hip. With my body still trembling, I try and reach for the breath leaping away from me.

All I want to do is give back. I want to make him feel this

way. Thinking that I won't be able to do to him what he just did to me hurts. It's a lot to live up to. What if I'm just not *that* good?

Brimming with lust, I grip his hair through the kiss as he moans into my mouth and gets on top of me. I fight the urge to remove his boxers. He didn't even have to take my underwear off to make me beg. I don't want to imagine what he could do to me if we lost the clothes.

I know how this is going to end if we keep this up, and I want it. I want him. Of that I'm sure.

I've never wanted something more in my whole life, but I can't give away something so precious to me without the promise of a tomorrow. I can't sleep with him unless I know that I won't be just a friend when I wake up in the morning.

"Haze, wait…" I exhale, my legs still shaking.

His face turns into a mix of confusion and worry.

"I want this. I really do, but… what does this mean? W-what are we?" When they fall out, the words aren't the only thing that leave me. He does, too.

He doesn't move a muscle, but I can feel him mentally pulling away from me, his mind traveling, once again, to a faraway place he'll never let me explore.

"Why are you doing this?" His face twists in irritation, and his features harden.

There are a lot of things I expected him to say after what happened, a lot of ways I expected things to go wrong, but this… this, I did not expect.

He speaks again. "I don't know what you want me to tell you, Winter. Why can't we just be us?"

"Are you serious?" is all I can utter. He can't be doing this right now. Not when I just trusted him in such a personal way. Not when I let him touch me like that.

He gets off me. "You know how I feel about you. I want you and you want me. Simple as that. Why do we have to put a label on it? Why can't we just enjoy this?"

Heartburn.

"I… Because it's important to me. What? Do you think I do this often? That I go around doing things with people for fun? That's not me, Haze. I don't do no strings attached."

He becomes irritated, the guy who whispered in my ear while I came apart a few minutes ago vanishing with each painful second that goes by. I can't speak. I just stare at him in shock. So if I hadn't brought it up, we would've slept together. He would've taken the privilege without the commitment.

"I'm going to go sleep in the guest room," he lets out and rolls across the bed to get up.

"Haze!" I call out to him, but he ignores me and walks out of the room, slamming the door behind him.

My mouth flies open as I sit up on the bed and stare at the emptiness in disbelief.

That did *not* just happen.

It feels like every drop of hope in my body is torturously being drained out of me. I squeeze my thighs where his hand used to be and clumsily wrap my arms around my body as if to shield myself from the pain threatening to reach my heart.

I shed a tear at the movie scene unraveling in front of my eyes: A guy walking away without an explanation. A girl sitting there, in her underwear, with her heart in her hands and one question burdening her: What did I do wrong?

Haze might've taken me to cloud nine, but I fell back down to earth and hit the ground. I remember what my aunt always used to tell me. She was right.

Love is both a blessing and a curse. It is both the best thing and the worst. When loving someone with all your heart.

The higher you fly…

The harder you fall.

ELEVEN

Before it's too Late

I'm woken up by the sound of the front door slamming. Immediately, I sit up and rub my heavy eyelids. A short moment of oblivion is the best I can do because, apparently, the memories are just as eager to come back as Haze was eager to leave me last night.

It was almost perfect.

It could've been a fairy-tale scene.

If, of course, Prince Charming hadn't told the princess that he wanted to sleep with other princesses all the while still having access to her *castle*.

I reach for the lamp next to the bed and flick the switch on.

Nothing.

Still no power.

But what truly bothers me is the roar of a car coming from outside the house and the way it keeps on getting farther and farther away. I run to the window and barely manage to see Haze's black car disappearing down the driveway.

What the hell? Where is he going?

I take in the front yard of the house. A small tree fell over, but it's nothing too bad. The fact that we don't have power yet tells me that the damage must've been worse elsewhere in town. I walk back to the nightstand and reach for my phone. I have one text message. It's from Haze.

> Had stuff to do.
> Be back tonight.

Short and cold.

I ignore the sharp pain in my chest as well as his message. Is this the part where I look for cameras? He can't be serious right now. You take me away from my family, bring me to a town I don't know, tell me you love me, and then hook up with me, only to freak out when I mention commitment and leave me alone in a house with no power the next day?

Nuh-huh, I don't think so.

I throw on the first clothes I can find and search the internet for a cab company in Colton Gate. I frown when I read the first name that came up on Google.

Adams Taxi Co.

Adams? As in Haze Adams?

Could the Adamses own the taxi company? Before I let myself fall deeper into a toxic question cycle, I push all Haze-related thoughts out of my head and dial the number.

The only places with power will probably be stores and restaurants, and I am not spending the entire day here alone while Mr. Afraid of Commitment is out there doing God knows what.

"WELCOME TO BECK'S. HOW MANY PEOPLE?" The waitress from the last time I was here forces a smile at the sight of me. I get it. I wouldn't like me either. It sucks having Haze Adams slip through your fingers. I would know.

"Just one, please."

"You didn't bring your friend this time?" she says, the arrogance in her tone covered up by fake politeness.

I can't deal with this right now.

"No, he's out with his boyfriend today."

Her jaw drops.

I do everything in my power not to laugh.

I just *had* to. She gave me no choice.

To my great surprise, she looks relieved. I bet she thinks that this is why he was ignoring her pickup lines. Whatever helps her sleep at night.

She leads me to my table and brings me a menu. I don't know why I came back to the restaurant Haze and I went to. When the taxi driver asked me, "Where to?" I went for the only place in Colton Gate that felt somewhat familiar.

A short while after the waitress brought me the menu, she comes back to take my order.

"What can I get you?" She holds her notepad in her hands.

"I'll have the breakfast combo."

She nods. "Would you like a drink with that?"

"She'll have a cappuccino. It's on me."

I look ahead to see a familiar set of eyes staring back at me.

I recognize the guy who bought me the black dress a week ago. He just sat down in front of me. I'm tempted to ask him who he thinks he is to choose a drink for me but bite back my words.

"Make that two, actually," he says to the waitress.

She raises her eyebrows at him the same way she did at Haze the first time she saw him and gives him a warm smile.

Uh-uh. Looks like she's found her next victim.

I do have to agree with her: this Ryder guy is cute. I'd have to be blind to say that his dimples and messy black hair don't give him a head start on the good-looking scale, but he's not Haze. That's all I see when I look at any guy now: *Not Haze.*

"Hey. Winter, right?" He smiles.

"Yes," I say with uncertainty in my voice. "And you're Ryder if I recall?"

"That I am. Sorry to interrupt. I just saw you sitting there alone, and I thought you could use some company. Hope you don't mind."

I'm tempted to tell him to leave me alone but decide against it. We're in a public place, and he seems pretty harmless. Plus, I might as well talk to some people instead of just roaming around town alone for the rest of the day.

"No, it's fine."

"So, how was the storm last night?" he asks.

"It was windy," I joke but can't even muster a smile. "Weren't you there?"

"No, I was out of town. Just came back this morning."

"Well, you didn't miss much."

A bunch of small talk comes next, and I'm not that bothered by it. He knows how to hold a conversation, and he's pretty nice.

"So, did your boyfriend like the dress?"

That's right. He saw Haze back at the store.

"He's not my boyfriend." I take a long sip of water, hoping that the wait will make him change the topic. It hurts to say the words. No, he's not my boyfriend. He's not my boyfriend because he wants the sex but not the title.

"Oh, I'm sorry. My bad. It's just…" He pauses, obviously uncomfortable. "Your neck."

Shit.

It comes back to me. Haze gave me the biggest hickey of all time yesterday. It slipped my mind the second his fingers slid under my underwear. He got away with it. I can't believe it.

I bring my hand to my neck, my eyes widening. I'm going to kill him when he comes back from wherever he went tonight. Then, I guess I'll call Kendrick and leave the lake house. What else is left for me to do? Stick around to let him break my heart even more? I can't be just another Bianca to him. I won't.

"It's complicated," I say quietly.

"Well, if that makes you feel any better, I'm sure he doesn't know what he's missing."

Oh, he kind of does, actually.

Because my stupid ass let him into my pants.

I'm so thankful that I didn't go all the way. I would've felt awful if he'd told me he didn't want a relationship after we'd slept together.

When he sees that I don't intend to answer, Ryder takes the hint that I don't want to talk about it.

"What are you doing here alone anyway?"

"Power's still out where I'm staying, so I thought I'd spend the day in town."

The waitress brings us our meals and bats her eyelashes at Ryder, who also doesn't seem to notice. Maybe it's just a female thing, and I'm the only one who sees what she does. Maybe Haze really didn't have a clue last time.

"Well, there's a fair in a nearby town, and I have two free passes, if you're interested." He gets two tickets out of his pocket.

"They have power?"

"The storm went right by them. Lucky bastards."

"What's to say you're not a dangerous killer who wants to kidnap me?"

"I'm not, I swear." He puts his hands up. "But I get that this is what every serial killer says, so we can get a cab there if that makes you feel better. It's on me." He grins.

"Don't you want to use the passes on friends and family?"

"My friends are back home. I've been here visiting my grandparents for a while now, but I'm not sure Grandma would enjoy the monster roller coasters."

I let out a small laugh and glance at my phone. I have no new messages from Haze. He obviously doesn't care that I didn't answer his previous one. The pain burdens my heart, and the words come out before I can think about it.

"Sure. Why not?"

Haze

The rumble of my car is all I can hear when I pull into Vic's parking lot. I glance up at the large apartment complex building ahead of me and stop in the visitor spot. I don't know why I'm here. And by here, I don't mean at Vic's place.

I mean, in this fucking town.

I shouldn't have brought Winter here in the first place. I think I always knew, deep down, that eventually I couldn't contain myself anymore and it would come to this. Of course she would end up wanting a relationship. Any other scenarios I fed myself before that were bullshit. Why does she need the damn title? It's like she needs to put us into a cage.

I push the gear to park, kill the engine, and get out of the car with the memory of her body convulsing in pleasure intoxicating me. I can't stop thinking about how insanely sexy she looked. I can still feel my fingers squeezing their way inside her. She says that she's not a virgin, but just by the way she felt and how her innocent brown eyes widened at my touch… I'd be surprised if she'd had more than one guy.

And I know I'm an asshole who doesn't deserve her, but I really, really, *really*… want to be number two.

Images of us crossing the line fill my already messed-up head, and I shut the unwelcomed thoughts out. I could get hard just *thinking* about her. Not the time, brain.

I text Vic that I'm outside and to buzz me in. Barely a few minutes after, I'm inside the building and knocking on his apartment door. That's just how good of a friend Vic is. He wasn't kidding when he said I could show up at his place anytime I wanted. He was right. I can't run from the truth anymore. Which is why I have to talk to him. He's the only one who can help me.

The door opens in a creak.

"Haze, man, what are you doing here?" He raises an eyebrow.

I stare at him and finally let myself articulate the haunting words that have been following me everywhere I go for the past two years.

"Have you heard from Riley?"

TWELVE

Relationship Status

Winter

"Anyway, enough about me. You never answered my question. What brings you to Colton Gate?" Ryder asks, bringing a piece of cotton candy to his mouth.

We've been going around the fair for several hours now. Believe it or not, I managed to have some fun and even almost went a whole minute without Haze's name popping in my head.

Ryder is the polar opposite of Haze. He's an open book. I know almost everything there is to know about him simply from the afternoon I spent with him. He's nineteen, he grew up in New York, both his parents are dentists, he has a golden retriever named Rosco and a maid called Marta, who practically raised him. His grandparents live in Colton Gate, and he decided to come visit them because his grandpa isn't doing too hot lately.

"I told you. I'm on vacation."

"Yeah, but that's the short, crappy version you tell strangers. Why are you really here?"

Because I fell in love with a street fighter whose psycho brother kidnapped me and wants my head.

"No other reason. Sorry to disappoint."

"Does it have something do with this guy who's not your boyfriend but gives you hickeys?" he teases.

"Shut up." I force a laugh.

"Does it?"

"Maybe," I say quietly.

"I knew it." He seems proud of himself. "Let me guess, he won't commit?"

At first, I find the fact that he got it right creepy, but then I'm reminded that being afraid of commitment is common behavior in all males on planet Earth.

"Something like that." I fidget with the big teddy bear Ryder won at one of the darts games. I offered to carry it while he got us cotton candy.

He seems to notice the frown on my face because he elbows me slightly to get me to look at him.

"Hey, I'm sorry. He's a douche if he doesn't see the great girl that's right in front of him."

I can tell he's hitting on me, but I don't care. It makes me feel better to know that not every guy is as complicated as Haze Adams. Maybe I'd be better off dating someone like Ryder. No lies, no bullshit, just honest and reciprocated feelings.

We glance around the fair that's slowly emptying. It's closing at eight and it's 7:30. I'm not sure what's next, but I know I'm not looking forward to confronting Haze. I sure hope that the power's back at the lake house.

"I had a lot of fun today," he says.

"Yeah, me too. Thanks for the invite." I nod halfheartedly.

"You can keep Mr. Peppermint." He points to the teddy bear in my arm. I laugh at the name he's chosen.

"Are you sure?"

"Definitely. Giant pink teddy bear? That wouldn't fit in my room." He smiles.

The sound of a phone ringing lifts my hopes up only to send them crashing back down. It's Ryder's phone. Of course it couldn't be Haze doing a decent thing like calling to make sure I was okay in a house without power all day.

"Just a second." He steps away to take the call.

I unlock my phone. It's at 20 percent. We better get back to Colton Gate before it's dead and I can't get a cab back to the lake house.

He comes back. "There's a really nice pub back home. I was wondering if maybe… you would want to get a drink?"

"We're not legal, mister," I joke.

"They don't card."

I hesitate, battling myself on whether or not it's a good idea to take this day further with him. I don't like him like that. I don't think I'll like anyone like that again in a really long time. Worst part is, I'd probably be very interested in him if it wasn't for Haze, but his hold on my heart is far too important to want somebody else. It kills me to think that Haze could be with somebody else just fine since he refuses to be exclusive. The thought is enough to tempt me. I guess one drink can't hurt.

"Okay."

Haze

"So… that's the whole story," I say, the look on Vic's face making me feel even more stupid than the story itself.

I can't believe he got the whole explanation out of me. Vic has this annoying ability to get me to open up no matter how bad I don't want to. That tends to happen when you've known someone since diapers.

He didn't say a word once. He sat there and listened. I told him about the way it all started and how she was never supposed to be more than a way to piss off Kendrick to me.

Things would be so much easier if that was the case.

He shifts in his seat, furrowing his eyebrows in silence. It's already dark outside. I had no idea I'd end up spending the day here. It's a good thing Bea's at her mother's until tonight.

"Are you going to say something?" I grow impatient.

"Yes." He clears his throat like he's going to share words of wisdom with me. "Are you fucking dumb?"

Okay. Not what I expected.

"What?" I frown.

"No offense, but this girl… she's clearly the one for you, and you're telling me you're going to ruin it all because you're scared?"

My composure dumps me.

"You don't get it. I can't risk it. I can't let it happen to her, Vic. Not her."

He widens his eyes. "Would you just listen to yourself? You're talking like you have some sort of evil curse following you around or some shit. You were just unlucky, man."

"Unlucky? Is that what you call it? Unlucky?" I scoff.

He lets out a deep breath. "That's not what I meant. I'm just saying that you can't be afraid of being with Winter just because there's a chance that something will happen. You can't run from happiness just because there's a chance that you might lose it. That's like wearing a fucking raincoat every time you go out for the rest of your life just in case it rains."

His last sentence sinks in and creeps under my skin.

"Yes, shit happens. Sometimes, things get rough. But news flash: not every good thing in your life is going to go wrong, Haze. And guess what? Winter? You're in love with her. You're not fooling anyone. So you can either put your big-boy pants on and be a man or let her go find love somewhere else."

I'm stunned and unable to answer. Anger boils inside me as the last scenario he's just given me starts playing in my head. I can't deal with the thought of her looking at another guy the way she looks at me. I don't even want to *think* of her in some other guy's arms. Some other guy who would've told her what she wanted to hear last night.

"What are you waiting for?" he blurts out.

"What? You mean like now?"

"Yes, now!" He puts his hands up. "Don't you get it? You left her alone in a house with no power all day after you told her you didn't want to be with her. You'll be lucky if she hasn't left town when you get home."

His words feel like a meteorite, a truck, and a wrecking ball hitting me all at once. He's right. Why does he always have to be right? I called the power company and they told me the power would be back an hour after I left, but I didn't tell her.

Of course she would think that I abandoned her in a house with no power.

And I did. I did abandon her.

Fuck, I'm such a moron.

"I'll talk to you later." I get up and rush to the door. I almost sprint out of the apartment, the urgency in my steps resonating through the silent halls.

I slide back inside my car and get my phone out of my pocket. She hasn't texted me back since this morning. I let my fingers type a quick text.

Winter, I'm so sorry.
Are you home??

Five minutes go by. No reply. Then five becomes ten and I can't get a hold on my nerves. I start the car and drive away in a roar, heading back to the lake house with just one hope eating me alive: that she'll be there when I walk in.

"And for the lady?" the pub employee asks me when we sit in a red velvet booth next to a pool table.

"I'll have what he's having," I say. The waitress nods and walks away.

Ryder turns to me. "Are you sure? I don't think you're going to like it."

"Whatever." I shrug and analyze the semi-empty pub.

Ryder was right. They didn't card us. Nor did they check the IDs of the clearly underaged girls in the next booth.

Overall, the place looks okay. I bet it can even get real crowded in here on Friday nights. The deafening music makes it hard to think. But thinking is the last thing I want to do right now, so it's perfect.

The waitress comes back with our drinks, and I quickly take a sip. Like I expected, it tastes horrible—no, horrible doesn't even begin to cover it. It tastes like death, but I let the alcohol run down my throat, the burning sensation taking over the pain in my chest.

"Well, someone's in a hurry." He laughs and I put the already one-fourth-empty glass bottle down. "So, it's not that bad?"

"Oh, no. It's absolutely disgusting."

He laughs harder. "Then why are you drinking it?"

I dodge his question. "Why not?"

"Wow, this Haze guy really did a number on you, didn't he?"

"Please stop talking about him," I say, almost rudely, but force a smile on my face to soften the blow. I don't need him to remind me of the guy I'm trying to forget every five seconds.

"Oh. Of course, sorry."

The drinks keep coming until Ryder and I start chuckling for no reason. I can already feel tomorrow's headache. Ryder's nice. He says things as they are, and I bet he's even the type of guy to introduce you to his family and ask if he can kiss you. Haze was never that guy. He just takes what he wants without asking, and I think this might be part of the reason why I'm such a fool for him. There's no getting bored with him. There's no such thing as a routine.

Winter, stop. He doesn't want you like you want him. When are you going to get that through your head?

On beer number four, Ryder suggests that we take a shot, and I'm more than happy to oblige. Just when I slam the tequila shot glass back down, my phone vibrates.

I have a message. From him.

> Winter, I'm so sorry.
> Are you home??

Oh, so now he gives a shit. I scoff and put my phone back down. I'm not answering him. The waitress brings us one more drink, and I stop caring about him. Allow me to rephrase: I stop *thinking* about him. Because I know I'll never stop caring.

When it vibrates a second time barely ten minutes later, I

can't fight the curiosity telling me to check what he has to say.

You're not home.
Where are you? You
better answer me.

And now he's making threats. My head is a bit dizzy, but even in this foggy state, my heart taunts my better judgment and I decide to text him back. Right as I begin typing a reply, my phone dies.

Crap.

I spend the next twenty minutes thinking of what he's been doing all day and why he suddenly seemed to remember that I exist.

"Everything okay?" a worried Ryder asks.

"Yes, everything's good," I lie. "Phone's dead. I'm going to need yours to get a cab."

"You're leaving?" he asks, disappointment clear in his eyes.

"Yes. I should probably go. I've had enough."

I don't want to give the guy any more false hopes. He's a sweetheart. He doesn't deserve this.

"Okay, well, I had a lot of fun today." He starts to lean in.

A loud voice in my head screams that letting him make a move on me is not the way to go. That it will only make things worse. But it's drowned out by the flashes of Haze walking out on me and the tears I wiped while trying to fall asleep.

Loving Haze Adams has broken my heart in so many ways

and I'm not even dating him. Ryder scoots closer to me and slowly brings his face to mine. I can't move.

He doesn't want you, Winter.

Not in that way.

Only a few inches separate our lips…

"What the fuck!" a familiar voice barks.

We both jump, almost spilling the beers on the table, and look up. In the dimmed red lights of the pub… I recognize him.

"Stay the hell away from my girlfriend!"

Before I can make sense of what's happening, Haze reaches for Ryder's collar and lifts him out of the booth.

"Fuck off. She said she was single," Ryder says, shock occupying his features.

"Haze, let him go!" I clumsily get up and try to separate them, but Haze doesn't budge, his eyes locked on Ryder. He's too strong. It's like I'm not even there pulling on his arm with all my strength.

Then, he takes a swing Ryder is not going to forget anytime soon. I screech when Haze's fist meets poor Ryder's cheek and he falls to the ground.

"What the hell's wrong with you, you psycho?" Ryder yells, holding his jaw that probably hurts like a bitch.

"Ryder, I'm so sorry." The words tumble out and seem to make Haze even angrier.

"We're leaving. Now!" he hisses through gritted teeth and wraps his hand around my wrist.

He doesn't bother looking at me as he pulls me toward the exit. How in the world did he know where to find me? Why is he saying he doesn't want a relationship one minute and then hitting a guy who's interested in me the next?

All I can do is drunkenly follow him to the car that's waiting out front, and, as stupid as it may sound, when we take off and the tires screech down the silent streets, only one thought haunts my mind…

Haze Adams just called me his girlfriend.

THIRTEEN

Dark Secrets

"What the hell was that for?" I blurt, my head spinning a bit more with every angry turn Haze takes.

"Are you serious right now? Bastard was going to kiss you. I can't believe you would do that to me." His hands are wrapped so tightly around the steering wheel that his knuckles are white as snow.

"Excuse me?" I scoff. "Just yesterday, you wanted nothing to do with me, remember? You wanted to have sex, sure, but then you decided you'd rather walk out on me than talk about freaking commitment. You have no right to give a damn who I kiss, Haze. None."

I feel the tears threaten to fall, and as much as I want to stop them, I can't. When he sees the water spilling out of my eyes, his anger decreases.

"Winter, I…"

"You what? What else are you going to say to hurt me? Haven't you done enough? Just when I think about all these times when you disappeared on me for weeks when you knew I was falling for you. Or all the times you refused to tell me anything slightly personal about you. Or the time you went to see Bianca the day after you…" A sob cuts me off. "God, I've been such an idiot. To think that you cared for me."

I hate drunk Winter. She's so loud and sensitive.

I wipe the tears away from my cheeks with my sleeve and curse myself for not wearing waterproof mascara today. I should've known this would be a crying day just from the way it started.

"Screw this," he says, pulls over to the side of the highway and parks the car. Great, he stopped so we can argue better.

"Please leave me alone. I really don't want to talk to you." I sob.

"Fine. Then just listen." He sighs. "You're right. I'm a piece of shit. I've been acting like a royal dick, and I'm sorry. I really am. I'm sorry that I suck so much. But you have to know… I do care about you, Winter."

I can't fight the need to look at him, turning my head and regretting it right away. His blue eyes cut me even deeper.

"I care about you so much that I wanted to rip that guy's head off just for being close to you. Just the thought of him…" He takes a breath to calm himself down. "It drives me insane. I don't want you with anybody else. Can't you see that? Please stop crying." He winces and looks away. He can't stand to see me like this. Well, good. Because these tears are his fault.

"So what? I can't flirt with other people, but you can? That's why you don't want to be exclusive, isn't it? Because you want to keep sleeping around?"

"What?" His face twitches in frustration. "No, that's not it. Not even close."

"Then what? What is it? Why would you tell me that you love me only to reject me like this? Why did you leave me alone last night?"

"Because I'm afraid. No, I'm fucking terrified, Winter." He raises his voice, and I'm surprised by the brutal honesty he's finally giving me.

"Afraid of what? Of being my boyfriend? Well, don't you worry about that, Haze. There's no chance you might see that happening anymore."

"Don't say that," he pleads, reaching for my hand that's resting on my thigh. I move it away. To think that I would've done anything to hear him say that he cared just yesterday. Now it all sounds wrong. He doesn't speak for a short while, his breathing all I can hear.

"Kingston…" he whispers, and my heart breaks all over again. *That damn nickname.*

"Don't call me that. You can't keep playing with my feelings. You can't keep acting this way when you made it clear that you don't want to be with me. Why did you call me your girlfriend just when it's convenient for you? Are you punishing me for trying to move on? Why did you punch this guy?"

"Because you're fucking mine!"

An impenetrable silence fills up the car.

I can't speak. I can't breathe. I can't think.

All I can do is play the words he just said to me on repeat. I know I should tell him that I don't belong to anyone. That I'm not his. But I can't. I loved hearing him say that. And I hate myself for it… but I want him to say it again.

"You're mine, okay?" he breathes out, his voice dropping. "I don't want you to move on. I know I don't deserve your forgiveness. I know I deserve for you to never want to talk to me again, but please… let me take you home. I'll tell you everything you want to know if you just give me a chance to explain why I freaked out last night." He gives me the puppy eyes. "Let me prove to you that I can be the boyfriend you deserve."

My mind sticks to the word *boyfriend.*

Haze Adams wants a serious relationship, Winter. And he wants it with you. Just let that sink in.

We're not okay, and I'm nowhere near close to figuring out all of his secrets, but he's trying. And he just said he wants a serious relationship. Could it be?

"Fine," I say, pressing my forehead to the tinted window. Without a word, he gets us back on the highway. I mentally curse myself for giving in so easily. This better be the best goddamn explanation I've ever heard in my life.

THE FRONT DOOR OPENS IN A shrill creak, and Haze leads the way to the living room. Apparently, he knew the power would be back an hour after he left but didn't think it would be a good idea to tell me. I guess it is slightly better that he didn't leave me alone to freeze.

A thick tension surrounds us. We know what's coming. For the first time, Haze is going to tell me the truth, and I hope for his sake that he's finally ready to spill the beans.

I don't say a word and sit on the couch. He tries to buy himself some time by asking me if I want something to drink. I decline all the offers he's got lined up for me until he has no choice but to come sit down, too.

"How did you even find me?" I ask before we get into the more serious topics.

"Find My Friends," he says, and I assume he set it all up when he bought my phone. I didn't even notice that I was sharing my location with him. "I didn't want to look until I checked to see if you were home. I was afraid of what I'd find."

"You thought that I left town, didn't you?"

He nods.

"I won't. Not if you tell me everything right now."

He sighs. "I just… I don't know where to begin. Ask me whatever you want to know, and we'll just go from there."

At first, I struggle to choose which unexplained mystery I want him to dive into as there are too many, but then, I make up my mind and decide I'll start with something easy.

"What's up with everybody in town calling you Mr. Adams?"

He laughs. I bet he could see that one coming from miles away.

"My family pretty much owns this town," he starts. "There used to be nothing here. When my father got his inheritance, he saw potential and started investing in the area. At first, he wanted to buy the lots around the lake to build houses that he could rent out. But when a lot more people started showing interest, he decided to build his own snobby town. There almost isn't a building that my dad doesn't own here. If it's not all of it, it's parts of it. The companies and businesses around town pay him a fortune in rent. One of the only places that has nothing to do with him is Beck's, the restaurant I took you to. That's partly why I like it so much."

I nod as the missing pieces complete the puzzle in my head. This explains the taxi company's name. The Adamses are like kings in this town.

"Hell, even Vic's place belongs to my family. He pays rent to my dad every month, can you believe it?" He scoffs in disgust and shakes his head. He clearly doesn't get along with his father. But why? That's another question I need to ask.

"Did you grow up in this house?"

"No, this was just a summer house. We came here every year from May to September. My childhood home was like thirty minutes away."

So, I was right. Colton Gate is his hometown.

"*Was* thirty minutes away? What happened to it?"

As soon as I ask, I feel his walls go back up. He doesn't want to talk about it. I reach for his hand and squeeze gently to remind him that I'm only trying to make this work.

He sighs. "My father got it torn down and rebuilt a new house on top of it. Barely a day after we moved out, it was gone." He clenches his fists. He's really mad about that. "It's much nicer here anyway. This was always my favorite place."

I smile at his remark and push the guilt crawling up my throat back down. He seems to think that this isn't that bad. What he doesn't know is this was the easy part.

He hasn't seen anything yet.

"I want to know about Riley."

A hush immediately descends over us.

He fidgets with his fingers, and I can tell he'd like to take his promise to tell me everything back. But he can't. Not if he wants this relationship to stand a chance.

I know that Riley's the girl he got pregnant, but she obviously meant something to him. Maybe she still does.

"Riley was my first girlfriend," he says and lets a pause stand between us.

"I thought you didn't commit."

"I don't."

I can't help the doubts creeping into my eyes.

"I mean, I didn't," he corrects himself when he notices my expression, and it makes me want to squeal in joy. "But Riley doesn't really count."

I wait for him to carry on with the story.

"Riley, Vic, and I all grew up here together. Riley's mother was close friends with Vic's, and so I met her through him when I was like nine years old."

He wasn't lying when he said that Vic's his oldest friend.

"Riley's family had just moved back into town and decided to reconnect with their old friends. We were just kids back then. I saw her as some annoying girl who followed us everywhere. But then, puberty came along and things just started happening. And if you're thinking that it was awkward, it was." He gets a chuckle out of me.

"She was my first everything. My first awkward hug, my first sloppy kiss. Riley was that friend that you've known forever and you kind of owe it to yourself to date her even if you don't really know what love is. All you know is your hormones are raging and she's right there. Eventually, one thing led to another and you know…" He doesn't want to say it, but I know what his silence holds.

She'll always be a significant person to him.

She'll always be his first.

"We didn't even know what we were doing, really. We were just messing around. Then, I got into a really rough patch, and I just… I stopped caring about a lot of things. I started acting out, and I broke up with her over text. My parents decided to move to Florida shortly after that. Just one week before I turned sixteen and left town, she told me that she was pregnant."

I knew what was coming, but hearing him say it somehow hurts a lot more than I anticipated.

"I was just a stupid kid then. My brain couldn't even comprehend what she was saying. I told her to get an abortion, but she kept refusing. She eventually gave in and promised that she would. Then, I moved and I started dodging her phone calls. I cut her off completely. I cut Vic off, too." He stops, clearly ashamed. "I'm not proud of it, but I didn't give a rat's ass about anyone. I just… wanted to forget about the past. And they were a part of it."

He just wanted to forget about the past? What could be so bad in Colton Gate that he had to destroy every possible relationship tying him to it? There has to be more than just not having a great relationship with his parents.

"I hadn't talked to Vic in years until we ran into him at the mall last week. The last time we spoke was when he called to tell me that Riley's parents had found out about the baby and kicked her out. It was her dad's doing mostly. Her mother didn't agree, so they ended up getting a divorce. Vic's parents offered to take Riley in because they considered her to be like their daughter, but she skipped town and vanished into thin air.

"I tried calling her, I did, but she never picked up. I get it though; I'd been ignoring her for months. She stopped answering everyone's phone calls altogether. I never heard from her again. I started a new life in Florida, Tanner got me into the fights, and eventually, I stopped thinking about it. Until recently… when Blake brought it all back up." He lets out a breath, a sign that he's done with his speech.

I can't help but be touched that he's doing this. That the closed book is finally opening up to me. I feel so bad for him. That's a lot to handle. Especially for someone as lonely as Haze. He was fifteen, for Pete's sake. I also sympathize with Riley, who had to go through this hell on her own. Haze just wasn't in the right place.

He couldn't even drive a car yet, so take care of a baby?

Not a chance.

I intertwine our fingers. I want him to know that I'm right here. That he has all my support. We exchange looks, and he musters a weak smile that's filled with pain.

"How come you never met Blake if you grew up with Riley?"

"He was the troubled brother. He was never around, either at a distant relative's house or at boarding school. That's what they said, at least. They sent him away when he was very young. Riley never wanted to talk about it, so I just assumed it was bad. I knew he existed, but I never met him."

Looks like Blake got "crazy" stamped on his forehead long before he started street fighting.

"Is that why he blames you for destroying his family? Why he followed you to Florida for revenge? Because his parents got divorced?"

He lets out a long sigh, and I know what it stands for. It's about to get worse. A lot worse.

"It's more than that. A little while after the divorce, Blake's mother was moving into a new place and she got into a car accident." He looks down. "She survived, but… she lost her legs. She can barely do anything on her own anymore. Blake probably thinks that if it wasn't for me getting Riley pregnant, his parents would've stayed together and his mother would've never been on the road that night."

I can't bring myself to speak. That's a lot to take in. How could he bear to come back to a town that carries so much tragedy?

"Do you think Blake was lying? When he said that she had the kid?"

He doesn't reply for a little while. "I sure hope so."

I can't lie to myself anymore. This doesn't make sense. She wouldn't disappear unless she had something to hide. I get that her dad kicked her out and it was probably really hard on her, but running away and dodging everyone she's ever met? That's a bit much. Especially since her mother left her father for kicking her out. Not to mention, Vic's family was also willing to help. She had all these people ready to take her in after she got the abortion. But that's just the thing, isn't it?

What if she didn't?

What if Blake's right and Haze has a kid?

I have no idea what it would mean for us.

Haze shakes his head, and his jaw hardens. I know that he's beating himself up over what happened.

"Haze, don't," I say softly. "Don't beat yourself up over this. You were fifteen. It's not your fault. You had to deal with an adult situation long before your time. There is not a fifteen-year-old boy in the world who would've done better."

"I was one week away from turning sixteen," he corrects me, and I know he's using that tiny detail to keep the guilt trip going.

"Big deal. You were still too young to know how to handle something like this."

He lifts his head up and looks into my eyes. The way he stares at me tells a story. I know he's never been this vulnerable in front of someone before. No one gets to see past his walls.

No one but me.

And the thought makes me feel lucky. It looks like he's telling me "I trust you. Don't destroy me."

Haze Adams is so beautifully damaged that you can see the cracks in his heart through his eyes.

All I want to do is hold him until his splintered pieces fall back together, but I know that's not possible, so instead I scoot closer to him, and he raises an eyebrow at my gesture. He pulls me onto his lap, hooking his arms around my waist to keep me in place, and I chuckle.

There are so many other questions I want to ask him. I want to ask about the missing picture in the frame on the fireplace, the empty kid's room I found, and the person who was removed from the family portrait. I want to know why his family tore his childhood home to the ground, why they would do that only to rebuild something new on top of it afterward.

"Anything else?" he asks.

"Why bring me here? Doesn't Tanner know about this place?"

He scoffs. "Trust me, he'd never think to look here. He thinks I'd rather die than come back to this town."

"Is he wrong?"

He scoffs. "If you'd asked me that a month ago, I would've agreed with him."

"You don't anymore?"

He shakes his head.

"What changed? Why did you take me to a place that brings back such painful memories?"

"I've been asking myself that for a while, actually."

"And?" I arch an eyebrow.

"I don't know. I guess… I thought I'd be strong enough to face it all over again if I had you."

I can't stop the biggest smile from spreading across my face.

"What about the kid's room upstairs?"

A sharp breath escapes him, and I can tell this is the one thing he doesn't want to discuss.

"Listen, Winter… I want to tell you. I really do. But I can't."

Like I just got hit by a huge wave of déjà vu, I start pulling away from him. Even after all of this, he won't completely open up. He notices my body language and tightens his hold on me.

"Ask me anything. Anything but this. Whatever you want to know, I'll tell you, I promise but… I'm going to need more time for this one, okay?"

The agony in his gaze makes it clear that he's had enough for one night. He's in too much of a painful place as it is.

"How bad is it?"

I can't believe there's more. It can't possibly be worse than what he's just told me. How many times does a person have to go through hell before the Universe leaves them alone?

"It's bad," he whispers.

"Don't you trust me?"

He seems to be pained by my question.

"Baby, that's not what this is. Of course I trust you. I trust you more than anyone, but you have to understand, everybody I've ever gotten close to ends up leaving or getting hurt. No matter what I do, I lose them one way or another. It's like I'm cursed. Every time I open up or I'm even the slightest bit happy, shit comes pouring down on me and everything goes to hell. I just need a little more time. Can you do that for me?"

Maybe I shouldn't. Maybe I should tell him that keeping some stories for later wasn't part of the deal. But I can't. He's trying to meet me halfway. He's doing what he's never done before… for me.

What kind of person would I be if I forced the truth out of him when he's begging me not to?

"Okay."

His shoulders loosen up.

"I think that's why I backed out like a scared little bitch yesterday. I was scared that if you became my girlfriend…" His fingers run up and down my arm, making me shiver. "I'd lose you, too."

"Well, too bad." I press my forehead to his. "Because I'm not going anywhere. You're stuck with me."

"Does that mean that you'll give this dumbass another chance?" He gives me the puppy eyes.

"Maybe." I smile.

"So… I have to ask, what does this mean? What are we?" he mocks me by repeating exactly what I said to him the night before.

I bring a hand to my chest and pretend to be offended.

"Why can't we just be us? Why are you doing this right now?" I also use his own words against him.

Biting back a smirk, he leans forward and presses his warm lips to my neck, leaving a trail of kisses from my collarbone to my jaw. I shiver in places I didn't even know I could, my body responding to him in the way it always does.

That's when he says it.

"Because I love you, Winter Kingston."

I almost can't believe what I'm hearing.

"I'm sorry, what was that? I didn't hear you."

He laughs. "Aren't you a funny gal?"

"So I've been told."

"I said I love you, Kingston." He looks into my eyes. "And I'd be the biggest idiot on earth if I didn't ask you to be my girlfriend."

I don't have it in me to even attempt to come up with an equally romantic reply, so my fingers travel from his arm to the back of his head and I lean in to place a peck on his lips. My cheeks are going to start hurting if I keep this smiling thing up.

"I love you, too," I say, emotional.

"Is that a yes?" he teases. "Will you be my girlfriend?"

"What do you think?"

I let our mouths connect, unable to wipe the smile from my face. I try my best to kiss him through the overflowing joy pouring out of me, but we're both smiling like absolute idiots. With every passing second, the soft and sweet kisses become heated, insistent. The tension keeps climbing, reaching a level I know all too well.

Haze's hands climb under my shirt. He sucks my lower lip in between his teeth as his fingers gently brush my skin. They stop right under my breast. He pulls on my waist to get me to straddle him, which I do without a second thought. I can barely recognize myself when I start grinding provocatively against him, rocking my body back and forth and causing an obvious bulge to rise in his jeans. His breathing grows heavier, and he clenches his jaw. I know that look.

He's not letting me go this time.

He raises his eyebrows and gets up without a warning, lifting me up along with him. I instinctively wrap my legs around his waist, feeling his hands on my ass as he walks and kisses me harder. It feels so easy. So effortless. I know exactly where he's taking me. I know what's going to happen, but I'm not afraid anymore. Because this time, there's nothing stopping us. This time…

We're official.

FOURTEEN

Burning Desires

Haze kicks the partially closed bedroom door open and lays me down on the bed roughly. We resume kissing like we'll never get to feel each other again, and his fingers venture under my shirt, brushing my stomach on the way up. He kisses down my jaw, his tongue searing the crook of my neck and igniting a blaze only he can put out. I flutter under him, light moans falling from my mouth.

If my skin is fire, his lips are gasoline.

When he pulls away and stares, I know he's once again admiring his work.

"I hate you for that, by the way." I punch him in the arm. His smile grows bigger.

"What? I told you. You're mine. I want the world to know." He slowly brushes the purple marks above my collarbone with the tip of his index finger and wets his lips.

Boy, do you need ChapStick, or are you trying to turn me on?

I need a T-shirt with that quote.

"Okay, that's cute and all, but do that again and I'll make your face a giant hickey," I threaten, and he chuckles, leaning forward to kiss me again.

Before I know it, my shirt is over my head and on the

bedroom floor. My jeans quickly follow. He squeezes his hand under me, and easily unclasps my bra. I'm thrown off by the fact that he's better than me. I've been struggling with my bra since the day I was old enough to wear one, but Haze didn't even bat an eye.

That's because he's got experience, Winter. You think you're the first one? He's unhooked many bras. He's seen many bodies. You're nothing new.

I despise the voice in my head telling me that this isn't as special to him as it is to me. I'm ripped away from my thoughts when I notice him staring at me.

"What's wrong?" He doesn't complete his task, his eyebrows drawn and the worry on his face unmissable.

"Nothing…" I lower my eyes to my body. Now is so not the time to be feeling like this. Why am I doing this right now? We're together. Together as in a couple.

Haze is my boyfriend.

That still doesn't register.

He must think that you're at least a little special if the guy who doesn't commit committed to you, Winter.

"Bullshit. Something's bothering you. What is it?"

"I… It's just… This is nothing new."

I can already hear him scolding me when the words break free.

"What do you mean?" He frowns.

"You know, this… me." I shift uncomfortably and curse

myself for feeling this way. I can't even put words on what I'm feeling. It sounds so lame. It didn't get to this level yesterday. I thought about it, but it didn't bother me that much. Probably because I had the safety of my underwear. I wasn't going to be fully vulnerable. In a way, I could still hide.

My body language seems to make things clearer. I can tell he understands when realization fills his gaze.

"Seriously? Is that what you think? That you're nothing new?" He's a mixture of angry and confused.

"It's just… you've been with a lot of people."

"So? You have, too," he says.

"It was just one," I whisper.

His eyes grow at my sentence, but he tries to hide it. I think he always knew it, deep down, but he just needed confirmation. For a second, my inexperience seems to scare him.

He inhales a sharp breath.

"Do you think that I did this with any girl?" He pauses, reaches for my hand and intertwines our fingers. He lifts them up to get me to stare. "Or this…" He slowly leans forward and presses his lips to my forehead. "What about this? You think I did that with them?"

He pulls my face closer and brings my mouth to his. My stomach flutters. I kiss him back, but he pulls away quickly, careful not to let the tension rise.

"I never, ever kiss during sex. I never looked into these girls' eyes. Not once. It's too intimate. So if you think that you're nothing new, you're wrong. This is more than new. This is a first. Winter, I might know sex, but I've never known someone like you."

I can feel the pit in my throat melting away with every word. I'm baffled by what he just said to me, completely dumbfounded by how adorable he can be when he tries.

He closes the distance between us and kisses me again, only to whisper something in my ear a few seconds later.

"You see, the difference is… I might've wanted them for a few hours, but I could want you for the rest of my life."

My mouth flies open.

Haze's eyes immediately portray worry at my reaction.

"That sounded way less like rushing things in my head, I swear," he says rapidly and I chuckle.

Is this real? Did Haze Adams just get scared that commitment would scare *me* away?

It's official. The world is upside down.

His words spin around in my head. *I might've wanted them for a few hours, but I could want you for the rest of my life.*

This is without a doubt the cutest thing anyone will ever say to me in my entire existence. Yes, *will.* I'm claiming right here, right now, that this will never be topped. That no one else will make me feel the way he just did with a few words.

Ever.

Haze just won that award.

But he also won something else.

Without a word or warning, I slam my lips to his. He seems surprised but immediately grants me access to his mouth, kissing me back. I let my hands explore his chest, and he grunts when my fingers tug at the black elastic waistband of his boxers.

I want him.

I'm done being afraid.

With his lips still on mine, he finishes what he started and removes my bra, throwing it all the way across the room.

Wow, if he was worried that I'd want to put my clothes back on, no need to worry anymore.

My bra's in another country by now.

He places a hand on my uncovered chest, and with just the touch of a finger, he makes me regret waiting so long. He slightly pinches my nipple, his mouth disconnecting from mine and focusing on the newly exposed area. I bite back a gasp. His tongue twirls around my left breast, sending jolts of energy to my lower stomach.

His fingers find the path they were on the day before and lead the way to my panties. He looks up at me. I know the look in his eyes—he's asking me if I want him to.

I nod and he pulls on the light fabric to remove it. I'm completely naked, letting him see a side of me I've never shown anyone before, because yes, no one's really seen me naked. Not even my first time. It was pitch-black; you couldn't see shit.

But now I'm exposed in front of Haze in the most defenseless way a human can be.

He looks up at me for approval. I give it to him, and he smiles mischievously. He firmly wraps his arms around my thighs and pulls them apart. He fixes his gaze on me, and a million thoughts cross my mind. What is he thinking? Is it okay? I never really thought I'd be self-conscious about well, down there…

"You're fucking perfect, Winter." He takes his lower lip between his teeth. My useless questions are blown to pieces when I see the way he's looking at me.

He looks at me the way I look at cheesecake.

I disconnect from reality when he leans in and I feel his mouth against me. He starts doing what he's proved to be so good at: circles, his tongue quickly swirling around me and sending me to cloud nine. If I thought what he did before was good, I clearly hadn't felt *this.*

When I feel him inserting a finger inside me, it seems we don't have yesterday's problem. He effortlessly adds a second one and goes back to the motion that was incredibly effective last night. He starts curling in and out of me, and I chew on my lower lip to stop myself from moaning. Haze stops abruptly and looks up at me.

"Don't."

"What?" I say, coming out of a trance.

"You did that yesterday, too. Don't hold back. I want to hear you moan." His voice is firm.

I feel the embarrassment rush to my cheeks. He's doing it again. I never pictured myself to be a "dirty talk" kind of girl, but with Haze… all of my beliefs fade away. It's just… the way he says it. I don't know why my instinct is to repress any noise I want to make. It's automatic.

Haze picks up where things left off, and before I know it, I'm throwing my head back and swallowing yet another moan.

"I told you not to do that." He stops again, the authority in his voice sending shivers down my spine.

"Or what?"

I can't believe the words that just came out of my mouth. He raises an eyebrow.

"What did you just say?"

"You heard me," I say, challenging him in every way possible. I can tell he's a bit taken aback by my response. He doesn't say a word. Instead he gives me one look.

And that one look… is enough to make me regret challenging him.

I'm in trouble.

"Fine."

He starts moving his fingers in and out of me so fast that I have to grip the sheets to contain myself. My stomach clenches in pleasure, and he scoffs at my miserable attempt to resist him. I know I don't stand a chance.

"Play strong all you want. I'm not going to stop until I hear you moan for me," he says and goes back down on me, his tongue moving like it knows exactly how to end me. I arch my back, unable to take it anymore. The mix of his tongue, dirty mouth, and fingers finally result in a loud moan escaping my trembling lips.

Shit.

He smirks.

"See, that wasn't so hard, was it?"

I want to punch the cocky grin off his face.

"I hate you," I whisper under my breath, and he cackles.

"Do you? Well, looks like your body didn't get the memo."

He's right. Even if I wanted to deny it, the moisture between my legs would betray me. Minutes later, I know I'm not far from the bliss I experienced yesterday, but the need to be as close to him as I can possibly be outgrows the urge to climax. I want to feel him. Now.

"Take it off." I look down at him, and he instantly knows.

"What's the magic word?" he asks. He's not going to stop torturing me.

"Really?" I pant.

"What's the magic word?" He speeds up his pace in and out of me to the point of making it impossible to even form a sentence.

"Shit, *Haze!"* I throw my head back.

"Say it," he says, and I can't fight him anymore.

I give in. "Please."

He smiles, satisfied with himself, and slides his boxers down to his feet. Now, just like I didn't expect Haze to be bad in bed, I also didn't expect him to be small. But it's a whole other story seeing it with my own eyes. You mean to tell me that *this* has to fit inside *me*?

My worries die down when I feel the familiar wave of ecstasy building up in my stomach. My body starts convulsing uncontrollably. Haze finishes the job, his tongue spinning around me so relentlessly that I have no choice but to come undone all over again. Every trace of self-control in my being vanishes. Speechless, I lie there with widened eyes.

This *never* gets old.

Haze gives me a second to catch my breath, but all I can think about is how ready he is. That doesn't look like fun. It must hurt at this point. Before I can talk myself out of it, I let my hand move downward and circle him. He sucks in a breath, surprised. He's warm. Firm. I can feel him throbbing under my fingers. I tighten my hold on him and he clenches his jaw. I've never touched him in that way before.

"Not yet, baby," he says and moves my hand away. "There's something else I want to do first."

I know we're approaching a turning point when he gets protection out of a drawer on the nightstand. He says he's clean, but it's a risk that's not worth taking. Not to mention, I'm not trying to get pregnant when I can't even find my other sock. I'll learn to take care of myself, first.

He quickly slides the latex down his length and gazes at me hesitantly. His eyes are asking me if I'm sure. I nod and quiver when he guides himself closer and I feel him press against me.

"Haze, wait." I blurt.

He stops, a worried look on his face. "Now, where have I heard that before?"

I grin. He's referring to what I said last night.

"If we do this, there's no going back. No more running away because you're scared. No more doubts, no more secrets. We're all in. Are you ready for that?"

He smiles like he finds me adorable.

"Oh, Kingston…" He pauses. "We both know there was no going back since the second I laid eyes on you."

Then he pushes himself inside me.

I immediately gasp at the overwhelming sensation and bite on my lip. Haze stills himself and clenches his jaw. This is… indescribable.

"Shit, Winter, you're so…" I don't give him a chance to finish and kiss him. I know what he was going to say. That's to be expected since I've only ever let one person do *that* before.

"It's going to be hard to move," he breathes. "I don't want to hurt you."

"It's okay. I'm okay. I promise." I place a small peck on his lips, and he looks deeply into my eyes as if to make sure that I'm telling the truth. He starts moving again, slowly squeezing in and out of me and picking up the pace with every second that goes by. My first time only hurt because I wasn't ready or comfortable. It was awkward, cold. There was no pleasure, but this feels great even through the initial ache.

"You feel so fucking good," he hisses, and a gazillion butterflies collide in my belly. I struggle to adjust to his size at first but the dampness his fingers created quickly helps me adapt. Every time he lets himself go faster and the pain diminishes, he slows himself back down.

"Winter, I… I don't know if I can go slow." He lays his mouth on my collarbone, probably trying to think of something else. "You drive me crazy. I can't…" He stops moving. "I want to be good to you. I just need to calm down."

He seems ashamed, and my heart drums in my chest at the thought that he literally feels bad for how much he wants me. I love him so much.

"Then don't." I hold my breath.

He frowns and I kiss him.

"Don't be good to me," I whisper against his lips.

It's nothing. It only lasts a second. It's just a look.

But we both know what it means.

Oh, it's on.

Without a word, he yanks my hair around his fingers and starts pounding into me almost violently.

Jesus Christ!

My eyes roll back at his reckless yet calculated thrusting. He moves like he knows every weak point. Every sweet spot. The pain completely disappears. I can't help but moan and give him what he so desperately wanted earlier: I call out his name. Over and over again. He goes faster every time I say it, like his name rolling off my tongue is music to his ears. He starts kissing my neck, then transfers to my earlobe, biting it and making me shiver tremendously.

"So, this is how you like it, huh?" he smirks. "Duly noted."

I flush and moan again when he pushes deeper. I know what he really means is *so you like it rough?*

And I do.

God, what has this guy turned me into?

I shudder while he does things I didn't even think were possible to me. I know we won't last long. We've been waiting forever for this moment.

This is like thinking about the food you've left in the fridge all day, coming home to see that it's still there and finally getting to eat it.

I really need to stop making food comparisons.

After a while, spasms take over him, and I know he's close. I whisper in his ear not to hold back, and he asks me if I'm sure. I love that he's thinking about me first. I nod and he gives in, speeding up the pace and blowing my mind as he grunts into my ear.

"Fuck, Winter." He rams himself inside me unbelievably fast until he starts to tremble. Then, he fills me with one last powerful shove and collapses on top of me. He nestles his head on my shoulder and breathes heavily, still lightly shaking. I love seeing him like this. The look on his face is everything. We're both panting, high on each other.

"We have a problem," he says the last thing I expected to hear.

"What?" I ask.

"I'm never going to let you leave this bed again."

I flush and let out a chuckle.

"That good, huh?" I tease.

"Beyond good." He kisses the corner of my mouth and rolls off me, pulling me into his arms. We don't move one bit, holding each other in complete silence as I listen to his heartbeat and he traces circles on my skin.

"I love you," he whispers.

My heart melts into a puddle.

"I love you too," I say right back.

I feel at peace, like nothing could possibly ruin this. Like nothing could possibly ruin *us*. I know he just set another one of my records. He just won another award. Not only will no one else ever make me feel the way he does…

I've also never loved anyone as much as I love him.

THE SOUND OF THE SHOWER PULLS me out of slumber, and I open my eyes a crack, memories of the previous night resurfacing along with my senses. I catch myself smiling like a fool and suppress a squeal of happiness at the sight of my shirt on the bedroom floor. Last night was so out of this world I don't think I could fully comprehend what the step we took meant. It was like a dream. A blissful, amazing dream. The soreness between my legs finally seems to be enough for the truth to hit me.

We're together.

Haze is my boyfriend.

My boyfriend who isn't lying next to me, might I add.

I hear the water running in the bathroom and know that's where he is. I probably would've spent another thirty minutes smiling like a dumbass if it wasn't for Haze's phone incessantly buzzing on the nightstand. I eye it and fight the curiosity boiling inside me. On text message number five, I give up.

Five? Seriously? This may be an emergency. I feed myself the excuse I need to capture the phone in my hand and peek. On his locked screen are a few messages. I frown when I read the name of the first sender.

Bianca.

> Why aren't you calling me back? Where are you?

> I don't believe what you said. We're not over. You're just confused.

> Are you with that Winter bitch? Is that why you left town? She's not at school either.

Haze?! Answer me

I wince at the texts. She's right though. He *is* with me. Poor girl's talking to herself. It's been a while since he told her that they couldn't be friends with benefits if she had feelings for him, but she's still acting like he broke up with her when they were never together in the first place. I use my thumb to scroll down to the sixth and final text message. My stomach lurches with nerves when I read the name of the sender. At first, I try to convince myself that I read it wrong. But then I read it again.

And again.

And again.

Riley.

It echoes in my head like a song I hate but still can't stop singing. Seeing Bianca's name was nothing… nothing compared to this.

But that's not the worst part.

Not even close.

The worst part is the text message that comes along with it.

I'll see you tonight

FIFTEEN

Truth And Exes

Haze isn't the type to take long showers, but for some reason, this one seems to last forever—and by forever, I mean the "I swear this class started an hour ago but the clock says it was five seconds" kind. I draw in a breath when the water stops. The few minutes he spent in there felt like years, and I've never been more nervous to see someone walk out of a dang bathroom.

So many questions eat at me.

Why didn't he tell me that he got in touch with his ex-girlfriend slash possible baby mama? When did that happen? How did he even find her? Is that where he went yesterday? To see her?

Is he cheating on me?

I mean, *come on*, we haven't been dating for a whole twenty-four hours yet.

This one is *not* funny, Universe.

I know I need to confront him if we want this relationship to survive the day. It's one thing that he might have a kid, but going behind my back to contact his first *everything*? I don't think I can take it.

I inhale when Haze turns the corner and walks into the room

with nothing but sweatpants on. I watch the water slowly cascade down his pecs. Of course, he *has* to look like that when I'm about to go off on him.

What? Just because I'm mad doesn't mean I'm blind.

I make sure to keep my eyes off his body. He smiles at the sight of me sitting on the bed in one of his many black T-shirts. I wasn't comfortable sleeping naked last night, so he tossed it to me before we passed out. It goes without saying that it's too big for me, which resulted in him constantly laughing and asking me how many villages I can fit in there.

The smile is slapped off his face when he lowers his eyes to my hand and sees what I'm holding: his phone.

Instantly, he understands.

He knows that I know.

"I was going to tell you," he says.

I appreciate that he's not playing dumb.

He walks toward me and sits on the edge of the bed, holding out his hand in my direction to get his phone back. I give it to him, and he reads the unanswered messages on his locked screen.

He completely ignores Bianca's miserable attempts at getting his attention—like he's *wired* to ignore her, like it comes naturally to him—and he scrolls down to the real problem.

"I swear I would've told you as soon as I saw her reply. Nothing was official. She hadn't texted me back yet." He unlocks his phone and pulls up the text conversation.

It's true. He's only sent her one message, and she's just replied now. His message basically reads somewhere along the lines of "Vic gave me your new number. Said you live in the next town over now. We need to talk. I'd like it if we could meet tomorrow at such place and such time."

I look up at Haze and ignore all the questions crushing me. He takes my hand. I don't remove it, but I don't welcome his touch either.

"So that's where you were yesterday? You were with Vic?"

"Yeah." He brushes my palm with his finger. "I just can't live with the questions anymore. I asked him if he'd heard from her, and he said that she reached out to him a few months ago. He was the only one who knew that she was back. He didn't want to tell me unless I brought it up."

"He didn't want to tell you that the possible mother of your child was back in town?" I arch an eyebrow. "What a good friend."

"He is a good friend, Winter. He did it for me. I made him promise to never talk about it."

He made his best friend promise not to bring up this painful period again. Makes me wonder how many other things his friends can't bring up; how many wounds Haze Adams refuses to open.

"What does this mean?" is all I can bring myself to say.

I'm confident that he can see the doubt in my eyes, and the way he smiles sadly tells me that he can't provide me with the comfort I need.

"I don't know." He sighs. "I'll know tonight. I didn't want her to tell me anything over the phone."

I articulate what he truly meant. "You mean you didn't want her to tell you that you have a kid over the phone."

He rubs at the back of his neck, obviously as uncomfortable with the idea as I am. "Yes."

The fact that this is even an option stirs up a bunch of unexpected emotions in me. Yesterday, it seemed like a distant memory and a problem destined to remain unresolved, but today, it's here.

Today… it's real.

"Listen, for all we know she had the abortion and she's going to laugh at me for wondering all these years." He squeezes my hand.

"Vic doesn't know if she had the kid?"

"She didn't say. She hadn't talked to him in so long. I guess that's not something you casually slide into small talk. He said that she was in a rush, too."

Yeah… *in a rush to ruin my life.*

I curse myself for feeling this way about her. She doesn't even know me, but I still feel threatened by her mere existence.

"What would you do if it turned out to be true?"

That scenario doesn't seem to enchant him, but I know under his tough exterior, he has a big heart. And she's the first girl it beat for. He'll deny it, but that means something to him.

He's not fifteen anymore. He wouldn't run… not this time.

"Well… I guess, I'd learn how to be a dad."

This is real. My first boyfriend, the first person I fell in love with, might have a kid…

I tell myself that it all happened before me. That he had no idea that he'd meet me and that I shouldn't feel this way, but the truth is, dating someone who has kids with someone else is something you usually experience when you're older.

Not when your life's just begun.

"I have to ask"—he looks down—"can you handle it?"

I'm at a loss for words when his eyes meet mine and he stares. Only one question comes to me.

Can I?

"Because… I get it if you can't." His voice weakens. "The last thing I want is for you to leave, believe me. But I'll respect your choice if you do. That's a lot I'd be asking from you."

He's giving me an out right here, right now…

An out that I can't take unless I know whether or not I need to in the first place.

"How about you save that speech for when we find out the truth?" I muster a small smile and press my lips to the tip of his nose. His entire being seems to relax, his shoulders going from tight and firm to laid-back.

"What were you thinking?" he murmurs, letting me sparkle his face with light kisses.

"What do you mean?"

"I know you. A lot goes on in that stubborn head of yours. What were you thinking when you saw the message?"

"I don't know. That, maybe… you were picking things up where you left off."

He shakes his head like I've just told him unicorns exist. "You have to understand it's not her I want to see."

I know what he means by that.

When he goes there tonight, it's not to meet her.

It's to meet his potential child.

"I'm with you, Winter. I'm all in." He reaches for my hand. "Don't ever doubt that again."

"Don't text your ex-girlfriend behind my back and I won't." I give him a smirk that he returns.

"Noted."

I open my mouth to answer, but the only sound breaking the silence is my empty stomach growling.

"Come on, we've got to get some food in you." Haze smiles, gets off the bed, and pulls me to my feet.

I groan at the effort. It's too early to move. We didn't get nearly enough sleep last night. He hooks his arm around my waist and presses his lips to mine. I search for a morning breath but can't find any.

"Did you brush your teeth yet?" I ask.

"No, why?" He looks a bit amused by my question.

"No reason."

No big deal. Just one more thing to add to my "proof Haze

Adams isn't human" list.

When my stomach grumbles again, I give up on taking a shower before eating, and we decide to go down to the kitchen for breakfast. I shiver when my feet merge with the cold kitchen tiles. Haze motions to lead the way and—let's pretend that we're surprised—smacks my ass really hard when I step in front of him.

"Ouch," I cry out.

Of course that's the kind of boyfriend Haze would be.

"Had to. It was calling my name." He puts his hands up, and I elbow him in the stomach. He pretends that it hurts, holding his stomach in "pain."

"You're even more annoying as my boyfriend. Who knew?" I roll my eyes.

He stops dead in his tracks.

He turns around and backs me up into a corner until the distance between us is nothing but a sheer memory.

"What?" I laugh.

"You just called me your boyfriend." A small smile tugs at his lips

"So?"

"Say it again." He leans forward.

This giggly look on his face…

I could get used to it.

"What? Boyfriend?"

He nods.

"Boyfriend, boyfriend, boyfriend. Hazie's my boyfriend," I repeat like an annoying child and he laughs.

"You're damn right I am," he says, a victorious expression covering his face as his mouth finds mine again. Hands start to wander, and kisses start to linger. Before I know it, he's throwing me onto the couch and getting on top of me…

Looks like we're not eating anytime soon.

THE FAMILIAR SOUND OF THE BELL hanging above Beck's front door rings in our ears as we walk into the tiny yet crowded breakfast restaurant. This isn't new. It's almost always this packed, but for some reason, today's worse than the last few times we were here.

After making out for like thirty minutes, we tried cooking but I burned everything I touched, so we opted for the lazy option.

The waitress—who we've seen so many times, I'm beginning to wonder if I should learn her name—greets us and displays the same reaction seeing Haze as she always does. Except that, this time, his undeniable sexiness isn't the only thing she focuses on. This time, she sees something else…

Haze's hand in mine.

She frowns, and I'm reminded of the little white lie I told her a few days ago.

Right. I told her he was gay.

She looks up at me, and I can feel her disapproving look piercing my skull. Completely unaware of the rather funny moment happening, Haze pulls me closer to kiss my cheek. I can hear her thoughts from here.

Yep, definitely not gay.

She clears her throat. "Table for two?"

Haze nods.

At around the same time, an older man wearing a badge that says "Manager" joins her and grabs something at the front desk.

"Don't forget to tell them about the promotion, Rita," he says and quickly disappears back to wherever he came from.

"Are you a couple?" Rita forces a smile.

Man, can this get more awkward?

Haze turns his head to look at me and smiles. "Yes."

My heart sings in happiness.

She says something about our drinks and any extras being free, but I stop listening halfway. I find a hint of humor in the fact that this complete stranger somehow witnessed key moments of our relationship without even knowing it.

She leads us to our table, but what I see when I turn the corner freezes me in place.

Ryder.

Sitting at a table with a girl.

But seeing him isn't even what sets me off. It's what I hear him say to the tall and gorgeous girl that triggers me.

"You deserve so much better than him. He's a jerk if he doesn't see the great girl that's right in front of him."

No way.

The pained features the girl displayed vanish, and she gives him a faint smile.

"Listen, I'm in town visiting my grandparents, and I just happen to have two passes for the fair. Would you be interested in joining me?"

Oh, this is going to be good.

My hand abandons Haze's, and he stops walking. He sees what I'm looking at and clenches his fists. He wants to go over there. I place a gentle hand on his chest to stop him.

"It's fine. I've got this," I say, and he nods faintly.

I take all the nonexistent courage I have and walk toward Ryder's table. His new conquest sees me coming. He has no idea that I'm about to destroy his miserable attempt at picking up sad girls.

"Really?" I intentionally raise my voice to get the attention of the people around us. Heads quickly turn. "This is what you do to me? After everything that we've been through? You cheat on me. Is this all five years is worth to you?"

The seductive smirk is washed off his face.

"What about the baby?"

His jaw hangs, and a wave of gasps runs around the room.

Don't laugh, don't laugh, don't laugh.

"She's crazy. I only went out with her once, I swear," he stutters, and I see Haze pressing his clenched fist to his mouth to stop himself from bursting out into laughter.

"Let me guess, he randomly sat with you, offered to buy you

breakfast, then told you that he had two free passes to the fair? That's how it all started for me, too. I did everything for you. Do you still have self-esteem issues? Is that why you're doing this? I told you size does not matter."

The second round of gasps hits us, and it hurts not to laugh. Every eye in the restaurant, without exception, is on us. The brunette's face twitches in disgust, and she gets up, grabbing her glass of water and throwing its content in Ryder's face. She walks away, rushing out of the restaurant while Ryder just sits there, soaked, with his mouth wide open. I smile widely and walk back to Haze, who can barely breathe as he howls with laughter. That's when we see the owner, Rita's father, speed walking toward us. Haze and I exchange glances.

We are *so* kicked out.

"YOU ARE NO LONGER WELCOMED IN here, and we will make sure not to serve you if you come back." That's what the very angry man spat before showing us the door. We were kind of bummed out because we were starving and Beck's is a nice place, but we quickly rebounded—and upgraded, to be honest—by picking another restaurant.

I didn't dare ask Haze if his father owned parts of the restaurant we chose, but the way the staff treated him answered my question.

Everybody in Colton Gate knows he's the Adams kid. They probably think that he could ruin their business with just one bad comment to his father.

"When's your date with Riley?" I play with the strings of my sweater and lean back into my seat.

"You know it's not a date," he corrects me.

"Yeah, yeah, what time?"

He glances at the clock on his car dashboard. "Four thirty."

It's almost time. Only fifteen more minutes. We've been driving around town with no direction for a few hours. We spent the afternoon singing along to random songs on the radio and discussing topics that are probably way too dark for such a beautiful day. The conversation went from "What's your favorite holiday?" to "What's the point of life?" and "What was the first guy who thought it'd be a good idea to drink what came out of a cow thinking?"

Overall, today's been a very simple day.

But I can't remember the last time I was this happy.

"So… Riley." I try to look unbothered. "What's she like? Let me guess, tall, thin, gorgeous?"

"Now, Kingston, I might be dumb sometimes, but I'm not *that* dumb. I'm not answering that." He pretends to zip his lips and throw away the key.

I laugh. He's right. This question has no right answer. I can't believe that I even care about that stuff.

"Clever boy. Picked up on a few of my tricks, didn't you?" I crinkle my nose.

"I'm starting to." He grins and takes a left, pulling up next to a coffee shop. He parks the car and kills the engine.

"So this is it, huh?" I read the sign above the building.

"Yeah."

I don't reply, staring ahead at nothing in particular.

"What is it?" He seems worried.

"What?"

"Something's clearly eating at you. Spill it."

I shift in my seat. "It's nothing."

He arches an eyebrow.

"Fine. It's just that you said you were going through a rough patch when you broke up with her. So, technically, you two didn't break up because you didn't love her anymo—"

"I love you."

An idiotic grin spreads across my face.

"I know exactly where you're going with this, and the answer is no, I don't have feelings for her anymore. I'm head over heels in love with you, Winter Kingston. Are we clear?"

My mouth falls open, and I find myself gawking at him like he's just told me I can eat whatever I want for the rest of my life without ever getting fat.

Again with the food comparisons.

I'm so glad the scared-of-commitment Haze is gone.

"Yes, I did have feelings for Riley. But in an 'I'm a stupid teenager who only wants to play video games' kind of way. We were so young. It seems like another life. And whatever I felt for her is not even close to what I feel for you."

"Why's that?" I'm just pushing it for him to keep telling me all these wonderful things at this point.

"I guess… I never really knew love until I knew you."

I swoon.

"You know you're going to have to pay a fine for that, right?"

"Pay a fine for what?" he asks.

"Stealing lines from whatever cheesy romantic comedy you got that from."

He rolls his eyes.

"You are so good at ruining our moments, you know that?"

"You love me for it." I kiss him. He welcomes my lips, per usual. In that moment, I want to forget about Riley. I want to forget that we might be doomed from the second he walks inside that shop. I want to think about us and us only.

The perfect kiss ends a lot faster than I would've liked when we pull away for air.

It's 4:25.

In a few minutes, my boyfriend has a date with his ex-girlfriend that he possibly has a child with.

In a few minutes, everything could change.

"It's time." He sighs.

"Okay. I'll wait for you in the car." I get my phone out of my pocket. "Great, my battery's almost dead. I'm going to be bored out of my mind."

"What?" He glowers. "You're not staying in the car. Not a chance. You're a part of my life; I'm not hiding you."

I'm instantly touched that he would even *consider* bringing me in to witness such a personal moment.

"Haze, do you really think that she'll be comfortable talking about the possible kid the two of you conceived in front of your new girlfriend, not to mention a complete stranger?"

He looks down, understanding my point, and nods. I don't want him to go alone, but it wouldn't be right if I tagged along for their reunion after years of questions.

I have to put myself in her shoes. He's the one who contacted her wanting to know more about his child. If she really is a mother, she's only doing this for her kid to have a father.

"You know what, there's another coffee shop on the other side of the street." He points to something. I turn my head to see the shop he's talking about. Two coffee shops facing each other? These two are obviously competing with each other. "I'll get a seat by the window. If you do, too, you'll be able to see us."

I laugh. "Are you suggesting that I stalk you?"

"Hell yes, if it's the closest thing I'll have to you being there." I know he meant for it to be sweet, but it only makes the situation more real. He notices my frown and captures my hand into his.

"You know the first thing I do after this conversation is introduce you to her."

Sure. Unless you look her in the eyes and fall in love all over again.

I smile unconvincingly, and we get out of the car. He enters the coffee shop while I cross the street to reach my creeping spot. I order a latte and sit by the bay window as discussed. He's got the seat he wanted, too.

He makes silly faces at me, and my lips struggle to shape a somewhat believable smile.

Twenty-four girls walking into the shop and making me wonder if they're Riley later, I'm beginning to think we dodged the bullet. It's 4:50. Maybe she got scared and skipped town again. Maybe she's not coming.

Then, I spot her on the sidewalk and I know…

This is Riley.

With my luck, the tanned dark-haired beauty that looks like she escaped from a Victoria's Secret show just has to be Haze's ex.

Her perfectly straight black hair falls down her back, and she's wearing heels that I could never even *dream* of walking in without breaking both my legs. She doesn't need the heels. She must be around five foot eight.

For a second, I dare hold on to the hope that the real regular-looking Riley is simply hidden by the giant model, but I'm quickly proved wrong when she pulls on the door and walks into the coffee shop.

I see her stop in front of Haze's table, and my suspicions confirm themselves. She seems to expect him to get up and give her a hug of some sort, but he doesn't move a muscle.

When she realizes that he's not going to stand up, she awkwardly slides into the seat in front of him. They start talking and that's when I realize that Haze's plan has one big flaw: I can't hear them. He should've given me a microphone.

I'm kidding.

No, I'm not.

After five minutes of what seems to be an incredibly serious conversation, Haze looks down and covers his face with his hands. He's upset.

What did she tell him? It can't be that he has a kid. Haze was prepared for the news. In some ways, he expected it. No, he's way too upset. This is something else.

He just realized that he still loves her and now he's wondering how he's going to dump me.

Stop it, Winter.

She stops talking, apparently as sad as him, and places her hand on top of his. I really wish that he'd move away, but he doesn't. All I can do is sit there and stalk—I mean, *watch*—while wondering what just happened.

The conversation seems to drift to lighter topics, and eventually, she gets a small smile out of him. He even laughs at some point. I can't stand that I feel bothered by such stupid things.

They finish their coffees and both pay for themselves. Riley gets up and initiates a hug.

He hugs her back.

When he gets his phone out of his pocket and starts typing, I know what he's about to do. Seconds later, I receive a text.

Come on over

He's going to introduce us.

I get up and walk out of the shop with a sharp fear in my chest. I cross the street and push the door leading to my own personal nightmare open. Haze's face lights up when he sees me. He greets me by pulling me into his arms.

I don't dare look up at her to see her reaction.

Does she hate me? *I would hate me.*

"Winter, this is Riley," he says and takes my hand.

"Hi," I say and glance at her.

She smiles. But she looks uncomfortable, disappointed. She even looks a bit sad. I almost feel bad for the girl. At least she doesn't look like she hates me. That's a start.

"Riley, this is Winter, my girlfriend," Haze says just in case the giant hug he gave me wasn't clear enough.

"Hi," she almost whispers. It gets awkward a lot faster than I expected, and I'm thankful to hear her phone ring.

She peeks at the screen.

"I'm so sorry. I have to take this. It's the babysitter." She picks up and distances herself from us.

Only in that moment does it hit me.

Only then do I realize that this is real.

Haze has a kid.

From now on, she's back into his life.

They're back into his life.

He'll see Riley frequently, probably trying to make up for the lost time with his child. It'll never be just me and Haze in this relationship ever again. It'll be me, Riley, Haze, *and* their kid.

Even if Haze and I do have a family someday, it won't be his first time. We won't get to experience that together.

And things will never truly be the same after today…

WE'VE BEEN DRIVING IN SILENCE FOR the past ten minutes. I've wanted to ask him a million questions from the very moment we left the coffee place but thought he could use a second. He's still upset. I've been holding his hand in the hope of bringing him a tiny bit of comfort. So many options have been bugging me.

Maybe she lost the baby.

But then, why did she say the babysitter was calling? I doubt that she had a kid with someone else after she skipped town.

"There were two of them," he finally says when he pulls up into the driveway of the lake house.

I wait for him to carry on, my mind sticking to the word *were.*

"Twins. One of them died at birth."

I hold my breath.

"I wasn't there. Because I was too stupid to be responsible." He clenches his jaw. "I wasn't there when my sons needed me."

Sons. *Plural.* That means he has a baby boy right now.

"Stop. You were so young, Haze. Do you realize how much of a big step having a child is? She ran away after she promised to get an abortion. How could you know that she didn't?"

"I should've looked. I should've been there. I left them like a coward." He kills the engine and turns to me. "My son's two. His name's Jacob, and he's never had a dad."

I don't know how I feel about this, but it doesn't matter. How I feel isn't important. Haze is the priority right now. When we get out of the car and step inside the house, I give him a hug. He's so tall I have to get on my tiptoes to wrap my arms around his shoulders.

"It wasn't your fault, okay?"

He holds me tighter.

When we let go, I ask him the burning question.

"When are you going to meet him?"

"Two days."

He proceeds to tell me all about his son like he's memorized every single detail Riley's shared with him. Apparently, the kid's a genius for his age, his mother calls him Jake, and he's terrified of Santa. We spend the rest of the night sitting on the couch and talking about everything but the one topic driving me crazy: What does this mean for us?

I glance at the time on my phone and know that the day Haze meets his child will be here before we know it. And I'll never say it to him…

But I've never been so afraid of the clock ticking.

I WATCH MY BOYFRIEND PACE BACK and forth around the house and have no choice but to admit my attempts at calming him down are useless. He hasn't stopped thinking about meeting his son since Riley told him about his existence. She just texted him that she's on her way, and he can't control his nerves. I've never seen him like this.

"Haze, calm down. It's going to be okay," I say softly.

"What if he hates me?" He fidgets with his clothes, still walking around the house with no specific direction.

"He won't. He's a kid. He probably likes everyone. Plus, it's impossible to hate you."

I mentally laugh. I might not be able to hate him, but it's very possible for other people to despise him. Ask the East side and they'll write you a book about it. My heart sinks when my cousin and the boys creep inside my head. The way things ended was far from perfect. I haven't contacted them once. Am I a terrible person for not wanting to deal with their judgment?

I know what Kendrick would do. I know what he would say. He'd call Haze every name in the book and try to convince me to leave him. My cousin has to know, somewhere deep down, that Haze would do anything to keep me safe. He can say what he wants, but Haze has proved that he cares about me many times in the past. He had to trust that wherever he took me, I'd be okay.

I find myself wondering if the guys found a new fighter to replace Blake, if Kendrick and Nicole are still dating, and I even wonder if Will is still a tactless jerk. *Probably.* No matter how afraid of their judgment I am, I have to admit: I miss the East side.

"He'd have every right to hate me. I abandoned him." He sighs.

"Didn't know of him—big difference," I correct him.

"What do you think he looks like?"

"I'm sure he's gorgeous. I mean, kid's got good genes." I picture the beauty that is Riley in my head. She couldn't just be normal. She *had* to look heaven-sent.

"You're right. It'll be fine. So what if he doesn't like me? We have forever to work on this relationship."

His words echo in my brain. This is forever. Jacob will be here forever. So will Riley. I don't know why it's so hard for me to wrap my head around that. He has a kid.

A kid!

A kid who's coming to the house right now.

My thoughts are interrupted by the doorbell. This is it. Haze's going to meet his son. I try my best to ignore the painful pit forming in my throat. I can't be selfish. I won't. Haze gets up and lays a shaky hand on the handle. He glances back at me one last time before opening the door. My jaw drops at the sight of the person standing on the other side.

"Missed me?" He smirks.

I can't believe it.

"Kendrick?"

SIXTEEN

Steal My Man

"No!" Haze drags Kendrick inside by his collar and shuts the door. "No way. You could've picked any fucking day to find us and you chose today?"

"Let go of him." I tear them apart before Haze breaks my cousin's nose, which I don't doubt for a second he can and will do. He tries to come at him again. "Haze, don't." I push on his chest with my palms and stagger at his strength. "Look at me. Haze!"

He glares at Kendrick with tight fists, his chest rising and falling along to his heavy breathing.

"Haze," I plea, and he finally answers my calls, gaping down at me as the rage in his gaze dissipates. Our eyes send each other signals only we understand. He inhales to calm himself down.

"Let me guess, you two are dating," my cousin says just loud enough for us to hear. Still operating as a wall between the two experienced fighters, I turn around to look at our unexpected guest and nod. "Ugh, *vomit*," he adds.

Part of me wants to yell at Kendrick for ruining what could turn out to be one of the most important moments of Haze's life, but then there's also this tiny, annoying, and persistent voice telling me to give him a hug.

The biggest, embarrassing *I haven't seen you in forever* hug.

I don't bother asking him how he found us because, frankly, I don't care. The important question is what he plans to do now that he did.

"What are you doing here?" I ask him.

"What do you think?" He grabs me by the wrist. "I'm taking you home. Where you belong."

"She's not going anywhere." Haze yanks me back to him, the suddenness of his pull freeing my hand from Kendrick's grasp. "Are you out of your mind? She's not safe in Florida. Tanner's still out there. It's the last place she should be."

"He's been taken care of." Kendrick's voice grows angrier.

"What's that supposed to mean? What did you do?" Haze growls.

"You didn't kill him, did you?" I say what I know Haze is thinking out loud.

"I probably should've since he seemed to have no problem with killing Winter or my entire family, but no, I didn't kill that waste of oxygen you call your brother. I made a deal with him."

"What deal?" Haze asks.

"It wasn't much of a deal, really. I just made him a promise. That Winter would go back to Canada in a few weeks where she'll be safe and away from anyone who could want to harm her. But, especially, where she'll be away from you. All she has to do is leave town as planned when school ends. He promised to leave her alone until then. He doesn't care about her. It was never personal. He just wanted to get you back. Now, let's go. We have a long ride ahead of us." Kendrick motions to the door.

Haze grits his teeth and steps forward.

"You're not her mother, asshole. She's a big girl. She'll go with you if she wants to," Haze says an inch away from Kendrick's face.

"A big girl? Please. She's a child. She knows nothing. She's so naïve she actually thinks you're in love with her," Kendrick shouts.

"And it's never occurred to you that maybe I am?" Haze shouts right back.

Silence ensues.

Kendrick opens and closes his mouth repeatedly in a desperate attempt to restore his composure. He's speechless.

Is this a bad time to swoon like a thirteen-year-old girl?

Haze sidles to me and intertwines our fingers as if to support what he's saying. My heart swells with happiness. Kendrick shoots me a suspicious look that's dripping with expectations.

"It's true, Kendrick. He loves me… and I love him. I'm not leaving."

Kendrick draws a sigh, rolls his eyes, and curses.

"I was afraid you'd say that…" Kendrick says. "So I prepared for the worst."

He walks back outside, bends down to get something he left on the porch, then drops it on the hardwood floor.

A suitcase.

"Hell no, you're not staying here," Haze immediately says.

"Yes, I am. We're a family package, Adams. Sorry." Kendrick closes the door.

Haze studies me. I know he wants me to tell him that it's out of the question, but I end up smiling timidly instead. The truth is, I missed Kendrick. I wouldn't mind having him around.

"Oh come on. Cheer up," Kendrick scoffs. "It's just until Winter goes back to Canada. Then, she'll be safe and never see you again. Everyone wins."

"How am I winning, asshat? I'll never see my girlfriend again."

"Oh, I'm sorry, I said everyone. Which means you have to be an actual person and not a piece of shit to be included, Haze."

Damn.

That's the strike Haze won't allow. He's about to put Kendrick in his place when—*because Life has a sense of humor*—we're interrupted by the sound we've heard too many times today.

The doorbell rings.

Haze grabs Kendrick by his collar again.

"Fine, you can stay. But if you make a single sound or ruin this moment for me, the next thing coming out of your mouth will be your teeth, got it?" he hisses.

Kendrick nods in confusion, and Haze sets him free with a push. Kendrick stumbles back a few steps as Haze opens the door. On his porch are the gorgeous Riley and the cutest little brown-haired boy I've ever laid eyes upon.

He has green eyes while Haze's eyes are blue but the resemblance still hits me like a truck. He's definitely an Adams, this one, no doubt. Jacob's gaze roams the house curiously. Riley takes his hand and gets him inside.

"Hello," Haze says and kneels down to his level.

Jacob smiles shyly, revealing the most adorable tooth gap.

"What's going on? Why is there a kid and a model on Haze's porch?" Kendrick asks, nudging me with his elbow.

So much for not making a sound.

His nonexistent subtlety skills cause Riley to glance our way. She frowns, probably wondering who Kendrick is.

"That's…" I pause and prepare for his disapproving glare. "This is Riley, Haze's ex. And that's Jacob. Haze's kid."

"What?" Kendrick exclaims obnoxiously loud. They all jump. Even Jacob stares. I apologize and motion not to mind us while I drag Kendrick into the bathroom so he can tell me all about how I'm wasting my life away and dating the wrong guy. I twist the tap on and hope the water will obscure my cousin's bad manners.

"Are you out of your mind?" he blurts the second I close the door. "You're staying with him? You're going to stay with a guy who has a kid? Winter, this is insane."

"He just found out. What am I supposed to do?"

"I don't know. Here's an idea: get in my car and run away from this madness. Come on, have some self-respect."

"I can't just leave him, Kendrick. I… I love him. Just because he made a mistake when he was younger doesn't mean I should give up on this entire relationship."

"Oh for fuck's sake, look at them. Just look!"

He swings the bathroom door open, giving me a direct view of Haze, Riley, and Jacob sitting on the couch. Jacob is playing with the toys Haze and I bought for him yesterday. He's radiant. They all are. Riley's smile grows with every laugh her son emits. As for Haze, he seems amazed by even the simplest moves Jacob makes. Kendrick does have a point.

They look like the perfect little family.

Like a *too good to be true* picture with no room for me.

I clear my throat, refusing to let my emotions come out and play. I'm fine. I can do this. *It's no big deal*, I tell myself.

"Can't you see? Literally the only thing standing between that model chick and Haze is you. It's only a matter of time before they reunite for the kid. What's it going to take for you to take a hint? Are you going to have to find them in bed?"

"Okay, stop. I got it, jeez!" I put my hands up like I'm hoping they'll shield me from his negativity and stomp out of the bathroom.

Kendrick follows me. "Where's my room?"

"There are a hundred in this house. Go find one," I grumble.

"If you want to sit with them and third-wheel like everything is fine, go ahead. But I'm not going to watch you." He pokes at me again. I sigh and watch him run up the stairs to explore his new home.

I mute his voice inside my head and join the happy family in the living room. I think I see Riley roll her eyes when I sit down next to Haze. Did she just…

Stop, Winter. It's probably nothing. You're just imagining things.

"Hey, beautiful." Haze quickly pecks my cheek and turns to the kid, who's observing me intently. "Jacob, this is Winter. My girlfriend." He introduces us in the cutest kid voice possible, and I giggle. Hearing Haze talk to a kid is so different, yet so *hot.* I don't know why it makes him even more attractive. Jacob simply smiles in return. I come to find out that he's a very quiet kid. Riley tells us that he only speaks around the people he's comfortable with. And by speak, she means he says a few words and makes noises.

"So… how did you two meet?" Riley asks and takes a sip of the coffee Haze brought her a few minutes ago. Haze and I exchange sideways looks. There is no way we're telling her the real story. *Oh, it's nothing interesting. I followed my street fighter cousin to a meeting and thought I was being super slick. Haze, who's my cousin's nemesis, decided to make a deal with me as the prize to destroy his enemies. More coffee?*

"School," Haze says, and I bite back a grin.

Technically, it's not a lie.

"And how long have you two been together?"

"A few days at most," I say and only realize how unserious our relationship sounds when a satisfied smile emerges on her lips. Is it me or… does she look strangely happy right now?

"We've known each other for a while but… yeah, let's just say we weren't expecting this." Haze takes my hand.

"Just a few days? Really? I'm surprised. He used to be a keeper, that one."

What's that supposed to mean?

"In fact, we were together for, what, two years?" She takes another sip.

Okay?

"Remember the night of Vic's birthday party? Oh my God, it was so awkward." She notices my confusion. "Oh, that's right, you wouldn't know. Sorry. That's when Haze and I first got together. Blame five minutes in heaven. Vic had gotten himself locked with Gloria and he…" She bursts out laughing, and Haze laughs along with her.

"I can still see the look on his face. He was completely freaked out," he finishes.

"Who's Gloria?" I ask.

"Some girl who used to crush on him. He wasn't interested," Haze explains.

"Oh." I nod.

"Then, Oliver dared Haze and me to go together, and you know…" She takes a sip. "Anyway, this wasn't as bad as what happened on the pier. Remember that one?"

Haze laughs harder. "How could I forget?"

They proceed to hop onto the memory lane train and leave

me standing alone in an empty station. They keep reminiscing about days I never once heard of and laugh until I want to bash my head against the wall. Every joke Haze makes, Riley snorts so loud my ears bleed. She's scooted over to him on the couch and keeps hitting his shoulder every chance she gets. After a few hours of Haze being a typical boy and dismissing all the red flags that make my eyes the size of golf balls, I have no other choice but to accept the truth. I always want to see the best in people, but I'm not stupid. I can't deny it anymore.

She isn't only here for her son.

She's here to steal my man.

SEVENTEEN

Mine

"Time to wake up," a voice I know all too well whispers in my ear, and I groan, the numerous sleepless nights that I've had recently making it close to impossible to open my eyes. Haze lightly tickles me, and I finally gather the courage to move.

"What time is it?" I rub my eyes.

"Eight thirty." He rests his arm on my stomach. "Riley says it's better to get there early if we want the beach to ourselves."

He leans in to kiss me, but I turn my head and offer him my cheek instead. I can't help being annoyed with him. He's so oblivious.

"Riley said this, Riley said that," I mutter under my breath and push the covers off me, rolling out of bed.

"What's that supposed to mean?" he asks, his voice still raspy from just waking up. I pretend not to hear him and walk to the door.

"I need a shower." I sneak out into the hall and lock myself in the bathroom. The past five days have been worse than I imagined. I haven't had a moment alone with Haze. He hasn't touched me *once* since our first time, and I'd be lying if I said that it hasn't been on my mind. I know from the way his hands linger on my body when we hug or the way he eyes me when he thinks I'm not looking that it's haunting him as much as it is me, but we haven't had the chance to act on it.

Haze and I both got tested a few days ago just to be safe. I made it clear that I wasn't sleeping with him without protection—even if the tests said he was clean. The pill isn't a hundred percent effective. I'm not trying to become Riley the second. The results recently came in and… it goes without saying that knowing we're both STD-free isn't helping me control my urges.

Riley's been around every single day.

Every single day.

Jacob's the definition of an angel, but the fact that his mother has to tag along with him is slowly driving me mad. Kendrick says that I'm pathetic for staying. That I should leave this sinking ship while I still can.

I'm starting to wonder if he's right.

The only good thing to come out of this hell is that I've had more time to focus on my online classes. It's made me wonder how Haze's going to graduate. He's missed so much school. He doesn't look too worried about getting held back, that's for sure. I think back to the way no teacher ever wrote down that he was absent and wonder how many corners he can cut just by being the kid of the school's biggest funder.

Riley's flirting is getting more obvious with each torturous day that goes by. Even Kendrick, who didn't notice for a week when his own sister dyed her hair red during freshman year, knows that she's trying to seduce Haze.

I don't want to tell him because I know what he would say. He'd tell me not to worry because he loves me. I'm sure from his perspective, Riley just seems like a caring mother who wants her child to have a father. On day number three, she asked Haze to go to dinner without me. Something about Jacob not liking strangers. I almost laughed. She said that like Haze wasn't also a stranger who Jacob met less than a week ago. Haze denied her request, which made her mad. She tried to disguise it, and she might've successfully fooled Haze but not me.

I get a towel out of the cabinet and curse when I realize that I don't have any clean clothes with me. One quick trip to the bedroom shouldn't be too hard. I just have to find a way to avoid Haze's questions. I open the door and walk back in the room to see him standing shirtless next to the bed. He's just put on sweatpants. He wasn't lying about always sleeping naked.

See why I'm struggling with my involuntary vow of abstinence?

He furrows his eyebrows, surprised to see me back so soon

"Just getting some clothes," I say, hoping to run back to the bathroom without trouble. My hopes quickly fall. The look in his eyes tells me he's not letting me get away that easy.

I grab whatever clean clothes I can find and speed walk to the exit, but before I can turn the doorknob, he wraps his hands around my hips and spins me around. My back hits the closed door as he presses his muscular body to mine.

Dang it. So close.

"What's wrong?" He gazes deeply into my eyes, and I can tell he's hoping to find the answer I won't give him in there.

I can't keep it in any longer.

"She wants you," I blurt out.

There's no going back now.

"What?" He frowns.

"Riley. I know you don't see it, but I do. Even freaking Kendrick sees it. She wants her perfect little family together and for me to disappear."

Then, as I expected, he looks at me like I'm crazy.

Yep. He's completely clueless.

Why am I even wasting my time?

"Forget it." I try to move away from his hold, but he doesn't let me.

"Winter, wait, talk to me."

Am I going to have to spell it out for him?

"She laughs at every single one of your jokes, she's touchy, she's constantly reminiscing about the good old days. Deny it all you want, but she wants you back and you know it."

The confused look on his face remains. He really has no idea what I'm talking about.

Guys…

Unable to take any more of this nonsense, I bring my hands to his chest and push him off me. I manage to slide back into the bathroom and shut the door. I remove my clothes and get into the shower in a rush. The hot water soaks and soothes my muscles as I close my eyes, trying not to think of all the ways this shower could've gone differently if there was no Riley. If there was no Jacob…

I'm caught off guard when images of Haze running his hands all over my body as he enters me corrupt my brain. Now is so not the time to be thinking about sleeping with him, but my hormones don't give a flying shit that I'm mad. I had a taste of him once, and now I'm addicted. My heart comes bursting out of my chest when I feel a hand sliding over my hip. I jump and jolt around.

Haze.

Completely naked behind me.

I didn't even hear him come in.

"Haze! You scared the crap out of me!" I place a hand on my racing heart. "How did you even get in?"

"Door wasn't locked," he says, his eyes boring into mine, and chews on his lower lip. His gaze travels downward.

Oh, right, I'm naked.

I clear my throat, the water dripping down his chest throwing me off, and find myself staring down at him, too. To think I was daydreaming about this very moment just a few seconds ago.

"So what?" he says with a stern voice.

I just stare at him in confusion.

"So what if Riley did want me?" He steps closer. "I don't give a shit, Winter. I don't care how many memories she brings up. I don't care how many times she laughs at my jokes. I want you."

Leave it to Haze to casually drop a super serious speech on me when we're butt naked.

His words affect me a lot more than they should. I don't speak, simply because I have no idea what to say. He still doesn't see it. He doesn't see that she's flirting with him. I know he's just telling me what I want to hear.

"I want you. I'm always going to want you, and I'm sorry if I haven't done what it takes to make you understand that."

I'm far from prepared for what he does next.

"So let me clear things up for you."

The air leaves my lungs when he backs me up onto the tiled wall of the shower roughly and yanks my face closer to kiss me. I instinctively kiss him back. Like my body's been desperately waiting for his touch, it responds in a way that surprises me almost as much as it does him. I press myself to him, leaving no room for questions or hesitation. This is happening and no one, especially not Riley, is stopping us. He keeps on kissing me, but I know his attention is down there. He's more than ready.

His lips find my neck, and I moan as he feathers my collarbone with burning kisses. His hands trail down to my stomach, but I stop him. I don't know if it's my ego, or if it's jealousy, but I want to touch him. I want him to feel the same way I did the other night. It's his turn. He's chosen me over Riley. I'm going to show him he made the right choice.

I grab him between my fingers, and his lips instantly part.

"Winter, you don't have to—"

I don't let him finish. Instead, I hold him tighter and start moving my hand up and down in the hope that I'm doing this right. He groans and sucks in a breath. I'll never get tired of seeing that look on his face. Seeing the ecstasy cross his features is almost better than feeling it myself. The disbelief in his eyes when I get down on my knees in front of him makes me feel powerful, in control.

I look up at him and bring my head closer, teasing him.

"Fucking hell, Winter," he says through gritted teeth.

"What?"

"Do you have any idea how many times I've fantasized about this?"

The thought of him wanting this as much as I do drives me wild. He stops breathing when my mouth connects with his length. My tongue is gentle at first. I'm testing the field. Then, when I feel comfortable enough, I go all in. I wrap my lips around him and opt for a pace I hope is not too quick or too slow. I assume I'm doing something right from the way he throws his head back with a grunt and clenches his fists. I analyze his facial expressions, adjusting to every slight change in the noises he makes.

"Fuck, Winter, you…" He seems at a loss for words, his breathing unsteady. "No fucking way you've only had one guy." He tugs at my hair and the heat rises in my stomach. I never thought my body could react this way to… anyone, really. Haze's changed me in ways I don't understand.

After a few minutes, I ask him how I can make it better, and he looks at me like he's wondering if I'm real. I guess not every girl he's been with was open to criticism. He gives me a few instructions that I'm happy to follow. I didn't expect to be a pro the first time, and the way he reacts to my additions is worth every awkward try. I grab him at the base, my mouth still moving up and down around him, and increase the pressure with each twirl of my tongue. His breathing grows heavier until he snaps.

"Stop!"

I can hear in his voice that he doesn't mean it.

Not even a little.

"Why?" I pull away, worried that I did something wrong.

"Because I won't be able to hold it," he pants, taking a deep breath as though he needs a second to regain his composure.

Confused, I say, "What would you hold it for?"

His eyebrows shoot up to his forehead like he's wondering how I can even be asking such a question. Then, he half-smiles as though he finds me adorable and wraps a hand around my wrist to get me off the shower floor. I get back up, confusion plastered on my face. Without a warning, he spins me around and bends me over.

"For this."

He uses two fingers to make sure that I'm ready, and I gasp. *Oh my God.* I'll never, *ever* know what to expect from this guy. I look back at him and conclude that he's happy with what he found from the smile on his face. He lifts one of my legs up with his right arm, and I instinctively put both my hands on the shower wall in front of me.

"I've been going crazy just thinking about this moment and all the things I want to do to you since the other night. It's not ending now," he says, and I feel him push against my entrance from behind.

"Haze, wait." I come to my senses. "Not without—"

"*Shit*, you're right." He stops. "Hold on."

He lets go of me and quickly slides the shower door open. He stretches his arm out to get something on the counter. I hear the sound of a condom packaging being torn open.

"Wait, did you leave that there?" I ask and watch him slip the condom on.

"Maybe." He beams and bends me back down.

I rest my hands on the wall again, feeling the warm water run down my spine.

"So, what? Did you plan for this to happen?" I grin, amused.

"I'm not an idiot, Kingston. Shower with my hot girlfriend? The thought crossed my mind."

I'm about to speak again, but he shuts me up with one strong and sudden move. He grabs my waist and fills me entirely. I gasp and bite back a moan. He takes a sharp breath and stills himself, the both of us taking in every mind-blowing sensation that comes with our bodies merging. He stretches me, but it isn't as painful as last time. I'm so ready I easily adjust to his size. When he starts moving in and out of me in the way he does so well, I ask myself, why did we wait so long to do this again?

"Does it hurt?" he says through slightly gritted teeth and slows down. The closeness between us sends my heart into an endless race. I love that he's always concerned about me.

"I'm good. I promise." I dig my nails into my palms while leaning against the tiled wall in front of me.

I'm more than good.

I let out a breathy moan when he uses his hand to pull my hair into a ponytail and speeds up his thrusting.

Oh my… And I thought last time was amazing.

For a second there, I almost forget that Kendrick's right down the hall. I let the pleasure fog the truth. We're not alone anymore. I hope that the sound of the water running is loud enough to drown out the very obvious noises we're making.

After a while, he pulls out and I wince at the emptiness he left between my legs.

"What are you doing?" I ask.

"Honestly?" He arches his eyebrow. He seems to be asking me if I can handle his honesty.

I nod hesitantly.

"I can't keep watching while I fuck you."

My mouth falls open.

He doesn't wait for me to reprimand him on his choice of words. "I won't last long, and I'm nowhere near done with you."

He spins me around and my back hits the freezing wall. I can't believe how turned on I am by his dirty mouth. I should've expected this from him. I should've known he'd be very blunt after passing the initial "I don't want to hurt you" period.

He circles my thigh with his arm, carelessly lifting one of my legs up and kissing the corner of my mouth. Then, he looks into my eyes as he fills me again. My eyes automatically close. *Wow.* He bites his lip in pure bliss, and I know I like this position a lot more than the previous one because it allows me to see the look on his face.

"You feel… so fucking… amazing." He groans between each word, breathing heavily, and cups my breast with his hand.

"We're so going to be late to the beach," I pant.

He nuzzles his face into my neck and plants hot kisses all over my collarbone. Then, he grips my ass and pushes harder, deeper.

"Oh, I plan on it."

Just like that, I'm reminded of why I could never take the "out" even if I wanted to. I'm reminded that I couldn't walk through the wide-open door even if I tried. I'm reminded that I couldn't dodge the bullet if I saw it coming.

And I'm terrified.

Because deep down…

I know it's coming.

EIGHTEEN

True Colors

Haze slowly turns into the parking lot situated near the shore, finds a spot, and stops the car. The engine dies in a low grumble, and he lets go of his hold on my thigh. He always holds it when he's driving. It's become a habit of ours. Kendrick insisted on tagging along, which annoyed Haze to the extreme. He can't stand having him around. Says it's like having a second child.

I have to agree. All Kendrick does is watch TV, empty the fridge, and provide us with unwelcomed remarks about Haze and Riley. But, even after all of this, deep down, I'm thankful that Kendrick's here. I feel supported, sane. He's the only one, apart from me, noticing Riley's behavior, and I'd lose my mind if I was alone with Haze and his incessant unawareness. I'd probably let him convince me that I'm imagining things.

I know Kendrick secretly came with us to watch over me. He won't admit it, but he's worried about me getting hurt.

I am, too.

I glance at the quiet and distant beach. Riley and Jacob have been waiting for us for a while now. Haze texted her a shitty apology about being late when we got out of the shower.

I mean… it's only five minutes.

Okay, fine, it's thirty.

What can I say? We got a bit carried away.

My gaze shifts to the calm sea, and I smile. I might hate the girl, but she was right about one thing: getting up early means having the beach to ourselves.

"You do know that your crazy ex's trying to ruin your relationship, right?" Kendrick casually says to Haze as we walk.

"Let me guess, you're the one who got that idea inside Winter's head." Haze locks the car doors with the remote.

"Me? Are you really that dumb, Adams?" Kendrick mocks, and I capture Haze's hand in mine as guarantee that he won't use it to punch Kendrick. His clenched fist relaxes under my fingers, and he takes a breath, trying so hard to control himself for me.

"Remind me why I'm letting your douchebag of a cousin live in my house again?" he asks me.

"Because I need to be there for when you fuck this up and Winter leaves your ass," Kendrick says with a smug face.

"She's just trying to be a good mom. You're both looking too far into this." Haze shrugs.

"Yep, he's really that stupid," Kendrick adds.

When Haze sees Jacob sitting on a towel with sand all over it, his face lights up. This… this right here is one of the reasons why I can't be mad about this. He's not here for Riley. He's here for his son.

"About time." Riley smirks at Haze, completely dismissing Kendrick and me standing behind him.

"I wish that girl would eat sand and choke," Kendrick whispers in my ear, and I hold back a laugh.

Also one of the reasons why I'm glad my cousin's here.

We lay down the few towels we brought into a circle and sit.

"What took you so long?" Riley asks.

Kendrick scoffs. "You mean, aside from having sex in the shower and thinking they're sneaky?"

When he says that, I'm the one who wants to eat sand and choke. Haze and I shift uncomfortably, both thinking the same thing: *Well, shit.*

Riley's mouth flies open, and her face twitches in anger.

"Excuse me?" she lets out.

This it is. She's going to expose herself.

She notices Haze's perplexed eyes stuck on her and covers Jacob's ears to make it pass as if he's the reason she's upset. Thankfully, he's way too young and focused on his sandcastle to even come close to understanding what's been said. I know damn well she wasn't being a protective parent. She was being a jealous ex-girlfriend.

Haze apologizes for Kendrick's behavior while my cousin beams, proud of the very awkward moment he just created. Riley is careful not to address anyone but Haze for the next twenty minutes. She asks him to help Jacob with his sandcastle, making sure to exclude us and scooting closer to him on the beach towel. Kendrick and I exchange glances.

Good to know at least one guy here isn't completely blind.

Kendrick and I decide to make a sandcastle of our own, well aware that Riley will surely cut our fingers off if we try to intervene in her picture-perfect family moment. After a few minutes of very bad sandcastle making, Haze turns to us and laughs.

"Not to be mean, guys, but… a two-year-old's castle looks better than yours."

Haze made a joke. That's Riley's cue.

Like she's on a timer, she bursts out laughing and punches him playfully. My gaze jumps to Haze, and I try to catch his eyes. The look on my face screams *"I told you. I freaking told you."* But, of course, he doesn't look my way, his attention drifting back to Jacob and his unsteady castle.

"Are you thirsty?" Riley asks Jacob after a while.

Haze jumps at the opportunity to go get us drinks at the food stand on the opposite end of the beach. It warms my heart that he's so caring and good with kids, but… it also destroys me that I had to find out this way.

"Not that I love your company, Kendrick, but I won't be able to carry five drinks by myself," Haze says, and Kendrick groans, getting up to help.

"I'll help, too," I say. I can feel Haze's insistent eyes on me, but I don't care.

I'm not staying alone with her even if you pay me back all the money I've spent on food in my entire life.

We're halfway there when he says it.

"Babe…"

"What?"

"You know what. You should go back there and try to talk to her. Give her the benefit of the doubt. I'm sure you'll like her if you give her a chance."

"I highly doubt that," I say to myself.

"Winter, please. For me. I really want you two to get along."

I can tell it means a lot to him.

"Fine." I roll my eyes, and he smiles. "But if it's hell on earth, you owe me big-time."

"Yeah, yeah. Now, get back over there." He slaps my ass, and I grin at him before walking back to the last place I want to be.

Riley's back is facing me. She appears to be on the phone with someone. She hasn't noticed my presence, and I can hear what she's saying from here. I can't help but slow down and eavesdrop.

"What?" she asks.

Silence.

"No, of course he doesn't know. What kind of idiot do you take me for?"

I stop dead in my tracks. Who doesn't know?

"He won't. I won't let him."

Him… Who's *him*?

"Okay. I'll catch you later, girl. Bye." She hangs up.

So many scenarios are spinning in my head. Who is she

talking about? Haze's words return to me. *Give her the benefit of the doubt.* It's probably a misunderstanding. She must be talking about a surprise she's organizing for someone.

I take a deep breath and join her, sitting down on my towel. As much as I love Haze, I won't force it. If she doesn't say a word to me until the boys return, so be it. She sees me but doesn't speak. Awkward and hateful silence it is. I get my phone out of my pocket and pretend to text.

That's when she turns to me.

"I can't believe you're actually still here."

There it is. She's finally showing her true colors.

"Excuse me?" is all I can muster.

"Wow, you really can't take a hint, can you? In a week tops, Haze will be mine again and you'll be nothing but a memory." She pushes her perfectly straight black hair over her shoulder.

I knew she was after Haze all along. But seeing her finally drop the act still shocks me. She's got some nerve, that's for sure. I open my mouth to speak, but she beats me to it.

"Let's be honest. Do you seriously think that you stand a chance against me? I'm his first love, Winter. Not to mention the mother of his child. I'm the one he's supposed to be with and you're just…" She pauses, looking me up and down. "A filler. A distraction."

I can't even form a sentence.

"You may have him thinking that he's in love with you right now, but sooner or later, he'll come to his senses and do what's best for Jake."

I finally manage to get a word in. "Let me guess, what's best is to be with you?"

She nods.

"Then what? You're going to get married? Have a bunch more babies and live happily ever after?" I say with mockery all over my face.

"Exactly." She smiles and fidgets with her manicured nails. "Why are you even fighting this? We both know this isn't what you want. It never was. You don't want to be the stepmom. You don't want to be with a guy who has a kid at your age."

For the first time since the beginning of her speech, she waits for a reply. But now that she wants one, I can't give it to her.

"So please… please do us all a favor and have enough self-respect to walk away."

My gaze shifts to Jacob, who's playing with his toys. He's not paying attention and is completely clueless as to how much of an awful person his mother is. How did such an evil woman create such a sweetheart?

"Or what?" I raise an eyebrow.

"Or I'll have to get rid of you myself."

"Do you really think that I'm scared of you?"

She laughs in a very creepy "I'll make your death look like an accident" way and stares up at me.

Okay. I might be just *a little* afraid of her.

"You should be."

I'm alerted by the sound of Kendrick and Haze's bickering. I turn my head to see them heading toward us. They're not holding any drinks. We got here so early the food stand probably isn't open yet. Riley notices Haze and Kendrick approaching and looks at me with a smile on her face. Just like that, I know…

She's going to do something.

"Why do you have to be so horrible to me?" she scolds me.

You have *got* to be kidding me.

"What's going on?" Haze asks, stopping next to us.

She gets back on her feet and glares at me. I'm certain that no one could ever fall for her show, until fake tears come pouring down her cheeks and she starts sobbing.

Shit, the bitch is good.

"Nothing." The words tumble out of my mouth.

"Nothing? You call threatening me *nothing*?" She wipes a tear away dramatically.

"What? That's insane. I didn't threaten her."

"Oh, I'm insane? Your girlfriend just told me that I was ruining her relationship and she wanted me gone. She said that she'd do anything for things to go back to the way they were. She wants to get rid of me. Of us." She points to Jacob and chokes on her false sobs.

"What? I didn't say anyth—"

"More lies. How can you live with yourself? All I wanted was to reunite my son with his dad." She starts stuffing Jacob's toys into her beach bag.

I expect Haze to see right through her game because he knows me. He knows I would never do something like this. But when I look up at him, the understanding eyes I imagined would be pointed at me are nowhere to be found.

His eyes are cold, torn.

"Come on, Jake. We're leaving." She pulls a very confused Jacob into her arms and starts to walk away. "Don't even think about seeing your son again as long as this psycho's in your life."

"Riley, wait," Haze calls out, and hearing him desperately call her name breaks me.

He believes her.

No. It can't be.

"I told you there was nothing to worry about." His harsh tone sends shivers down my spine. "Why did you have to make a scene?"

Kendrick intervenes. "Excuse me? Are you kidding me right now? You're seriously going to believe that girl instead of Winter? She loves you, for some un-fucking-believable reason. There isn't a single bad bone in her body, you know that."

"Shut the hell up, Kendrick. I'm not talking to you," Haze hisses angrily and turns to me.

"I can't believe you… Tell me you're not actually considering this. You know me. I'd never do anything to make you lose Jake. I didn't say any of these things, she did. She said that in a week tops, you'd be together again. That I'd be out of the picture even if she had to get rid of me herself. How can you believe her?"

"I…" He stops speaking, a bit angrier with every passing second. "Fuck, I don't know what to believe, okay?"

My heart splinters into a million pieces.

Don't cry. Don't cry.

"I believed you. When everybody on the freaking planet told me not to. When every sign pointed to you being guilty. I always believed you and you can't even believe in me for two seconds!" Tears build up in my eyes.

I wish I could stop the words coming out of my mouth. I wish I could swallow them before they do any damage. But I can't. Because Riley's right. Deep down, I don't want to be the stepmom. I don't want to be with a guy who has a kid. I tried. I really did. But it's too much for me.

So I let them fall.

I let the words destroy us the way Riley wanted them to.

"This doesn't work. We… We don't work."

His jaw drops.

Then, I walk away. No last word, no last look. I leave Haze stranded on the beach, and Kendrick follows. I wish he'd say something. I wish he'd say that he believes me. That he has no idea how he could ever doubt me in the first place, but he doesn't. He just stands there.

I was wrong before. When I said that nothing would ever be the same after Riley came back.

Things will never be the same *now.*

Because now…

He made his choice.

NINETEEN

Losing You

"Do you want to talk about it?" Kendrick asks, his voice breaking the thoughtful silence keeping me company since we left the beach. We've been walking for a solid forty minutes with no goal, direction, or purpose. Or should I say, *I've* been walking with no goal, direction, or purpose and my poor cousin's been following.

"Nope," I say and try to swallow the painful pit in my throat. What's there to talk about? Haze believed her. He believed the girl who ran away with his child instead of me. What's done is done.

Shortly after we left the beach, I turned off my phone. Not because Haze was texting or calling me, but because he wasn't.

And that silence…

That silence means he doesn't regret it. That silence means that we really just broke up.

"What do you want to do now?"

"I don't know. Walk off the face of the earth," I whisper to myself.

He sighs. "He's not worthy of you, Winter. Never has been, never will be."

I don't answer, staring into the emptiness. We're in the middle of nowhere. A few buildings can be seen in the distance but none that I recognize.

"You never should've met the guy in the first place. It's my fault. All of it." He kicks a rock on the sidewalk with his foot.

"Don't say that. Everything happens for a reason. Maybe I had something to learn from him. Maybe Riley's just the Universe giving me a chance to escape before this relationship ruins me."

It kills me to say that. Hell, it kills me to even *think* that. It pains me that Haze Adams might just be a lesson. That he might be just a page in a book that's still out there.

"And what lesson could that be?" he asks.

"I don't know. Stay single for the rest of your life? Give up on men?" I try to joke. "I'll let you know when I figure it out."

Another tear runs down my cheek, and I can tell Kendrick's hurting for me.

"Want me to kick his ass?" he offers.

"Yes," I say, but then retract myself. "No, it wouldn't be right."

"See? That's exactly what I was trying to avoid. This is why I wanted you away from him. You don't deserve to cry because he's too much of a dumbass to see through that girl's lies. Just say the word and I'll take you far away from here."

The thought spins around in my packed-with-regrets head. Maybe this is for the best. Because no matter how much of a liar

Riley is, I can't be the obstacle standing between a son and his father. She'll never let Haze see Jake again if I stay.

"Take me home." I contemplate how much these three little words are going to change my life.

"Home?" Kendrick asks, hesitant.

I immediately know what he means.

"Home." I nod, my already fragile heart breaking for good.

He knows I'm not talking about the lake house.

THE CAB STOPS IN FRONT OF the wood-built house for the last time, and the simple sound of the tires screeching makes me want to cry out all the water my body contains. I hoped Haze's car wouldn't be in the driveway. I hoped I could go in quickly, pack up my things, and be out of there.

Unfortunately, he's home. I know me leaving without a goodbye would've been harsh. But so is not being chosen by your own boyfriend.

I pay the driver, drag my feet to the front door, and push it open. Kendrick follows behind me. I turn the corner and see Haze sitting on the couch with his face covered by his hands. He looks up quickly when we walk in. His eyes are bloodshot.

Shit. I can't do this.

How did we go from there to here? How did we go from in love to completely shattered? How are we so broken when just this morning he picked up my pieces and put me back together?

"I'll get our stuff," Kendrick whispers and heads for the

staircase. The second Kendrick's footsteps fade up the stairs, Haze speaks.

"Where have you been?"

His eyes are filled with pain.

"Nowhere. Just walking around."

"Oh." His voice is weak.

I don't force the conversation.

"Can we talk?" He pats the couch.

I sigh, walk to him, and sit down farther away from him than I usually would've. He doesn't speak for a few seconds.

"I want you to tell me what really happened," he whispers.

Here we go again.

"I already told you. She lied. I didn't do any of those things. She was the one making threats. Not me."

He sighs, his pale blue eyes begging me to come clean.

"You still don't believe me." I can't stop the tears from coming back. Really? I *just* got them to leave.

"I want to. I really fucking do, but you have to admit it's a little weird that you were so upset with Riley just this morning and then… then this happens. I wouldn't be mad, Winter. I get it. We just started this relationship, and now everything's changing. I wish things would go back to the way they were, too, but they can't. Jacob's here now, and he's not going anywhere. Just tell me the truth, please," he begs.

That's when I snap.

"I did! I did tell you the truth, but you won't listen. You won't believe me. You refuse to see Riley for who she is because you know that if it's true, if she really is a horrible person, you won't be able to get to know your son. Do you still have feelings for her? Is that what this is about? If you want to be with her, then please, please just go ahead and put me out of my misery."

I don't mean that in the slightest, but I'm so angry I can't help it. Shaking my head, I try to walk away, but he gets up and stops me, circling my arm before I can take another step.

"You can't be serious right now." He raises his voice. "I've done *nothing* but try to show you that I'm in love with you. I don't want her. I wouldn't want her in a million years. She could sell her freaking soul and I still wouldn't want her. Don't you get that?" he barks at me, and I can tell he's fighting the urge to break something.

"Then why? After everything she's done, why do you still believe her? After she ran away with your twins and didn't even bother to call when one of them died? Why are you choosing to trust her over me?" We're both shouting at this point.

I know he has no idea how to answer that. So I say the first thing that runs through my mind before he can gather a response.

"How do you know that Jacob is even your son?"

Color depletes from his face.

It was impulsive, and yes, I didn't watch my mouth, but in the end, I mean it. A few days ago, I would've never doubted that Jake is Haze's. They're so similar I was sure Jake had to have

Adams blood. But today, I saw what Riley's capable of. The girl could lie her way out of anything.

"I heard her on the phone with a friend earlier. She didn't know that I was listening. She kept talking about not letting someone find out the truth. It sounded like she was hiding something from some guy. Have you ever considered that maybe she's lying to you?"

Haze's stunned. He stares at me in silence, his chest moving up and down rapidly. I know my words hit hard.

"Look me in the eyes and tell me you're a hundred percent certain that Jake's yours."

He tries to speak but fails. The truth is, he has no clue.

"He looks like me. You said it yourself."

"So? He's so young. It's too early to tell. You just... you can't really be that gullible, can you? She left town when she had no reason to. The whole world was on her side. Why would she do that unless she had something to hide?"

"Winter, stop." He refuses to look at me.

"If she lied about me, then what's to say she didn't lie about this?"

"I said stop!" he snaps, his tone catching me off guard. Surprisingly, his anger doesn't scare me. It just shows me that I'm getting under his skin. He's angry because he knows there's a chance I might be right, and the thought terrifies him.

"Even if she did lie about what happened on the beach, she wouldn't lie about something like this. I can't..." He runs a quick hand through his hair. "I can't believe that she could be so cruel."

"Well, I can."

He flinches. I give the shock in his eyes a few seconds to dissipate. He reaches for my hand and traps it in his. For a split second, I think he's going to tell me that he believes me and apologize. Then maybe we can at least *try* to fix this.

But he proceeds to break my heart instead.

"You have to understand… He's my son. I don't give a shit about never seeing Riley again. But I can't abandon Jacob. Not again. If to see him, I have to see her, then I'll see her every day. I'm… I'm sorry."

"Don't apologize. You should never have to feel guilty for wanting to know your kid, Haze. And I'm not asking you to choose. I would never do that."

I remove my hand from his grasp.

"But you have to." Realization flashes in his gaze.

"Yes." I look down, my throat hurting. "I have to choose because you can't."

"What does that mean?" He takes another step forward, and I turn my head, watching Kendrick pass through the kitchen with my stuff. He motions to our suitcases and walks out of the house. He's going to pack the car.

"It means I have to go." I turn away.

"Winter, wait, please…" he begs. "We can still make this work. We'll find a way. We'll—"

"Then what? What happens when she tries to tear us apart again and there's nothing you can do about it because you're terrified of losing your son? What happens the next time you don't trust me? Haze… you didn't even give *me* the benefit of the doubt," I repeat as if saying it again will make him understand how much it hurt me. He asked me to give it to her but let me down when I needed him.

"I know and I'm a dumbass. I'm a fucking idiot for not listening to your side of the story. I'm sorry. I should have trusted you," he says, the desperation in his voice torturing me.

"But you didn't," I murmur.

I know I can't hide the truth anymore. The real reason behind it all. This isn't about Riley lying. This isn't even about him doubting me. It's something else.

"I don't want to be the stepmom, Haze."

Saying it out loud finally pushes me over the edge.

I lose the war. I put down the weapons and admit a defeat that was evident from the start. The tears come streaming down my face. His features soften when he sees me wipe my eyes. At this point, breathing properly feels like a task you need a degree for.

"I don't want you to have a kid with somebody else. I thought I could do it. But I can't. I'm sorry."

All hope is drained from the atmosphere.

There isn't anything he can say to make this right. Because even if Riley stops lying, even if, for some unknown miracle, she stops wanting to be with him, she'll still be the mother of his kid. There is no happy ending for us. There never was.

This is *always.*

And I can't take always.

"All I see when I look at you is this life that we'll never get to have together." I choke. "All the firsts that you will give to her, and even when you do something as simple as smiling at Jake… it kills me. I don't want to be this person, Haze. I don't want to be the jealous girl on the outside looking in. I hate myself for it, but… it bothers me, and I can't change that."

He looks like he's trying his hardest to think of the right thing to say. He's searching for the one line that will somehow make all of this okay, but he won't find it.

He won't find it because it doesn't exist.

"I was mad at Riley for wanting to spend the rest of her life with you, but I get it." I place a hand on his cheek, look into those piercing eyes, and wonder if I'll ever see them again. His eyes close at my touch, like he's enjoying our last moment before it runs away and never comes back.

"I would've wanted forever, too."

He clenches his jaw and fists to try and stop his feelings from breaking down his walls. Even in a moment like this, he won't let himself be vulnerable. Seeing pain in his blue eyes suddenly feels like the saddest thing in the world. He looks down, staring at the floor. All I want to do is kiss him. I want him to drag me back to the bedroom where we'll fix this without words. I want to run to him and tell him that everything's going to be okay.

But I can't. Because it's *not* okay. None of it is.

I can't bear to spend another second with him knowing it'll be the last, so I turn around and start walking. I can hear the distant roar of Kendrick's car outside.

Every step I take feels like a dagger to the heart. I lay my hand on the doorknob, but just as I'm about to turn it, he says the words that truly end me.

"So that's it… I'm just going to lose you?"

My heart splits right in the middle.

I can't answer. I just stand there, with my back facing him and my eyes flooded. I'm afraid if I turn around, I'll fall back into his arms. If I turn around, I'll stay.

"Say it."

His words echo in my mind.

"Say you don't love me anymore."

Please, don't do this to me.

"Haze…"

"Say it because it's the only way I'll ever move on."

Please, don't make this worse.

I can't do worse.

"Winter, please," his voice cracks.

This is my breaking point.

The tears evolve into sobs.

"Well, then, I guess you'll never move on."

I turn to look at him one last time and see a tear escape his eye. I can barely believe it. He's crying. *Haze is crying.*

"Because I'm never going to stop loving you."

Next thing I know the door's closed behind me and I'm watching the lake house disappear in Kendrick's rearview mirror along with our memories. They grow distant until they're completely out of sight. Until they're just that: memories. Memories of a time when we still stood a chance.

Kendrick doesn't dare speak, just listening to me sniffle like a maniac. I'm crying so hard I'm legally blind at this point. He eventually turns on the radio to cover up his awkward witnessing of my breakdown.

What are you doing, Winter? You should be happy. You dodged the bullet, I tell myself.

But then why…

Why does it feel like I didn't dodge it at all?

TWENTY

Blocked Numbers

"I'm starving," Kendrick says, pulling up to a fast-food restaurant's drive-through and rolling his window down. We've been on the road for way too many hours to count. Haze really did take me to the middle of nowhere. My cousin and I haven't exchanged a word since we left the lake house. I've decided that I'm not in the mood to talk to him or anyone ever again, *period.*

"Hi, can I get four cheeseburgers—extra cheese, no ketchup—large fries, and a Coke?" Kendrick says.

I'm surprise that he got me two burgers. I'd barely eat one.

"Do you want anything?" He turns to me, and I scoff.

Of course this is all for him.

"You're a pig, you know that?"

"There it is," he says, proud of himself.

"What?"

"That smile."

He's right. I've almost never truly smiled since the day Riley showed up. It's been a while since my life's been nothing but tears and constant worries.

"Sir? Your order, please?" the employee insists.

"Right. Sorry. She'll have a salad and water."

"I'm sorry, what? Are you putting me on a diet?" I punch him in the arm.

"You'll need to look your best for your next boy." He wiggles his eyebrows, and I shudder, the thought stamping down my rib cage.

My next boy.

My next boy that won't be Haze.

We get our food, and Kendrick parks the car.

"Come on, you're driving." He unbuckles his seat belt.

"What? Why?"

"I want to eat."

"So I get to drive while you stuff your face? Thanks a lot." I roll my eyes and switch to the driver's side against my will. "How the hell am I going to eat a salad while driving?"

"I guess I'll have to feed you." He laughs.

"I hate you, you know that?"

We get back on the highway. We're ridiculous. Kendrick trying to feed me while I drive, covering me in salad dressing and croutons, is a show I should probably pitch to Netflix. He makes sure to mock me every time he gives me a bite, and after a miserably long while, he says that my driving makes him sick and we switch places again.

What? I'm a good driver.

Sometimes.

After a few years, the GPS informs us that we only have one hour left on the road.

"Hey, did you guys find a replacement for Blake?" I ask.

"Yes."

I wait a second for him to go on, but he doesn't, so I say, "That's it? That's all I get? Who is he?"

"Some guy." He shrugs.

I can tell he's dodging my questions, but I don't have the mental and physical strength to play detective today. *Or ever.*

"What about the boys? How are they?"

"They're good. Alex's got himself a girlfriend. And Will is still… well, *Will.*" He chuckles.

"Oh, a girlfriend? Is she nice?"

"Don't know, never met her. Alex's barely ever around anymore. His girlfriend's keeping him busy."

I ask Kendrick about Kass. Apparently, she's still working at the animal shelter, and last he heard she was seeing Luke Jenson, a jock from school who's been crushing on her forever. She's been texting me during my time away and asking why her mom was clearly lying to her about where I was. I get it. Maria doesn't know how much Kass is aware of. She's trying to protect her.

I didn't text her back once. I didn't text any of them back. Not Will, not Kendrick, not Kass. The phone call with Maria was the best I did. It's like I was caught up in a dream and I didn't want to wake up.

As for Kendrick, he tells me that him leaving town without a reason—or at least, a reason that he could share with her—didn't sit well with Nicole and they're over… *again.*

"My phone's dying. I need your GPS," he says, but it's more of an order than a request.

I dread turning on my phone. I turned it off so that I wouldn't know if Haze contacted me. I do as Kendrick asked and ache when I see the many new voicemails and texts on my screen. They're all from him.

"Don't listen to them," Kendrick says.

"What are you talking about?"

"He left you voicemails, didn't he?"

I don't even have to ask him how he knew for him to tell me.

"That's Haze Adams we're talking about. He's not going to stop fighting for you. Eventually, he'll find out Riley's a dirty liar and come running back."

"Maybe I should just listen to one." I can't help but crave his voice. Just one more time. Then I'll get him out of my system.

"If you want my advice, don't do this to yourself."

He's right. There's no point. It takes everything I have to delete his texts. No matter how many times he apologizes, he can't just "unhave" a kid. His apologies wouldn't change anything. This can never work. We're a lost cause.

My finger selects his number, and I take a deep breath…

Before pressing the Block This Contact button.

KENDRICK PARKS THE CAR IN MARIA'S driveway, and I'm tempted to tell him to get back on the road. Here we are. Back to the place where it all began. Both Kass's and Maria's car are here. Kendrick said they both took the day off work when he told them about our return.

"You ready?" Kendrick asks.

"Not even close," I say.

We pull the trunk open to grab our luggage, and I'm exhausted just *thinking* about all the questions Maria and Kass will ask us the second we step foot inside the house.

The first thing we see walking through the front door is my aunt cooking dinner. I salivate at the smell of her food. I'm still starving. My salad didn't want to be in my mouth and apparently much preferred being on my clothes.

Her face lights up when she sees us.

"Winter. Thank the Lord." She runs to me and pulls me into one of her familiar hugs. When her arms close around me, I want to cry an ocean. I've been holding it back since I left the lake house. Since I left *him*… I knew Kendrick wouldn't understand, so I pushed it down, but I can't do this anymore. I could use Allie, my best friend, right about now, but she's back in Toronto. I've been texting her the entire time I was in Colton Gate, but it's not even close to the real thing. There's so much she doesn't know. She doesn't even know about Haze. Only she can make me laugh even in the saddest moments. I wish she was here.

But she isn't. I'm alone.

No matter how surrounded I am.

Kendrick says something about going to meet the boys—who he hasn't seen in a while—and quickly leaves. He slams the door, and I start apologizing to Maria, trying to somehow make up for all the worries I've forced on her without meaning to in the past few weeks.

"Is that Winter?" I hear Kass call from the second floor.

Footsteps come stomping down the stairs, and my cousin turns the corner rapidly. I catch a glimpse of myself in the mirror in the hall. I look like hell. My eyes are still puffy from crying. When Kass sees me, she doesn't say a word. One quick look at my face is all she needs.

She captures me into her embrace. Again, the hug awakens in me this undeniable urge to cry, but this time, I surrender. I let the tears flow. I cry, and I cry, and I cry until I can't breathe. Maria joins in on the hug, and they hold me in silence, telling me that everything is going to be okay.

Maybe… I'm not completely alone, after all.

"I GET IT. HE WAS TRYING to do right by his son. His hands were tied." Kass throws herself back onto my bed and stares at the ceiling. "Oh, and what's that Riley bitch's address? I just want to talk."

I laugh at her question. I don't know what I would've done without her. It felt so liberating to pour my heart out. I told her everything that happened between Haze and me, from the first day at the lake house to the last—okay, maybe I didn't mention our steamy times—and she turned out to be way more understanding than I anticipated. I can barely recognize her.

She's far from the girl who once chastised me for sleeping at Haze's place forever ago. It's like she can relate. Either her relationship with Luke is more serious than I thought, or she's been with someone else. Kass was always quick to judge, but somehow she's different now. She understands boy drama.

Maria couldn't stick around for the story. Turns out the emergency at the hospital didn't care if she'd taken the day off. They desperately needed staff, and she ended up going anyway. She asked me if I was okay thirty more times before leaving, and I told her that I'd be fine. We all have to experience heartbreak one day or another, right? Only, the word *heartbreak* doesn't seem appropriate. This feels like a heart*explode*, or a heart*destroy*, or maybe even a heart*hammer*. Someone add these to the dictionary.

"Canada, come say hello!" a voice shouts from downstairs.

Will. I missed the idiot. As soon as she hears Will's voice, Kass hugs me, says that she has to do homework, and walks out of my room. I'm a bit surprised by her sudden departure but don't think much of it. I walk down to the kitchen and see Will and Alex standing next to the door. It feels like I haven't seen them in ages. I hug Alex first. Then comes Will's turn.

"Wow, you look like hell," he says mid-hug.

"Still completely tactless, I see." I pull away.

"Always." Will smirks. "Hey, where's the new guy?"

"He's outside. He had to take a call," Alex replies.

"Oh, the new guy's here?" I ask Kendrick, curious to see who they chose as a replacement for Blake.

Immediately, his face changes and he rubs at the back of his neck, which has always been a gigantic red flag when it comes to my cousin.

"Winter, about that…" He seems uncomfortable.

Will's eyes widen. "Wait, you didn't tell her?"

"Tell me what?"

"Will, shut up," my cousin hisses.

"Well, that's not going to be awkward at all," Will scoffs.

"What's going on?" I ask.

Kendrick steps forward. "There's something you need to know about the new guy. He's…"

He doesn't have a chance to finish his sentence. The front door opens and someone walks inside Maria's kitchen. But it's not just anyone. It's the one person I thought I'd never see again. The boys turn to me, waiting for a reaction of some sort, but I can't bring myself to give it to them. All I can do is call his name.

"Ryder?"

TWENTY-ONE

Back For You

Haze

I used to laugh at the dudes who left a girl a hundred voicemails. I could never wrap my mind around it. I remember calling Vic whipped once or twice during his falling-in-love-with-Bea days. The idea that I'd end up like one of these idiots never crossed my mind. *It's impossible*, I thought. *I don't do love.*

Now that I'm standing alone in a house that's way too big for one person, staring at my phone like it's a passion of mine and hoping that she'll deign to return just *one* of the four voicemails I've left her, I have to admit…

I'm fucking whipped.

Yep, I'm one of these guys.

When did I become such a pussy?

I rub my eyes and collapse onto the bed where I used to hold her, the bed where I first felt her. I haven't slept in twenty-four hours. I couldn't sleep in my room because the sheets still smell like her. Scratch that, the entire fucking house smells like her, and it's driving me mad.

I fidget with my phone impatiently. I don't know what's

taking Riley so long. I called her a few hours ago and asked her to come alone. She said that she'd get a babysitter and be on her way. I hate to say it… but she did seem oddly happy to hear that Winter is gone. I don't know if I'm just imagining things.

I don't know anything anymore.

I sigh in relief when I hear the doorbell.

She's here.

I glide downstairs and open the door. As soon as I see the girl standing on my porch, my stomach lurches with discomfort. She's dressed up, wearing a short red dress that clings to her skin and a full face of makeup.

Riley smiles. "Hey."

"Hey. Thanks for coming." I step aside to let her in. My voice reflects my mood, but she doesn't seem to notice my tone, the grin widening on her lips. I motion to go into the living room and shift when she sits a little too close to me for my liking. I feel like I owe it to Winter to move away; then I have to remind myself that she dumped me.

That I lost her.

"So… you dumped Willow?" she asks.

I bite back the harsh words wanting out of my mouth. She knows Winter's name. She has to be doing that on purpose.

"Winter," I correct her. "And no. I didn't. She dumped me."

My statement seems to shock her.

"She did?"

"Yeah, she can't handle being the stepmom, and I get it,

which is why I asked you to come over."

Her eyes grow bigger.

"I need to ask you something."

"Of course. Anything," she says and lays a hand on top of mine. I know she might mean for the gesture to be supportive, but it only makes me uncomfortable.

I move my hand away and clear my throat.

"I want a paternity test."

Her reaction is immediate.

Her face twitches in anger. "Excuse me?"

I'm taken aback by her response. It's been years since I saw her. She can't seriously tell me that the eventuality of such a request hasn't crossed her mind.

"What? You don't believe that Jake's your son? How can you doubt your own flesh?"

"Riley… Honestly, it's not him I doubt."

If I thought she was angry before, I hadn't seen anything yet.

"What's that supposed to mean? That you don't trust me?"

"I want to. I've known you my whole life, Rile. I want to believe that you'd never lie to me about something so important, but I can't take any chances. What's the problem? If Jacob's my son, then you have nothing to worry about."

"I…" She's speechless at first. "Okay."

I'm surprised.

"Really?"

"Sure." Her lips agree, but her body language tells another

story. She leans back into the couch, playing with the fabric of her dress.

"All right, let's go right now then. I have an appointment," I lie and get up. If she's being dishonest but has somewhat of a soul, she'll come clean before we get to the doctor's office. This is the oldest trick in the book. She'll feel the walls closing in on her and spill.

She hesitantly follows me to the door, dragging her feet and letting the anxiety in my stomach hit the roof. She's reluctant. Bad sign.

No, no, no.

Don't let it be true.

Don't tell me I lost her for fucking nothing.

I walk to the door and get my keys out of my pocket. I reach for the doorknob and begin to tur—

"I just wanted him to have a father." Her voice comes out in a whisper.

I freeze in place, the dreadful truth dawning on me, and turn around to see red, teary eyes staring back at me.

"What did you just say?"

She doesn't repeat, lowering her gaze to her feet.

"Riley, what did you say?" I ask again.

She looks up at me and tears start pouring down her face

Shit, shit, shit.

This can't be happening.

I did not just lose Winter over a lie.

"It meant nothing." She chokes on the sobs.

The implications accompanying what she's saying punch me in the gut. Inexplicable moments start to make sense. Questions start to find answers. All these nights when she was working late, she wasn't working…

"You cheated on me?" I ask, but it still comes out as a fact.

"Baby, please. It was a mistake. You have to believe me. I regretted it as soon as it happened. I didn't love h—"

"Wait. Hold on. Are you… trying to spare my feelings right now?" I cackle in anger. "Do you even hear yourself? That's not what I'm mad about. I don't give a shit that you cheated, Riley. I care that you lied about me being the father. How could you do this to me? To Jacob?" I can't help but raise my voice at her, so furious I could destroy everything within my vicinity.

"As soon as I found out he wasn't yours, I went to his father and he wanted nothing to do with him. He kicked me off his porch into the pouring rain, screaming that this wasn't his problem. Then, when I told you, you didn't want him either, and I… I freaked out. I didn't know what to do, so I left. I thought I could start over until…"

"Until recently. When I texted you," I finish. She nods, sobbing louder. "And you decided to pretend Jacob was my son again. How sick are you?"

"You don't understand. I can't do this anymore. It's hard raising a child by myself. I don't have the means."

I know that by "means" she's referring to cash.

"Money?" I spit in disgust. "You did this for a damn check?"

"Haze, baby, please." She grips my clothes. "Okay, maybe in the beginning it was all I wanted, but then… then I saw you with that bitch and I remembered how amazing you are. I saw the way you looked at her and… I want that. I want you. I want what you guys had."

I get away from her grasp, my brain unable to decide which abomination to focus on first.

Winter…

What have I done?

"Do you have any idea what you just did? What I just lost because of you and your fucking lies?" I spit.

"What? You mean *her?* She's nothing. Anything she's done to you, I'll do better. I can be the one you need. I was the one you needed once."

I don't even hear a word she's saying, the memories of her walking out the door haunting me.

"She was right." I break with each word. "She was right, and I didn't believe her. How could I not believe her?"

When Riley sees my semi breakdown, she doesn't say anything and stares, her expensive mascara rolling all the way down to her neck.

"Get out."

"What? Haze, please. You don't mean that."

"I said get the fuck out!" I have to shout to get her to listen.

When she realizes that her tears aren't making a difference

and the mess she's made isn't this easy to clean up, she finally walks out of the door. I don't let a second pass me by and run upstairs. I don't know what I'm going to do, how I'm going to do it, or when I'll do it. I don't know anything, but I don't care. I know the most important thing of all.

I'm going to get her back.

Winter

"HOW MANY TIMES AM I GOING to have to say it? I'm sorry," Kendrick begs, following me around the kitchen and doing what he does best which is annoying me until I wish I was deaf. We're on day two of me ignoring him. It's as apparent as the bags under my eyes that I'm not ready to talk to him, but he won't take a hint. He keeps saying that I should be over it by now, which only makes me angrier.

I don't know how exactly he expected me to react to the news that he's the one who sent Ryder to Colton Gate to start shit between Haze and me. Yes, turns out Ryder doesn't have family in Haze's hometown. The only thing he had was a desperate need for his leader's approval.

He claims that everything else he told me was true and apologized. I hate that I can't even be mad at him. He was a pawn in Kendrick's game. He just wanted to be accepted. Kendrick said he needed a way to test Ryder, their newbie who was dying to be in the East side main fighters' close circle, whatever that means.

My cousin called it an initiation. He talked about needing to make sure he was trustworthy. I don't care what he says to justify it. That was a lame move and he knows it.

Apparently, Kendrick and Ryder spent a long time in Colton Gate following us every time we went out and thinking of ways they could mess things up. While Kendrick and I were staying at the penthouse, Will and Alex recruited Ryder. Kendrick called them and sent his new puppet after us as soon as he woke up in Tom's apartment and saw that I was gone. Kendrick arrived to town shortly after Ryder did. I have no idea how they tracked us down so quickly, and I was way too angry to ask. This explains Ryder randomly buying me a dress and offering me passes to the fair. But what this doesn't explain is his recycling of the "fair passes" trick on another girl the next day.

My guess is… he's just an asshole.

Kendrick tried to hide behind the fact that this was partly Maria's request. She called and asked him to go watch over me even after our phone call because she couldn't sleep not knowing if I was okay. What she didn't know was… he was already in Colton Gate creeping on us. Maria or not, I'm still mad. He could've just made sure that I wasn't dead like she asked instead of adding "let's ruin Haze and Winter's relationship" to his mission description. This is on him. He has to own it.

Alex walks into the room. "Still not talking to you?"

"She's stubborn." Kendrick rolls his eyes.

Alex's been waiting around the house for twenty minutes now. He got here way too early. We're all supposed to go to the movies together today, and I'm nowhere near ready.

But what I'm even less ready for is returning to this hell they call school tomorrow. Tanner agreeing to leave me alone unfortunately means going back to my regular life, which includes school. Kendrick said Tanner promised to make good use of his contacts all around the street fighting community to get people off my back. It's time to start living again. I can't spend the rest of my senior year in hiding.

Plus, Maria said that I have to prepare for the finals if I want to stand a chance at graduating. I feel like I've missed so much. At least, now that I'm single, I'll have plenty of time to catch up with my online classes.

I put my cereal bowl away—that I couldn't fill all the way because Will drank all the milk again—and walk out of the kitchen. I'm in desperate need of a shower and silence, which doesn't exist in this house since Will's been staying with us. It's been a few days now. He said something about needing a break from some family drama. As the overly nice person that she is, Maria said yes. I think the guys are starting to grow on her.

I wince, thinking back to Haze alone in Colton Gate. I haven't heard from him since I left town.

I mean, you did block his number. It must be pretty hard to contact you.

Inner Winter?

Yeah?

Shut up.

I can't stop wondering what he's doing. If he's seen Riley again since I left. If she finally got what she wanted. I bet she was very pleased to find out that I was gone.

The bathroom next to the kitchen is occupied, so I try the one on the second floor. Just before I can turn the doorknob, voices flare on the other side. Two voices to be exact. I press my ear to the door.

Riley at the beach and now this.

Eavesdropping is my new thing, apparently.

I can barely discern a low voice saying, "I'll talk to him. I promise. No more lying."

I hear nothing for a while, then footsteps. I hide in my bedroom, which gives me a direct shot of the show, and peek through the partially closed door. Someone walks out into the hall.

Kass.

Who was she talking to? I swear I heard a guy's voice. She looks around as if to make sure that nobody saw her, goes back into her bedroom, and closes the door. My doubts turn into facts when someone else walks out of the bathroom.

Will.

It hits me.

I remember running into him in the morning a day before the fight. He was leaving the house in a hurry and looked like he'd been caught red-handed.

I can't believe I didn't see this sooner.

He was probably sneaking out of the house after spending the night with Kass. Something's going on between these two. They've totally been shacking up behind Kendrick's back. This might also be why Kass has changed recently. She looks freer, less uptight. More *Will.* When it's not me and Haze, it's Kass and Will.

Oh, well. Kendrick is going to be pissed, but I ship it.

I lock myself in the bathroom and ignore the unwanted flashbacks of the rather *heated* moment Haze and I shared the morning before everything went to hell. Thinking that this will never happen again feels surreal… impossible.

After a quick shower, I dry myself, throw on a sweatshirt and leggings, and pull my brown hair into a messy bun that makes me look like a homeless man. My lack of sleep is showing. I need to fix whatever's happening with my face. My eyes jump to my makeup bag on the counter, and I make the effort of opening it. Yes, *effort.* Any possible trace of confidence or motivation I had disappeared when I left Haze. I feel like there's no point to even trying to look somewhat cute if he isn't there to see it. He's the only one whose eyes I want to catch.

"Canada! Hurry or we're leaving without you. The movie's starting in fifteen," Will calls out, and I run downstairs.

"SHOULD WE TELL HER THAT SHE accidentally used Nesquik as foundation?" Will mocks a girl passing by when we step out of the movie theater. Ryder, Alex, and Kendrick cackle at the sight of the young girl who, indeed, is wearing a foundation way too dark for her skin tone. It's okay, girl. We've all been there. Or at least, I have. I used to wear dark chocolate foundation and think I was fooling everyone.

The movie only increased my annoyance with anything that rhymes with love. It was supposed to be an action movie, but, of course, the main character fell for the hot girl who can kick ass and… *there goes my mood for the rest of the day.*

The guys don't want to go home just yet, but Kass and I have had enough. Ever since I witnessed Will and my cousin sneaking around this morning, I've been noticing them sharing glances that are packed with desire from time to time. The tension is unmissable. How long has their secret love story been going on right under our noses?

The boys suggest that we go to the arcades next to the theater, but since Kass and I aren't in the mood, we opt for the nearby coffee shop instead. Kendrick and Will decide to send Ryder on coffee duty while they burn the very little brain cells they have left playing video games.

I haven't really said a word to Ryder since two days ago when he and Kendrick confessed to everything, but I have to admit he isn't too bad. He's still the nice guy I spent a day at the fair with. I just wish our entire relationship hadn't started with a lie.

Just before we walk away, Kendrick receives a message. He checks his phone and turns to us.

"Party at Rose's tonight," Kendrick reads out loud.

"Who's that?" I ask.

"Tanner's ex. They've been on and off for like two years." He shrugs and proceeds to reply to the text. "You up for it? I know I am."

I'm not surprised by his willingness to go. Kass said that Kendrick's been on the rebound since Nicole broke up with him. Everybody agrees to his unexpected plans except for me. Kendrick raises an eyebrow in my direction.

"Winter?"

"Will Tanner be there? I'm not trying to die tonight."

Will laughs. "No, I think she dumped his ass for good a month ago. She's seeing some other guy now."

I hesitate at first but decide I have nothing better to do than cry about Haze tonight anyway.

Oh well, I'll watch movies and stuff my face some other time.

"Count me in."

They nod, satisfied with my decision. Kass, Ryder, and I cut across the street, and I push the glass door to the coffee place open. We enter the very modern shop that gives me Pinterest vibes and sit by the bay window. Ryder offers to order for all of us since the line is long. I promise to pay him back. As soon as Kass and I are alone, I drop the bomb.

"So… you and Will, huh?"

Her face grows pale, and she wiggles in her seat. "Me and Will what?"

"I saw you this morning."

She bites on the inside of her cheek.

She knows she's busted.

"Don't tell Kendrick."

"Why?" I ask. I've never known Kass to care about Kendrick's opinions. I had the proof of that when she dated Blake.

"Will doesn't want him to know."

So, this is all him.

"How long?"

"A while." She fidgets with her phone. "He promised that he'd talk to him, but he never does. I'm so sick of this."

We're interrupted by Ryder coming back to the table with way too many drinks. The guys have been treating him like their service boy. That's the price to pay for being the newbie, I guess.

Kass says she has to go to the bathroom and leaves us alone. A blonde I noticed Ryder was chatting with while waiting in line comes up to him and drops a Post-it on the table. It has her number on it. Ryder cracks an uncomfortable smile as she walks away.

I laugh at his expression. "What's wrong?"

"Nothing. She's just… not really my type."

She's absolutely gorgeous. The guy must be blind.

"And what exactly is your type, Mr. High Standards?" I take a sip of coffee.

"I don't know. I have a very specific type, and she's just not it, I guess. I prefer brunettes." His voice is full of suggestion.

Is he talking about me? I don't have the energy to overthink it. I wasn't into him then, and I'm not into him now.

"Hey, listen. There's something I need to tell you." He glances at the bathroom like he's afraid Kass will come bursting through the door any second. I don't reply, sinking in my seat. "I'm sorry… for the way it all started. I know you must think I'm a jerk. Truth is, that day at the restaurant, me pulling the same trick on another girl was a dare. Kendrick and I were bored out of our minds, and he challenged me to try and see if it could work again. It was wrong of me, and I felt guilty as soon as it happened. I just want you to know that." His dark eyes seem sincere. Ryder's a really attractive guy. To most girls, at least. Like I said, I'd probably be into him if things were different. I know he's probably close to Haze in the looks department but not in my heart, he isn't. I begin articulating a reply, but I'm interrupted by an unexpected text message popping up on my screen. I furrow my eyebrows. Apart from Kass, Maria, and Allie, I don't have lots of people to text.

This is the part where I wonder where to buy myself a life.

I pick my phone up, and worry devours me. It's from an unknown number. I've never been the luckiest with unknown numbers, that's for sure.

This prick again? I thought you had better taste, Kingston.

My heart stops.

I glance around the coffee shop nervously.

There's no way.

No way that he's here.

I would've seen him. You don't just *miss* Haze Adams.

Ryder asks me what's wrong, but his words are wiped out by my heart pulsing in my brain. My eyes refuse to stop searching for his face.

He's here.

He has to be.

That's when I see him.

Walking inside the coffee shop with a smug face and wandering eyes. Just like that, I lose track of, well, *everything*. Heads begin to turn. I hear one of the girls—who I recognized from school—at the table behind us whisper, "Is that Haze Adams?" and her friend snorting, "Yes, I heard he got back yesterday. I wonder why. No one's seen him in a while."

He raises his eyebrows at the sight of me and smiles. It's that easy. With just one look, all the lies I've been feeding myself since I left Colton Gate crumble to pieces. They're right.

The notorious bad boy is back in town.

But what they don't know is…

He's back for me.

TWENTY-TWO

Unforgivable

"Is everything okay?" Ryder, whose back is facing the door, asks. He has no idea that the person responsible for the dark bruise under his eye just walked into the coffee shop.

I try to speak, but my lips remain sealed despite my best efforts. Haze is looking right at me, not even slightly bothered by the countless eyes set on us. He looks breathtaking. Facts are facts. My miserable brain might've tried to convince itself that he isn't all that during the past few days, but it didn't stick one bit. It's clear now that I've been lying to myself.

He's all that and more.

Dark circles reside under his eyes, giving away that he hasn't been sleeping as much as he should. Is he half as messed up as I am? Is it because of the breakup?

Relax, Winter. Maybe this is just a coincidence. Maybe you just happened to be at the same place and he texted you.

You blocked him, dumbass. That would mean he got a new number just *to text you.*

Yeah, definitely not a coincidence.

Please don't walk toward me.

Please don't walk toward me.

And… he's walking toward me.

Does my brain still function? I'm not sure. *This freaking guy*. He could straight-up ask me if I like cheese and still make me doubt my capacity to speak English. He stops next to us, and Ryder's face flutters in shock. I assume mine is worse.

"Still hanging out with this asshole, I see." He stares at Ryder like he's hoping it will make him disappear. "Going undercover to ruin a relationship—that's low, dude. Even for scums like the East side."

God, I missed his voice.

I don't bother questioning how he knows about Ryder's stunt. He's still the West side's main, which according to Kendrick is just a less formal way to say leader, and his guys probably filled him in the second he came back into town. Will told me the East side rebounding after Blake's betrayal was the talk of the street fighting community for a while after we left.

I almost forgot, while we were away, about this whole street fighting mess. For a second there, when Haze kissed me the night of the storm, he was just a guy I'd fallen in love with. Not the leader of the West side, not a dangerous heartbreaker with attachment issues. We were just two stupid kids living the dream.

Until reality came settling in and we were forced to wake up.

"What are you doing here?" I ask, avoiding his persistent gaze on me.

"We need to talk." His voice is firm, low.

I want to say no, but the mere sight of his blue eyes, that are crammed with guilt, is enough to change my mind. I know it won't make things better. We're hopeless. We were hopeless from the very second Riley came back, but I still tell myself that there's no harm in one quick talk.

Ryder speaks on my behalf. "You wish. She's done with you, man. Forget it."

"I've punched you once—are you looking for round two? You still got one good eye. I'm down," Haze threatens, and I know the girls at the table behind us are hanging on to every word. Ryder's fists turn into weapons.

"Go ahead, try. You just got lucky last time." He gets up.

This is *not* happening right now.

"Guys, stop." I bounce up, place a hand on Ryder's chest to stop him, and instantly feel Haze's eyes burning where my fingers meet Ryder's shirt.

"Seriously, Haze, why are you here?" I move my fingers away from Ryder, and Haze's shoulders drop.

He exhales. "To fix the biggest mistake of my life."

Man… why does he have to say things like that?

"Five minutes. That's all I want," he says when I don't reply.

I take in a sharp breath.

"Five minutes," I agree.

Haze's face lights up like he's surprised—no, *in disbelief*—that his begging actually worked. As for Ryder, he stares at me disapprovingly, but I overlook his drawn eyebrows and head to the door with my ex. The whispers following us like shadows make it clear that the news of Haze's return will travel almost as fast as my heart is beating right now. *Haze Adams back in town and after the new girl! Who knew he could care?*

We have to distance ourselves from the shop to get somewhat decent privacy. We don't need them gawking at us during such a painful moment. I walk by his side, the wind blessing me with a draft of his cologne and causing me to get weak in the knees.

This freaking guy part two.

We come to a stop in an empty parking lot. Now that we're finally alone, without everybody's eyes on us, without the whole world's disapproving comments stinging in my head, I know it'll take all the willpower I have not to fall back into his arms.

He speaks after a few seconds of us staring at each other. "You blocked my number."

"Five minutes. Is that really what you want to talk about?"

He slides his hands into his jeans pockets and sighs.

"I'm an idiot," he says.

"Don't say that."

"No, I am. I'm more than an idiot, actually. I'm a *blind* idiot."

He gets a faint laugh out of me.

"I'm an idiot because I didn't believe the only person on earth who believes in me."

Why do I feel like he's about to drop a bomb on me?

"You were right."

My pulse quickens. "What?"

"Jake's not mine."

I can't believe the words coming out of his mouth.

"I confronted Riley. I asked her for a paternity test. She freaked out, confessed to everything. She cheated on me when we were dating. I don't have a kid. I never did."

I was right.

I was right.

I tried to tell him, and he dismissed me like I was crazy.

This could technically change everything. Not wanting to be the stepmother is the main and most important reason why Haze and I couldn't work. But I've had nothing but time to think during the past sleepless nights. The father thing was a problem, yes, but there's also everything else.

There's the fact that I feel betrayed. I feel like I gave him my trust in a heartbeat, and he couldn't give me his when it mattered the most. The fact that even when he promised to tell me everything, he couldn't. He still didn't want to open up about the mysterious kid's room in his house.

"That's great. I'm happy you got the truth." I ignore the tightening of my heart. I can literally see the hope draining out of his blue eyes.

"It doesn't change anything, does it?" he asks, but it comes out as a statement.

"What did you expect, Haze? That I'd just fall back into your arms and pick up where things left off? You hurt me. I'm glad you got the truth, but it doesn't change the fact that it took you this long to believe me."

"Winter, please…" He tries to grab my hand, but I don't let him.

"Sometimes, I think about how much I love you and it scares me. Because then I realize that you're never really all in. You say you feel the same, but somehow you're always two steps away from backing out. One step forward can mean five steps back any day with you, and I don't know if I can take it.

"Then there's also the fact that I barely know anything about you. I've never seen or heard anything about your parents until the lake house. It's like they don't exist. What's the deal with them? You promised to tell me about the room I found back at your place but never did. You're still so afraid of opening up to me while I'm over here telling you everything you want to know without blinking. That's not fair, Haze. It's okay to have issues. We all do, but I guess… when you didn't give me your trust, you lost mine."

He doesn't reply right away, probably wondering what part of my outburst to focus on first. That's a lot to take in.

"I guess, what I'm trying to say is… unless you're willing to sit down and tell me everything, and I mean *everything*, I don't think a second chance is possible for us."

I bite my tongue and fight the urge to take it all back. Losing him once almost completely destroyed me. I can't imagine what it'd do to me if I were to let him back into my life and get even more attached only for something like that to happen again.

I can't keep falling for him unless I'm sure he'll be there to catch me.

I'll also be going back to Canada soon. I didn't bring that up because I know it would make him feel pressured, and I wish he would come clean because he wants to, not because he *has* to.

"You asked for time and I gave it to you, but I need you to tell me everything now. Can you do that for me?" I beg. His eyes drop to the concrete, and I know from his stance and silence that he's not going to give me the answer I desire.

I want nothing more than to see the pain leave his marvelous face, but I know what I'm about to do can only have the opposite effect.

I place a gentle kiss on his cheek, fighting tears that are hell-bent on paying us a visit, and walk away. I know to anyone watching the scene, this probably would've seemed like my way of forgiving him.

But it's not.

Far from it.

It's my way of saying goodbye.

LYING ON KASS'S BED, I WONDER if I should start working on my will since I'm obviously not getting out of here until I'm seventy. I've been waiting for her to finish getting ready for an hour now. It didn't even take me half the time that it's taking her. I chose to wear a very simple black dress and slapped on a bit of red lipstick. Pretty bold, I know. But I wanted to try something different.

I watch her straighten her already perfectly straight hair and absently scroll through social media. I've seen Rose's party mentioned a few times already. Everybody's going. I'm not stupid. I know Haze will probably be there, too.

I literally have to force Kass to drop the mascara when the boys threaten to leave without us for the third time. We get in Kendrick's car, and Will turns up the radio. Will says something about Ryder, Alex, and his girlfriend meeting us there through the blaring AC/DC music.

Will's the designated driver for tonight. As for Kendrick, he's already started drinking. Will's mouth opened so wide when he saw Kass earlier that he could've easily swallowed two families of flies. The reaction she got must be why she dressed up. I think she's trying to get him to wake up. Or to torture him for not telling Kendrick about them. Now that I know about their secret, the chemistry is so obvious it seems impossible that I'm the only one noticing.

Twenty minutes later, the car stops in front of a two-story white house with way too many people standing on its front yard. I catch myself looking for Haze's car in the full driveway. I don't see it. Maybe he's not coming. An unwanted mix of relief and disappointment shoots across me, and I never thought such a combo could exist.

We step inside the house without knocking, and the first thing I see when crossing the threshold are two girls dancing on top of the kitchen counter. I scan the crowd, recognizing many people from school and trying to stick names to the countless faces around me.

A few girls next to the minibar notice me and elbow each other. They shamelessly stare. I recognize the tallest one.

Natasha.

Bianca's best friend.

I think I've seen the other two girls hang out with Bianca at school. Natasha runs a hand through her wavy ginger hair and raises an eyebrow at me. It looks like she's thinking, *"So, this is the girl who got Haze Adams to commit?"*

She gets her phone out of her pocket and starts typing. I'd bet a hundred dollars that they're alerting Bianca, their evil clan leader, of my presence. Luckily, I'm dragged out of the room when Kass pulls on my arm and goes up to the second floor where she says Ryder, Alex, and his girlfriend are waiting for us.

As promised, they're standing by the pool table. We're introduced to Mia, a short brunette with a bright smile. She keeps on cracking jokes, which instantly makes me like her. Once we get the introductions out of the way, the guys offer to go get us drinks. Kass, Mia, and I keep the conversation going until the first delicate question falls out of my cousin's mouth.

"So, how well do you know Alex?" is the only way she can put it.

Mia chuckles. "If by that, you mean, do I know about the fights? Then, I know him very well."

"Great. She's one of us," I say, and the girls laugh.

"How did you guys find out?" Mia asks.

"Well, as far as I'm concerned, I live with a dumbass who can't keep a secret to save his life. Wasn't too hard to put the pieces together," Kass says.

"What about you?" She turns to me.

Kass scoffs and I know she's wondering how I'm going to summarize such a long and messy story into a few sentences.

"Oh boy, I followed the guys when I thought they were lying about going to a party. News flash, I was right. It turns out they were going to some creepy meeting. I had no idea when I got into the car that night that it was the beginning of—"

"An epic love story."

I freeze in place.

I know that voice.

"Haze," I say to myself.

I turn around and, because I'm the luckiest girl on earth, come face-to-face with the one person I was afraid to see tonight.

Shit, he looks hot.

It's like the more I try to convince myself that he has no effect on me, the more handsome he looks. He's wearing a plain black T-shirt. How is that enough to make me dizzy?

"What are you doing here?"

"Hello to you, too, gorgeous. I'm good. Thanks for asking." He beams.

"Who's this?" Mia asks.

I take a sip of my drink. I'm not *nearly* drunk enough for this.

"Me? Oh, I'm no one. Just her future husband."

I start coughing, the liquor in my mouth going down the wrong pipe.

"Don't choke, babe. We haven't even gotten to *'til death do us part* yet."

Mia swallows a laugh and arches an eyebrow like she's waiting for me to confirm his story. Problem is, I'm too busy trying not to suffocate. I finally manage to breathe properly again after a few seconds.

Did he just say that?

Like he can hear my every thought, he fills the distance between us, wraps his tattooed arm around my waist from behind, and presses his body to mine. I slightly gasp but don't move away. I can't. The truth is, I want to stay there. I wish his embrace didn't feel this good. I wish he didn't feel like home.

I finally gather the strength to step away from his hold when I notice a few people staring.

Mia laughs. "Future husband, huh?"

"Absolutely. She just doesn't know it yet." He takes a sip out of the red cup in his hand.

"Boyfriend?" Mia guesses.

"Ex," I correct her.

Haze leans in just enough to brush my jaw with his lips and whisper in my ear, "Baby, you're breaking my heart."

Don't you dare shiver. Don't you dare sh…

Crap.

"Excuse me." I throw Mia a polite smile before dragging Haze to a quiet spot—or as quiet as a spot can be in such a monster party—and push him into the corner, away from prying eyes. A deep laugh leaves his lips.

"You know, if you wanted to get me alone, all you had to do was ask." He steps dangerously close to me, and I know from his even-more-cocky-than-usual behavior that he's had a few drinks. I'm proved right when I smell the liquor on his breath. "You look stunning, by the way." He captures my waist with both his hands, brings our bodies together, and draws circles over my stomach with his thumb. I catch myself wishing I wasn't wearing a dress just so I could feel his fingers on my skin. I can't lie. I still want him. *Bad.* Special thanks to my inhibitions for bailing on me when I need them the most.

"Don't do that." The words itch in my throat as I step back.

"Do what?" He pushes a strand of my hair away from my eye.

"Stop being so… charming. Nothing's changed."

"Yet," he taunts.

"I thought I'd made myself clear earlier."

"You did. You were perfectly clear. I don't have your trust anymore. So I'm going to get it back. I'm going to earn it."

"You mean you're ready to tell me everything?" I let myself hope for a brief second. As always, he becomes uncomfortable and shuts down as he balances his weight from one foot to the other. This is my answer. "I see. Enjoy the party, Haze."

By the time I find Mia and Kass, the guys are back with our drinks and already done with theirs. I bring the plastic cup to my lips and take a huge sip I'll most likely regret in a few hours. Maybe it's the heartbreak. Maybe it's to feel better. I don't know. But one thing's for sure…

I want to forget.

Haze

The heat is unbearable. The house is so packed it's nearly impossible to move around the crowd without smelling what everyone had for dinner. She doesn't seem to mind, drinking and laughing with her friends. She's the most beautiful girl here, and she doesn't even know it. She's completely clueless, as always. *That's just Winter being Winter.*

I've been talking with some guy from school for over an hour now, but I can't stop glancing in her direction. Not going to lie, I only came to this lame party because I hoped that she'd be here. She says she needs space. I can give her space.

I mean, I'm like five feet away from her.

That's enough space, right?

She's drinking a lot—like *a lot*—and I hate it, but I don't have a say in anything she does anymore. *Damn it, Haze. What's wrong with you? Why can't you just tell her? Why are you so messed up?*

I notice a guy from the varsity team walk by her and turn around to get a second look. He's staring at her ass. Anger tears through me. I know exactly what he's thinking. She's wearing a black dress that shows off all the right curves, and I don't know if it's the fact that I can't have her anymore, but I've never wanted to take her upstairs and make her scream my name more than in this very moment.

This is new for me. I've never missed someone's presence. Yes, I miss her body, but for the first time, I also miss… *everything.* I miss her sticking her freezing feet to my legs at night. I miss her smell. I even miss her trying to push me off the bed in her sleep.

I'm brought back to reality by my phone buzzing for the twentieth time tonight. The guy I was talking to says something about needing another drink, and when I don't reply, he walks off. I press ignore on Trevor's call and push my phone deep in my pocket. My guys have been harassing me all day. Word that I was back in town spread a lot quicker than I would've liked. They weren't supposed to find out this fast. I get it. I've been the worst leader possible, and I know me leaving out of nowhere and feeding them bullshit excuses is not going to go unpunished.

I did it because they wouldn't understand. Hell, *I* don't even understand. I've tried, but I can't possibly comprehend what this woman did to me. How she and only she can make me want to change. *To be better…*

"Hey, sexy." A high-pitched voice rings in my ear, and I curse under my breath.

Bianca.

I analyze her smudged makeup and her lipstick, that's so bright it could blind you, then focus on her outfit. She's definitely dressed to impress.

"Hey," I say, my eyes wandering back to Winter.

"Hey? Is that all you have to say? Hey? I've been texting you nonstop. Did you not get my messages? Where have you been?"

"Around." I shrug.

"How could you not tell me you were back in town?"

A guy the size of a giraffe steps in front of us, his frame blocking the view. And by view, I mean Winter.

"I was busy." I take two steps sideways to see around him.

Great. Guess I'll just add "turned me into a stalker" to the list of things Winter Kingston did to me.

"Well, now that you're back…" She bites down on her lip. "There are other things you could get back to."

"Thanks, but no, thanks."

Winter laughs at something that Ryder douche said, and I wince. *Come on, Winter, it's so fucking obvious that he wants you. Can't you see? I know because I used to look at you that way. I used to and I always will.*

Noticing that I'm somewhere else, Bianca follows my eyes.

"Don't tell me you're hung up on the new girl."

I take a sip of beer as a reply.

"I was right, wasn't I? You two were together this whole time."

Well, isn't she smart?

"What? Are you like dating or something?"

"We will be" is all I say.

I'll find a way to get her back. *I have to.*

"Come on, she's clearly flirting with that guy." She points to Ryder, who keeps devouring Winter with his eyes, and I clench my fists. "Don't you want to go upstai—"

"I said no thanks!" I interrupt her. How many times am I going to have to reject her for it to stick?

"What's wrong? You used to like it." She presses her breast to my arm, and her fingers trail down my chest. Her hand takes a very inappropriate direction, and I gasp. Is she insane? I'm about to push her off when she stops moving and whispers the worst four words I've heard today.

"*We have an audience.*"

That's all it takes.

My eyes jump to Winter.

In her gaze are anger, disappointment, pain. She looks down, shakes her head, and walks off.

Shit.

"There. Problem solved." Bianca grins victoriously.

I don't waste a second listening to her nonsense and walk around her to follow Winter—no, wait, I try, but Bianca stops me, sinking her five-foot-long fake nails into my arm.

"Where do you think you're going?"

"What don't you get? I don't want to fuck you," I snap. "I didn't even want to fuck you back then; you were just too easy.

Now get the fuck out of my face."

I squeeze my way through the crowd, the hateful words I spat leaving a bitter taste in my mouth. That was harsh. I know it was. After telling her a hundred times that we weren't happening, I lost my temper. I've tried to let her down easy, but nothing I do ever seems to work. I guess I thought maybe rejecting her the hard way would do the trick. I push all Bianca-related thoughts out of my mind and turn the corner, desperate to figure out where Winter went. I need to explain myself. She's got this all wrong. I walk into the living room and curse at the endless sea of heads surrounding me.

How am I ever going to find her now?

Winter

Sitting on a bench I found while wandering around in Rose's backyard, I swallow the sobs filling my throat and shiver in disgust at the scene playing on a loop in my head. We aren't dating. He's not my boyfriend anymore, but I still couldn't stand to see him with her. Bianca, out of all girls? That's low.

I hate him.

I really, really, really hate him.

Okay, fine. I *want* to hate him.

No matter what I do, I can't seem to convince my heart to mirror my brain. You'd think seeing Bianca try to grope him in public would pave the way for my hatred but *nope*, I'm still an idiot hung up on a guy I can't want. What's it going to take to get these feelings out of me? A freaking heart transplant?

"There you are," a familiar voice calls behind me.

Ryder.

Disappointment runs through me. Even after what happened, I hoped it would be Haze. I hoped he'd be the one following me.

"I'm fine. Go back inside. I just need a second." I turn my face to conceal my teary eyes.

"Don't do that. Don't push me away. I want to help."

"Ryder, I mean it, go back inside."

He doesn't listen, sitting down next to me.

"I'm not leaving. I saw what happened. He sucks. He doesn't deserve you."

I take in his concerned features. He's worried. That's nice of him, but I truly wish he'd leave me alone. What part of *"Go back inside"* doesn't he get?

"Winter…" He clears his throat. "I know we might've gotten off on the wrong foot, but me trying to kiss you at the pub, it wasn't…" He searches for words. "It wasn't a part of Kendrick's plan. It was real. I like you."

Awesome.

And the award for the world's worst timing goes to Ryder.

"I'm way too broken to like anyone like that again, I'm sorry." I try and reject him in the nicest way possible.

"It's okay. I can wait. I can fix you. I can fix what he broke."

When he tries to take my hand, my bullshit meter explodes.

I reach a limit I knew was coming for a while. I can't take any more. I've been through so much recently. I am *not* adding awkward unrequited love to the list.

"I can't do this right now. Listen, I'm flattered, I really am. But you and I… it's not happening," I say and get up.

Something snaps in his eyes.

Something I've never seen before.

I start to walk away, but he jolts up, wraps his hand around my wrist, and forces me back to him.

What the hell?

"What are you doing? Let go," I warn.

He doesn't budge.

"Every time. Every single fucking time." He raises his voice, obviously trapped in his own head. "It's always the same thing, isn't it? You're never going to change."

"What are you talking about?" I glance around the backyard in the desperate hope of capturing someone's attention. No one's looking our way. We're in an isolated spot, and the music's so loud they probably can't hear a thing.

"What's the thing with girls and assholes, huh? Please enlighten me. What's so attractive about heartless pieces of shit? It's like you enjoy being treated poorly. Why does the nice guy always finish last?"

Fear cripples me.

Ryder obviously has a lot more issues than he lets on. For a second there, I thought he was too squeaky clean and damage-free to be involved in street fighting. Now, I know. The guy's got problems. Like they all do.

I'm reminded of the words he said to me at the restaurant when a gorgeous girl showed interest in him and he said he had a very specific type. What is his type? The challenge? The broken girl? The one who already loves someone else? The one he can't have? *All of the above?* I try to get out of his grasp, but he tightens his hold around me. I wince in pain.

"Ryder, you're hurting me. Let go!" My shouting seems to pull him out of whatever anger trance he was stuck in. I see it in his eyes. The realization, the regrets. He's going to let me go. But he's too late.

"Get your fucking hands off her!"

Someone does it for him.

Haze.

Ryder's hand leaves my body and he crashes to the ground. Haze is on top of him, pummeling his face with hooks that are so strong it's a wonder that Ryder's still conscious. He can't fight back, all of his attempts unsuccessful.

"Haze, stop!" I scream, but he doesn't hear me, his sight and common sense destroyed by pure rage. It's like he becomes this entirely different person when he fights. He's on autopilot, empty, no feelings, no second thoughts, just *instincts.*

All I can do is hope that my despair will stop him from beating Kendrick's fighter to a pulp. Yes, Ryder has issues. Yes, what he did was wrong, but I don't think he's a bad guy. I think what just happened has nothing to do with me and everything to do with him. I think he's miserable. And you wouldn't believe the toll misery can take on someone's life…

I realize that the commotion has attracted the attention of the mass when I see a thick crowd of teenagers gathering around us.

"Fight, fight, fight!" a wasted jock from school shouts through the air, and the varsity team joins in his chanting. The same guy pulls his phone out of his pocket to record the scene.

This is why I hate social events.

No, this is why I hate people, *period.*

Students start to spill out of the house, curious to see what was important enough for the jocks to stop drinking. This is getting completely out of control. Ryder manages to get a few punches in, but his face still makes the saying "you should see the other guy" look like it was invented for him.

"Haze, stop, you're going to kill him!" My begging only increases the crowd's chanting.

It can't possibly get any worse than this.

Then, because the guy up there likes to prove me wrong, the definition of *worse* stumbles out of the house.

Kendrick, Will, and Alex.

I might not always listen to my cousin when he gives me lessons on the street fighting rules—or ever, really—but I remember this one: In the main fighters' close circle, one's problem is everyone's problem.

One's fight… is everyone's fight.

"Haze! Please. I'm begging you," I belt out, blinded by the tears.

That finally seems to be enough to grab his attention.

He hears me and looks up.

Our eyes lock.

Still on top of Ryder, he stops, his white-knuckled fist hanging in the air. The same way I did during the fight at the Downside, I recognize him… He sees the tears in my eyes, and his arm drops to his side. He's going to stop. He's going to let Ryder go.

But the guys intervene before he can do so.

Kendrick and Will both pounce on Haze while Alex helps Ryder off the ground. I know they technically don't have a choice. Haze attacked one of their own, but if they'd seen how Ryder acted, they'd be attacking him, too.

"Guys! Stop it," I cry again. Haze might be a solid fighter, but it's four against one. This is inhuman. The very unfair fight quickly turns around as Haze takes Ryder's place on the ground and the guys kick the hell out of him. It starts with a cut on his eyebrow. Then it's a cut on his lip. The wounds multiply along with my fears. Haze eventually stops fighting back, grunting in pain as he holds on to his stomach. He can't take them all.

God, I love that idiot.

I have to do something. Anything. It all happens too fast for the crowd to catch up. Will pulls Haze up by the grasp he has of his collar and aims for the final punch. Haze can barely stand. What I do next will probably not go down as one of my finest moments.

I step right into the chaos.

"Stop!" I've never screamed louder.

"Winter, get out of the way!" I hear Kendrick's voice.

I don't know how it happens. Who pushes me or how quickly my body hits the ground. All I know is the pain and the panic spreading in my chest when my head hits something.

"What the fuck did you do?" a familiar voice barks.

Then, my senses go numb…

And my eyes close.

TWENTY-THREE

Stolen Touch

White.

It's all I can see. At first, when I peel my eyes open, I think I'm in the hospital since the walls are bare and cold, but I quickly realize that I'm wrong. My sight clears up and I glance down at the queen bed under me. I'm in a bedroom. A very empty, untouched, and quiet bedroom.

"Thank God you're awake."

My eyes jump to the door that just burst open. Haze's standing in the doorway, his bruised face and cut lip twisting my heart in my rib cage. His bloodstained T-shirt's a bit ripped from the fight, and his perfectly messy hair only adds to his roughed-up look. Even like this, he manages to take my breath away.

"How are you feeling?"

"Where are we?" I feel my head with my hand. It hurts so bad.

"In my apartment." He sits on the edge of the bed.

Since when does Haze have an apartment? How much did I miss while I was locked away in Thomas's penthouse? I try to sit back up—to demand much-needed answers and clarifications—but fail, my body weighing a million pounds and practically embedding me into the mattress.

"Hey, easy. You hit your head. I'm not letting you move until a doctor looks at you." He gently pushes me back down. "I called somebody. They're on their way."

"What happened?" I ask.

"What happened is you're crazy, Kingston. What the hell were you thinking stepping into the fight like that? Don't ever do that again. Not for me." He flinches at the reminder and runs his fingers along my jaw. His guilty eyes fall to my mouth for a few seconds. I sigh in relief. He's okay. I did stop the fight, even if it took me almost getting into a freaking coma to do it.

Don't ever do that again. Not for me.

For who, then, Haze? If not for the goddamn idiot I love more than I thought possible, *for who?*

"Kendrick pushed you out of the way before Will punched you. You fell and hit your head on a stupid bench."

So, this is what I have to thank for the pounding in my skull. Hitting my head on a bench. *Yep, that'll do it.*

"I'm so sorry I brought you into this." He takes my fingers and brings them to his mouth. He kisses the back of my hand, and I want to melt at the sweet gesture. Then, because I have the worst timing on earth, a rather evil idea comes to me.

"I'm sorry… Who are you?"

His jaw hangs.

"What? What do you mean? I'm Haze. I'm your boyf—" He stops talking. "Was your boyfriend."

I appreciate that he's not lying about our relationship status. He could've tried to take advantage of my "amnesia" to get his way, but he didn't. I burst out laughing at the look on his face. His shoulders sink with relief as he lets out a disapproving sigh.

"So not funny."

"Oh come on, it's a little funny. Admit it." I grin, the smile on my face eventually rubbing off on his. I laugh quietly and try to sit back up again, only to fail… *again.* "Since when do you have an apartment?" I glance around the room. It's barely been lived in. The only pieces of furniture are a bed and a lamp.

"Since my psycho brother slash roommate kidnapped the girl I love and tried to have her killed. Not exactly an ideal living situation, you see?" he teases, barely holding my hand like he's afraid I'm going to break if he squeezes.

Hearing him refer to me as "*the girl he loves*" serves as a detonator to the truth I've been keeping locked away. It threatens to break through my barriers and the concrete walls I spent days building around my heart.

Why am I not dating him right now?

Why aren't we back together?

The thought of his incessant secrecy and the images of Bianca drooling all over him seem like distant problems now that he's looking at me with the world's worries in his eyes. It's crazy to me, that Haze Adams can say shocking, inappropriate, *scandalous* things one minute, then be so sweet and heart-melting the next. He can be this charming, flirtatious, and confident person one second, then completely fall apart if you pull the right strings. But no one gets to see that. No one ever gets close enough to see what's hiding behind his layers of cockiness.

Except for me.

I've seen the damage. I've seen the scattered pieces. I've seen the mess and I didn't even blink.

I'm so far gone. I'm *too* far gone.

"Where are the guys?" Realization finds me. Kendrick would've never left me alone with Haze in a situation like this. He begins to answer, but he's stopped by Will walking through the door with a bunch of bags in his hands.

"I got her something for everything. Stuffed nose, muscular pain, headache, dizziness," Will says, holding a bottle of pills up to his eyes. He notices me. "Oh, good, you're awake."

"It's just my head that hurts, Will."

"Well, then, you'll be prepared for next time." He shrugs.

"There won't be a next time. This is never going to happen again." Haze scowls at Will and stares back at me.

"Says the number one reason for Winter's life constantly being in danger," Will taunts under his breath, and Haze tries to shake off his remark, but I can tell it affects him. He already feels guilty. This isn't helping.

"Where are the guys?"

Discomfort shoots across Will's face.

"It's really not that big of a deal, okay?"

"Will, what is it?"

"Well, Kendrick kind of took off. Alex's out looking for him. Kendrick was super pissed when a witness told him why Haze attacked Ryder, by the way. I think he's going to kick him out."

"He took off?" I repeat like there's no possible way that I heard him correctly.

"Yeah, he freaked out when he saw you on the ground. He's the one who pushed you so that I wouldn't punch you. He said it was all his fault and that he had to fix it. Then he left."

That he had to fix it?

What does he mean by that?

"That's it? He just left me?"

"Yeah… but I'm here!" Will puts his hands up and smiles.

I offer him a sad smile in return, and he walks out of the room to take a call. I decide not to question Haze's miraculous access to a doctor at this hour. I know he'd tell me not to sweat it. I have no idea how I'll even pay for this. This isn't Canada. Here, health problems mean *No big deal. Just sell your house.*

"Why did you run?" Haze asks.

"What are you talking about?"

"Earlier, when you saw me with Bianca, you ran. Now, for someone who doesn't want to be with me, you sure seemed upset." I catch his smirk. He just wants to hear me say it. He wants me to admit that I was jealous.

"Why did you punch Ryder?" I give him a taste of his own medicine.

"Gee, I don't know. It's not like I care about him hurting you or anything."

"Oh, so you care about me? Tell that to Bianca."

"I did. Multiple times. Crazy pants just can't take a hint. If you'd stayed two more minutes, you would have seen me very loudly tell her to fuck off."

So he rejected her in front of everybody…

Now who's the idiot who made a scene for nothing?

"Oh." I stare at my fingers.

"What about you, Kingston? What's your excuse?" He scoots closer to me on the bed.

I find myself drained of any strength, emotional or physical, that might've resided in my body when our eyes connect. I don't want to fight it. Haze and I are wrong in too many ways to count. We're wrong, but we're real. Many walls still keep us apart, and I don't know about tomorrow but tonight… I want to kick them down. Tonight, I don't care.

"I love you, that's why."

His mouth drops open. He doesn't reply. Nor does he react. It takes a second for my words to sink in. Then, without a warning, he smiles and gets on top of me. I didn't expect any less, but I still struggle with something as basic as breathing when he lays a hand on my cheek and leans forward. He stops two inches away from the high only he can give me.

"Give me one good reason why I shouldn't kiss you right now."

I'm afraid if I give in to the temptation, it'll never let me go.

I know if I kiss him now, I'll never stop.

"The doctor will be here soon and… Will's in the next room and… you can't. I'm still mad at you," I stutter, my attempts at convincing him not even enough to convince *me.*

Dang it. Why is this so hard?

"Uh-huh." He nibbles on his lip and leans in some more.

"Haze, don't." I muster all the will I have left.

He stops and glances up, his eyes asking me the questions I'd never ask myself. He's saying, *"Do you really want me to stop?"*

The last of my self-control is blown to pieces.

I cup his face and give in to what I'm terrified to want. I kiss him with all I have. He pulls away at first, surprised that I made the first move, but quickly brings my face closer again. His lips meet mine, and my mouth responds in the only way it knows how: by kissing him back. I missed this. *I missed him.* I'm supposed to be mad. I'm supposed to be getting over him. This is everything but getting over him. What's wrong with me?

The guilt in my stomach dissolves when his tongue asks for access, and I grant it to him. His fingers tug at my dress, slowly sliding along my thighs…

"Sorry to interrupt," a deep voice says.

Haze jerks away from me, his face going from confused, to surprised, to *horrified.* In the doorway is a man that looks around forty-five. Next to him is Will. He's probably the one who let him in. He must be the doctor Haze called. He seems familiar. I think I've seen him before… but where?

"What are you doing here?" Haze asks, and I'm tempted to elbow him. He's the one who called this doctor guy here. Why is he being rude?

"Did you really think that I wouldn't be notified of you calling at one of my clinics? To ask for another doctor than me, to make it even worse. Of course I'd take the opportunity to see you." The man raises an eyebrow in my direction and stops speaking while he analyzes me thoroughly. He looks repulsed. "Still a ladies' man, I see."

Well, excuse me.

"No, I'm done with that, actually," Haze hisses, the coldness in his tone incomparable to all the times I thought he was being cold. He wasn't being cold. *This* is Haze being cold.

"Is that so?" The man looks at me like I'm garbage one more time. "Well, you see, I wouldn't know about that because you never call or answer the phone."

"What's going on here? Do you two know each other?" I ask, the word *confused* an understatement when it comes to how I'm feeling.

"Yes, I agree with your conquest of the week, Haze. Don't be rude. Introduce us," the man says. I don't let his offending words get to me.

"Richard, meet Winter," Haze says.

Uncomfortable, he rubs at the back of his neck and glares at the man in silence. Then, he brings his eyes back to me.

"Winter, meet my dad."

TWENTY-FOUR

The Chase

I observe the man standing in front of me, my gaze shifting from his cold blue eyes that show absolutely no sign of kindness whatsoever to his black and slightly gray hair. Now I know where Haze's eyes come from. I was certain I'd seen this man before, and I was right. He was in the family portrait back at the lake house.

His severe and tired features somehow make his purpose as clear as the sun in the sky. This man's goal in life is to make money, nothing else. From what he just said, he's a doctor who owns several medical clinics, which explains how he could afford to invest in Colton Gate and real estate in the first place. I know Maria's friend, Thomas, is rich with just one clinic. I can't even imagine having several.

"And by the way, I never answer your texts or calls because they're always about the same thing," Haze growls at his dad.

"And they'll always be about the same thing until you come to your senses and realize that we're right."

Haze sighs. "Can you just do your job and make sure that she's all right?"

His father's eyes stop on me, and once again, I get the feeling that he's judging me. Maybe he thinks I can't possibly be rich enough for his kid. Maybe he thinks I'm temporary. Whatever the reason is, he hates me.

"Under one condition." Richard crosses his arms. "You show up to the reception your mother is organizing for her new collection Tuesday after next week. It starts at seven. You should have plenty of time to explain to us why on earth you moved out of the house we bought for you and your brother," he says dryly.

God, if he only knew.

I assume he has no idea about the fights. I can't possibly imagine Tanner coming clean to his parents. *Mom, Dad, I kidnapped Haze and his girlfriend and tried to kill them. Might be why baby bro moved out and doesn't show up to family dinners anymore. But, hey, it's just a guess.*

My mind sticks to what Richard said about a new collection. I assume that means Haze's mother works in fashion.

"Will he be there?" Haze frowns

"Of course he will. He's part of the family and the only one who still visits us."

"Then I'm not coming."

"You will if you want me to examine your lady friend here." Richard raises his eyebrows, and I have to admit his arrogance is familiar. His son had to learn it somewhere. Haze clenches his jaw, irritation covering his face, and looks my way. I'm fine. I won't let him manipulate Haze for a checkup I probably don't even need.

"I feel fine, really." I force a smile.

"I don't care, Winter. You fainted," Haze says.

"I promise I'm okay."

Richard cackles. "Or so you think."

It's been two minutes and I already hate the man.

No wonder why Haze gets irritated at the mere mention of him.

"You're not seriously going to listen to her, are you? She hit her head so hard she fainted. She might have a concussion. Is a little evening with family so terrible that you won't even make sure your girlfriend is okay?"

I know we're not technically together, but I don't see the point in correcting his father. He's clearly an asshole, and if I tell him we're not dating, he'll find great pleasure in saying that Haze's an irresponsible player who can't commit to anything. Haze stares at me from the corner of his eye, like he's waiting for me to deny the title, but I never do. A small smile spreads across his face.

"Oh, and one more condition."

"What now?" Haze rolls his eyes.

"Your girlfriend will also be joining us."

Is he serious? Did he really just invite me to a party where I'll see the guy who got me kidnapped and locked in a basement? *Thank you, but I'll pass.*

"Not a chance," Haze says.

"Why's that? Isn't she your official girlfriend?"

Again, Haze looks at me and waits for me to deny the claims, but I refuse to give his father the satisfaction.

"Let's just say, Tanner and Winter don't get along. She's not coming, period."

"I'm assuming you're referring to the big fight you had with him about her. He told us about that. I believe he's ready to move past your issues, and he misses his brother more than he hates his enemies," he says with a straight face.

A fight? Is that what he called it?

He probably told his father that he hates my cousin and disapproves of me and Haze all the while being very careful not to mention the illegal slash psycho aspect of it.

I wish I knew how the two incredibly wealthy Adams boys ended up street fighting. You'd think kids from families like this couldn't be further away from the wrong side of the track. So many untied knots, so many stories that don't add up, so many mysteries in need of unraveling.

Haze grows irritated. "Why do you care if she comes or not?"

"I mean, if you really are serious about her and she's here to stay, we might as well get to know her. Plus, your brother's ready to make amends if you just let him. He's been working on himself. He's even bringing a new girl home this year."

Simply hearing him talk about Tanner like he's somewhat of a good person sends chills down my body. I almost died because of him. Blake almost shot me in the head under his order.

"I'll come, but leave her out of it."

"Very well. Then I guess I'll be on my way." He turns away and walks to the door. Haze curses under his breath, and the sorry look in his eyes tells me everything I need to know. He's going to break. He's going to give in.

"Fine."

His father stops dead in his tracks, then turns around. "So… do we have a deal?"

Haze stares at me for a few seconds, and I can tell his conscience is responsible for this. It's playing tricks on him. His father made him feel stuck. I know he couldn't live with himself if he didn't get me checked up and something happened to me.

"Yes."

I glare at Haze. He did *not* just force me into having dinner with my kidnapper.

"But the second she's uncomfortable, we're leaving," he adds, trying to make me feel better and failing miserably.

"Fantastic, I'll let your mother know," Richard says and lays his medical tools on the bed.

He had no right to say yes on my behalf. I know I said yes for him when Vic asked us to go to his party in Colton Gate, but this is different. Vic didn't kidnap and lock Haze in a cave. I guess his father will be very disappointed because there's no way I'm going to their party from hell.

Richard walks me through the usual checkup he promised, and Haze doesn't look at me once. He knows I'll be giving him a piece of my mind as soon as his father leaves. I can't help but want to know more about his family. Seeing Tanner and Richard makes me wonder how Haze managed not to go crazy.

"So?" he says the very second his father finishes.

"I believe she's okay, but further tests in an actual clinic are required if you want to be sure. I can get you an appointment tomorrow."

"You would do that for her?" Haze frowns in suspicion.

Richard looks at me from head to toe in disgust. *What's new?*

"Not for her. For you. You truly seem to care for that girl," Richard states, still acting like I don't have a name.

Haze's blue eyes travel to me.

"I do. Very much."

My heart lurches against my rib cage.

"I figured. Why else would you bring her to the lake house?"

We both stop breathing.

He knows.

"Don't give me that look. You must've known deep down that we'd find out. We have eyes everywhere, son. Especially in Colton Gate."

We can't bring ourselves to speak.

"Did you really think we wouldn't try and figure out where you ran off to when you're so close to graduating? This earned us a very big and annoying..." He pauses like he's searching for the right term to use. "...*conversation* with your school, by the way."

Conversation's obviously code for something else.

"So what? A 'conversation's' nothing you can't afford." Haze does the air quotes with his fingers.

That's how I know that I was right.

His parents are basically buying Haze's way out of everything. Is it for the reputation of their brand? Or out of love for their son? Whatever it is, one thing's for sure, money really does speak. *And it speaks louder than anyone will ever know…*

"Let me make a quick call for her appointment." Richard walks out onto the balcony linked to the bedroom and closes the door.

"Not exactly a ray of sunshine, your father." Will's voice reminds us of his presence. He's been so quiet I almost forgot he was here this whole time.

"Tell me about it," Haze says.

"Will, could you give us a second, please?"

"Oh, I see. You need a second to fight."

I almost laugh at his blunt remark. He's absolutely right. Haze needs to know that I don't care what he says. I'm not going to the stupid reception even if he pays me.

"I'll be in the living room. Then, I'm taking you home. Kendrick may have freaked out earlier, but he'll lose his shit if he doesn't know where you are."

"Okay. I won't be long. Promise."

He shuts the door, and I turn to Haze.

World War Three is beginning.

"I know what you're going to say, but please just hear me ou—"

"No, you hear me out." I raise my finger at him, ready to drop my guilt speech on him, but when I get back on my feet, the dizziness takes a hold of me and my knees give out.

"Easy." Haze instantly wraps his strong arm around me to keep me from falling.

"Let go." I brush off the humiliation clinging to me, avoiding his blue eyes. I can't be having a brain-dead moment. Not right now.

"I'll let go of you when I'm sure you can actually stand, Kingston," he says, mockery lacing his voice.

"I told you, I'm fine." I ignore the close proximity that would usually temper with my ability to speak. I'm too mad to let his charms push my *dumb Winter* switch on.

"No, you're not. Which is why I'm taking you to the clinic tomorrow." He pulls me back to the bed. I sit down.

I'm still upset with him for saying yes.

"What else was I supposed to do, Winter? I got stuck in his games. I'm sure he won't even remember it in two weeks."

"You can't honestly believe that," I say, and he sighs. I'm right, whether he likes it or not. His father's not going to let us out of the deal.

"I'm sorry," he breathes.

My anger was obviously never mine to begin with because it vacates my body as soon as he apologizes. I can't be mad at him.

He was trying to look out for me. In his own messed-up, clumsy, and *Haze* way.

I nod. "It's fine."

He sits down next to me, apparently relieved that I'm not angry, and reaches for my hand. I'm reminded that we were making out—*hard*—before his nightmare of a father walked in.

"Haze, I don't… I don't want you getting the wrong idea." I move my hand away. "I know you want us to get back together, and I do, too, but… I told you, I need time and most importantly, answers."

"I know that. And I can give you time. But…"

"Let me guess, you can't give me answers."

He clenches his jaw and fidgets with his bloodstained shirt.

"I get it, Haze. You have a dysfunctional family. So what? Do you really think that would've been enough to scare me away? I fell for you even through the horrible things people told me about you. At this point, it's pretty clear that I'm stuck on stupid for you."

"You say that now, but you don't know what you're talking about." He looks away. There he goes again, slamming the door in my face right when I think I finally have one foot inside.

"Okay. That's it. Look at me." I grab his face. "You're going to listen to me very carefully because I'm not going to say it again. There is nothing, *nothing* that you could ever tell me that would make me love you less. Do you understand me?"

In that moment, when I look into his eyes, I swear I can see one of the walls he put up around his heart come down. I can see his shield partially disintegrating and hitting the ground.

"Nothing, huh?" He looks at me like he's thinking, *"Oh, Winter, you have* no idea *what you're getting yourself into."*

He looks at me like he was meant to ruin my life.

"Nothing." I intertwine our fingers. "So please… please just come clean so we can put this nonsense behind us."

He knows what I truly mean is *so we can get back together*. He's about to say something when Richard walks back into the bedroom, creating a wonderful tension that reeks of unfinished business.

"Be at this clinic at four." He hands Haze what appears to be a business card. "You'll need to be with her as proof that you're my son. We're booked months in advance. She's lucky we're accepting her."

"Got it," Haze says coldly.

This is his way of letting his father know that they're not anywhere near okay or on good terms.

"Oh, and please don't fool yourself into thinking you can bail on the reception once you go to the appointment. We can easily have another and very different conversation with your school, son. Remember that," he says before he walks away and leaves the apartment.

Great, now he's blackmailing Haze, too. Threatening your own kid to keep him from graduating just so you can get what you want? That sounds like a well-adjusted human being.

Will comes to tell me that he's heading home shortly after Richard walks out.

"I guess I'll see you at school, then," I say awkwardly while Will helps me up.

"Yeah, see you." Haze sways from one foot to the other, hiding his hands in his pockets.

I know we're both fighting the need to kiss goodbye, or to at least hug, like we used to. Not touching him feels so strange. Will and I walk out of the large building, heading for his car parked in the visitor spot.

"You know… for what it's worth, I think you're being hard on him," Will says when we pull up into Maria's driveway thirty minutes later. He kills the engine and turns to me.

"You're defending him now?"

"I know, I know. I'm as shocked as you are, believe me. The guy was never anything more than an asshole to me, but I guess… when I started seeing him all the freaking time because *someone* had to fall for the enemy, I realized he's not so bad." He hits my shoulder playfully. "I had my doubts at first, but I think he really does love you."

"Who are you, and what did you do to Will?" I laugh.

"Go ahead, mock me. But seeing him so openly say what he wants, it's just made me think."

"And what are you thinking, may I ask?"

"That maybe I want that, too."

He doesn't know that I'm aware of his story with Kass. I

don't think I should tell him that I witnessed them this morning. Kass made me promise not to tell anyone about this. Not even him.

"What? A complicated bad boy with a secret past?" I tease.

"No, a girl that I'd chase forever if I had to. A girl I'd chase like he's chasing you."

I almost tell him that I know he's already found that girl. It's none of my business, but I hope these two figure things out. They've both changed each other for the better. What he said resonates with me, although I can hardly believe that Will said something wise. Haze is far from perfect, but he tries… and maybe, in the end, it's all that matters. We sneak back into the house that's dark and completely silent. It's past midnight. I find myself in bed, tossing and turning, while my brain comes up with a hundred scenarios that will most likely never happen.

I wonder what Haze was going to say before his dad walked in earlier. I wish he'd have had the chance to finish speaking. I really thought, for a second there, that I got through to him. I hook my phone to the charging cable next to my bed. It's been dead since I left Haze's. My heart jumps when the screen lights up and I see the one message I've been dying to read.

> I'm taking you out to dinner after your appointment tomorrow. I'll be waiting out front after school. You want to know everything? Fine. Be ready.

I throw myself back onto my bed, the giddying speed of my pulse making me feel like a kid on Christmas morning. I bring a pillow to my chest and take a deep breath, thinking that maybe, *just maybe…*

We still stand a chance.

"GOOD MORNING, SLEEPING UGLY," WILL SAYS, ripping me away from a dream I wish had never ended. I yawn, pull the cover over my head, and groan. When he sees that I'm awake, he walks out of my room and makes sure to slam the door.

Since Will's been staying with us, he's taken it upon himself to wake Kendrick, Kass, and me for school in the morning. Needless to say, his waking techniques aren't the most delicate, and he annoys the heck out of everyone, but he doesn't care.

He wouldn't be Will if he did.

I spent the entire night dreaming of my date with Haze. Will interrupted the best dream yet. The date ended up in the bedroom. *Need I say more?*

He's going to come clean, for good this time. The possibilities are endless and, quite frankly, terrifying to think about. I push the warm blanket off my skin and run a hand through my knotted and messy morning hair. I glance outside my window. The sun's shining, birds are singing. What could possibly go wrong?

Oh, right. I'm going back to school today.

That's what could go wrong.

Twenty minutes later, I'm walking into the kitchen and ignoring Will's yapping about how excited I should be to go back to school. He knows how nervous it makes me, and so he just has to annoy me.

"Where's Kendrick?" I change the topic as I head for the fridge.

"Don't know. He left early this morning. I'm giving you a ride." He takes a mouthful of cereal.

"What about Kass? Does she ride?"

He chokes on his food.

"W-what?" he says after he finally manages to stop coughing.

It physically hurts not to laugh. His face is priceless.

"Does she ride with us to school?" I arch an eyebrow.

"Oh, hm… yes, she will," he stutters.

I promised Kass I wouldn't tell him that I know about them; I'll just have to let him figure it out on his own. Until then, I'll keep dropping hints that will make him beyond uncomfortable and completely paranoid. *Payback's a bitch, Willi.*

"Kendrick does know that never facing me again doesn't erase what happened yesterday, right?" I attempt to ease the stinging sensation in my chest. I still can't believe he left.

"You know he only pushed you so that you wouldn't get punched. He never meant for you to hit your head."

I nod faintly. What Will said about Kendrick wanting to "fix it" has been bugging me ever since last night. I'm worried he did something stupid. This is *so* Kendrick. He doesn't think before he acts. Especially in a moment of panic.

I slide two slices of bread into the toaster and sit around the kitchen table. I know Maria's already at work from the empty spot in the driveway. She left us some money for food on the counter, per usual. When I get up to fetch my toast, my phone buzzes. I have a message from Kendrick.

> I'm so so so sorry.
> Sorry. Sorry. Sorry. Did
> I say I was sorry?

I can't smother a smile.

> I think you might've
> mentioned it.

> I'm a dumbass for leaving. I
> never meant for you to pass
> out. I'm sorry about Ryder, too.
> I took care of it. He won't
> bother you again. Let's make it
> fair, next time you see me,
> punch me in the face.

> Kendrick, I may be mad,
> but I'm not that mad.

No, I insist. Please, punch me in the face real hard.

Okay:)

Huh? I was kidding

I wasn't.

"So, you ready for your first day back?" Will asks.

"Nope," I say and rest my phone on the table.

"Don't worry, I'm sure Haze will be there to protect you if anything goes wrong." He wiggles his eyebrows. "Not that anyone will try to come at you after what happened last night."

"What do you mean?"

"Oh, come on, he got into a fight for you. He beat up a guy, Winter. Word travels fast. Everybody knows you as Haze's girl now—no getting out of it. Sorry."

"Great. That's just great," I mutter.

As if I already don't have enough people hating me at school. I'm not sure Bianca and her minions were happy to hear about Haze getting into a fight for me.

Only then do I realize that Haze hasn't texted me yet today. I don't know why I somehow expected a message from him. A good-morning maybe?

I'm so pathetic. Maybe I should text him first.

Winter, you told him you needed space just yesterday.

What if I don't want space?

What if I want his gorgeous body on mine and his lips to kiss every inch of my skin?

Make up your damn mind, woman.

I decide to step on my pride and text him first. I wait and I wait, but he never replies. I try not to think too much into it.

Kass rushes into the room, panic flowing out of her. "I'm so late." Her hair and makeup aren't done, and anyone who knows Kass knows that she's not one to take off-days. These don't exist in her life. She takes very good care of herself and always has.

"Good morning, control freak." Will smirks, and I'm tempted to let out a very loud "*Aw*" at the fact that they have nicknames for each other—as weird as they may be—but I decide that probably wouldn't be appropriate since I'm not supposed to know about their relationship.

Kass flushes, locks herself into the first-floor bathroom, and all Will and I can do is hope that we'll make it to school on time.

"HEY, WINTER, WHO ARE YOU TEXTING?" Kass asks when I check my phone for the fifth time since we left the house. I glance out the window at the passing palm trees and curse under my breath.

"Who is she *not* texting, you mean." Will glances at me in the mirror.

I throw my head back. "How did you know?"

"Please, you're not fooling anyone with your sad puppy eyes," Will says.

I know Haze isn't one to always have his phone in his hands, so worrying is probably pointless, but I have this gut feeling that something is wrong. I can't quite put my finger on it.

"I'm sure he's just busy," Kass tries to reassure me.

"Yeah, or he's dead. We all know that's the only way Haze would ever leave Winter alone."

I force a laugh, bothered that I'm not the only one who thinks this is weird behavior for Haze.

"We're here."

The two dreadful words hit me a lot harder than I expected. The stress is real. I search for air as I get out of Will's car with a heavy bag of books on my shoulders. I caught up with school as much as I could but still feel like I missed a lifetime of classes. So many questions eat at me. I have no friends in this school whatsoever. Not to mention that the prom is coming up. Am I supposed to go? The answer reveals itself to me as quickly as the question did. I just can't see myself going. There's no point in trying to live the Cinderella dream. There are only two weeks left before the school year comes to an end and my old life comes calling my name.

Two weeks.

Fourteen days.

Then, I'll be on a plane back to Canada.

NOTHING. NOT EVEN A QUICK TEXT. I haven't heard a peep from Haze once today, and I'm beginning to think something is seriously wrong. He wasn't at school. This used to be typical behavior for him, but that was before… *everything.* I'm sure he knows better than to do that anymore.

Will was right. To everyone, I'm Haze's girlfriend. People stare. Girls hate me from afar. It's nothing I didn't see coming, but it still makes me uncomfortable. I just have to be thankful that I haven't run into Bianca and her evil Barbies yet.

On the bright side, I talked to the majority of my teachers and was relieved to hear them say that they were willing to figure something out with me for extra credits. I also met up with the principal, who said I'll be able to take part in the finals like everyone else.

I shut my locker and squeeze my way through the crowd of eager-to-go-home teenagers. At least Will suggested to drive me home if Haze doesn't show for my appointment. I step outside and the way people look at me tells me that he's here. I don't even need to see his face. I simply follow their very obvious stare… to him.

He's just standing there, casually leaning back against his parked car with his hands in his pockets. His face lights up when he sees me, but mine only darkens.

He's bruised. And the wounds look fresh. They're not from his fight with Ryder. He must've gotten them today. I stamp down to him.

"Hey, you." He grins.

"What happened?" I immediately ask.

He sighs. Did he really think I wouldn't acknowledge his bleeding eyebrow?

"Get in." He opens the door for me and I climb inside the car. Shortly after, we drive off. I watch as the creepers outside the school become blurry shapes.

"So?" I insist. "Mind telling me what happened to your face?"

"I'm the West side's leader, Winter. I got back into town after a while. What did you expect?"

Great. He's in a mood.

"Gee, I don't know. Not that my boyfriend would show up with blood dripping off his face, maybe."

I only realize what I've done once it's too late.

I called him my boyfriend, didn't I?

He smiles, his bad mood instantly slipping away.

"What did you just call me?" He raises an eyebrow.

"Nothing, I… That's not the point." I blush. "Don't change the subject. What happened?"

He can't stop smiling. "No, really, what did you say? Because it sounded like you called me your boyfriend."

I choose not to entertain his ego and cross my arms over my chest. My cheeks are burning up. *Stupid brain!*

"Fine." He grins. "My guys made me pick things up where we left off. They always do when I leave for a while. Call it an insurance policy. They need to be reassured that I'm still with them."

He wiggles in his seat. Something's bothering him.

"What is it?"

"It's probably nothing."

"Haze…"

"It's just… They usually give me the benefit of the doubt, but this time, it's like they don't believe a single word I'm saying. They're real fucking obsessive. They don't trust me anymore. I have to prove myself to them. I mean, goddamn, they wouldn't even let me use my phone when I was there."

That explains it.

"Do you think a guy in the East side could've told them something about us? Like confirm it to them?" he asks.

"What? No, they wouldn't do that."

Haze nods halfheartedly. He's not convinced.

"You have no idea the bullshit I had to come up with just to be here right now. I thought they'd never let me get away."

"But I mean, can you blame them? They're right, aren't they? You *are* in bed with the enemy."

He places his hand on my thigh and I shiver at his touch, but for the first time in a while, I embrace it. We both know I never came close to *un*loving him. Now that he's ready to tell me everything, nothing's holding us back.

"I'm not in bed with the enemy, Kingston." He squeezes my leg, his hand traveling upward slightly. I hold my breath, my heart hammering in my rib cage. Then, at a red light, he turns to look at me and smirks. "Not yet."

I CAN'T AVOID THE WAVE OF nostalgia pouring over me when Haze and I walk into the familiar fifties diner where we had our first date—if you can even call it that. The memories are still vivid in my mind. This was shortly after Tanner went crazy on me and Kendrick went to beat him up, only to get beat up himself. The guys had set up a date with Haze through my phone so that I could convince him not to tell the whole world about Kendrick's state. This is where I told Natasha, who was flirting with Haze, that he had STDs.

Ah, *good times.*

"You remembered?" I smile.

"What do you mean? We've been here before?" He frowns.

"Yeah, on our first date that wasn't a date," I say, feeling a bit hurt that he forgot.

"Oh, that was you? I thought it was Bianca," he jokes, and I roll my eyes. He pulls me to him and kisses my cheek, his warm laughter wrapping me up. "Of course I remembered."

The lady whose uniform makes her look like she came right out of *Grease* shows us the way to our table. The doctor's appointment turned out to be waste of time. I'm completely fine and there is nothing wrong with me apart from a sore bump on my head. Which means we made a deal with the devil for nothing.

"So this is where you tell me everything? A bit crowded in here, don't you think?" I glance around the room.

"I'll tell you at my place. I thought we'd enjoy one last meal before I reveal all of my darkest, deepest secrets and send you running for the hills." He smiles, but I know, deep down, he means it. He fears my reaction.

It can't possibly be that bad, can it?

"Fine, one meal. But then you tell me everything."

He hesitates for a second before finally giving in.

"Yes. Everything."

"STOP!" I LAUGH AS HAZE THROWS yet another overcooked fry at me. We've been cracking jokes for a good twenty minutes. The food wasn't the best I've ever had, to say the least, but Haze made it better. It's taking him a ridiculously long time to finish his nonappealing plate, and I'm this close to losing my mind.

"I swear, you've been eating that same fry for ten minutes."

"I haven't."

"Please, you'rc totally stalling."

"I'm not stalling. Oh, look, a puppy!" He stares out the window, and I have to force myself not to do the same. He's changing the topic again. He knows exactly what stupid thing to come up with to distract me. My brain immediately went on *"Did someone say puppy?"* mode.

"Haze, please, can we leave now?" I huff.

"There's this really nice place I'd like to show you."

"No, you said we'd eat, then go home so you can tell me everything. We ate, now let's go. And once we get there, no more stalling. You sit down and tell me the truth."

He pouts. "Damn, really? I thought we could Netflix and chill."

"More like Netflix and don't touch me."

"Ouch." He grins and brings his hand to his heart like I just shot an arrow right through it. The waitress places the bill on the table, and I try to reach for it, but per usual, Haze is too fast.

I stare at him with disapproval all over my face. One day I'll get him. I'll never stop trying.

"Too slow, Kingston. Better luck next time."

HAZE UNLOCKS THE DOOR TO HIS rich-kid apartment and throws his keys onto the counter. My poor ass, who still can't believe how huge his place is, trails behind him. Haze kicks his shoes off, sending them flying across the hall, and crashes onto his leather couch. I take off my shoes, as well, and follow him. I can literally feel the burdening weight of silence on my shoulders, the haunting anticipation in every sharp breath, the fear in his stance. We know this is now or never.

"What did your fighters make you do?" My fingers hover over his marked cheek and recent bruises. I don't dare touch him.

"We picked a fight with Ian's guys."

I remember Ian, the leader of the North side—the street fighters that go by *the Scars.*

"We've been enemies since the East side and I attacked them to find you. We thought they were responsible because Tanner sent us down the wrong path. Our alliance went to shit, and the entire time I was gone, they pulled random attacks on us. I should've been there for my guys. I've been a terrible leader."

"What do you mean you picked a fight with them?"

He sighs. "I can't tell you any more than this, baby. We have a code."

He says that like he's not breaking his "code" by being here with me right now.

"Fine, then tell me this. What's the deal with your family? What's with the kid's room in your house?"

His face changes. He probably prayed that I wouldn't ask about that, but I owed it to myself. I can't go on without knowing what made Haze so miserable. I need to figure out what made Haze… *Haze.*

He takes a deep breath. "I was fourteen when it happened."

Why does this sound like the beginning of my heart breaking?

"My parents never talked about it. They were so focused on keeping up appearances and looking like the perfect little family that they went on with their lives and never mentioned it again. 'We've got to maintain our image, Haze. We've got to do it for the business, Haze.' They moved, tore the house down, got rid of the pictures like it was that easy. They just… erased her."

Her. It was a girl.

"God, Winter, I just… I hate them so much." He clenches his fists, talking about it clearly stirring old, buried, and undealt with feelings. He looks like he could cry tears of rage.

I trap his hand into mine and squeeze. I want him to know that I'm here. I'm here for whatever he's about to say to me, for the lows and the highs, for the good and the bad. I'm here for whatever comes next. And I'll still be here after he says it.

"I'm sorry. I know this doesn't mean anything to you." He runs a trembling hand through his hair and sucks in a breath. "I… I had a sister."

He has such a hard time pronouncing these three words that I almost tell him to stop right there. I hate seeing him like this, but part of me feels like this might actually be good for him. He could use talking about it. He hasn't in years.

"Desiree. That was her name. Des for short."

I don't speak, the hundred shattered pieces in my mind falling back together. She's the one whose picture they removed from the frame. She's the one who was cut out of the family photo. *They cut her out.* Their own kid. What kind of monsters are they?

"She was five."

I catch myself holding my breath when his blue eyes singe mine. I'm impatient, yet reluctant, to learn why he said "*had*."

"Tanner got involved in the street fighting mess long before

I did. Our parents were never around. I mean, they were but… not for the stuff that mattered. Tanner started acting out, and he was the first of both of us to try and break free of the cage they put us in. We had to be perfect boys who would eventually take over Daddy's business and make some more money when the time came, but we didn't care. Tanner more than me."

The bomb's about to drop. I'm about to discover what turned Haze Adams's heart into a block of ice. What stole his smile away between the picture of him at twelve and the one at fifteen.

"I was babysitting her. Tanner was out selling God knows what drug to some sicko, and my parents were at a fancy-people cocktail party for the night."

He stops and looks at me. Like he's afraid that I can't handle what's coming. Like he wouldn't blame me if I walked out the door right now and never returned. So, before the walls come down and the mask comes off, I hold on to him. I intertwine our fingers and hope to bring him the comfort he needs. He smiles through the resentment…

And tells me the story I will never forget.

TWENTY-FIVE

Revelation

FLASHBACK

Haze Adams woke up with a start, unusual noises he couldn't identify pulling him out of brief but much-needed slumber. The clock on the wall read 2:00 a.m. The young boy frowned as he eyed the flat-screen TV in front of him. It was nowhere near loud enough to bother him, let alone wake him when he was this exhausted. His mind wandered to his sister sleeping upstairs.

He'd been watching her almost every single night that week. His parents loved to confuse their youngest son for a babysitter whenever it was convenient for them, but, as opposed to the majority of fourteen-year-old boys, Haze didn't mind. Desiree was easy to babysit. She always had been. All she wanted was for her brother to read stories with happy endings to her. Haze didn't have the heart to tell her that she wasn't born into the right family to get one.

Since Desiree had officially entered her "monsters under my bed" phase, Haze had learned to sleep with one eye open to be ready whenever she called. Heaven knew he was the only one who'd come running if she did. Indeed, Haze had been like a parent to his sister for as long as he could remember. He couldn't possibly count the amount of times she'd accidentally called him "Dad" or snuck into his room after she'd had nightmares. It was nothing new. It was an everyday thing at this point. Desiree's father constantly promised his daughter that he'd play with her, only to back out and leave her big brother to comfort her. She pretended that she didn't mind, but she held back tears every time her dad closed his office door in her face with the promise to play tomorrow.

The noises hit again, interrupting Haze's foggy thoughts.

He cursed. This had to be Tanner trying to get in through a window again. This was the fourth time this week. It sometimes seemed like Haze's older brother's mission in life was to forget his keys. Like it was on his everyday to-do list. Or maybe his parents had changed their minds and decided to come home from their snobby friend's reception instead of spending the night at the hotel.

When the noises sounded once more, this time louder, Haze got up. Something was wrong. He knew it, but he still tried to keep the whirlwind that was his mind from jumping to conclusions. Surely, if someone was breaking in, the high-tech and expensive security system his parents had installed on the house would've gone off. They'd paid a fortune for it. If something was going on, he would've known, right?

His heart jolted in his rib cage when the power went out, soaking the teenage boy and the Adams mansion in complete darkness. *No power equals no high-tech security system*, a voice in the back of his head reminded him.

Something was definitely *wrong.*

His pulse quickening, the boy grabbed the first thing he could find that somehow resembled a weapon—which, in this case, turned out to be a large marble vase his mother kept in the living room—and started walking to the kitchen where he hoped to find a knife. With trembling hands, he got his phone out of his pocket with the intention to dial 911.

Little did he know he'd never get a chance to press Call.

Someone launched at him from behind, spinning him around and punching him in the face with a strength Haze couldn't match. His mother's vase shattered into a million pieces as his cell phone fell a few feet away from him. The pain was nothing compared to the fear he felt when he looked up.

There they were.

Standing in his kitchen.

The silhouettes.

They were masked, dressed in black, tall, broad-shouldered, and very probably armed.

"What the fuck? You said no one was home," one of the men shouted as he analyzed the terrified teenager on the ground.

"They were supposed to be out tonight, I swear," his partner replied in anger. They had somehow forgotten that the Adamses had kids. "We can't have him in our way. Tie him up."

Haze put up the fight of his life, his every attempt at hurting the intruders useless and unsuccessful. They were too strong. He was fourteen. They had years on him, and every punch he threw resulted in him getting kicked down, beaten up, and thrown to the ground.

His body surrendered when a very sharp and heavy object hit the back of his head, and he collapsed onto the cold ceramic floor.

"Fucking stupid kid," one of them spit.

Barely conscious, he could feel the blood dripping down his forehead as his senses escaped him. The masked man who'd knocked him out held a gun to his temple. Haze didn't doubt for one second that they'd have what it took to shoot.

"Listen, boy, we don't want to kill you, but keep this up and we will."

Realizing that he'd come at them again if they gave him the chance to recover, the masked monsters took Haze's choice away by tying him to a kitchen chair and circling his hands with tight ropes. Then it was the tape on his mouth. They'd thought of everything.

One of the thieves started filling large black bags with random items lying around the house. His father's autographed baseball, his mother's expensive necklace. Everything they could get their hands on seemed to be a good match. Meanwhile, the other monster kept the teenage boy at gunpoint.

"I've got upstairs," the masked man who had tied him up said and climbed up the stairs.

Haze screamed as loud as he could, trying to warn Desiree, who was fast asleep in her bedroom. The duct tape blocking his mouth made it impossible. He was praying that she had heard the commotion downstairs and hidden. Her bedroom was on the opposite end of the house, and it was so big he wouldn't have been surprised if she hadn't. *Why was the damn house so big? Why did his parents need eleven bathrooms?*

Somehow, this statement alone made this attack easy to believe for Haze. The Adamses were beyond wealthy and shamelessly flaunted their money to anyone who had eyes. This robbery had probably been planned for a while.

"Man, you have to see this," the thief called from the second floor.

"If you try to escape, we'll come back and kill your entire family. Do you understand me?" the man holding the gun warned through gritted teeth before joining his partner.

A lot of noises. Their footsteps running up and down the halls. This was all Haze could hear as he fought to free his wrists to the point of bleeding. He didn't care about his life. He didn't care about the pain.

He only cared about her.

Then, he heard the worst sound he could've ever imagined. It was barely audible. It was a creak. A door opened. He would've never heard it if it wasn't for the complete absence of sound due to the power loss.

"Haze?"

Desiree.

That's when he heard the gunshot.

"What the fuck did you do?" one of the masked men belted.

"I-I don't know. I panicked. It came out of nowhere."

Hesitant footsteps followed.

"What the fuck, Marc? You said we wouldn't hurt anyone. You said… I didn't sign up for this." Panic could be heard in the man's tone.

Haze held on to every word, praying, hoping, *dying* to hear them say that they missed. He just needed something. Anything.

He kept on trying to free himself from the chair he now called his prison and eventually ended up knocking it over. Still tied to the chair, he landed on his side and groaned in pain as the pieces of marble from the shattered vase on the floor cut his skin.

"We have to go to the police," the man barked.

No. No. This can't be happening.

This isn't real.

This can't *be real*, Haze thought.

"Are you insane? What do you think they're going to say, huh? What's going to happen? Thanks for your honesty, you're free to go? No, fuck no. I'm not dying in prison."

"Damn it, Marcus, you just killed a kid."

And just like that…

Haze's world stopped turning.

Distant sirens roared outside. Colton Gate was a small town.

A gunshot at 2:00 a.m. wasn't an everyday thing. The neighbors had probably called the police the second it had happened.

"We need to get out of here."

"Are you insane? We can't just leave her like this."

"Listen to me. Listen… Do you want to be locked up for the rest of your life? Is that what you want? Because that's what's going to happen if we let them find us here."

Silence.

"That's what I thought. Come on, we have to leave. Now!"

And so they did…

They left, running back down the stairs and exiting through the exact same window Tanner always used to sneak in. This was probably how they'd found out about it in the first place. Burning tears filled up the teenage boy's eyes as he started to hyperventilate, his throat tightening with every forced and agonizing breath. This wasn't real. This couldn't be real.

From there, he acted on instinct, using the pieces of marble on the ground to cut the ropes holding him prisoner. The blaring police sirens were getting closer. He ran upstairs, ignoring his blood dripping on the squeaky steps. When he reached the second floor, the boy screamed… the loudest, longest, and most heartbreaking scream of his life.

There she was.

On the ground.

Haze had never considered himself to be squeamish when it came to blood. But this was a whole other story. He'd never seen so much.

"Des!" he choked out. "No!"

He ran to the child, picking up the pale, blood-covered five-year-old into his arms and swaying her in a miserable attempt to comfort her, the way he always did when she had nightmares. Except that now her skin was freezing, and the nightmare was real. She was still conscious, crying and shaking as she fought for each gasp of air.

"No, no, no, stay with me. Des, don't close your eyes. Des, don't leave me, *please!*" he begged, shaking her as though he hoped it would change anything, patch up her wounds, and give her back her life. The life they'd stolen from her.

The blue-eyed little girl didn't speak. She couldn't.

"I'll make them pay for this, I promise." He sobbed harder. "I'll make them pay."

She squeezed her big brother's sleeve as a reply, her delicate fingers holding him for the last time.

Then she stopped.

The shakes left her, the tears ceased, and the life spilled out of her eyes.

And, in that moment…

He knew.

She was dead.

His baby sister was dead.

Because he wasn't strong enough. Because he couldn't stand up to the intruders. The teenager cried, all the water his body contained. He cried enough tears to match the blood on the floor, and he held her, until the police forcefully removed him from the scene. Even then, he fought with all he had. As they took him away for questioning, he recalled the words the thief had said to him.

If you try to escape, we'll come back and kill your entire family.

But there was no point…

His family was already dead.

TWENTY-SIX

Together Again

Winter

Haze slouches against the couch and conceals his face with his right hand, as though he's hoping it'll make him any less vulnerable, any less *broken.* I've never seen him clearer. His life made him this way. Not just his parents, not just Desiree, not even crazy Tanner. Everything he's gone through shaped him into the man he is today. He's been blaming himself ever since that night. He thinks he's responsible for his little sister's death, and he's been living with that guilt. This guilt that no sane human can possibly carry without shutting down.

"I'm so sorry," I whisper.

Tears of anger glint at his eyes. The story isn't over, I can tell. But he needs a minute. So I give it to him.

"She was cold. She was so cold." He chokes on the words, and I feel like I'm right there, with him, alone in the darkness of the Adamses' mansion. I feel like I'm the one watching the life being sucked out of my sister as the capacity to hope leaves my body forever. "I didn't know what to do. She was crying and… there was so much blood. So much… So I just held her until she… she…" He can't seem to say it at first. "I watched her die, Winter." Then, he can't take it any longer. Tears cascade down his face, and I find myself crying, too. I open my arms to him, and he accepts my embrace, leaning into me. He doesn't say anything. He lets me hold him.

I've never seen Haze *really* lose it before. I've seen him shed a tear, yes, but I've never seen him have a full-blown panic attack. He can barely breathe, his chest moving up and down uncontrollably fast in my arms. Do you ever truly know someone until you've seen them *completely* fall apart? He's fighting his tears… fighting himself.

"Hey, it's okay. I'm here. I'm here," I repeat and hold him tighter. "Just breathe with me. Breathe." I inhale and exhale repeatedly until, eventually, he matches my breathing patterns and clears his throat. He sits back up and looks in the opposite direction. He hates being vulnerable.

"Seven days later, the house was gone. We moved to Florida two weeks after. My parents never cried in front of us. Not once. The night of her funeral, I heard my dad say to my mom that I was weak. That I should've saved her. He never looked at me the same way again."

This is why he started fighting.

"Tanner suggested to train me. I started working out every single day so that I'd never be weak again. I refused to be a helpless little bitch who couldn't defend himself anymore. Then, when we moved here, we heard about the fights and… you know the rest."

He started fighting and training every day so that he'd never lose someone else. He was fourteen years old, for Pete's sake. He was so young. It's no wonder he couldn't stand up to two grown men with guns. Why do I feel like becoming a fighter was secretly his way of punishing himself?

"Did they ever catch him? Marcus?"

He clenches his fists at my question. That's my answer. The combination of so much pain and anger in one person can't end well. The way his life turned out is the mere example of that.

"No."

It all makes sense now.

"I wanted to tell you, Winter, I swear. You have no idea how many times I almost did. But… you're the brightest thing in my life, and this is the darkest one of all."

I have no reason to doubt him anymore. He told me about the biggest trauma of his life. My eyes descend to the numbers tattooed on his forearm. *04/16*. I've been wondering what it meant since the day I met him.

"Is that the date she died?" My fingers gently brush his skin.

"No. God, no. She deserved better than that." He shakes his head. "That's the date she was born."

I wait for him to elaborate.

"I didn't want to remember the day that I lost her. I wanted to remember all the years that I didn't."

I understand what he means by that. He didn't want to ink

himself with the tragic date when she was taken away. He wanted to honor her life by celebrating the time he got to spend with her.

"It wasn't your fault. Please tell me you know that." I interlace our fingers and run my thumb along the palm of his hand. He draws a breath. I know better than to think me saying it to him once will be enough to end a lifetime of Haze blaming himself.

"Yes, it was. She'd still be here if I'd just been stronger. I could've saved her." He blames himself some more.

"No, that's the thing, you couldn't have. You were a kid, Haze." I lift his chin up with my right hand. "None of this is your fault. None of it."

He doesn't argue with me, even though he clearly wants to, and stares in silence like he's having an awakening. Then, after a few seconds, he speaks.

"I love you so much."

I don't say it back. I smile through the pain and let my body do the talking. I push the void between us aside and kiss him like I'll never get a chance to taste his lips again. I want him to know how much what he just did means to me. His mouth recognizes mine as he circles my wrist and pulls me on top of him to deepen the kiss. My legs fall on both side of his body while his fingers venture into my hair. His hands clinging to my waist make me feel like an addict relapsing after working so hard to get clean. He's a drug, and deep down I know… I could spend the rest of my life trying to get sober from Haze Adams.

His fingers wriggle under my shirt and dig into the hollow of my hips. If we keep this up, this will end the same way the dream I had this morning did.

He whispers against my mouth. "Does that mean that we're back together?"

"I don't know. Does it?" I say, unbuttoning his shirt.

He knows we're back together. This isn't even a question. My hands slip on his bare torso and trace the definition of his stomach. They curve around his muscular body, roaming downward and stopping right above his belt. I rest my fingers on the buckle and analyze his expression carefully.

Are we doing this?

He gives me the green light by pushing my head back to his and kissing me again.

We're interrupted by his phone ringing.

He scoops it up, takes a quick peek at the screen, and declines the call, but it immediately rings again. He curses and presses the Decline button once more. He goes back in for a kiss but—big surprise—it rings for a third time.

"It's one of my guys. It must be important." He sighs and I nod in disappointment. I start to move off his lap, but he grips my hips and presses me down onto him. "Don't. It shouldn't be too long." He strokes my bare arm.

He picks up.

"What?" he snaps.

I can't hear what's being said on the other end.

"You've got to be shitting me," he growls, obviously not pleased with the news he's getting. "I told you, I'm off to try and fix things with the North side."

So that's the ridiculous excuse he had to come up with for them to let him go…

"I'm not with her. How many times am I going to have to say it?"

They're onto him. They know something's going on. He won't be able to keep lying for long.

"What? Trev, hold on, slow down."

This makes me realize that I don't know anything about his fighters. He never brings them up.

"Okay, damn! I heard you."

He hangs up, throws his phone on the couch, and curses.

"Let me guess, you have to go," I say.

"I'm sorry. Trust me, you have *no idea* how much I'd rather stay and strip you naked right now." He tightens his grasp on my waist for a second, fighting himself. Then, he curses and takes his hands off me. "I'll get you a cab. We can't risk them seeing us together. They're way too suspicious."

I shift away from him.

"So what if they find out about us? What are they going to do? Kill me?" I joke, but Haze doesn't laugh, which tells me that this is a lot more serious than I thought.

"You don't need to worry about that because that's not going to happen. I won't let it." He smiles and furthers himself from me to call a cab.

He comes back two minutes later.

"The cab will be here in five."

I nod. His eyes flash.

"Hold on."

He sprints to his room. I hear him move stuff around until he finds what he's looking for. He walks back into the kitchen with…

Is he serious?

"I want you to have this." He hands it to me.

I crinkle my nose. "Pepper spray?"

"Keep it with you at all times, okay?"

"Is it really that bad?"

He knows where I'm going with this. Are his fighters coming after me? Should I be worried?

"No, it's just… you never know what could happen. Promise me you'll carry it everywhere."

I exhale. "Haze…"

"Winter, promise me." His piercing pale eyes drill into mine.

"Okay. I promise." I give in and go drop my new friend into my backpack. When I come back, Haze pulls me into his familiar arms, kissing my forehead and playing with my hair. He doesn't want me to worry, but I can't help it. He's kidding himself if he thinks he can be with me and still lead them.

If there's one thing that I learned about the street fight

community… it's that they'll find out eventually.

They always do.

TWENTY-SEVEN

Disappearing Act

Marching down the crowded hall like a prisoner walking to their death, I try my best to seem somewhat excited that I'm going home. I'm usually the first to squeal in joy when the bell rings, but strangely, I can't even muster a smile. Today is Friday and I have nothing—and I mean *nothing*—to look forward to. I don't have plans with the guys, I don't have plans with Kass, and I *especially* don't have plans with my boyfriend.

That would require having one.

As though this day isn't bad enough already, I turn the corner and see her leaning against my locker. Bianca. I've been avoiding her at school for five days, and I'd say I've been pretty successful so far. At least, until now…

"What do you want?" I groan and attempt to access my locker, but she won't budge.

"Don't mind me. Just came to see the miracle woman up close." She snorts and cocks her head to the side.

"You've seen me. Now, move."

"You know he never let me spend the night. Never. Not once." She twists her dirty-blonde hair around her finger and checks out her nails. I'm really *not* in the mood to hear her talk about Haze right now.

"Move," I repeat, and she finally takes a hint.

"He never introduced me to any of his friends. He wouldn't even allow me to be seen with him in public, can you believe it?"

"That's fascinating, really." I open my locker and start shoving its content into my backpack.

"But with you"—she completely ignores my obvious annoyance with her—"with you, it's different. He rejects girls, he gets into fights. He would do anything for you. And so, I just had to come and see for myself. What is it about you that makes you so damn special?" She steps closer as she speaks.

If she only knew that I haven't heard from Haze in four days.

"I remember the first time I saw you. You were at my party, and Haze and I had just finished fucking." Her words make me want to vomit. "I ran into you after he kicked me out because he didn't want us to come out at the same time. That's how meaningless we are to him. All of us," she spits harshly, but her pale eyes are tainted with a distant sadness that could almost make you feel sorry for her. Almost.

Memories of that night claw at me. This was the party where Haze saved me from some enemies of Kendrick who wanted my head. We never did get to find out who they were, but my guess is it was Tanner's guys. This is when it all began. He took me to his house and offered me a place to sleep. I had no idea, back then, that I'd end up falling for him. I wanted nothing more than to get this troubled guy out of my life. I'd overheard their conversation after they'd… *yeah*, and he'd said something about making it clear that he just wanted to sleep with her from the start. She'd rushed out of the room in fury. It's crazy to think of Haze in this light. He really did treat her like trash. But with me… he's this entirely different person.

I don't know how to feel about this.

"Then, when the cops showed up, he grabbed your arm and ran away with you. Just like that. He protected you, Winter Kingston, the random new girl. A perfect stranger. His first instinct was to save you."

Okay, I've heard enough.

"Listen, I'd love to stay and listen to your side-chick story, but I have better things to do, so if you'll excuse me…"

Anger tears through her face.

"Side chick, huh?"

Here it comes.

"Is that why, when you left town for some reason, he didn't chase you and came to see me? Because I'm the side chick?"

My stomach churns. Will telling me that Haze was seen at her place the day after I left pops into my head.

"Or did he not tell you about that?"

"No, he did. He told me everything. He told me how he couldn't even kiss you and left you standing there barely two minutes after showing up."

"And you fell for it." She chortles loudly. "Of course you did. Let me tell you what he truly did that night."

Fear grips my insides.

"He fucked my brains out. He took me from behind, and we did it again and again and again. He fucked me so hard I couldn't get enough. And let me tell you, it was good."

Projectile vomit in 3, 2, 1…

"But I assume you know that. You did sleep with him, didn't you? He really is mind-blowing in the sack, that one." She smiles as if she's reminiscing.

Haze said that he didn't sleep with her.

He said he couldn't even kiss her.

He promised.

It feels like multiple bullets are piercing my heart. I wish she didn't get to me. I wish it didn't hurt. But it's pretty hard not to doubt Haze when I haven't seen or heard from him once since the night he told me about his sister. I've been texting him—more like I've been texting myself—and he's been ghosting me. I'm getting tired of his disappearing acts. I'll be on a plane back to Toronto next Friday. We don't have time for this. *We don't have time for anything.*

"So, let me ask you, princess. Who's the side chick now?" She offers me a self-satisfied smile, turns on her heels, and disappears into the moving crowd. I fail to ignore the bitter taste lingering on my tongue. I can't take it anymore. I get my phone out of my pocket to see I have a message from Kass. She's giving me a ride home from school per usual. She's waiting for me outside. I text her that I'll be right there and select my conversation with Haze. My fingers type the message I've been wanting to send all week.

> Is this your way of telling me you don't want to get back together anymore? If so, please be a man about it and tell me in person.

"HEY, CANADA. WHERE'S THAT BOYFRIEND OF yours?" Will says, throwing himself onto the couch with a bag of ketchup chips in hand. That's his go-to snack, and I honestly have no idea where he finds those. I know we have them in Toronto, but I haven't seen them anywhere since I moved to the US. Does he get them shipped?

"Yeah, we haven't seen him in a while," Alex adds.

"Oh, you don't know?" Kendrick mocks, walking into the living room and sitting right on top of Alex. "Prince Charming forgot that he had a girlfriend recently." Alex pushes him off and they laugh, wrestling each other like kids.

Kass walks in, too. "I'm sure he's just busy."

"Busy flirting with all the girls in town," Will says, and I throw a pillow at him, my fake smile faltering.

"Seriously, though, what's his deal?" Kass says and throws herself on the couch next to me. "You two just got back together, and you haven't even had time to talk about what's going to happen in a week. You know, when you *literally* move to another country? What is he even doing? I don't understand this guy."

I sigh. "You and me both, sister, you and me both."

She's right. I've been trying not to think about it, but the clock ticking is bringing us closer to the inevitable goodbye with every passing second. The finals are next week. I'm already drowning in studies and all these papers I have to write for extra credit. I have no clue when or *if* Haze and I will even have time to spend time together before I leave. Then there's his parents' awful reception on Tuesday. I assume we're not going anymore since it would mean seeing each other, and we're particularly lacking in that department.

"He's here." Kass jumps up when she gets a text message.

"Who's here?" I look at her.

"Luke."

I immediately gaze at Will, who can't erase the anger on his face. Kass's seeing Luke Jenson again? Why? What happened to my favorite forbidden couple?

"You seeing him again?" I ask before she walks out.

"Yes. He's taking me to prom next week. *Somebody's* got to." The emphasis she puts on the last part isn't lost on me. Will probably doesn't want to take her because it would mean telling Kendrick about them. He keeps his eyes glued to his phone, but I can tell he's falling to pieces with each step Kass takes toward the door. He couldn't keep his promise. But why? It's so obvious that he's head over heels in love with her. He needs to wake up before it's too late… I get it though. How do you tell your best friend that you've been sleeping with his sister behind his back, when he's specifically forbidden you to?

Kassidy's eyes lift to Will. Then, she looks at the ground, pain coloring her traits, and walks out. Next thing we know, a car's screeching down the street.

I receive a message shortly after that. It's Haze. He texted me back.

Well, that's a first.

I'm so sorry, sweetie. I can explain. Please come over to my place.

Sweetie? Since when does Haze call me sweetie?

Where have you been?

I'll tell you everything in person, I promise. I love you. Can you come over?

I stare at the screen for a few seconds, uncertainty growing inside me, and decide I owe him a chance to explain himself.

I'm on my way.

"THANKS AGAIN." I UNBUCKLE MY SEAT belt and climb out of Will's car. He was nice enough to drive me.

"No problem, Canada. You good to get back home?"

"Yes, don't worry. Haze will drive me, or I'll get a cab."

Will nods and I slam the door. He drives off in a roar as I make my way to the entrance of the alluring brick-built building with my backpack hanging off my arm. I thought I'd bring Haze the assignments and notes he missed from the classes we have together. I notice two guys that look my age smoking next to the building and watching me but don't think much of it.

I text Haze to buzz me in since I can never remember his apartment number. The familiar sound quickly resonates in the wide entrance hall, and I pull the heavy door open with a million thoughts swirling around my brain. He texts me to come in without knocking.

I have no idea what I could possibly say to him at this point. Every time I think we're making progress, he takes us back to square one. The elevator ride isn't long enough. I need more time. More silence. I need another chance to figure out how to casually bring up that I'll be on a plane taking me to another country in a few days. The ding indicating that I've reached his floor only accentuates my panic. The painful lump in my throat makes itself known as I count every step I take religiously. I haven't been able to get rid of the doubts cutting through my stomach since earlier. What Bianca said stayed with me. I can't shake her. What if it's true? What if he did sleep with her?

I suck in a breath, lay an uncertain and shaky hand on the handle, and turn it. As soon as I walk in and close the door, I'm struck by a darkness I did not expect. All lights are off. Engulfed in gloom, I let my hands explore the walls in search of a light switch.

"Haze?" I call.

No reply.

At first, I think maybe he's pulling a prank on me. But I quickly realize I couldn't be more wrong. The lamp comes on and I see him.

The guy that should be Haze but isn't…

He's tall, brown-haired, and buff. He looks at me with a smug face and arched eyebrows. His nose is crooked, but it doesn't seem birth-given. It looks like he broke it. I've never seen him in my life.

"So, it's you, huh?" he says casually like I'm not completely terrified.

"Who are you?"

"I mean, I get it. Great ass. I'd hit that, too." He eyes me up and down, my previous sentence going in through onc car and out the other.

"Where's Haze?" I ask louder.

"Oh, don't worry about him. He won't bother us." He smiles and gets up, walking toward me. "I made sure of it."

Oh hell to the no.

I don't have even the slightest idea as to who that is, but it doesn't matter. He's bad news, I know that much. I try to make a run for it, but he beats me to the door like he's had time to prepare for my every move. "Hey, where are you going? We've still got so much to discuss, you and I."

I get my phone out of my back pocket, but he sees me coming from a mile away. He wrenches it from my hands and lobs it across the room.

"Rude!" He glares at me. "I'm talking to you."

I'm paralyzed.

"What do you want with me?"

"I want what we all want. To get our leader back and for you to stop being a pain in the ass."

To get our leader back…

This… this is one of Haze's fighters.

"You know, it's funny. Even your goddamn cousin doesn't want you together, but you two idiots still can't take a hint." His fingers trace the curve of my jawline, and I tremble in fear. "Don't get me wrong, we're happy that he told us everything, really. It exposed Haze for the lying son of a bitch he really is."

Kendrick.

Kendrick told them about us. Haze was suspicious that someone in the East side had snitched. I didn't want to believe it. This has to be what Kendrick meant by "fixing" it. This is where he went the night of the party. This is why Haze said his guys were even worse than before. They knew he was lying for a fact. I bet Kendrick thought he was keeping me safe. That

Haze's guys would force him to walk a straight line again and get him away from me. If he only knew…

"I'm sorry, where are my manners? I didn't even introduce myself. Name's Ryan, but I go by my last name. Everyone calls me Sutter. Maybe your boyfriend told you about me?"

No, he didn't. If he had, maybe this wouldn't be happening.

"Where is he?"

"Haze? He's fine. Trev's keeping him busy while we take care of you." He cackles. "Bastard has no idea. He still thinks he lost his phone."

It all becomes clear. Haze didn't send me those messages.

This guy did.

I knew something was off. He never calls me sweetie.

Wait, Winter, he said "we." I think back to the guys I saw outside. Could they be with him?

"He actually thought he could fool us by staying away from you for a week, can you believe it? He really does take us for a bunch of brainless imbeciles."

That's why he hasn't been around. He was trying to convince them that we weren't together.

"I gotta give it to him. The guy really does love you." He steps forward and corners me. "It's fascinating, really. We didn't think he had it in him."

"I'll scream. Don't think I won't." I gather all my courage, my throat so dry it hurts to speak.

"Scream all you want, darling. There isn't a soul in the

building." He twists a piece of my hair around his index finger, and I wince. "Do you know how easy it was to get everyone out for a few hours? All we had to do was go from door to door, claim the landlord sent us, and tell them we suspected there was a gas leak. They didn't even bat an eye."

Only then does realization crumple me.

They thought this whole thing through. I'm not strong enough to fight this guy. My only chance is to outsmart him.

"What are you going to do to me?" I quiver in fear.

"We don't know yet. See, the initial plan was to get rid of you but…" He smirks. "Maybe we don't have to go to such extremes. Maybe we can get rid of Haze's feelings for you instead."

"What does that mean?"

"What do you say you show me how that pretty mouth of yours turned Haze Adams into your little bitch?"

Instant gag reflex.

"What? You screw my leader but not me. A bit unfair, don't you think?" He shoots me a cocky look.

I have an idea.

"Then I'm free to go?" I bat my eyelashes.

"Yep. I'm sure Haze finding out that I fucked his precious Winter in his bed would do the trick."

It takes an unparalleled strength for me to crack a giggle, step toward him, and run my hands down his chest.

I pray that I'm believable.

"That's more like it," he says, satisfied.

I stand on my tiptoes and whisper in his ear, "I have protection in my backpack. Let me grab it."

He beams. "I knew there was a reason Haze liked you so much."

Just like that, he lets me bend down and grab my backpack lying on the floor. *Freaking idiot.* I unzip my bag and dive my hand deep into it, my fingers searching for it. Where is it?

I know I brought it.

"What's taking so long? My dick isn't going to suck itself," he hisses.

The moment Haze and I shared in this exact spot five days ago haunts me.

"I want you to have this."

"Pepper spray?"

"Keep it with you at all times, okay?"

I am *so* glad that I listened to him.

"Why don't you suck on that?" I spin around and spray the monster in front of me right in the face. He stumbles back a few steps, screaming in agony as he covers his eyes with his hands.

That's my cue.

I slam the door to Haze's apartment open and leap into the hall. I know there's a very good chance the guys I saw outside will be waiting for me, but I don't care. I have to try.

"You bitch!" I hear him yell as I go down the stairs. The adrenaline kicking in gives me the super speed I so desperately need. I can hear his distant thumping behind me. He's probably blinder than my great-grandma right now.

I swing the front door of the building open. I'm running so fast I can't even begin to see my feet hitting the ground. Night is falling upon us. Luckily, the guys outside weren't expecting me, which gives me a head start.

"Get her!" I hear one of them shout.

They're not too far behind. The road's empty, no cars to be seen. Haze's building just had to be in an isolated spot. I wish I could lose them, but the way the street borders the apartments makes it impossible. I'm exposed, darting in the center of the road. There's no escape. I try and reach for my phone in my pocket, but then I'm reminded that Ryan tossed it. I left it upstairs. I signed my own death warrant.

A car roars loudly behind me. It's getting closer and it's going fast. *Too fast.* It's one of them, it's got to be. What am I going to do? I can't outrun a car. My heart is beating so rapidly it seems impossible that I haven't had a stroke yet.

In a scene worthy of an action movie, the car passes me and loudly hits the brakes right in the middle of the road, screeching as it stops and blocks the way. I desperately search for a way out. I search and I search, but there's nowhere for me to run.

This is it…

I'm going down.

TWENTY-EIGHT

Dilemmas

Tears. It's all I can see when the door flies open and a broad-shouldered silhouette rushes out of the car. It takes me a second to recognize him, for the familiarity of his tall frame to sink into me.

Haze.

He's here.

I don't recognize his car. Without a word, he runs to me, his eyes telling a million stories, and goes straight for my face. He cups my cheeks with his hands and examines me obsessively. "Thank God. Are you okay? Did he touch you?"

"I'm okay. I'm okay." I nod in distress and hold on to his jacket as if I need to make sure that he's real.

"I'm so sorry, Winter. I'm sorry. I had no idea, I…"

In that moment, I don't care about what he did. I don't care that he disappeared. I cry in relief and throw myself into his arms. He holds me as tight as possible, but our reunion is short-lived when footsteps come running down behind us. We turn around.

There they are, a few feet away from us. Three guys. A redhead, a guy with black hair, and Ryan. His eyes are red, burnt.

He glares me with a hatred I'd recognize anywhere. Murder lies in his gaze. He walks toward me, but Haze steps in front of me, his arm and body immediately shielding me.

"Don't even think about it," he says through gritted teeth, and Ryan stops dead in his tracks.

"Get out of my way, Haze."

"You're not touching a hair on her head."

The tension fills any empty space it can find and renders the air toxic.

"Let me guess, Trev told on us," Ryan says.

Haze doesn't reply, but the answer is all over his face.

"I knew we couldn't trust him," Ryan says to his friends. "He's weak. His guilty conscience always gets the best of him."

"At least he has one," Haze spits.

"Listen…" Ryan starts. "This doesn't need to get messy, man. We just want the girl."

"You're going to have to kill me."

I compress Haze's bicep. He's basically challenging them into killing him. He needs to stop.

The red-haired guy next to Ryan speaks up and steps forward. "That's what you call not seeing her anymore? You're a liar, Haze. This girl needs to stop being a fucking problem."

"Really, Andrew? You too? I'd expect that coming from Ryan, the piece of shit, but you…" Haze says in disgust. "You were my friend. I trusted you."

"I wish things were different, Haze. I really do." Shame

radiates off Andrew's stance. "But we can't trust you anymore. We told you what would happen if you didn't give up on her."

"Fine, I lied. But it doesn't have to change anything. Having her in my life doesn't change who I am. I'm still me, guys," he begs.

"Still you? Please, you're throwing fights, disappearing on us, working with the East side."

Haze's words leave him.

"Yeah, we know about that. Turns out the East side's just as against your relationship as we are."

Haze peeks at me from the corner of his eyes, waiting for me to validate their accusations. I nod and he clenches his jaw.

Damn you, Kendrick.

"Thanks for starting shit with the North side, by the way. You cost us our best alliance. All over some stupid girl." Ryan huffs and puffs, glancing at the guys over his shoulder. He's clearly the brain behind the operation. The other two seem to hate the situation unraveling before their eyes. "We don't want to kill her, and we won't have to if you agree to get her out of your life."

"What is this? An ultimatum?"

"Maybe it should be. Choose, Haze. The girl or us."

Haze's face hardens, his gaze gliding from them to me. My heartbeat races when I get lost in the blue of his eyes. Finally, he smiles faintly.

"Then, it's settled."

He captures my hand into his.

"I'm done fighting."

My lips part.

Wait, what?

Ryan fails to hide his joy. "Fine. I'll lead the West side."

"Now, we both know the only way to get the title from me is to beat me. Either you fight me, or you win the most fights. No other way to become the main. That's the rule."

"I don't have to. You just quit. I don't have to challenge the main if he's a quitter. *That's the rule.*" He spits Haze's words back to his face.

There are so many rules I'm not even close to understanding. Maybe I should start listening to Kendrick's speeches.

"Oh, come on, humor me. You think you have what it takes to lead? Prove it."

Ryan tightens his fists and looks over at the guys. They nod in approval. There's no avoiding this fight.

Haze makes me step back. Seconds later, Ryan runs to us, putting up a fist no one wants to be on the receiving end of. I yelp as Haze easily intercepts his attack, punching the breath out of him and pushing him to the ground. Ryan groans in pain but quickly gets back on his feet. Seconds later, Haze is twisting Ryan's arm behind his back like it's nothing—like *he's* nothing—and shoving him back down. The other guys don't move one bit, guilt scorching their faces. Helpless, they watch Haze destroy their future leader on repeat.

It quickly becomes clear why Haze was the main. He's winning the fight by far, effortlessly dodging every upper cut Ryan comes up with and returning the punches to sender ten times harder.

"Really, Sutter? Using my own moves against me? In case you forgot, I fucking made you." Haze pulls Ryan by the collar of his clothes and sends him flying with one strong and final hook. Ryan whimpers, struggling to get up, as he wipes the blood off his mouth. "That's who you want as your leader? Be my guest," Haze scoffs.

Haze's fighters are speechless, which is understandable. What can you possibly say when your new leader just got their ass handed to them by the one you're trying to kick out?

"Now, here's what's going to happen. You're going to go home with your excuse of a leader and never come near me or my girl ever again."

Ryan spits more blood. "And why would we do that?"

"Because you know damn well I could ruin your lives with all the dirt I have on you."

"We have dirt on you, too," Ryan grunts.

"Yeah, but you won't use it. You don't have Daddy's money to save your ass. I, on the other hand…"

On their faces is pure and undeniable defeat. They know he's right. Whatever they have against him, he can find worse, and he'll always come out unscathed on the other side. They can't take him on. They'd most likely end up behind bars, but Haze…

his parents would get him the most expensive lawyers just to save their company.

"If I find out that even just one of you is plotting against me, I'll have everyone's dirty little secrets sent to the police in a heartbeat, you got it?"

No answer.

"Did you fucking get it, yes or no?" he snarls.

Frustrated, they nod.

Haze places a hand on my back, applies pressure to get me to start walking, and opens the unknown car door for me. I quickly climb onto the leather seats. Next thing I know, we're driving down the street and watching Haze's old life disappear in the rearview mirror.

"PLEASE TALK TO ME," HE BEGS, squeezing my thigh with his hand. I'm speechless from everything he's just told me. Ryan may be a psychopath, but he wasn't lying about Haze staying away to keep me safe. Apparently, they even sabotaged his car so that he couldn't come to my rescue if he found out about their plan. We're in some guy called Trevor's car. "I wanted to tell you, I really did, but I couldn't. I had to play perfect leader for a week to get them off my back. I thought I was protecting you. Even if it turns out the bastards knew all along. Don't be mad."

I inhale and take my hand to his.

"How could I be mad?"

He gave up the only thing that made him feel better after his sister's death. He quit fighting when he's been training his whole life. He didn't even hesitate.

"You didn't have to give it all up for me, you know."

"Yes, I did," he says. "They were basically asking me to choose between the fights and your life, Winter. That wasn't an option."

"You could've just never seen me again."

"Like I said…" He interlaces our fingers. "Not an option."

I flush.

He clears his throat. "I think it's for the best anyway. I realized that maybe… I don't want this life anymore."

"Why not? What happened?" I say softly.

He turns to look at me at a red light.

"You happened."

My stomach turns into a fuzzy mess.

There he goes again with his damn swoony lines. Do they come naturally to him, or does he rehearse?

"You know you could've just told me you couldn't see me for a week, jerk," I say, ignoring the heating up of my cheeks.

"It had to be believable, *prude*," he teases.

"Trust me, it was. I really thought we were done."

He starts laughing.

"What's so funny?" I ask.

He shrugs. "Nothing, it's just cute."

"Cute? What's cute?"

"How you thought I'd be stupid enough to ever let you go again."

My heart flitters in my rib cage as I look outside the window to hide the idiotic grin on my lips. I mean, *come on.* Is he trying to get me to take his clothes off right here right now?

Someone give this boy a cuteness award.

When I look back at him, I squint my eyes and notice he's bleeding. His cheek is wounded. It looks like Ryan did nudge him after all.

"You're hurt." I lean in.

"This? It's nothing."

"We need to clean you up."

"You can play nurse all you want when we get home."

"Home?"

"You're sleeping at my place tonight," he states. "I mean, unless it's too hard for you to go back there after what happened."

"No, don't be ridiculous. I'm fine."

He nods. "We're stopping at your house so you can pick up clothes. We only have a week left. You're staying with me."

So he does know.

"Kendrick won't allow it."

"Kendrick almost got you killed tonight because he put his dirty nose where it didn't belong, so he'll have to deal with it. I'm not letting you out of my sight, girlfriend."

"You are aware that the girlfriend title doesn't give you the right to control everything I do, right?" I ask.

"Yes, of course. We're just making decisions as a couple. So we're going to make the decision *together* to have you stay with me."

"In other words, you're choosing."

"Yep." He grins and I laugh.

HAZE SIGHS WHEN I GRIP HIS arm and drag him to the bathroom against his will. He says he doesn't need me to clean his wounds, that he's fine, but I don't hear a word he's saying. I haven't been able to stop looking at his cut since we got to his place.

"What are we doing? Please say taking a shower." He circles my waist with his arm from behind.

"You wish. I'm cleaning your wound."

"I told you I'm fine. I'm starving. Let's order a bunch of food instead."

"Sit!" I motion to the corner of the bathtub. He obeys but makes sure to complain while I get alcohol out of the bathroom cabinet. "This is going to hurt."

"No, it won't."

I press the cloth to his wound.

"Ouch!" He winces.

I suppress a laugh.

"Shut up." He smiles and gets up to tickle me.

I accidentally drop the cloth into the bathtub when I try to move away from him and bend down to get it.

"Winter…" I feel him shift closer behind me.

"What?" I say, still trying to get the cloth.

"You might want to stop doing that in front of me."

I freeze, suddenly very aware of the position we're in.

My ass is barely two inches away from him. I didn't even think of that. We haven't seen each other in four days, and considering how long it's been since the last time we had sex, I'm not surprised the stupidest little things turn him on.

"Or what?" I get up. He's so close that his torso crashes against my back. His hands creep under my shirt, and chills scamper down my spine. His mouth stops next to my ear.

"Keep doing that and you'll find out."

I let out a soft gasp when his lips find my neck. He knows exactly how to drive me insane.

"Haze…"

"Something wrong?" His breath bounces on my skin, and I know I won't be able to survive the usual teasing. We keep getting interrupted lately, and it's been so long. Too long.

I jolt around, bringing his face forward as my lips close over his. We're both eager, starving. Our tongues converge and he groans when I suck his lower lip between my teeth. He pulls me up and wraps both my legs around his waist, his mouth never once leaving mine as he carries me out of the bathroom. We're both so busy making out that I only realize we're in the kitchen when he drops me on the stone-cold table.

Wait, *the table?*

"Why the table?" I giggle in between kisses.

He smirks and goes back to kissing my neck like he spent his entire life studying my sweet spots. I bite my lip when he sucks on the skin just under my collarbone.

Then, he takes on my earlobe and whispers in my ear, "Because I'm having you for dinner."

Goodbye, world. It was nice knowing you.

I laugh again and take his T-shirt off. I toss it across the living room as his hands tug at my tank top, pulling the fabric up…

"I'm guessing this is a bad time."

We both jump, staring at the wide-open door.

I can't believe who's standing in Haze's kitchen.

TWENTY-NINE

Troublemakers

"What the hell are you doing here?" Haze spits, getting off the table and pulling me along with him. His brother hasn't changed one bit, his face still unreadable, cold… *lifeless.* Haze steps in front of me like he expects him to pounce, but Tanner doesn't move a muscle, his gaze straying between Haze and me numerous times before he speaks again.

"Don't worry. I'm not here for her. Not this time."

"What do you want? How did you even get in?"

"You seem to forget who taught you everything you know on picking locks, brother," he says, the smile creeping on his lips enough to give me nightmares. How long has he been standing there? "Look, I'm not here to start a fight. I'm here to end one."

Everything he says sounds like a lie. Haze doesn't bother replying and raises a suspicious eyebrow at him.

"This has been going on for too long. Clearly I can't keep you away from the East side ch—" He stops. "From Winter," he corrects himself. "I don't care anymore. I want my brother back."

Haze crows, "Right, well you should've thought about that before you kidnapped my girlfriend and almost murdered her."

"I was a fool. I thought this was the only way to get you back, but I was wrong. I'm sorry. If you're going to believe anything I say, believe that."

"Okay, let me spell it out for you. If you're here for forgiveness, you're not going to get it."

He doesn't reply for a good five seconds, and I can tell Haze is close to losing his temper.

"I heard you're done fighting," Tanner says after a while. "Rumor has it your guys kicked you out."

How does he know that? It's only been a few hours.

"Word travels fast," he adds like he's reading both our minds.

"What's it to you?" Haze asks.

"Word on the street's that someone's been asking around the community about you since you skipped town. They've been very discreet; even I couldn't trace them."

"So what? You came here to warn me?" Haze raises an eyebrow.

"Yes, I did. Someone's after you, brother. It's not the North side, it's not your guys. It's not even the West side. Can you think of anyone you pissed off lately?"

I repress a snort.

I mean, has he met Haze? The list goes on and on.

"Thanks for the brotherly concern, but I'm good." Haze walks to the door and swings it open, beckoning him to leave.

"No, you're not. Even if I'm wrong about the psycho after

you, you just became the number one target to all your enemies, can't you see that? By tomorrow, the entire world's going to know that you're on your own. That makes you vulnerable. You'll be dodging attacks left and right."

"What's your point, Tanner?"

"My point… is that you need to join my circle."

This makes Haze scoff.

"Thanks, but no, thanks."

"Haze, you don't understand…"

"I do understand. I understand that my traitor of a brother is looking for an excuse to get my trust back and screw me over again."

"You do realize that people will find out why you quit, right? It will lead back to her, Haze. Everything will."

Haze's anger fades, Tanner's warning finally puncturing his walls. He glances at me. He's worried.

"No one's touching her," he says.

"I can help you protect her if you give me a chance."

"Protect her? Spare me the bullshit." Haze points to the door once more.

"I know what I did was fucked up, but… things have changed since then. I've changed. I want to make this right. At least tell me that you're coming to Mom's reception on Tuesday."

We haven't had a chance to discuss that yet. Haze transports his weight from one leg to the other uncomfortably and shakes his head no.

"You have to come. We're making a big announcement."

"So?"

"It's important."

"What is it?"

"You'll have to come to find out." Tanner uses the only leverage he has.

"Why would I come for some stupid announcement that doesn't affect me?"

"Oh, it will." Tanner pauses. "In fact, it already has."

Tanner makes his way to the open door, his steps echoing in the barely furnished apartment. He turns around a few seconds before he walks out.

"I'll see you there, little brother. Actually, I hope to see you both there." He doesn't dare look at me. The door clicks shut, and we wait for his footsteps to fade down the hall.

"Don't tell me you're actually considering this," I say, recognizing the look on his face.

"Aren't you?" Haze walks to the living room.

"That's the curiosity talking. That's exactly what he wants. What if it's a trap?"

"He'll be dead before he hurts you," he says, still aimlessly roaming his apartment. He won't admit it, but seeing his brother again wasn't easy.

"He's still your brother," I breathe.

"I don't care. He sure as hell didn't seem to care when one

of his guys put a gun to my temple. I… I need some air."

I follow him onto the balcony, the rage radiating off him making me rethink my every word before they even come out.

"Haze," I whisper behind him.

The lean muscles of his back stretch to the rhythm of his unsteady breathing, his hands gripping the railing so tight that his knuckles turn white. This is a fresh night, and he's still shirtless. He looks completely unbothered by the chilly temperature.

I, on the other hand, am starting to understand what Jack must've felt like in *Titanic*.

"I lost my brother…" He finally speaks after a few seconds. "Who, as crazy as he is, was pretty much the closest thing I had to a family since Des died. Then, I lost my fighters. This may not mean much to you, but I thought they were my friends. And now…" He looks ahead into the emptiness. "Now I'm going to lose you, too."

"What are you talking about? You're not going to lose me." I press myself to him. He wraps his arms around me, and even in this ice age, his skin is smoking hot. I relish in the searing of his body on me and take in every bit of his cologne.

"Do you think I don't know that we only have a week left?" He tells me the words I've been dreading. "In that week, we have finals and prom and my parents' stupid reception. We barely have any time together. What about after? When are we going to talk about this?"

I break away from his hold. "Don't pin this on me. I tried talking to you, but you've been gone for days. It's pretty hard to communicate when there's only one of us talking."

"Yeah, well, maybe I wouldn't have to pretend I'm not seeing you anymore if you weren't the damn East side girl!" He raises his voice at me.

I fall silent, disbelief crushing me. Are we really doing this right now? Is he seriously blaming me for being, well… *me?*

"Do you think I want this? Do you think I asked to be in the middle of your stupid war?" I shout. I know he's going through something right now, but that doesn't give him the right to speak to me this way. "If you wanted nothing to do with the damn 'East side chick' as you so nicely put it"—I create air quotes with my fingers—"then maybe you shouldn't have made a deal with her as the prize in the first place."

The argument keeps escalating. Overwhelmed, I don't wait for it to reach a higher level and walk back inside the apartment. Haze doesn't miss a beat, mirroring my actions.

"What about me? Do you think I wanted this to happen? Do you think I planned to fall in love with you?" He trails behind me. "You were supposed to be a game. A way to destroy the East side. You were supposed to be nothing to me. Nothing," he snaps, and I blink back the tears forming in my eyes.

"Oh yeah? Well, I'm sorry that you hate loving me so much," I scream and head for his bedroom. "Let me spare you any more trouble."

"Where do you think you're going?" he calls as I grab the bag of clothes I packed to stay with him and throw its strap over my shoulder. I stride toward the front door, but he's too fast. He easily steps in my way, his hard chest blocking me.

"Move." I try hitting him, pushing him, tackling him, but nothing gets me the results I seek. He picks the strap off my shoulder and my bag meets the floor. On punch number three, he steps sideways, but it quickly becomes apparent that it's not because he's letting me go.

Not even close.

He grips my waist before I can twist the handle, spins me around, and slams my back to the door. He forcefully jacks his body to mine to immobilize me. We're both angry messes. Two stupid kids in love, blinded by the fear of losing the only thing that matters. The only thing the whole world denies us. Every sign, every moment… they point us toward the colossal and impending truth. That maybe we really aren't meant to be together. That the Universe keeps on pulling us apart for a reason. It'd be so much easier if we just let it go, parted ways, and remembered the brief, passing romance we shared during our senior year. It *should* be easy… but love never is.

"You are not leaving me!"

"Yes, I am!" I relentlessly punch his torso until he grabs my wrists.

"Just fucking stay!" he shouts, pinning my arms on each side of my head. His chest rises and falls rapidly as his pleading eyes sink into mine. Eventually, his anger flops, leaving room for a desperation that shatters me. "*Please…*"

I can't think. I can't speak.

A lapse of judgment. That's what hits me. *Just fucking stay.* The words pry their way out of my mouth before I can stop them.

"Make me."

His lips part. All we do is stare at each other in silence.

I look at him.

He looks at me.

And we realize the same thing at the same time.

What the hell *are we doing right now?*

The breath is knocked out of me when his lips roughly slam against mine and one of his hands slips into my hair. I should get him off me. I should push him away after all the horrible things he just spat in my face. But I can't. *I don't want to.* Instead, I do the wrong thing for even worse reasons. I find myself kissing him back, our moving tongues making me forget the words we didn't mean… *the words we should've meant.*

I don't know how we find ourselves on the couch. I don't know how he ends up on top of me, tearing off my underwear with his teeth, and I *especially* don't know how I end up moaning into his mouth while he pushes himself inside me. I don't know why my body responds to him this way, to the strong roll of his hips, to his tongue on my burning skin. Truth is, I don't know anything when it comes to Haze… and I want it to stay that way.

I don't want to know. I don't want to *think*.

If I do, I'll be reminded that we're doomed. That next Friday, I'll be on a plane taking me far, far away.

Away from this place.

Away from my family.

Away from *him*.

He rests my leg on his shoulder and takes it further, deeper.

I hate him.

I hate him so fucking much.

But I love him more.

"You're not leaving me," he grunts into my ear and speeds up his thrusting to the point of making me shake. He once told me that I was his, and, when he pushes so deep that my eyes roll back, I know it's true. I hate it. I hate it more than words can say. But he's right. He's right and he always will be…

I'm his.

Haze

A phone.

That's what wakes me up. I stretch, my hand automatically wandering to her side of the bed—let me rephrase—the side where she should be, and frown when the silk sheets skim the tips of my fingers. She isn't lying next to me. I rub my eyes and peel them open, ignoring Winter's phone going off on the nightstand.

I sit back up, the memories of how she felt around me

converting my confusion into lust. Last night was different. It was hateful, angry sex, filled with resentment and desperation. She wanted to resist. I could see it in her eyes as I rammed myself inside her. She wanted to be strong, but she couldn't. We both couldn't. *We never can.*

I swear this girl is going to be the death of me.

I hear motion in the kitchen and smile, scooping her phone that's still annoyingly buzzing off the table and carrying myself out of bed. The first thing I see when I march out of my room is Winter standing in front of the oven, cooking breakfast, or should I say, *trying* to cook since she's a self-proclaimed queen at burning pastas.

"Smells good in here." I walk to her and rest her phone, which just stopped ringing, on the counter. She's wearing my shirt. She's the cutest thing in the entire freaking world, and anyone who disagrees will have to fight me. "I didn't know you cooked."

"I don't. Which is why I'm hoping you don't die from food poisoning." She giggles.

"You're not eating with me?"

"I already ate."

I nod and kiss her. She barely pecks my lips and pulls away.

"That's it? That's all I get?" I pout.

"Sorry. My morning breath says I can't kiss you longer. I want you to live."

I laugh.

"Any plans today?" I ask.

"Yeah, Kass's picking me up in less than an hour to go dress shopping. You know… for prom. She already got her dress, but I didn't."

"I thought you weren't going to that."

"I wasn't going to, but Kass's dragging me, so I thought maybe…" She stops talking. "Maybe we could go together."

I pretend to hesitate, which only accentuates the worried expression on her face.

"If you're going, then I'm going," I say, and she rejoices, the most beautiful smile I've ever seen lighting up her face. She throws her arms around me and kisses my cheek multiple times. I don't care much for prom—I never have—but I care for Winter, which makes the choice easy.

She turns off the stove and goes to get a plate out of the cabinet. I find myself staring when she gets on the tips of her toes and the shirt rises, giving me a quick but much appreciated sneak peek of her ass.

"Nice shirt." I smirk and lean back against the counter with my arms over my chest.

"I grabbed the first thing I could find. Hope you don't mind." She comes back with a plate. "It's so big, I never get cold. I like it."

"Keep it if you want. You're going to need it when you move to the North Pole."

The smile is instantly slapped off her lips.

I know that was a low blow. I couldn't help myself. We haven't talked about her leaving yet, and it's weighing on me a bit more every day.

"I'm sorry. I've been good since last night. I'm stopping now." I put my hands up in surrender.

"No, don't. You're right. It's time we talk about it." She places the plate down next to the sink. "Let's just put it out there, shall we? I'm leaving next Friday. What then?"

Her affirmation punches me right in the face. I don't know why I somehow convinced myself that she'd flinch and decide to stay. To me, the possibility of her leaving was just that: a possibility. But now it's real… *too real.*

"Don't tell me you're actually considering leaving," I let out.

"Of course I am. Florida was never a permanent thing for me. Toronto's my home. It's where my family is, my friends. My whole life. The college I chose."

"I thought your life was here… with me." My throat itches.

"It is. You're a big part of my life, but… they are, too."

"So what? You're just going to leave? We're just going to break up in five days?" The words *break up* echo in my chest.

"I don't want us to. We can find a way."

"I'll give you a way. Stay here. Find a college here. Let's build a life here. Screw Canada. It's cold all the time anyway." My anger speaks for me.

"But it's my home…"

"And Florida is mine."

An impenetrable tension surrounds us.

"Long-distance relationships are a thing, you know?" Her voice breaks.

"Is that really how you want to live? Winter, this isn't an 'I see him on the weekends' kind of long distance. This would be an 'I see him once every six months.' We can't do that. Don't you want this to work?" I move over to her.

"Are you even listening to yourself? You're the one sounding like you don't want us to work right now. I'm trying and you're just… downing every solution I come up with," she says, tears welling in the corners of her eyes.

Shit. Great job, Haze.

I sigh. "You're right. You're right. I'm sorry. Hey, look at me." I lift her chin up. "We'll cross the bridge when we come to it. We still have a few days to figure this out. And we will. We're strong enough. I promise." I open my arms for a hug that she doesn't decline. She wipes her tears and hides her face in my neck. My baby's just as scared as I am.

She only leaves my embrace when her phone vibrates for the millionth time.

"It's been going off since I woke up," I say.

She nods and picks it off the counter. She reads the many texts on her screen, and if I thought the look on her face was heartbreaking before, I'd clearly never seen the pain envelope her like this.

She just read something. But what?

"What's wrong?" I ask her.

"Nothing." She moves from side to side.

"Winter."

"It's nothing, I promise. I have to shower. Kass will be here soon." She turns on her heels, but I steal her phone away from her. She's not quick enough to stop me. She has a few texts from Kendrick and Will, all asking her the same question. They want to know if the rumors are true. They're asking if I really gave up fighting.

The most recent one, which is also the text that turned Winter's smile upside down, rubs me the wrong way.

It's from an unknown number.

> Heard you're leaving next week. Can't wait for Haze to pay me another visit;)

What the fuck?

"Who's that?" I ask.

"I… I have no idea how she got my number." She doesn't directly answer my question, but she says enough.

I put the pieces together.

"Bianca?"

She nods.

"What has the psycho been saying to you?"

What's it going to take to get that damn girl off my back?

Am I going to have to personally find her a new boy to stalk?

Or file a restraining order?

Because I will if I have to.

"Winter, tell me," I insist when she doesn't answer. "What has she been saying to you?"

"Oh, you know, nothing much. The usual. That you slept with her the day I left town. That you had sex with her over and over again and lied to me about it." She looks at the ground.

Anger consumes me.

Then surface the memories…

My footsteps are fast-moving, both hesitant and determined. Both too slow and too fast. I have no idea why I'm here right now. I know this isn't going to fix anything, but I still find myself going up the stairs leading to Bianca's porch. This time feels different. I *feel different. I repeatedly pound on the door until she opens up.*

"Haze? You're here," Bianca states, but it sounds like she's having a hard time believing it. She steps aside and I walk in, silently staring at this girl who isn't that good-looking now that I really think about it. Sure, she has a nice body, but she doesn't have the nice mind to match. What's a nice house if the rooms are empty? What's a nice book cover if the pages are blank?

"I've missed you so much, babe." Her fingers cling to my shirt, spreading all over my chest as she presses her breasts to me. "I knew the rumors weren't true."

"What rumors?" I finally speak.

"Oh, it's nothing. Just a bunch of nonsense. People are saying you're with that Winter bitch."

Gee, I forgot how much she talks. It never bothered me before since I don't listen and easily shut her up, but right now, for the first time, I want her to keep talking.

"What's that supposed to mean?" I frown.

"They're saying that you have a thing for her or some shit." She doesn't wait for me to deny nor confirm her claims and straight-up gets down on her knees in front of me. I'm too stunned to react. People are saying that I have a thing for Winter? How come the whole fucking planet seems to see it except for me? Bianca unhooks my belt the same way she did many meaningless times before, except that now, I'm repulsed. I could gag. Confused, I circle her wrists and get her back on her feet.

"What's wrong?" she asks.

"Nothing."

Nothing's wrong. I'm still me. Nothing's changed, right? She nods and grips my collar to press her mouth to mine. It just takes a second. My mind is the victim of a hundred flashes. I see us at the motel. I can still hear her moaning while I kiss her neck.

Winter… Kingston…

I'm lying. Everything's changed. Everything. I pull away, looking at Bianca's face, her eyes, her lips. I look for traits that remind me of her. This girl who could be anywhere in the world right now.

"I have to go." I walk away.

"Haze, wait! Why are you leaving?" she calls, but I don't stop, swinging the front door open. Her words echo in my head. "Why are you leaving?" Deep down, I'm afraid… I'm afraid because I know exactly what my answer is…

"Because you're not her."

"She's lying. I didn't sleep with her." I take her hand, my eyes grazing over her perfect face, and pray that she'll believe me. "I promise you. She'd say anything to break us up."

She blows out a breath and looks up at me.

"I believe you."

My shoulders loosen up.

"I just wish she'd stop trying to ruin our relationship. She's gone too far, Haze. She's borderline obsessed."

"Don't worry about her. The girl's harmless. Just give it a few weeks and she'll find some other guy to transfer her daddy issues onto."

She nods, but she's not convinced.

"Come here." I capture her into my arms once more and kiss her forehead. After a minute, she tells me she has to hop into the shower before her cousin gets here. I watch her drag her feet to the bathroom and struggle to swallow the annoying lump occupying my throat.

My parents' reception is on Tuesday.

Then there's the prom, and on Friday, she'll be leaving me.

We're strong enough, I told her earlier, but I know we're both wondering the same thing…

Are we?

THIRTY

Betrayal And Champagne

Winter

"Please don't make me go," I whine as I climb inside Haze's car reluctantly. This is it. Tonight's the reception I've been having nightmares about.

I pull the sleeveless black dress Haze got for me back up to hide my exposed cleavage and curse. It's beautiful, it really is, but no dress could ever be beautiful enough to shake the bad feeling in my stomach. Nothing could numb the voice in my head whispering that the world's about to end…

"We'll be there one hour tops. Just long enough to know what the stupid announcement is," Haze says for the third time as he joins the traffic.

"What if it's a trap? What if he blows up the room and kills us all?" I say, aware of how overdramatic I sound. I don't care. I wouldn't put it past Tanner after what he's done.

"And risk hurting my parents? No, he's smarter than that. He's way too desperate to inherit the company. He changed his mind a few years back. He's been licking their boots forever."

"Do you think he was right?"

"About what?" he asks.

"About your enemies coming after you now that you're on your own." I fidget with the soft fabric sticking to my thigh.

"I don't know… but I need to get out there and show them that I'm not afraid. I'm not going to be looking over my shoulder for the rest of my life," he says and ironically does just that to check his blind spot and switch lanes.

"You better take me out to eat after this," I pout and look out at the neighborhood as it runs past the window.

"Behave tonight and I'll buy your cute ass as much food as it wants." He grins.

"And I want cuddles when we get home. A lot of cuddles."

"Then cuddles you shall have."

"I'm sorry, but I'm going to need you to pinky swear on that one."

"You're a child." He laughs.

"Pinky swear or I'm staying in the car." I cross my arms.

"We both know you'll eventually get hungry and come inside for the free food," he mocks.

Haze knows how much he's asking from me. When he told me he was going, I went back on my word. I can't let him go through this alone. His family is too much of a delicate topic. He says he's only going because of his father's threat to call the school and stop him from graduating, but I know it's because he's curious about the announcement. So, during the past few days, he's been at my beck and call, treating me like his life purpose is to fulfill my every desire. He's always been attentive to what I want but this… this is something else. He lets me choose the music during every single car ride and doesn't even bat an eye when I put on the cheesy pop songs he usually can't help commenting on.

It took a lot to convince Maria to let me stay with Haze. I have to call her every day after school to catch her up on how my exams are going. Most of them went a lot better than I expected. I didn't run out crying once, and, for me, that's a good sign.

The only way I could get some quality studying time living with Haze was by locking myself into his bedroom for a few hours every night.

I knew if I didn't, we'd end up studying each other.

Time flies, and before I realize it, Haze is pulling up to the longest driveway I've ever seen. High fences keep me from feeling poor at the sight of the most likely huge property they conceal. Haze stops the car in front of the black gate blocking the way and rolls his window down.

"Identifications, please," a deep voice says. I squint my eyes, looking for the intercom. It's well hidden by thick roots growing on each side of the gate.

Haze smiles.

"No way. Daryl, man, you still work here?" he asks.

The person on the other end doesn't speak for a while.

"No, it can't be. Haze, is that you?"

"In the flesh."

A loud beep follows and the gates open in a shriek. Haze speeds onto the road he seems to know very well, the distant house bordered by what seems to be acres of land taking my breath away. A water fountain stands in the middle of the driveway, making me wonder what other crazy luxurious things the Adamses own. This is the kind of house you see in the movies.

And I thought their lake house was big…

"Your house's bigger than the White House," I say.

"My parents' house," he corrects me. "I know, it's way too big for two people."

I scoff. "Oh, it's not just two people. There's the maid, the gardener, the butler, the chef, the—"

"Okay, smart-ass. I get it." He grins. A large number of cars—all equally expensive-looking—are neatly parked in front of the house. The driveway's packed, which is why I'm not surprised to see valets patiently waiting for us. I assume they have an underground parking or something.

Of course they do.

Add up the value of this house and the cars in its driveway and I'm pretty confident you'd get more than Kendrick, Kass, Will, Alex, Maria, and I will ever make in our lifetime combined.

Out of place. That's how I feel when one of the valets opens up my door and helps me out of the car.

"Miss," he says politely.

Haze gets out as well and throws the keys at a valet he also seems to recognize. Everybody looks so happy to see him it makes me wonder how long they've been working for his parents. Haze kisses my cheek when he notices the nervous wreck that I am and offers me his arm to hold. Here comes the scary part. We're going inside.

Quickly, heads turn and eyes grow in size. The *oh so fancy* people holding cocktail glasses look so uptight, my instinct is to look for the sticks coming out of their asses. They're judging us. They're judging *me.*

That's when the need to disappear really hits.

Under the ridiculously expensive dress I'm wearing, I'm still me. The same old Winter who couldn't buy herself another phone for months, and still wouldn't be able to get one if it wasn't for Haze, after she threw it in the toilet. I know that my stepfather, Harry, has been saving up to send me to college ever since I was a kid, but I'll only access that money when I move back home. And even then, it's an amount people like this probably make every twenty minutes.

I don't belong here. I never will.

"One hour and we're gone," Haze reminds me, sensing my panic. A waiter walks by us with a tray of champagne and stops dead in his track.

"Mr. Adams, we had no idea you were coming. It's a pleasure to see you again," he exclaims.

The whole staff is apparently in love with him.

Haze smiles. "Lawrence."

"I'm sure your father will be very happy to see you," he says.

"Well, that makes one of us." Haze makes a face, and the waiter only lets himself laugh for a second before he forces his serious face back on. He probably shouldn't be laughing at a joke about his boss. Something tells me Haze was the only member of the family treating his parents' employees like human beings.

We step into the large reception room, which I assume only exists to host events like this, and are immediately scrutinized by the masses. I spot them. Haze's parents. They're faking smiles and forcing laughter, probably trying to land an investor of some sort, while nodding their heads along to what looks like a very boring conversation.

They see us.

His mother's face lights up. She has pale brown hair and soft features. She's like a female version of Haze. He told me that she created a very prestigious clothing line—that Richard paid to launch—a year back and that if it wasn't for her husband, she wouldn't be working. She looks decent. Not nice, but decent. At least she can smile. God knows Haze's father doesn't understand that concept. Speaking of Mr. Block-of-ice, he glares at me from afar.

"They hate me," I whisper to Haze.

"No, they don't."

"Please, I'm a peasant to them. I'm a peasant trying to date the prince," I say in a high-pitched voice, and he laughs.

"If it makes you feel any better, they hate everyone. I don't even think they like each other." He sends us into a fit of giggles.

We finally come face-to-face with the two monsters hiding behind expensive clothing and jewelry. His mother slowly eyes me from head to toe, analyzing me, while Haze's father doesn't bother looking at me.

"You came." Richard speaks first, laying a hand on Haze's shoulder. Haze winces and wiggles away.

"Tanner was pretty convincing," Haze says.

"You two finally stopped fighting over stupid things, then?" Richard huffs.

Because trying to kill someone classifies as *stupid things…*

"Not even close." Haze's smile reeks of arrogance. He accepts the champagne a passing waiter offers him, takes a huge sip, and finishes the drink in one gulp.

Well, this is off to a great start.

"Aren't you going to give your mother a hug?" His mother opens her arms to him. Haze doesn't step into her embrace, which leaves her no choice but to very awkwardly force hug him. He doesn't return her hug, standing as still as a brick wall, until she pulls away. This is heartbreaking. It reminds me of my mom. Only difference is my mother doesn't hug me.

At least Haze's mother tries.

I inspect the room and find myself enlightened as to why they're talking to us. Everyone, without exception, is staring.

The Adamses are trying to make a good impression. My guess is they wish to look like a united family in front of potential business partners. I mean, he is their son.

"How handsome you've become, sweetie," his mother says and pretends to get emotional. Yes, *pretends*. There are no tears. Always look for the tears.

She's talking like she hasn't seen him in years. It can't really be that bad, can it? Doesn't Haze come home for Christmas? Is that why he said he never gets presents? Because he doesn't show up? Sadness gains control of me. My baby doesn't deserve to spend Christmas alone.

"Well, what are you waiting for, darling? Introduce us to your girlfriend." His mother clears her throat and looks at me.

"Mom, Dad, this is Winter," Haze says, disinterest obvious on his face. He sees right through their game.

"Call me Anita." She smiles as we shake hands. Richard stares down at our handshake like he's afraid my dirty peasant fingers will rub off on hers.

"I didn't know you had a girlfriend." She forces a bigger smile on her lips, her mouth stretching while her eyes remain empty.

"How could you? He never calls," Richard grunts, the remainder of the awkward tension from before coming back at full force.

"Where's Tanner?" Haze finds something, *anything* to fill the silence. I can't imagine just how desperate he must've been to change the subject to bring up his brother, out of all people.

"Oh, he's here somewhere with his new girlfriend."

"Rose? How is she new?" Haze asks his mother.

"Not Rose." She takes a sip of champagne and looks out onto the dance floor. "I have to go back to my guests, but you two enjoy yourselves," she says before walking away. As for Richard, he straight-up leaves without a goodbye or reason. *Charming.*

"They seem… nice," I say to Haze, and we both break out into laughter. I'm not mad. Nor am I offended. Sometimes in life, you just have to accept that some people suck and there is absolutely nothing you can do about it. So, you keep your head high, move on, and let them take their "*suckery*" elsewhere.

"You have no idea how glad I am that you're here right now." Haze brings his mouth to mine, and I kiss him back, the slight taste of the alcohol he just chugged lingering on my lips.

"Aren't you two adorable?" A voice I'd recognize anywhere makes us jump.

No way.

Will.

And Kendrick.

What the hell?

I've barely talked to my cousin since Haze told him his snitching to the West side almost got me killed. He apologized a hundred times. And although he definitely didn't want me to go live with Haze, the guilt eventually won him over.

"What are you two idiots doing here?" Haze asks.

"You bring Winter into a party that's literally an open invite for someone to attack and think we won't come?" Kendrick scoffs. "You're funny, Adams."

They're both wearing tuxedos. William Martin and a tie? Not an everyday combo. He keeps on playing with it, clearly uncomfortable.

"You gave up fighting, man. Everybody knows it. She's not safe with you anymore." Will shrugs.

"How did you even find out about this? Or get in?" I ask.

"Believe it or not but Haze's lovely brother put us on the guest list. He came to us and said he was afraid someone might give their revenge a shot and Haze might need backup to protect you," Kendrick explains.

"You're telling me that Tanner came to you?" Haze asks a lot louder than he intended to. Tanner did say that he wanted to make things right. That he'd even help protect me if he had to. But Haze doesn't buy it.

"Yeah, don't worry, we're not buying his nice-guy act for a second either, but we figured it was way too suspicious not to come," Will says. "Oh, alcohol." He picks a drink off a nearby waiter's tray.

"Sure. Let's get drunk to protect Winter." Kendrick rolls his eyes. Will doesn't listen, taking a sip of champagne.

"Oh, come on, from the size of this crib and the amount of rich people in the same room, the police will be here before any fighter even steps foot inside this house."

"You guys literally just walked in," I mock.

"Shh!" he dismisses me. "Do you think there are any billionaire chicks looking for a boyfriend somewhere around here?"

Oh, I see what's happening. He's on the rebound. He's crushed over Kass and acting out. He's obviously heartbroken. This can*not* end well.

"I'll go check." Will smirks and dives into the crowd. Kendrick says something about free food and catches up to him. I laugh. If it isn't to look for a girl, it's to look for the buffet.

Boys will be boys.

"SO WHAT DO YOUR PARENTS DO for a living?" A lady wearing golden earrings—that I'm pretty sure are actually made of gold and not the cheap stuff I always buy—looks me up and down.

"My mom's a hairdresser, and I never knew my dad. Not that it's common to have a present dad when your mom got knocked up at sixteen, you know?" I say and enjoy watching her face fall apart. She smiles uncomfortably. Everyone I've talked to tonight, *every single one*, has somehow asked me if my parents are rich by subbing the words "to be rich" with "for a living." I've been having the time of my life making them crazy uncomfortable since I caught on. Haze and I are officially the talk of the night. The Adams son is dating a non-millionaire.

How could he stoop so low? I already know what they think of me. Might as well have fun with it.

"You'll have to excuse me. I have to go sell drugs. Have a wonderful night." I turn away and pull on Haze's sleeve to get him to come with me. He's laughing so hard he's suffocating.

"I can't believe you just did that."

"Nothing but the truth, Hazie, nothing but the truth." I smile as he finishes his seventh glass of champagne. He's been drinking a lot. I didn't comment because he actually seems to be having fun, which, *news flash*, was very unlikely to happen tonight. I'd be on the floor right now if I'd had this much champagne. I think it's his way of coping. He's hurting. I'll definitely be the one driving since I only had half a glass hours ago.

"Dance with me." Haze sets his cocktail glass on the buffet table and holds out his hand in my direction.

"You're drunk," I laugh. He pulls me closer to kiss the corner of my mouth.

"I'm drunk on you, baby," he whispers.

I'm about to kiss him when the sound of someone repeatedly hitting a cocktail glass with a spoon rings out in the room.

"May I have everyone's attention, please?"

We look up to see who's talking.

Tanner.

He's standing on top of the massive spiral staircase built in the center of the room. We haven't seen him once in the few hours that we've been here. We haven't seen much of the East side either. Last I remember, Will was off talking to some blonde and Kendrick was eating his body weight in food somewhere. I almost forgot about his announcement.

"First, on behalf of my wonderful parents, I'd like to say that we are incredibly happy that you could all make it tonight." He smiles. When the guys said Tanner invited them earlier, I saw the tiniest light glow in Haze's eyes. It was a short, fleeting moment of hope. Even after what Tanner did, Haze would still like to believe his brother can be redeemed. I grab his hand and intertwine our fingers to show him my support.

"As you all know, we are gathered here tonight to support my dear mother's new clothing collection. But before we proceed with her speech, I have a big announcement to make."

Haze doesn't seem to realize how tight he is squeezing my hand, but I don't budge one bit and let him drain the blood out of my fingers. He needs it.

"Maybe some of you don't know, but I'm the eldest son. I'm twenty-two. And I feel like the time has come for me to start building a life for myself by pursing the Adams legacy."

A heavy hush descends over the reception room, the chatters and whispers dying down abruptly.

"My father once told me, the son who married first would become the legal heir of Adams Inc."

Haze's jaw drops.

"And so, it is my pleasure to tell you that I have found the woman I want to spend the rest of my life with." He clears his throat. "This woman and I go way back, and even though we lost our ways when we were younger, we've recently found each other again. Honey, come join me," he says to someone on the second floor. We can't see them from where we are.

Then it happens.

She walks down the stairs, and I immediately want to stick the collapsing pieces of Haze's heart back together.

"Everyone, meet my wife, Riley Evans."

Color drains from Haze's face as his brother cuts the very last thread still holding their relationship together. As he daggers him right in the back. As he shoots the final bullet.

The bullet Haze will never heal from…

Nothing makes sense. Tanner and Riley? When? How? Where did this even come from?

"But that's not all," Tanner adds.

Riley climbs back up the stairs for a second, and joins Tanner again, but this time… she's holding the familiar angel that I've grown to love even through the hell Haze and I went through. One second is enough.

Everything falls into place.

Every lie finds its truth…

"This is our son, Jacob."

THIRTY-ONE

Flames And Revenge

Tanner's eyes haven't moved. They're stuck on Haze. He's staring. He's waiting for a reaction, for Haze to break something—*everything.* And I know I'd be lying if I said that I'm not waiting, too. Haze hasn't moved a muscle. Or spoken. Not once. He's in shock.

"Haze." I call his name because, frankly, it's all I can do. I want him to look at me. Just me. I want him to know how sorry I am, even though sorry doesn't come close to scratching the surface of how I'm feeling right now.

Only Kendrick understands how bad this is. Will is completely clueless. My eyes meet Richard's for a second. He's not surprised. I think he knew. I always said that Jacob had to come from the Adamses. I was right. He did. *Just not from the Adams we thought…*

"Get him out of here," Kendrick tells me, and if he thinks Haze is about to lose it, he won't have to ask me twice. I turn to my boyfriend, who seems to be in some sort of a trance. He's fighting every nerve in his body not to explode.

"Haze, let's just leave, please," I whisper and grasp his arm.

He sees right through me.

"You fucked my brother?" he finally shouts, his voice resonating across the huge reception room.

There isn't a guest that doesn't gasp. Tanner included.

"Haze, brother. No need to make a scene. Let's talk about this like adults," Tanner begs.

He's embarrassed. *Good.*

"Don't you dare pretend that he's overreacting," I say, surprised at the words coming out of my mouth.

"Winter, with all due respect, this is none of your business," Tanner says rudely.

That's what makes him snap.

"With all due respect?" Haze cackles. "I'm sorry, when did you ever respect her? Was it before or after you tried to murder her?"

An even louder wave of gasps cuts through the air.

"Haze, stop!" his mother exclaims. This isn't good for business. She may be the queen of false emotions, but this… this she can't fake. Even Richard looks panicked.

"I'm sorry. Are Daddy's partners not in on the criminal sons' secret?" Haze asks. "Wait, what am I saying? Of course they're not. I'm looking at the people who saw the murder of their five-year-old daughter as bad business."

Here comes wave of gasps number three.

I swear this is better than TV.

So, Haze's parents do know about the fights. I assume they

don't know everything, but they are aware of their boys dipping their toes into a few shady things.

Riley's standing back with Jacob as he hides his head into his mother's neck. He never liked shouting. He's the truly innocent one here. He can't help that he was born into such a dysfunctional family. He shouldn't be witnessing this.

"It's him? The guy you cheated on me with?" he addresses Riley. "My own brother?"

Tanner turns to his "wife" and motions not to answer.

"Haze, let's put all this nonsense in the past and move forward, please. Or if you want to talk about it, let's take this outside," Tanner says.

"You'd like that, wouldn't you? For me to stop airing your dirty laundry to possible investors? Well, too bad. I'm not going anywhere. How long? How long did this last?"

Tanner fidgets with his tuxedo sleeves.

"I said how long?" Haze screams.

"The whole time," Tanner finally breathes out.

Ouch.

Haze shakes his head in disgust.

"Did you two know about this?" He gazes at his parents. "Did you know back then that my girlfriend was pregnant with my brother's kid?"

People hold their breath, as though they fear the sound might keep them from hearing what Richard will say next.

"Yes, we knew," he admits. "We caught her sneaking out of

the house once."

There goes another bullet straight into Haze's chest. They knew he was beating himself up over it, and they didn't say anything.

"But that doesn't mean you and your brother shouldn't talk this out," Richard has the audacity to add.

"Talk this out? You want us to talk this out. Okay, fine, what do you want to talk about, bro? The fact that Riley was my first girlfriend and now you're married to her? Or the fact that you were sleeping with her the whole time we were dating? Or maybe you want to talk about the fact that she got pregnant with your kid but pretended that it was mine because you refused to pay for your son?"

"Haze Christopher Adams, that's enough!" His father raises his voice at him. Haze's middle name is Christopher?

"So, to all of you rich investors, I have one question to ask. Is my brother really the type of person you'd like to invest millions in? I suggest you don't. Because he'll fuck your wife, get her pregnant, and then marry her to steal your company."

Holy shit!

"Security!" Richard yells, but we both know it's too late. Haze's already said too much and probably cost his family a colossal amount of money. A tall man that's shaped like a fridge starts to walk toward us, a pained expression on his face. He doesn't want to do this.

"Don't bother, Daryl," Haze tells the man, "we're leaving."

He looks back at his family. "Don't ever contact me again. None of you. I'd rather be an orphan than have a family like this," he says through gritted teeth and rushes to the exit. "Desiree would be real fucking proud."

As if Desiree's name is a knife jamming into her stomach, Haze's mother pulls an agonized face. I suppose it's been forever since she heard her daughter's name. That tends to happen when you do everything in your power to cover up your kid's death.

Kendrick, Will, and I carefully follow Haze. None of the guests move. They watch us walk away in silence. We've barely stepped foot outside the house when we hear someone chasing after us.

"Haze, wait, I'm begging you," Tanner calls from afar.

Haze turns around very calmly and waits for his brother to reach us, but I know better than to think it's because he's ready to hear him out.

"I never meant for this to happen. I was stupid. She's the one who snuck into my room one night when you were out with Vic. She came on to me. She said she liked older guys and…"

Bam!

Haze's fist repeatedly grinds into his brother's face. Tanner falls to the ground like a magnet drawn to his other half. It takes both Kendrick and Will to get Haze off him, but the damage is already done. That's going to leave one heck of a bruise. Tanner groans in pain, still on the ground.

"Haze, please. We're brothers. I didn't know Riley meant this much to you. I…" Tanner's words trail off.

"Don't you fucking get it? She didn't!" Haze screams louder than ever before. "*You* did…"

Just like that, the curtain drops and the lights come on.

The truth settles around us and we know… *that's* what this is really about.

Haze doesn't care that Riley cheated on him. He cares that his brother, who he secretly considered to be the last of his family, could do something so horrible to him. He would rather die than say it, but deep down, he hoped that maybe one day, years from now, he'd be able to save their relationship and get his brother back. But, tonight, Tanner proved him wrong.

Tonight, he showed him that he has no one.

That he never did.

"We're not brothers anymore. You're dead to me. Dead. If I ever see you again, I'll end you. Are we clear?" Haze spits and darts to his car that the valet just parked out front. I tell him to let me drive, because he drank way too much to even go anywhere near the wheel, and he nods, climbing into the passenger seat and shutting the door closed.

MY STEPFATHER ALWAYS SAYS THAT THE road to inner peace can be very lonely… but that, sometimes, a little loneliness is precisely what you need. I never really understood just how true that is until now. That's what Haze is. A lonely soul desperate for peace. A lonely kid who doesn't know how to handle *not* being lonely anymore. He spent his entire life alone, and now that he has someone who cares, he's waiting for things to go wrong. For the rain to come pouring down and wash away the love he's been given.

He hasn't said a word to me since we left his parents' house. He slouched into his seat, rested his forehead to the window, and let his mind wander to a place I could only wish to uncover. I can't stand seeing him like this.

"Do you want to talk about it?" I finally ask.

"Nope," he says.

"Is there anything I can do?" I slow down in anticipation of the light turning red.

"Just… stop talking, please."

Harsh.

"Haze, I'm just trying to help."

"Then stop trying."

Immediately, my self-respect screams that I can't let him talk to me this way. I turn into a random and deserted mall parking lot. It's late. It's almost midnight.

"What are you doing?"

I turn the key in the ignition and let the engine die while I unbuckle my seat belt and turn sideways to face him.

"Let me make something clear. I'm a lot of things, Haze. But I'm not the girl you take your anger out on. If you want to be alone tonight, it's fine, you can tell me. But not like this."

He throws his head back with a deep sigh. “I’m sorry. I’m being an asshole.”

This is too much for him. *Tonight* is too much. The alcohol, the announcement. This day needs to end.

“No, I get that you’re mad, Haze. I would be, too. I want you to take all the time you need, but I’m not the enemy. I want to be here for you, but if you want me to g—”

He cuts me off. “Believe me, that’s the last thing I want.”

I’m about to answer when he shoots up in his seat.

“What was that?”

I frown.

“What?”

He unbuckles his seat belt. “Get out of the car.”

“Why?” I ask, freaked.

“Winter, get out of the fucking car! *Now!*” he shouts.

I know that look. That panic.

Something’s wrong. This isn’t about our silly fight anymore.

From there, everything’s a blur. I’m barely aware of how fast I rush out of the vehicle. I’m barely aware of Haze catching my hand in to his. All I know is he starts to run. So I do, too.

I run.

As far and as fast as humanly possible.

Then I hear it…

The click.

But it’s the explosion… that really stops my heart.

Haze tackles me to the ground, his body shielding mine as

we hit the concrete. Uncontrollable sobs fill my throat. But pain has nothing to do with it. For once, I'm not crying because I'm sad. I'm crying because I'm *horrified.*

"Look at me. Are you okay?" His hands are shaking from the rush of adrenaline. He keeps analyzing me the way he always does as he looks for a wound of some sort. "Are you hurt?"

"What just happened?" The words trickle out of my mouth.

"What everybody said would happen." His voice shudders as he wraps his arms around me. He doesn't want to say it, but he doesn't need to. I know…

Someone just tried to kill us.

He holds me against his chest and apologizes, over and over again. That's all he can do. Passing cars pull over to the side of the road. Witnesses run to us, asking us if we're okay, if we're hurt, but I can't bring myself to answer. Hell, I can barely bring myself to *breathe.* I think I hear a girl say help is on the way, but I'm not sure. We should be dead. We *would* be dead. If Haze hadn't heard whatever the hell it was that gave the bomb away, they'd be pulling our burnt corpses out right now.

I watch as fire rises in the empty parking lot, the pile of scrap that used to be Haze's car melting away under scorching flames, and remember what Tanner said to Haze a few days ago. I can still hear his voice as he says it. *"Someone's after you, brother."*

And I'm terrified…

Because he was right.

THIRTY-TWO

Traitors And Last Days

"No way. I'm not going on that." I cross my arms over my chest and ogle the *death* ride—I'm not exaggerating; that's literally what it's called—Haze's been talking about since we stepped foot inside the amusement park.

"Yes, you are. We only have two days left together. You're not just standing by while we have fun." Haze circles my shoulder with his arm, and I peer at Kendrick, Alex, Will, Mia, and Kass walking behind us. When Haze showed up at my locker after this morning's exam and suggested that we go enjoy ourselves for a change, I knew I had to spend at least one of my last days in Florida with my family. He's not the only one I'll be leaving on Friday, and although I'm glad that he did, I still can't believe that Haze let the East side tag along.

"Fine. But when I throw up all over your jacket, just remember you asked for it."

He smirks. "I promise I'll hold your hair."

I laugh as we walk to the overly long line of people waiting for their dose of *Death*. We've been here for a few hours already. I went on as many rides as I could with them, but I'll gladly have Will and Kendrick call me a chicken until I'm eighty to escape this one. Giant steel balls tied to wires being thrown hundreds of feet into the sky? Thanks, but *hell no.*

I glance back at Kass, who's been conversing with Will for a few minutes now. They're laughing. I'm not up-to-date with their scandalous forbidden love story, but I'd say things are going better. As for Kendrick and Alex, they look like kids, amazed by the lights, the commotion, the music. Man, the East side really needs to get out more. And by get out, I mean to places that don't include dark alleys, abandoned buildings, or creepy sewer fighting spots.

Mia, Alex's girlfriend, easily fit right in with us. She's the one who suggested that we set a *no phone* rule for the rest of the day. Haze and I were happy to oblige. One, because it allows us to truly live in the moment, and two… because we don't want to receive any more calls from the police asking us to come back to the station. The investigation's still ongoing even if they labeled it a random attack. Someone tried to blow up two kids, and it's got people talking. The detectives assigned to the case haven't been much help, but it's only because *we* haven't been much help. From the second they showed up at the scene, we knew we couldn't tell them the truth.

Oh, it's actually quite simple, Officers. You see, my boyfriend here used to be involved in very high-paying illegal street fights and is also, overall, just an asshole who gets people mad. Good day!

It looks like Tanner was right. Someone is after Haze. But who? We're not anywhere closer to figuring that out. The list of suspects is endless. Who knows how or when the bomb was even placed under his car. As soon as Maria was informed of what happened, she forbade me from sleeping at Haze's place again. She says it's gotten out of control. That being near him is too dangerous, but has that stopped me from letting him sneak in through my bedroom window every night since? *Nope.*

She's right. About everything.

My brain knows it.

But my heart doesn't care.

I dodge flying cotton candy when Alex and Kendrick start throwing food at each other. I smile. I can't help it. I'm going to miss these idiots. But most importantly, *my* idiot.

"I can't believe that in a few days I'll be back in my bedroom full of boy bands posters," I mutter to myself, and Haze's hand grows rigid in mine. I know he hates hearing me talk about it. He's still hoping that I'll change my mind. "Haze…" I pine for his forgiveness. Now's not the time to get into a fight. The closer we get to the big day, the longer and bigger our arguments become. I think we're finally starting to feel the walls closing in on us.

"What are you two lovebirds fighting about?" Will asks, noticing Haze's frown.

"Is that even a question? She's leaving Friday," Kendrick says.

Haze doesn't reply, his jaw tightening. He might have said yes to the East side coming, but that doesn't make them any less annoying to him. We wait for a few more minutes. As the line for *Death* lessens, the nerves in my stomach expand. The employee finally motions to come closer since we're next.

"You guys go ahead. I'm not dying today."

Haze smolders his eyes at me and stops me right before I wiggle my way under the red rope marking the line's perimeter.

"I'll stay with you," he says to be a good boyfriend, but I know how much he wants to do it.

"No, go. I'll be fine. I promise."

"Are you sure?"

"Absolutely. I'll go get something to eat. I'm starving."

"You're the best." A riveting smile tugs at his lips.

I love seeing him like this. I love seeing him smile.

Really smile.

"I'm hungry, too. Get me one of whatever it is you're getting," Kendrick says.

"Me too," Will adds.

"Same for me," Alex joins.

And… I'm feeding them all.

The usual.

I laugh and watch them get inside the giant balls—*no cute way to say it, sorry*—as the worries on my mind slip away. It's been so long since we've just been happy. No problems. No attacks. No crazy girl trying to ruin my relationship. There's always some kind of disaster recently, but not today. Today's our day.

"I love you." Haze turns his head to look at me as he walks.

"I love you more," I say right back. Kendrick starts gagging as Will and Alex break out into a fit of chuckles. They think we're cheesy, but I don't care. Right now, we're happy.

And it's all that matters.

I walk toward the food court, my stomach grumbling loudly, and stop in front of the soft pretzels stand. I get in line behind a family of five and fidget with my shirt, my only source of entertainment a rock on the ground. Intent on winning the *no phone* challenge, I kick it, roll it with the tip of my shoe, and wait for my turn to come. The young girl in front of me drops a teddy bear I assume she won today, and I pick it up, giving it back to her.

Then, I see him.

A few feet away from me.

The person I'd somehow convinced myself had stopped existing the day we left him behind. The one guy whose betrayal I will never forgive.

Blake.

He's looking right at me, standing completely still in the dense and moving crowd. I can't tear my gaze away, the deep blue of his eyes taking me back to the last time I saw him. He was going to pull the trigger. He was this close to killing me. Then he got shot in the leg. Kendrick told me about the rumors. The whispers on the street. People said that Blake had left town. He sure couldn't come back to school anymore, not when Kendrick had promised to destroy him if he ever saw him again.

But he's obviously returned. Along with his ability to walk.

My fear turns into terror when he does the simplest yet creepiest thing I've ever seen.

He smiles.

"Miss, are you ready to order?" the stand employee asks, and I nod, stepping forward to tell her what I want.

By the time I look again… he's gone.

I'm not hungry anymore, but I still order seven pretzels double the size of my hands for everybody. At the same time, I spot them in the distance. They're laughing, radiating happiness.

"You have no idea what you just missed," Kendrick says, wrapping his arm around my neck to tousle my hair. I have to punch him twice to get my freedom back.

"He's right. You would've had the time of your life if you weren't such a chicken," Will mocks.

"Don't listen to them." Haze smiles as I distribute the food among the pigs—I mean, the *guys*.

I consider telling them about Blake. I made the mistake of not telling them about the unknown number texting me once, and we all know how that turned out. I'm about to, but when Will pies Kendrick in the face with the pretzel and the group howls with laughter, I can't go through with it. Blake's presence might be a pure coincidence. I know they'd want us to leave when there really is no need to overreact.

It can wait until we get home.

"Is everything okay?" Haze asks suspiciously.

He knows me too well.

"Yes, everything's fine," I lie, getting on my tiptoes to kiss his cheek. "For the first time in forever, everything's fine," I repeat.

The night has fallen, and the colorful lights spreading all around the site fascinate us almost as much as it does the many children still dragging their parents around. They'll be going home soon and surrendering the amusement park to older crowds. The teenagers looking for a thrill will come flowing through the front gates soon.

"What about the Ferris wheel?" Mia claps her hands in excitement and points to the rotating ride.

"Why not? I could use a nap," Haze mocks, and we laugh, as in all of us. Even Kendrick. I never thought I'd see the day these two would *kind of* get along.

"I wouldn't mind," Kass says, peeking at Will from the corner of her eye.

"Me neither." He clears his throat.

I smile. Can they be any more obvious?

I bet these two are just *dying* to secretly hold hands up there.

"Why is it so far though?" I wince. I've been wearing my new shoes all day and my feet are killing me.

Haze doesn't say anything, just steps in my way and beckons me to climb on his back, which I do without so much as a second thought. I laugh and wrap my legs around his waist as he runs across the crowd too fast for the guys to catch up. I snort like an actual pig and suddenly give the expression "piggyback rides" its meaning. We're both howling like idiots. *Yep, it's official.* We've just reached a whole new level of cheesy.

He lets me down, and we wait for the group to meet us in front of the line. When they do, we form the teams. Haze goes with me, Will goes with Kass—*shocker*—Alex with Mia and… Kendrick finds himself alone.

"What about me?" Kendrick complains.

"Don't worry, I'll go with you, handsome." A sixty-something-looking lady in front of us turns around and offers Kendrick a toothless smile before taking his hand. "Come on, we're next."

Kendrick widens his eyes as she drags him to their seat. We're all laughing so hard our stomach hurts. Minutes later, we're good to go, the sound of the engine roaring indicating the beginning of very slow motion. The view is mesmerizing, top of the wheel or not. I look at Haze to see him already staring at me.

"View's this way." I smile, and he opens his mouth. I cut him off before he gets a chance to speak. "I swear to God if you say something cliché like 'My view's better,' I'll slap you in the face."

"Why you always got to ruin my lines, Kingston?" he teases and puts his arm around me.

"I had to." I put my hands up. "Before someone calls the cheesy couple police on us."

He doesn't reply, silently staring at me. Today's been perfect. *He's* been perfect. On his face is the smile that started it all. The smile that put my dumb ass into this mess in the first place. The only smile with the power to shake me, make me, and shatter me all at once.

"Is this the part when you kiss me on top of the Ferris wheel?" I ask, but I already know the answer.

He chews on his lip, his eyes falling to mine, and smirks. "You bet your ass it is."

When his mouth meets mine and his fingers brush my jaw, I want to die. Not because I don't love him. Not because I don't care. But because I do. Too much. Too hard. Too *everything*. The love, the familiar taste of his lips, the feverish need only he gives me. It makes my heart bleed.

Because I know in a few days, I'll be on a plane. A plane taking me somewhere he won't be.

"Attention please. We kindly ask the couple in the back to get a room. Thank you," Kendrick calls from afar. Will, Alex, and Mia burst out laughing. We stop kissing. Kass and Will have been so busy mentally stripping each other down it's a wonder they even noticed we were making out.

Then, the magical moment ends. We come back down to earth, the pressure of all the things the next day will bring weighing on me. I can't believe that prom is tomorrow.

We spend the rest of the night talking with Irene, the kind granny Kendrick rode the Ferris wheel with. She's sixty-eight years old, and her husband proposed to her on top of this exact Ferris wheel forty-seven years ago. They constantly came back for their anniversary until he passed away from cancer. Today is their anniversary. She still comes. Every year. Without exception. She does it to remember him. The love of her life.

This is the most beautiful story I've heard in a long time.

The drive back to Maria's place feels heavy, stressful. It's been like this since I told Haze that I was leaving. When night falls, marking the end of yet another day, he becomes this dry, cold person.

"Thank you for today." I smile when he parks his new car on the side of the street. Maria's working a night shift tonight, which means that Haze might actually be able to get in using the front door.

"Why?" He smiles.

"You didn't have to say yes to them coming, but you did. Thank you for making a compromise."

"Yeah, well, maybe I'm hoping you'll do the same for me when the time comes." He isn't smiling anymore. He's icy. It doesn't take a genius to understand what he's talking about.

"Haze, can we just…" I pause. "Not do this tonight?"

"Then when? Tell me. Please. Because I can feel you slipping through my fingers a bit more every day, and it's driving me insane. Are you really going back?"

I sigh, well aware that the answer he so desperately wants is not one that I can give him.

"I tried today. I really did." He speaks again. "And it worked. For a second there, I let myself forget that in less than forty-eight hours, the only person who makes me happy will be on a plane taking her miles away from me, but I can't ignore it anymore, Winter. The happier we are right now, the harder it's going to be when you leave."

"If it were you in my shoes, right now. What would you do? If your entire life, your family, your friends were in another country. What would you do?" I reach for his hand.

"I'd stay. Because I love you." He takes his hand back, his anger eating him whole. He says that now… but he doesn't fully understand what it means to have a family. People that he can trust. To feel *safe*. I have that back home.

"Haze, I just… you know where I stand. I'm homesick. I miss being able to sleep at night without wondering if someone's coming for me. I miss my stepsiblings, my stepdad. I miss my best friend. They matter to me."

"But I don't…" he says quietly, like he's talking to himself, and doesn't wait for me to tell him how wrong he is. Instead, he reaches over to unbuckle my seat belt, and I stare at him in shock.

"I can't. I can't just stand by and wait for you to leave me. I'm sorry." His words cut me open.

"Haze, please don't do this. We don't have much time left," I beg. "Come inside, we'll—"

"Have a good night, Winter." He stretches and opens my car door for me. I can't believe him. He's kicking me out.

"Fine, be mad at me. But I love you. More than anything. So

when you're sleeping alone tonight, it's by choice. I'm not going to apologize for missing my home."

"Just like I'm not going to apologize for loving mine. My life is here, Winter. Not in some snow-buried country." Emotions deplete from his voice. He's shutting me out. The way he always does when things get hard.

"Fine. Then we're clear." I close my watery eyes, take a deep breath, and get out of his car without looking back. No one's home yet.

Kass's going to Morgan's birthday party tonight, and everybody was riding with Will, which means the guys have to drop off Alex and Mia on the way back. I hear the roar of Haze's car echo as it screeches down the street, and it takes everything in me not to fall to my knees right there and cry all the tears my body allows me to. I insert the key into the hole but curse in annoyance when the door opens by itself. Kass must've forgotten to lock up again. I enter the house and drop my stuff on the counter.

"Hello, Winter."

I jump and look up.

He's right there. The guy who gave me nightmares. He's casually standing in my kitchen. And the only thing on my mind when he takes a step toward me is the fact that this could've all been avoided.

If only I had told the truth…

"Blake?"

THIRTY-THREE

Prom And Disasters

I've regretted fighting with Haze a lot in the past few weeks. I've wanted to get a second chance at a conversation and slap some sense into myself way too many times to count. But I've *never* regretted fighting with him as much as I am regretting it right now. Because the row I was in with him… is the reason I find myself alone with a psychopath.

I should've told the guys. But I didn't. Because I wanted this perfect day to last. I wanted us to be careless teenagers. Just *once.*

"How the hell did you get in here?" I ask, finding the pepper spray in my purse and holding it up to his face. I've been cherishing it ever since the Ryan incident.

"Easy!" He puts his hands up in surrender. "The door was open. I was worried someone broke in."

I scoff at his pathetic excuse. The only intruder in this house is him and he knows it.

"You need to leave, right now." I try to sound as threatening as I possibly can.

"I'm not here to hurt you, Winter. I promise, I just want to talk."

"Not interested. Get the hell out!"

He holds his hands up to his face—probably in anticipation of getting sprayed in the eyes—and steps forward. But the last thing I want is to get into a fistfight with him when I'm home alone, so I jerk away, reach for the door, and swing it open… but I can't run out of the house.

Because Will's standing in the doorway.

I have never been happier to see this buffoon.

I might not die today.

"What's wrong? Have you seen yourself in the mirror?" he mocks, but his bad joke flies right by me. He quickly spots what I was running from—or should I say, *who*—and his face collapses. Kendrick walks in seconds later and displays a similar reaction, but the rage crawling out of him allows me to prepare for what he intends to do.

"Kendrick, no!" It takes every ounce of strength in my body to stop my cousin from pouncing on Blake. I'm not sure Maria would be pleased to see her white welcome mat has turned red when she comes back tonight.

"What the hell are you doing here?" Kendrick barks as Will pulls me behind him.

"I came here to apologize," Blake dares to lie.

"Apologize? Are you serious right now? You didn't push me on the sidewalk. You tried to kill my family. You can shove your apology up your a—"

Blake interrupts him. "I heard you're a member short."

"So?" Kendrick's fists are weapons. Weapons that Blake will

be closely introduced to if he doesn't leave soon.

"I want back in. Please, I'm sorry. Betraying you was the biggest mistake of my life."

He's lying. That's all he knows how to do.

"Get the hell out of my house before I kill you." Kendrick strides to him and stops barely one inch away from his ex-fighter's face.

"Kendrick, we were best friends," Blake says, upset that his plan to get our trust and murder us in our sleep isn't working.

"We weren't best friends." A tiny bit of emotion peeks through my cousin's voice. "We were brothers… and you betrayed me. You betrayed all of us."

Understanding that sweet-talking Kendrick isn't his way in, Blake turns to me. He's even dumber than I thought if he believes he has better chances with me.

"Winter, when I saw you at the fair today, I just… I realized how much I missed the East side. I had to at least try," he says. "You have to believe me, I never meant to hurt you."

The laugh Kendrick emits next is loud, throaty—chilling.

"I'm sorry, you mean to tell me that you accidentally tied her up and pressed a gun to her head? You don't just trip into a fucking murder attempt!"

The fist Kendrick puts up causes Blake to finally take his warning seriously.

"Fine, I'm leaving." He walks to the door. "But I really am sorry. I learned from my mistake. I'd do anything for a second chance."

"Yeah, and I'm the queen of England." Will rolls his eyes.

Probably because he'd like to leave with his two legs, Blake exits Maria's property as Kendrick carefully watches through the window to make sure he gets back into his car on the other side of the street. Then, when the threat goes dormant, they turn to me.

"When he saw you today at the fair? What the hell is he talking about?" Kendrick reminds me of what Blake said.

Busted…

I LIE AWAKE IN MY SOON-to-be empty bedroom and replay the conversation I just had with the guys in my head. So… to sum it up: I'm a moron. They wouldn't let me hear the end of it, and what's worst is I can't even blame them. They're right. I should've told them. Who knows what could've happened if Will hadn't walked in when he did?

Plus, because my guilt isn't unbearable enough as it is, Haze decided to take up all the remaining room in my brain and steal any chance of sleep away from me. I can't stop thinking about him alone at his place.

I haven't had the guts to ask him if the two of us are still going to prom together tomorrow.

Or if there's even still an *us* at all…

I'm about to pick up my phone to text him when it vibrates.

I'm an idiot.

I let out a huge breath of relief.

Why?

The girl I love is leaving soon and we're fighting

I sit up on my bed and type a reply inhumanly fast.

That sucks. Who's the lucky girl?

Her name's Winter.
She's beautiful, funny but beyooond stubborn.
Maybe you've heard of her.

Just saw her actually. She told me she loves you too.

I wish I was with her now.

Yeah? What are you going to do about it?

Not sure. I'm thinking sneak in through her bedroom window and give her the best makeup sex of her life

I blush.

Well, that escalated quickly.

She says to text her when you're almost there.

He stops replying and leaves me hanging. A minute later, my phone vibrates again.

No need.

I'm at her window.

Of course.

I run to the glass, and sure enough, he's right there, looking at me with puppy eyes. I push my window open.

"What are you doing?" I find myself laughing, trying not to wake up everyone with my dying seal laughter. Seriously, there is no such thing as a cute laugh. There's the laugh at 3:00 a.m. when you're alone stuffing your face to a Netflix movie, and there's the laugh when you're in public.

"I've always been told to follow my dreams." He throws me one of his *oh so famous* pickup lines, and I pretend to gag.

He chuckles at my reaction.

"Maria isn't home yet. Get in through the front door."

"Why?"

"So that you don't risk breaking your back, duh."

"But, Kingston… where's the fun in that?" He smirks and does what he's done almost every night recently, easily reaching my window and sneaking inside a bedroom that clearly wasn't expecting him. I've spent the last two hours packing. He doesn't acknowledge the mess once, standing tall next to my bed as his blue eyes travel from my face to my Disney pajamas. He smiles at my outfit but doesn't comment.

"I'm sorry," he breathes out after a few seconds of silence.

"Sorry? Is that all you got?" I taunt. "You think I'm going to forgive you that easy?"

His eyes grow in shock.

"I *know* you're going to forgive me that easy."

"Well, you're wrong."

"Is that so?" He tilts his head to the right and steps closer to me. I make it a point to tease him by stepping back although I know my average-sized bedroom won't allow this *You push, I pull* game of ours for too long.

"Yes," I say unconvincingly. When my back hits my closet and his body meets mine, we both put down the weapons and give in to the need—the urge.

We can't control it.

We kiss.

But it's not soft. Or gentle. It's both eager and sloppy. Both sad and happy. We're miserable and desperate for this kiss, tugging at each other's hair, clothes, faces. We're desperate for forever, and we're terrified, horrified, *panicked*… because forever ends tomorrow.

His fingers dig into my shoulders as he pushes my hair away to kiss my neck. Taste it. Breathe it. Then, he stops. And for the same reason I won't let our clothes hit the floor, he looks into my eyes. We're thinking the same thing. We need to talk—*really talk*—before we go too far.

If we don't, we'll be fine for a second, panting into each other's arms while we disconnect from reality. For a minute, we'll forget that the plane taking us to the sky is going to crash. We'll forget that everything that goes up… comes back down.

And I don't know if we can survive this fall.

"We can't keep fighting," I say.

"I know."

"What happened earlier?"

He sighs. "Every time we're happy, there's a voice in the back of my head telling me that it might be the last time."

"It doesn't have to be."

He pulls away, the hope illuminating his gaze breaking my heart. It's small, but it's there.

"Did you decide to stay?"

"No."

Nothing in this world could make being the reason the light

in his eyes dies easy.

"Oh."

He nods and turns away.

"But I'm asking you to come with me." The words come out as a quick, crammed mess. His back is facing me. I can't see his expression, but it's a good thing since I'm pretty sure his pain would pulverize my courage.

"Before you say no, just think about it. There's nothing here for you anymore. You're done fighting, your brother's with Riley and taking over the company. Your family betrayed you, and you have people lining up to hurt you. What's keeping you here, Haze? Please tell me, because I don't get it."

He swivels around to face me.

"Winter, it's my home…" he murmurs.

"No, it's not." I raise my voice. *"I am."*

His mouth falls open.

"Home is where your heart is. Can't you picture it? Us moving in together and arguing over what colors to paint the walls? Because I can. I can see every moment of it." I cup his face with my hands. "I can see us unpacking our boxes and me getting a pet even though you said no until you eventually get attached and want to keep him. I can see you complaining about the cold weather but forgetting all about it the second you come home to me. I can see me graduating and getting a job, while you figure out what you want to do and finally step out of your family's shadow. I can see all of it. I can see us being happy. But

I need you to see it, too…"

I'm crying. I don't know how or when it happened, but I am. If my enormous speech hit him half as hard as it just hit me, we might stand a chance.

I guess, imagining us together in a whole new life without the constant danger made me emotional. He stays silent for a "math class" eternity. He's conflicted.

Please don't say no.

Don't destroy us.

"I'll… I'll think about it," he barely says.

His voice lacks everything: excitement, determination, hope. But the wave of joy that washes my pain away when the words leave his mouth is unexplainable. I jump into his arms, and I cry. His muscular body hovers over mine, making me feel like the safest and most vulnerable girl on the planet all at once. A tear comes rolling down my cheek and crashes on his shirt.

"Why are you crying?" he asks, worried.

"I'm not. My eyes are sweating," I joke.

"Winter…" He dabs at my tears with his thumb.

"Fine. I'm happy that you're even considering it," I admit.

He smiles faintly and pulls me back to him to kiss my forehead.

I welcome his touch the way I always do and dare believe that we still have a shot at forever.

It's not a yes…

But it's a start.

I WAKE UP TO THE SOUND of the birds singing and the sunrays filtering through my bedroom window. *Nah, I'm just kidding.* I wake up to the sound of Will and Kendrick chasing each other around the house and screaming about Will losing a bet and refusing to shave his head. I gave up trying to understand these two a long time ago.

Stretching, I look to my right and see Haze sleeping soundly next to me. I gently push a piece of his brown hair off his face and hear Maria and Kass chitchatting downstairs. Haze will have to leave the same way he came in: through my window. I hate that I have to wake him up, but Kass and I have a long day ahead of us. My lovely cousin has scheduled a million appointments for tonight. We need to get our hair done, our nails, our makeup. She has a list—an actual list that's been on the fridge since last week—of all the steps we have to go through to achieve our princess status.

"Wake up." I sprinkle Haze's face with kisses. He groans like something that came out of *Planet of the Apes* and hides under the pillow. "I have to get breakfast before we leave. Plus, you probably shouldn't be lying in my bed naked when Kass rushes inside my room in thirty minutes."

I glance at our clothes scattered all across the floor. I can't help but grin. Way to be predictable. The couple fight, the guy comes and says sorry, the girl forgives, and they have sex. Ladies and gentlemen, I present to you: *Every single love story summed up in one sentence.*

Haze groans again as an answer and keeps ignoring me.

"How about this? If you get up right now, you won't have to wear a tie at prom."

"Not good enough." He shrugs. "If I get up, I get to do whatever I want with you *after* prom." He gets his head out from under my pillow and lets our eyes mix. His stupid sexy smirk gets me every time.

"You wish."

"All right. Good night, then." He pulls the covers on top of his head. If he falls asleep again, there's no way I'll get him out of my room in time.

"Fine, fine, you win," I laugh.

"Wise choice." He grins and transports himself out of bed. He wanders around the room naked and, because he notices my eyes on him, makes sure to take his sweet time picking up his clothes off the ground. Nothing new, here. *Just Haze being Haze.*

"Meet me at school at four. Don't forget." I wrap the covers around my bare body, get up, and kiss him.

"I would never. Especially after the deal we just made." He wiggles his eyebrows, and our lips collide for a brief moment. He opens the window and turns around. He's stalling on purpose. He wants to stress me out.

"Go, you jerk!" I hit his arm playfully.

"I love you, Kingston." He looks at me one last time.

"I love you, *Adams*." I use his last-name habit against him.

I watch him make his way down the house and disappear

behind the high bushes surrounding the property. I shower quickly and head downstairs for breakfast. Kass is already dressed and ready to go. She's standing in the kitchen, cooking what I assume to be eggs.

"Haze didn't want to stay for breakfast?" she asks when I walk in.

My eyes widen.

"Don't look so surprised." She turns off the stove. "You guys were crazy loud last night. Man, he must be really good."

Apparently, the face I make is hilarious because she bursts out laughing right away.

"Chill, I'm totally messing with you. I saw his car leave just now."

"I hate you so much." I bring a hand to my heart to soothe my panic and sit down at the table.

She laughs harder and asks me if I'm ready for the few things we have to do today. I nod and mentally try to prepare for the busy day ahead.

SIX HOURS. SIX FREAKING NEVER-ENDING hours. This is what Kass meant by "a few things." I yawn my head off as we pull into Maria's driveway, and get out of the car in a rush. *Man, trying to look pretty is exhausting.*

We only have about an hour left before we have to be at school. Haze and I have been texting all throughout the day. I can't stop thinking about him possibly coming with me to

Toronto. I know he didn't say yes—it was more of a maybe—but he said he'd think about it. Tonight, he'll give me the final answer. Soon, I'll know what the future holds for us.

Kass and I hurry inside and change into our prom dresses and shoes. I have to reassure her that she doesn't have back fat close to twenty times before she agrees to come out of her room. I struggle to walk with my three-inch heels inside the house and fear it'll be even worse in a large crowd. I don't know what I would've done if it wasn't for Maria offering to pay for half my dress. Those things cost a fortune. My stepdad, Harry, transferred me the first half of the price as a surprise to celebrate my graduation. I'm so grateful for him. Heaven knows my mom wouldn't have done that.

We spend the next hour bowing to Maria's every demand. She compliments the guys on how handsome they look in a tux, takes way too many pictures of us, and asks Kass and Luke, her date to prom, to change locations every five minute. Will is beyond jealous, and Kass knows it. I think that's what she wants. She's desperate for him to grow some balls and tell Kendrick the truth. I really wish Haze could've come, but Maria forbade me from seeing him again. Having him show up would kind of defeat the whole purpose of Haze sneaking in through my window every night for the past week.

Then, when 3:45 p.m. comes, I give Maria the biggest hug—since she'll be working tomorrow, and we won't see each other again before I leave—and we scramble inside Will's car to embark on the road leading to my very last night in high school. To my last moments in Florida.

To my last hours… with him.

THE HIGH SCHOOL GYM IS BIG—like *how many calories can I eat when I'm bored* big. But there are so many of us, the students crowd every inch of our personal space, leaving Kass and me no choice but to hold hands to get to the photo booth on the other side of the room. We lost Alex and Kendrick shortly after we arrived. I haven't found Haze yet.

Kass spots him first. He's standing in the corner with his hands in his pockets. I've seen him in a tux before, but the fact that he's wearing it because he agreed to take me to prom—something he once told me he would never go to—makes him all the more irresistible. He looks like the definition of droolworthy, the tux fitting his hard body in all the right places and owing him a few—okay, a *lot*—of glances from any female present. I'm so caught up in checking him out that I don't even notice the tanned girl standing right next to him. To my defense, she wasn't obvious from this angle.

Bianca.

I look back at Kass, waiting for one of her usual "I hate that bitch" comments, but she isn't where I left her. I glance around and see her getting dragged into a room by someone.

Will.

Well, shit. I sure hope they brought *prom*tection.

That's it. I'm going to hell for this pun.

I eye Bianca, who's wearing a glittery and gorgeous red dress that puts my sleeveless white dress to shame. I wasn't sure about going with white at first since I thought it was a well-known unspoken rule that white should be saved for weddings, but Kass changed my mind. *"Is it a law? No? Then break the fucking unspoken rule."* She made me laugh. Mind you she was in a mood that day, but she was right. She always is.

Maybe it's time we make rules of our own.

I take a breath and weave my way to Haze, my heels already killing me. I catch the last sentence Bianca tells him.

"I'm giving you one last chance here. Think about what you're going to do. Think carefully."

Unbothered, he doesn't reply and looks around the room. His eyes find mine and go from uninterested to huge as he looks me up and down. This look right there. This is the reason some girls dream about this night their whole lives.

"Winter, you're..." He desperately searches for words for a few seconds. "*Everything.*"

I flush.

"Thank you." I smile and wrap my arms around his neck. "You're very *everything*, too."

He laughs and kisses me. I can feel Bianca's hateful eyes on us, but I couldn't care less. When we pull away for air, *I'm* pulled away from him, tumbling a few steps back. Haze catches me before I lose my balance.

My eyes quickly find the person who just roughly slammed her shoulder into me. Bianca. *Who else?* She turns around, forces a smile that's full of arrogance on her lips, and spits a bitter "sorry" as she walks away. I sigh and look back at Haze, who just tells me to ignore her. I ask him what they were talking about, and he replies that it's not important. I insist and he tells me that she somehow heard through the grapevine that he was thinking of leaving town with me. She gave him one last chance to choose her. One last chance to choose *right.*

How did she even know about this? Haze brushed it off, but I'm so creeped out it takes me a good minute to forget about it and enjoy the rest of the night.

THE DANCE FLOOR IS CRAWLING WITH people by the time the slow songs come flowing out of the speakers and the lights go from blinking to dimmed. Haze and I have been dancing, mocking the DJ's upbeat song choices and laughing until our stomachs hurt for a few hours now. I haven't seen Will and Kass once since he dragged her away, which tells me things either went very wrong or very right. As for Kendrick and Alex, they drank way too much of the obviously spiked punch and are probably trying not to puke somewhere.

"May I have this dance?" Haze holds out his hand to me when couples start forming around us.

"You may," I agree. We're as close as can be, slow dancing along to lyrics that say "*If we can't have tomorrow, let us have right now.*" The irony isn't lost on me.

I want to enjoy this with all of my being, but I'm afraid. Everything is too perfect right now, and if there's one thing I learned about fairy tales, it's that after the ball comes the fall. Soon, the clock will strike midnight and the glass slippers will vanish. Along with my life in Florida. Along with our story.

"Did you think about my offer?" I ask, pulling away and admiring the reflection of the pale gym lights in Haze's eyes.

"I did." He nods.

Ten seconds until midnight.

"And?"

Five seconds…

Three…

Two…

One…

"I can't come with you, Winter."

Here's midnight.

"Why not?" I ask.

"This is my home. I'm not ready to give it all up."

"But… don't you want to be with me?" My voice cracks.

"Of course I do. But life is constantly standing in our way." He stops dancing. "Maybe it's trying to tell us something. Maybe we weren't meant to be more than this."

I take a step back, the tears threatening to ruin my overpriced makeup, as I fail to mentally grasp what he just told me.

"What?" is all I can say. "What do you mean?"

"I mean that… maybe we were meant to be a fling."

If words could stab you, I'd be hemorrhaging right now.

"A fling?" I spit with disgust. "You mean to tell me that we went through all of this… for a fucking *fling*?" I yell and cause the students dancing around us to stare.

"Winter, I…" he begins but stops speaking too soon for any real apology to come out. He's staring at something in the distance. Someone. "I'm so sorry, I have to go," he says quickly and leaves me and my broken heart stranded in the middle of the dance floor. I don't even bother to look, or care, to see who was worth ditching me for. I don't want to care. Not about him.

Not anymore.

I let the waterfall building up in my eyes flow freely and push my way through the thick crowd of students. I can see the door from here. I tell myself that this will all be over soon. That I'll call Maria and be out of this school—no, out of this country—in no time. I'm about to walk out of the gym when someone spins me around. Worried eyes are pointed at me. Kendrick's.

"Winter, what's wrong?"

"I think Haze and I just broke up for good." My lips quiver.

Saying it out loud hurts even more. I didn't even know it *could* hurt more. How is that possible?

"What? I'm so sorry. What happened?" he asks.

"Please, don't pretend like this isn't the best day of your life," I scoff and remove my arm from his grasp. He has no right to play the "sorry" card on me. He's been trying to sabotage us from day one. I run outside the gym and into the empty parking lot with a gigantic lump in my throat. As I move away from the building, I want to scream. I want to shout at the top of my lungs, but no sound comes out. A fling? *A fling?*

I'll show him a fling by flinging him off a bridge.

I begin to dial Maria's number but am interrupted by my phone ringing. The caller ID rips my heart out of my rib cage.

Haze Adams is calling.

I press the Reject button, but he calls again two seconds later. We go through the *hang up on me, I'll call right back* cycle a few times before I lose my temper and pick up.

"What?" I snap, but I can't hear his reply.

What I hear instead is the vehicle loudly hitting the brakes behind me. The screech of the tires resonating through the empty parking lot. The swinging of the van door, the pumping of my blood when strong arms close around me, and I drop my phone. I hear someone curse while I fight back. I hear the moans when I kick the stranger where it hurts.

"You fucking bitch." He grabs my hair and bashes me in the face twice. I can taste the blood on my tongue.

"Hurry up!" a female yells from inside the car.

I hear the sound my body makes when it gets thrown in the back of the van, and I curse myself for falling for the wrong boy. I hear the roar of the engine when it takes off. I hear a lot of things… but the sound that sticks with me is her voice. The high-pitched voice I'd recognize anywhere, even with my eyes closed, even in the dark, even when I'm passing out because of yet another stranger. I hear it over and over…

That voice belongs to Bianca.

THIRTY–FOUR
Farewells

Haze

Heading toward the front door with my phone glued to my ear, I recall the conversation I just ruined and think of the thousand smart things I could've said instead of "Maybe we were meant to be a fling." I'm such a fucking idiot.

Why am I such a fucking idiot?

I panicked and the worst reverse psychology of all time came bursting out of my mouth. I didn't mean it. Not even for a second, but I was so desperate for her to stay I thought maybe… if I scared her, she'd change her mind.

What's wrong with me?

The fear of watching her get on that plane is changing me. It can make me do the craziest, stupidest things.

Kendrick told me she ran outside. I have to see her and explain why I left in the middle of the conversation. She needs to know that Trevor was there, looking at me from the corner of the room. We've been keeping in touch since my guys kicked me out. He's the one who told me they were going for Winter last week. He even lended me his car when Ryan ruined mine.

He's the reason Winter is okay right now. I knew he wouldn't have come if it wasn't important.

He begged me to come back and lead the West side again. He said things are going to shit now that Ryan's the main. I told him what I told Winter: that I don't want this life anymore.

I just want her.

But I can't leave with her. Not yet. There's so much she doesn't know.

"Damn it. *Pick up!"* I mutter to myself, calling her back for the fourth time in a row. She keeps hanging up on me.

"What?" Her voice comes down the other end, and the air returns to my lungs.

"Winter, thank God, where are you? I'm coming to you."

She doesn't reply. Noises erupt on the line. Too many to identify. First, the squealing of tires. Then a door being slammed.

"Winter, what's going on?"

Her phone just hit something. The ground.

That's when the adrenaline kicks in.

I don't think. I bolt down the hall, halfway to the front door, and push every student roaming around the school out of my way. I can hear the struggle down the line. Someone's fighting her.

"Winter, answer me!" I yell again even though I know the chances of her replying are near inexistent.

A groan of pain every guy knows reaches my ear. She just

kicked him in the nuts. *That's my girl.*

"You fucking bitch," the guy—who's going to get a slow and very painful death later—hisses.

"Hurry up!"

He's not alone. There's a girl with him. I leap out onto the parking lot and barely have time to see a van taking off at full speed. She's in there.

Fuck, fuck, fuck.

I pick her shattered phone off the ground. I need to follow them but how? I didn't bring my car. I had a cab drop me off earlier. I knew I'd be drinking.

"Did you bring condoms?" a girl giggles as she and a guy I recognize walk out of the school. They have no idea what atrocity just happened here. They don't know that the girl I love just got taken… *again.* I recognize them. There's Jackson Miller, a dorky, nerdy guy I used to be paired with in science, and Tina Jones, a cheerleader. They're walking to his car. My guess is he's about to lose his V card.

Sorry, bro, not happening tonight.

I run to him. "Give me your keys."

The poor guy's gaze fills up with fear. He hands me his car keys with a shaking hand. Everybody here really is creeped out by me. I mean… *everybody except Winter.* I ask him which car it is, and he points to a red Honda. The next second, I'm exiting the parking lot in a loud growl and driving down the road a lot faster than the law allows me to. I used to be such an idiot when it came to speeding, but I stopped when I fell for her.

I guess meeting Winter Kingston was like finding something to stay alive for.

I can't believe how lucky I am when I see the back of the van from afar. I have to be smart about this. They can't know that I'm following them. Winter's phone starts to ring shortly after.

Kendrick is calling.

I put the call on speaker. "Kendrick, for once in your life, you actually have good timing." I take an unexpected right turn, trying to keep up with the rattling white van speeding down the street.

"Haze? What's going on? I can't find Winter. Are you with her?"

He's about to lose his shit. *There it goes.*

"She's been taken."

He proceeds to let out the loudest *"What?"* I've ever heard.

"I was on the phone with her when it happened. I heard everything. I'm following them right now. I need backup. I'll use Winter's phone to share my location with you." I speak so fast I'm impressed he understood any of it. He agrees, and I hang up, my eyes fixated on the car.

I try to keep a good distance between us, but the traffic is terrible and I'm afraid I'll lose them if I don't drive up their asses. I can't help but think that the timing was too convenient. Circumstances got me away from her exactly when they needed her alone. What if Trev's pathetic speech wasn't a coincidence?

What if he was distracting me while his allies got to her? It wouldn't surprise me.

What if, after he told me about the guys' plan to get rid of Winter, they wanted to put his loyalty to the test by forcing him to betray me? This is so like Ryan.

They were right. In the street fighting community, love is weakness. It's the deadliest weapon of all. And taking my girl is probably their way of punishing me for choosing her over the fights. But I would do it again. In a heartbeat. In the blink of an eye.

I would always choose her.

After a while, the van hops onto dirt roads—that I know Tanner used to take for shady transactions back in his drug-selling days—and distances itself from society. These roads are small, deserted. I turn off my headlights so that they don't notice me following them, but I'm not quick enough. They're onto me.

They start taking unexpected turns, speeding down the dark streets ahead of us. I eventually lose them and completely panic. I've been in this area before. There is only one place where they could be taking her. So I slam on the gas…

And hope that I'm right.

Winter

"Wake up, you trash."

I can't get a grip on my senses when my eyes snap open and the pain from the punch that knocked me out pulses in my brain.

I try to move, but my hands and feet are tied together. I feel the tape obstructing my mouth, and the fear slams against my rib cage.

I got kidnapped… *again.*

God damn it, everybody needs to stop kidnapping me!

What is this? This year's new trend?

The large doors of the van squeak apart. Two shadows are standing idly in front of me, but I can't discern their faces. Everything is blurry. The abundance of crickets outside hints that they took me to the middle of nowhere.

I have *no idea* how I'll get out of this one alive.

"Finally." I recognize Bianca's silhouette. "Get her out of the car." She motions to the guy responsible for my momentary dizziness, and he painfully drags me out by my hair. He's wearing a mask. *Coward.*

Bianca… I always knew there was more to this girl. She couldn't take a hint no matter how many times Haze pushed her away. She's been obsessed with him for so long, I guess finding out that he might be leaving town for me was her breaking point.

She snapped.

How could we not see it? She literally came up to Haze tonight and offered him one last chance to love her back. To choose her.

And he chose wrong.

I finally recover my sight and get a good look around. We're on top of a cliff, surrounded by miles and miles of empty fields.

I can hear the waves loudly crashing against the rocks from here and imagine how my body colliding with them would feel. There is nothing around except an old barn that's barely standing. No one to swoop in and save me.

No hope.

"Took you long enough to wake up." The unknown guy pushes me to the ground, and I frown. That voice. It's familiar. "How nice of you to join us for your last moments."

He takes off his mask, and when I see his hateful blue eyes staring back at me, I wish I could say that I'm surprised… but I'd be lying.

Blake.

Of course it's him.

Traitor one day, traitor always.

I blink back the tears burning my eyelids, wishing, *praying* that my death will be quick. At least I'll die knowing I kicked him in the nuts and possibly ruined his chances of reproducing.

"You know, I'm actually kind of surprised that we succeeded. Don't get me wrong, I'm happy that we did, but I thought the East side would have learned their lesson by now. This is, what, your second time being kidnapped on their watch?" He laughs.

I glance at Bianca, who's standing a few steps back with her arms over her chest and a satisfied smile on her lips. She changed back into regular clothes. *Imagine wasting the only prom of your life for a guy who doesn't care.*

"It was almost too easy, really. All I had to do was show up to your house, sneak a microphone in, feed the guys some shitty redemption lines, and *voilà*." He puts his hands up as if he's expecting applause.

This is why he was at the house that day. He's been planning this for a while.

"Guess how we found out about your very convenient departure to Canada? Man, you must really be mind-blowing in bed for Haze Adams to consider swapping the palm trees for snow." He laughs. I know that the microphone is how Bianca found out about this. We talked about it in the kitchen last night. "Oh, I'm sorry. Where are my manners? We're missing the best part. Her afflictions, her torments. We don't get to hear her beg for her pathetic life."

I hold back tears when Blake tears the tape off my lips violently. He stares like he expects me to say something. But I do what any sane person would do instead. I scream. I scream as loud as I can. They don't flinch. Blake even starts laughing. My despair is pointless. No one's going to hear me.

"Really? You have nothing to say to me? I remember you being a lot chattier the last time your life was in my hands." He cackles.

"Why are you doing this?" I finally whisper. I'm shaking.

"Do you really have to ask?" Anger takes over him. He pulls me off the ground brutally, his face barely two inches away from mine. The air gets lodged in my lungs. "You ruined my life, that's why. Do you have any idea how hard it is to get back into a fighter's circle once you've been labeled a traitor? Especially when the side you betrayed ended up beating you? You made me a joke in the community. You took the only thing that I cared about away from me!" He spits in my face and pushes me back down to the rocky ground. "No circle means no fight. No fight means no money. I went from a high-up fighter to selling drugs to high school kids and stealing shitty cars to survive, for fuck's sake!"

This is where he went. When he left town. He probably couldn't afford his place anymore. I recall the story Haze told me about him back at the lake house. His mother is invalid because of a car wreck, and he doesn't speak to his father. He doesn't have his parents supporting him. He has nothing.

I stare into the emptiness ahead of me and contemplate my death. I look it right in the face. He's waiting for me to cry, I can sense it. If this is how I'm going to go, I sure as heck am not going to give him that pleasure.

Blake refrains from saying more and goes to get what appears to be luggage from the van. But it's not just any luggage. *It's mine.* I recognize my floral suitcase. This is my stuff. I finished packing earlier today. They probably broke into the house while Maria was at work and grabbed it. He tosses my things on the ground.

It all clicks in my head.

They're covering their tracks.

They're probably going to shoot me, throw my body into the water, and get rid of my things. It'll look like I didn't want to leave my boyfriend, freaked out, packed my bags, and ran away. They've though this whole thing through. The police will close the investigation and quickly hop onto the next case.

They'll never know that I was murdered.

"Who else are you working with?" I ask.

"No one. It's just me and B, over here." He turns to Bianca. "Oh, and the West side for like two seconds. They were very useful tonight. Got Haze away from you just when we needed it. They really hate him."

This is what distracted Haze when we were dancing. I should've known he wouldn't have left if it wasn't important.

"You two? Really?" My eyes stray from Bianca to Blake.

"Not your everyday duo, I know, but I ran into her when I got back into town. She told me all about you and Haze living the dream in fairy-tale land, and I knew I had to do something about it. You see, I'm *really* getting sick of you two standing in the way of my happiness." He carries on with his incessant blaming of the entire universe.

His annoying habit to call everyone but himself guilty makes me realize something. Haze has nothing do with Riley being pregnant and Blake's mother losing her legs. It was Tanner all along, but Blake doesn't know that. He's got this all wrong.

"Enough chitchat. Time to die." He makes his way to the van, opens and closes the driver's-side door with a slam, and comes back. In his hands… is a gun. He carelessly loads it right in front of me.

"It wasn't Haze!" I blurt out when Blake points the weapon at me. He frowns. I've got his attention. "He's not the one who got Riley pregnant. It was Tanner."

Pain colors his face for a second, but it vanishes when he shakes his head.

"You're lying." His voice is firm, cold.

"I'm not. She was sleeping with Tanner the whole time they were dating. Haze had nothing to do with what happened. If you don't believe me, go ahead and ask her. She and her kid just moved into town to live with Tanner. They're married."

"What?" he blurts out.

This is working. I'm getting to him.

"I know it's a lot to take in, believe me. We were just as shocked." I feign compassion.

"No. This is bullshit. This… She's not in town. She'd have come to see me. She…" he stutters.

"She was looking for you. But she couldn't find you." I feed him the lie he so desperately wants to hear. "See, you didn't lose your family, Blake. You have a chance to make things right. A chance that you'll lose if you pull that trigger right now. You know Kendrick and the guys will never stop trying to expose you if I go missing. You'll end up in jail one way or another. Can't you see? There is no scenario that involves killing me in which you end up winning."

Hesitation spreads across his face.

"Don't listen to her. She's getting inside your head," Bianca screams at him. "She ruined your life, remember? She'd say anything to save herself. Kill her!"

She obviously doesn't want to do her own dirty work.

"Blake, this isn't the way. Think about it. You can have the family you deserve if you just untie me. You can't kill me."

An army of anger and pain lead the war in his eyes. He's conflicted. After a few unbearably long seconds, he puts the gun down. I let out a gigantic breath of relief, my heartbeat returning to my rib cage. But when something hits the back of his head and he collapses to the ground, I know the nightmare is far from over.

Bianca just knocked him out.

She drops the sharp and heavy rock she just used to silence her partner and looks at me.

"You're right. He can't kill you," she says as she steps over Blake's unconscious body and picks up the gun that escaped his hands. "Which is why I'm going to have to do it myself."

Great.

"Bianca, please," I say in a hurry. "We can talk about this."

That's when I see the motion.

Right behind her.

I see the shadow hiding behind the million-year-old barn.

It's him.

The man I'll love until my last moment, even if my last moments are soon.

Haze.

I can't hold it back anymore. Warm tears come rushing down my cheeks. But they're tears of joy. How did he find us? I can't believe it. He's here. Haze is *here.* Our eyes meet. He motions to remain quiet by pressing a finger to his lips.

"Now, I'm going to let you choose." Bianca checks out her perfectly manicured fingers with her available hand. "You tell me how you did it and you get the bullet to the head, quick and easy. Or, you don't, and we do this the long, painful way."

"Tell you how I did what?" I sob, my lips trembling.

"Don't play dumb with me. You know what. How did you get him to commit, huh? How did you turn the heartless player into a good man?" She carefully analyzes my face as though she really thinks she'll find the answer somewhere in my features.

This girl is completely insane.

Haze and I exchange glances from afar. I gather from his body language that he's been dying to intervene, but he's waiting for her guard to be down. He doesn't have a gun. She does. One wrong move and it's curtains for both of us. He needs to be smart about this.

My hope dies when Bianca speaks again.

"It's all right, Haze, you can come out now!"

No.

Shit, shit, shit.

How did she know?

With a look of defeat all over his face, Haze exposes himself.

"Please." She chortles at his shock. "I knew it was you from the second we noticed someone following us." She points the gun at him, and he has no choice but to put his hands up in surrender.

"Bianca, please, listen to me, you don't want to do this," he says.

"Shut the fuck up." She makes it clear that she's not asking. "Get over here." Haze obeys, walking toward us. He's still wearing his tux, the same way I'm still wearing my white dress—which is now brown due to the dirt on the ground. I can't wrap my mind around how quickly our prom turned into a living hell. How fast the Cinderella dream became a nightmare.

"You've come to save your precious Winter, I suppose?" Bianca asks, anger and jealousy flowing out of her. "What does she have that I don't, huh?" She begins to cry as her once perfect mascara covers her face. Her arm is shaking. I desperately pray that she won't pull the trigger.

A part of me feels bad for her. The truth is, I don't know why he chose me over her. Why do things happen the way they do? Why is life the way it is? She's seeking answers that don't exist.

"Is it because she's skinnier than me?" She gasps for air. "Because I can lose weight. That's not an issue."

Wow, the girl needs help…

And she needs it fast.

"Bianca, put the gun down. Please." Haze tries to take a step toward her.

“Not another step.” She shouts so loud he freezes in place.

“We both know you don’t want to shoot me,” Haze says.

I scowl at him. Damn it, Haze. This is exactly what *not* to say to her. Now is not the time to test how far she’s willing to go.

“I had Blake put a bomb into your car just to get rid of her. I knew there was a risk it’d kill you, too. You really think I won’t shoot?”

Comprehension hits Haze and me. It was her, working with Blake. They are the people Tanner said were after Haze. Blake was the one asking around the community. Seriously? That old *“If I can’t have him, no one can”?*

“Do you know how many times I cried for you? Every single night when you showed up to my house, used me, and then left without a goodbye when you were done.” She’s hyperventilating at this point. My heart aches at the way she talks about him. Haze really was an entirely different person back then.

I know he’d say that he told her what he wanted from the start, that he never lied to her or slept with her under false pretenses, but we both know he should’ve stopped this relationship the second she caught feelings. Haze said they were friends with benefits for six months. To an unstable girl like her, that’s a lifetime.

“But her…” she says through the sobs. “She’s got the kisses, the I love yous, the promises. You’re even considering moving to another fucking country for her.” She makes herself angrier with every word.

Realization flashes in her eyes.

"You. This is all your fault." She jolts around abruptly and points the gun in my direction. Haze immediately steps in front of me, his hands still up in the air.

"Haze, don't!" I cry.

"You're right, Bianca. You're right. I'm an asshole. It was me. Not her. *Me*." A bunch of words tumble out of his mouth. I know he'd say just about anything to calm her down and get her attention off me.

Her sobs grow louder. "Why can't you see that no one will ever love you like I do? I'm so much better than this skank. Deep down, you know that, don't you? I'd do anything for you. Haze, I love you."

He doesn't reply, glancing at me from the corner of his eye. He seems to be ready to pounce, to take any bullet coming my way, and it terrifies me.

"But you don't." Her voice is quieter. "You don't love me because of her."

"Bianca, please," he begs.

"Admit it!" she shouts.

Haze

"But I do," I say and look her right in the eyes. "I love you, Bianca."

"What?" she chokes, her sobs reducing in intensity as the fire decreases in her stare.

"I love you. I was just… lying to myself." I take a step toward her, which she allows. That's a good sign.

"What about her?"

"She's nothing to me. She's a distraction." I keep stepping forward. I'm getting closer. I can take the gun away from her if I act fast. From there, all I have to do is knock her out.

No, Haze, you have to at least try and get her to give it up by herself. You know what could happen if you fail. You can't risk it.

You can't risk Winter.

"You love me?" she repeats again, disbelief spreading across her features as she starts crying hysterically like she can't believe that her dream is coming true.

"Yes, I promise."

Just one more step.

One more and I'll knock her out.

I can do this.

"And you don't love her?" She stares at Winter.

"No, I don't. I never did. I love you."

When I say the three magic lies, I anticipate a million things from her. I somehow convince myself that I can handle everything she'll throw my way. But I was wrong. I wasn't prepared for what was to come. I would never, *not even in a hundred lifetimes*, be prepared for what was to come…

"Great. Then you won't mind if I do this."

It barely lasts two seconds.

But it's enough.

The gunshot echoes in the silence of the night and I fall apart, shouting at the top of my lungs.

"No!"

Two seconds.

One move.

That's all it takes for my world to come crashing down.

THIRTY-FIVE

Home Is You

Winter

"No!"

I close my eyes, anticipating the gunshot, anticipating the pain, anticipating the *end.* But nothing happens. I'm not dead. How am I not dead? The gunshot hisses in my brain as my hand jumps to my right ear. Blood comes dripping down my palm. The bullet grazed me.

She missed.

When he runs to me, Haze's face is indescribable. His eyes are bloodshot, his mouth open. He captures my face in his hands and breathes heavily, his entire body trembling as he wraps his arms around me and holds me so tight it's hard to breathe. He looks like the weight of the world has just been lifted off his shoulders.

"What were you saying? She means nothing to you? You're a fucking liar, Haze." Bianca sniffles. "It's your fault. You're making me do this. You're giving me no choice." She cries louder and points the gun at the guy she claims to love.

There's nothing we can do. We exchange glances that are

filled with defeat. We don't need to speak. Our gazes are saying goodbye. We're saying "I love you" for the last time. We both close our eyes in anticipation of the inevitable. We hold each other and pray that this will be quick.

That's when a loud noise startles us.

Another gunshot.

A bullet ricochets on the ground next to Bianca and she jumps.

We all turn our heads to see a car speeding toward us, its glimmering headlights blinding us as it approaches. The person responsible is stretching their arms out the vehicle window. Then, the driver of the car strikes the brake and all doors are swung open as three silhouettes climb out of the vehicle. Relief. That's all I can feel.

Will, Kendrick, and Alex.

"About fucking time." Haze glares at them. Panicked, Bianca stares at the three witnesses who just showed up and looks for a way out. The boys are surprised, shocked that the girl they've been going to school with since they were kids is behind this.

She's cornered and she knows it.

"Bianca? Y-you did this?" Kendrick asks, and the seriousness of what she's done finally dawns on her.

The truth crushes her like a pile of bricks.

She glances at the gun she's holding and drops it.

She falls to her knees and starts to cry. That's all she does. She cries uncontrollably.

Here comes the breakdown.

"What the hell am I doing? I almost…" She sobs to herself as she shakes. "What's wrong with me? I'm sorry. I'm so sorry." She wraps her arms around her body and rocks herself back and forth. "What have I done? What have I done?"

The guys look at us as if they expect some sort of explanation, but they figure it out for themselves when they notice Blake passed out on the ground. Haze summarizes the previous events as best as he can. Then, without wasting another second, he gets me off the ground and into his arms. We're still shuddering from the trauma.

"I'm so, so sorry," Haze whispers against my hair, and I let my tears wet his neck. I can't believe this is the second time we've escaped death. The second time we've stood this close to the edge and somehow managed to see another day.

"It's okay. We're okay," I sob, and he presses his lips to mine. We make out in front of the boys, but there isn't even a slight part of me who cares. "So much for being just a fling, huh?" I tell him when we pull away and he sighs.

Kendrick stops him from answering. "Get her out of here. Now!"

"What about them?" Haze eyes them.

"We'll handle them. Go."

Haze has no choice but to trust that they'll do the right thing as he picks up my suitcase—that I'm really glad Blake didn't throw into the ocean—and motions to get into a car I don't recognize. I don't ask questions. Just as he's about to join me, Kendrick calls out to him.

"Hey, Adams?"

Haze turns around and stares at my cousin.

"Thanks for always looking out for her."

This sentence holds so much more than it leads on. I remember the day Haze told my cousin he was in love with me. Kendrick didn't believe him.

He believes him now.

Haze stops, his mouth agape, and finally puts an end to the war that's been raging for far too long…

Haze nods. "You know I always will."

"WHOSE CAR IS THIS?" I NARROW my eyes when Haze pulls up into Maria's driveway and kills the engine. We've been driving in silence for a few minutes now. I think we needed a moment to ourselves. What happened tonight seems unreal, impossible. My brain keeps rejecting the information. It doesn't want to be told that I almost died again. That Haze's crazy friend with benefits took being jealous to a whole other level.

I can't keep living like this. This can*not* be my life, no matter how much I love this guy. No matter how many promises we make… It really is time for me to go home.

"You're not going to like it." Haze half-smiles before telling me he stole the car from Jackson Miller just as he was about to lose his virginity to a cheerleader. Poor guy. I hope he got lucky.

"You have to give him his car back," I say.

"Yeah, yeah. I will." Haze smiles faintly. "Maybe."

He gets a small grin out of me, which is only something Haze could do in such a serious moment, and helps me out of the car. He refuses to leave my side in case I'm hurt. He insists on helping me get around. We then step inside the house that I'll be leaving tomorrow.

When I open the door to my bedroom after changing out of my dress, I fight every nerve in my body telling me to beg Haze to come with me. Because I know what his answer will be. He made it clear when we were dancing.

He's not coming.

Whether or not he follows, I'll be on a plane back to Toronto first thing in the morning, and there's nothing no one, not even Haze, can do about it.

It used to break my heart but not anymore. After what happened tonight, after I got kidnapped for the second time and almost lost my life *again*, I'm finally ready to accept that going back home is for the best.

Home is safe.

Home has my stepfather and stepsiblings.

Home has my best friend, Allie, who I bet is just *dying* to get me to binge-watch cheesy shows with her again.

Home has everything.

Except for one thing…

Home doesn't have Haze Adams.

"How's your ear?" I ask Winter when she comes back from the bathroom with her prom dress in her arms. She hangs my tux, that I've just swapped for a pair of sweatpants, and puts her dress away.

"It's okay. I sterilized it. It barely hurts." She lies on her bed. Silence streams down on us, and we welcome it. Or at least, I do. Because I know what will happen once it leaves us.

After a few seconds, she says it.

"What does this mean for us?"

My heart twists in my chest. I sit on her bed and look at the hardwood floor like I'm waiting for it to slip from under my feet. I can't face her. I know I wouldn't survive her teary gaze and sad smile.

"It means that I'll be visiting you as often as possible. That we'll spend Christmas and every holiday together. That we'll FaceTime, text, and call every day. It means that you won't even have time to miss me." I gather what's left of my courage to look into her eyes. Just as I expected, it kills me. No, it *crucifies* me.

It destroys me because she starts to cry.

"Don't cry, baby, please. This isn't over. You hear me?" I lift her chin up. "We're not breaking up. I'm never going to stop fighting for you. I mean it."

She wipes a tear away.

"At prom, you said—"

"It was bullshit. All of it. I freaked out and told you a bunch of lies because I'm a fool. I'm a fucking imbecile who would do the craziest thing to keep the girl he loves by his side."

She doesn't reply right away, chewing on the inside of her cheek.

"Please say something," I beg.

She takes a breath and gives me what I want.

"*Something.*" She does to me exactly what I once did to her, and I laugh in relief.

"I bet you were just dying to plug that one in, weren't you?"

She chuckles, the tiniest smile warping her lips. I wrap my arms around her body, feeling this fervent need to tear the oversized hoodie she's wearing off her. I need to feel her, even if it means that I'll hate myself even more for letting her go tomorrow.

"You really think we can do this? The long distance?" she whispers into my neck.

"I know we can."

I mentally smack myself for putting her through this.

Damn it, Haze. Why can't you just tell her?

"I'll… I'll miss you," she chokes out.

"Winter, please… you're killing me right now." I'm so busy trying to swallow the painful lump in my throat that I don't even realize tears are welling in my eyes.

I didn't want to admit it, but I've known it for a while now. The bastards are right. All of them. This girl has changed me.

She's made me vulnerable. She's taught me to feel when I didn't want to. When I didn't even know that I could.

"I love you," I whisper, and she sighs.

"I love you, too, you goddamn idiot." Her voice shatters as she climbs onto my laps and encloses my lips with hers. I immediately kiss her harder. I know what she's doing. She's giving our bodies a chance to say goodbye.

She's giving them a chance to do what we can't.

The kisses go from soft to hard. From slow to fast. The rising tension reminds me to enjoy this moment to the fullest. I dig into the dips of her hips, and she grinds relentlessly against me. I groan into her ear.

Fuck, I'm already rock hard.

This is going to be torture.

I decide to skip the agonizing teasing and go straight to the good part. I impatiently get her out of the hoodie hiding her perfect curves and my eyes want to pop out of their sockets when I see that she's not wearing a bra under it. I desperately take in her body, memorizing, engraving, and relishing in every inch of her skin.

My fingers find her nipples while I suck on her earlobe and kiss my way down to her breasts. I circle my tongue around her and feel her melt into my hands. She's holding back. I hate when she does that. Nothing gets me hard like hearing her moan for me. Don't even get me started on watching her come. I grip her waist, flip her over, and pin her down under me. We keep kissing until she tugs at my sweatpants and removes them.

"Someone's ready." She bites on her lip and takes me between her fingers. I hold my breath when she starts to pump up and down.

Shit.

"Ladies first." It takes all my willpower to take her hand off me. "How long until they come home?" I whisper and pull the short shorts she loves to wear as pajamas down her legs. She's not wearing underwear either. *I'm so hard it hurts.*

"We have like thirty minutes tops before the guys come bursting through the front door."

My lips quirk into a smile.

In a sudden move, I toss her shorts across the room and grip her thighs apart. Our eyes meet.

"I'll make you scream in ten."

Her cheeks flare, but I don't wait for her to reprimand me. I know she likes when I'm raw. I press my tongue to her and focus all my attention on the spots I know she likes best. She whines and squirms at the strong pressure of my mouth. I don't take it slow. We're way past the "is that okay" phase. I know what she likes by now.

The familiarity of her taste doesn't help me in the *hard as a rock* department. The bliss on her face when I slide two fingers inside and start thrusting in and out of her quickly tells me that my lonely nights are only going to get worse. How the hell am I supposed to go back to being alone after her?

After *this*?

She gasps for oxygen. "I want to feel you. Please."

"Not yet," I smile.

"Jerk," she pants.

"*Prude*," I say before going back in.

My tongue continues to twirl around her until she starts to tremble. She's close. She grips the sheet and closes her eyes, but, just as she's about to reach the peak, I guide myself inside her and start to pound so fast even I'm shocked. I press my lips to hers as she gasps in surprise. She moans so loudly into my mouth I'm afraid that sound alone will cut our moment short. I could come just listening to her.

"Oh my God, *Haze*." She claws at my back recklessly. That's for sure going to leave a mark, but I don't care. *Fuck, she feels so good.* I don't want this moment to end, not yet, so I try to think of something else. Something that'll take my mind off how tight she is.

I roll my hips harder, faster, and her mouth drops open. She moans louder when I take a fistful of her hair and she finally reaches the sky. Her eyes widen as she shudders in my arms. She's out of breath, overwhelmed. Slowly coming back down to earth, she whispers that she loves me.

So I say it back.

I say it back and show her just how much I mean it.

I say it back and make her mine…

One last time.

HAS ANYONE EVER BEEN HAPPY TO hear their alarm in the morning? Has anyone ever said, "Yeah, time to wake up!" while jumping out of bed? Probably. But that someone has definitely never been me. Indeed, the sound of my alarm usually annoys me. It always has. But this morning is different.

The alarm doesn't annoy me. It guts me.

Its buzzing tells me that the time has come.

This is it. I'm leaving.

I peel my heavy eyes open and slam the snooze button of my alarm clock. It's five in the morning. My flight is at eight, which means we have to be at the airport soon. Haze's naked body is sprawled across mine, his head on my chest and his arm around me. I enjoy the warmth of his skin and trace down the curves of his stretching back muscles. How am I *ever* going to find the strength to get out of this bed?

We barely got any sleep last night. We spent the first half of it making love and the second… worrying that it might be the last time. The boys came home at around 2:00 a.m. I rushed downstairs, the worry that something had gone wrong eating me whole. They told us everything.

Apparently, as soon as we left, Kendrick called the cops claiming to have been driving by when he heard a gunshot. The police showed up at the scene and found nothing but an unconscious Blake on the ground. They called Kendrick to let him know about what went on later and thanked him for doing his citizen duty. It turns out that Blake wasn't lying when he said his only means of survival was selling drugs. He had an unimaginable amount on him and in his van. They also matched his prints to a bunch of car thefts all over town.

He's going down, even if it's not for the right crime, and that's all that matters.

As for Bianca, Kendrick gave her an ultimatum: go get the help she needs or face the consequences of the law. She could check herself into a mental institution for young adults, or Kendrick could tell the police and her family all about her murder attempt. She chose option number one. He's been going to school with her ever since they were five. I think that's why he went easy on her.

Kendrick and Will offered to drive Jackson's car back to him last night. Will knew where he lived, so the boys left fifty bucks in his mailbox. Consider it a *"Sorry we're the reason you didn't get laid on prom night"* gift.

"Winter, are you up?" Kass asks from the hallway and knocks on my door. They all promised to get up early to say their goodbyes. Alex even spent the night for it.

"I'm almost ready," I call and nudge Haze with my elbow.

"Five more minutes," he groans.

"I'm going to take a shower, and you better be up when I come out." I place a handful of kisses across his face and walk off. By the time I make myself presentable and put on an airport-appropriate outfit, Haze is sitting on the edge of my bed and playing with his fingers. He's wearing the clothes he found at my place last night. It's a good thing he's so territorial and left a bunch of stuff behind the numerous times he snuck in through the window. One can't wear a tux forever.

The impending pain in his eyes breaks me. He runs a hand through his messy hair and pats the bed. I join him. Ten minutes of making out and feeling sorry for ourselves later, we're walking down the stairs and bickering about how heavy my suitcase is.

"How many rocks are you bringing back home?" Haze taunts, and I punch his arm.

I'm a known overpacker.

Hell, if I could, I'd bring *him* in my suitcase.

In the kitchen stand Will, Kendrick, Alex, and Kass. They look beyond tired, but first and foremost, they look sad, like "someone just died" sad.

"I'm going to miss you." Kass steps forward with her arms open. She's smothering tears. I won't be able to keep my composure if she starts crying.

"I'll miss you, too." I hug her and fail to swallow the painful pit in my throat. Alex and Kendrick are next in line for the "It sucks that you're moving to another country" hug.

"You'll come visit every summer, right?" Kendrick whispers when we pull away.

"Every summer. I promise." My voice uncovers a pain I didn't expect. I never knew this would be so hard.

"Don't get into too much trouble in penguin land, okay?"

I laugh at my overprotective cousin and think back to the way it all started. To the day I followed him to his creepy meeting with no idea that it would mark the beginning of a crazy adventure. The events that changed *everything* play through my mind, and my heart cracks open. I can't glance Haze's way. I won't survive it.

He's the goodbye I can't say.

My gaze jumps to Will, whose eyes are red.

"Will, are you… crying?"

"What? Don't be ridiculous, Canada. There's just something in my eye." He rubs his eyelids.

He's crying.

That's it. I can't hold it in anymore. Tears begin to flood my eyes and soak my cheeks.

"Come here." He opens his arms to me, and I walk into his embrace with a painful laugh. It kills me to see them like this.

They're not just Kendrick's friends anymore.

They're family.

"You know what? Group hug," I add.

The guys grumble at how cheesy this is but still participate in our ridiculous embrace. I walk out of the tiny but welcoming house that I came to with no other plan than survive my senior year. I didn't know, back then, that it'd turn out to be a much harder task than anticipated.

Haze circles my shoulders with his arm as we make our way

to the car. He sees me fighting the tears. But, this time, they're not for him.

I'm going to miss seeing them every day, yelling at Will for eating his ketchup chips like a pig and making a mess, rolling my eyes at Kass when she complains about having back fat, and going off on Kendrick and Alex for wrestling each other all around the house. Regardless of the hell that we went through, I'm still going to miss Florida.

I'm going to miss the good parts.

I slouch in my seat and lecture myself for being this torn. They're my family. I see them five to six times a year for holidays, family gatherings, and birthdays. We visit each other every summer.

This isn't goodbye, Winter.

It's until next time…

Haze

THE AIRPORT IS STUFFED WITH PEOPLE. You'd think showing up at 6:15 a.m. would earn us some calm, but the commotion clearly disagrees. I don't know what I expected, really. School is over and summer is at our doors. If the packed building is everything but quiet, Winter hasn't said a single word since we left her aunt's house. I wish I knew what she was thinking.

It feels like the oxygen is being sucked out of my lungs when she speaks for the first time to tell me she's going to print out her boarding passes. It's like every step she takes is bringing me closer to the edge, closer to losing it.

She's leaving, Haze.

For good.

Unless you do something about it.

I mentally battle myself and watch her long brown hair swing from left to right as she walks away from me.

From us.

An airport employee shows up to help her with any questions she might have. I'm about to follow her when my phone rings. The number on the screen immediately sends me into a whirlwind of panic.

This isn't the time or place.

I glance around nervously, making sure that no one is close enough to listen, and pick up.

"Not a good time," I drone.

"When is it ever?" he scoffs. "You know I wouldn't have called if it wasn't important."

"It better be worth it," I spit.

I'm not risking Winter finding out about this. Not when she's leaving soon. I'll tell her. But not like this. I've been busting my ass making sure that she never overheard one of these calls.

I don't want her to see that part of me.

That hateful, stuck-in-the-past, after-revenge part of me.

I look at the only girl I've ever loved. She said there's nothing here for me anymore, and she's right. *Of course she is.* I want to go with her. I want nothing more than to get on that plane but I can't. I can't give up just yet. I can't betray my sister.

I think back to all the times when I would disappear on Winter for days when we first started talking. It was to follow leads. It got me into so much trouble, it might as well be worth it.

That's the last thing I have to do before I can leave my messed-up days behind. Before I can be happy with her. Before I can be free.

I can't break the promise I made to Desiree that night. I have to find the guy who stole her life away.

I have to find Marcus.

"We know why there hasn't been a single trace of him in the past months, Haze." My source's words flow quickly.

"Ricky, just spit it out, already."

"There isn't a trace of him because he's not in the country anymore."

An unpleasant feeling in my stomach quickly dominates my usual curiosity. I almost wish that he hadn't called. I wish I didn't hear him say these words because of what they imply.

It all makes sense.

The piece of shit stopped leaving clues behind. No credit card transactions, no whisper on the street, nothing. It was like he'd just vanished from the surface of the earth. I thought he might be dead. I was wrong.

"Where is he?" I keep my eyes glued to Winter, who's smiling at me from afar. She's completely oblivious, waiting in line to check her luggage at the counter.

What I wouldn't do to keep this girl out of harm's way.

"Listen, man. I made a mistake. I'm sorry. This one's on me," he says in fear of my reaction.

"Ricky, I'm only going to ask you one last time. Where's the bastard? Where's Marcus?" I hiss at his endless stalling. He lets out a long breath that makes me want to rip his head off. I don't need the dramatic effects. It's like he's holding his tongue precisely to piss me off.

Then, after the longest five seconds of my life, he says it.

"You don't happen to be planning a trip to Canada anytime soon, do you?"

My mouth falls open as my ability to think, breathe, speak—overall be a human being—escapes me.

All I can do is look at her. Just her.

Are you fucking kidding me?

"I have to go." I hang up before he can even think of getting a word in and weave my way through the thick crowd of travelers. My feet go up against my brain, my pulse quickening as I shove my hand into my pocket and grasp my passport. My stomach knots.

I find myself behind her. I cut the line, not giving a single fuck about the people huffing and puffing.

"Haze, what are you—"

I don't let her finish, crashing my lips to hers. She's surprised, stunned, but she kisses me back. She welcomes my mouth the way she always does. I break away from her and catch the confusion burning in the back of her eyes. I don't say a word, aware that what I do next can either change everything…

Or ruin it.

I get my passport and the boarding pass I printed out yesterday out of my pocket. Up until now, I was convinced that it was pointless. That I couldn't possibly change my mind at the last minute and decide to go. But I still booked a flight the second she told me she was leaving. Maybe because, deep down, I knew it would come to this. I knew I'd end up chasing this girl to the end of the world.

Even if she's not the only one I'm chasing…

Her hand jumps to her wide-open mouth. Her watery eyes stray around like she's looking for cameras. Like she's waiting for a crew to jump out and scream, "You've been pranked!"

The words she once said to me spin around in my head.

Home is where you heart is.

She's right.

She was always right.

"What are you doing?" she asks, but it comes out as a plea. She's begging me. Her eyes say, *"I swear to God, if you're messing with me right now, you're not having children."* I know she's forbidding me from answering the question wrong.

So, I give her the only right answer there is…

"I'm going home."

ABOUT THE AUTHOR

Eliah Greenwood is a Canadian 21-year-old author who started writing books online when she was fifteen years old. When her book "The Bad Boy's Rules" and its sequel gathered up to 30,000,000 reads on the internet, she decided to give her loyal readers what they'd been asking for and self-publish. She's currently working on the third book in the Unwritten Rules series. It is expected to come out in 2019.

ALSO BY ELIAH GREENWOOD

Unwritten Rules (Book 1 in the Unwritten Rules Series)

Unbroken Rules (Book 3 in the Unwritten Rules Series) – *To be published*

Heartbreakers For Hire – *To be published*

Sign up to Eliah's Newsletter to be the first to know when the third book is **OUT!**

https://www.eliahgreenwood.com/subscribe

Enjoyed the book? Please consider leaving a review for **Unspoken Rules** on Amazon!

Follow Eliah on Instagram for previews of the next book and your Haze and Winter fix!

Instagram: **@EliahGreenwood**

ACKNOWLEDGEMENTS

To my Wazers, my babies… thank you. I realized while reading this exact section in the first book that I didn't give you nearly enough credit. You have changed my life. From the drawings you send me every day, to the pictures you take of yourselves holding the first paperback, to the handwritten letters you guys give me at meet-and-greets, you have shown this small town girl that anything is possible. I will never find the words to express how grateful I am for your support. I cherish each and every one of you. Haze and Winter would've never ended up on paper if it wasn't for your constant love and dedication. Thank you for somehow making it through the internet version that now makes my eyes bleed. All my love.

To my boyfriend, Tommy, thank you for knocking some sense into me when I needed it. God knows I almost didn't finish this book, and the world owes these pages to you. You laughed at the fact that I gave a 45-year-old character your name in this book, but just know that I swore to never name a character after someone… unless that someone is you. I love you with all my heart, Tom. Always.

To Sandra, my editor, thank you for dealing with my tired brain and its weird tendency to mess up the same words on repeat.

To my sister, Marie, you did it again! Thank you for calling me out and telling me I needed to fix the ending if I didn't want to get hunted by readers. I appreciate you always being there to advise me.

To my father, thank you for stopping me when I'm ready to throw my computer out the window. I know, as a dad, it's your job to cry when your daughter writes steamy scenes, so… thanks for crying with class. Also… I know you'll skip straight to this part to see if I thanked you, so, while you're here, piece of advice, don't read the book with petals on the cover. **laughs nervously**

I love you, Dad. Thank you for everything.

I wouldn't be here without you.

Printed in Great Britain
by Amazon

61143588R00293